Books by Bill Fitzhugh

HIGHWAY 61 RESURFACED
RADIO ACTIVITY
HEART SEIZURE
FENDER BENDERS
CROSS DRESSING
THE ORGAN GRINDERS
PEST CONTROL

RADIO ACTIVITY

BILL FITZHUGH

HarperTorch
An Imprint of HarperCollinsPublishers

❦

HARPERTORCH
An Imprint of HarperCollins*Publishers*
10 East 53rd Street
New York, New York 10022-5299

Copyright © 2004 by Reduviidae, Inc.
Excerpt from *Highway 61 Resurfaced* copyright © 2005 by Reduviidae, Inc.
ISBN 0-380-80637-1

First HarperTorch paperback printing: April 2005
First William Morrow hardcover printing: April 2004

HarperCollins®, HarperTorch™, and ❦™ are trademarks of Harper-Collins Publishers Inc.

Printed in the United States of America

Visit HarperTorch on the World Wide Web at www.harpercollins.com

10 9 8 7 6 5 4 3 2 1

To Sergio Fernandez for teaching me what I needed to know in the production room and for helping me get my first job in radio. This is all your fault and I can't thank you enough.

For the late Wayne Harrison, the late Dave Adcock, and all the jocks who worked at WJDX and WZZQ, 102.9 FM, Jackson. We rocked.

And finally for Kendall: This one goes out to you.

Acknowledgments

Once upon a time there was an FM rock radio station in Jackson, Mississippi. Originally WJDX-FM, the call letters later changed to WZZQ-FM. It was by all accounts one of the best free-form and, later, album-oriented rock radio stations in the country. It was staffed by people who knew, loved, and played an astonishing variety of music. I grew up listening to this station and later, thanks to the Junior Achievement Program, I worked there. It would be an understatement to say this changed my life.

In addition to my personal knowledge of the artists and music of the sixties and seventies, I relied on the following sources for information: All Music Guide website (www.allmusic.com); Joel Whitburn's *The Billboard Book of Top 40 Hits;* and John Tobler's *100 Great Albums of the Sixties.*

Special thanks to D. Victor Hawkins, with whom I worked at WZZQ, for constant consultation on every aspect of this story. Many of the segues alluded to in these pages sprung from our Tuesday evening get-togethers while I wrote this book.

Also to Steve Larson, fellow ex–rock radio guy, for helping with programming and music issues from a larger market perspective. And, belatedly, for putting *Radio Free Comedy* on the air in Seattle at KJET.

Regarding matters outside of radio, my thanks to the following for their help: Chris Purser, Geoff Purser, and Steve Shirley for sharing their knowledge of the Mississipppi woods; Cynthia Speetjens, Al Nuzzo, J. Brion Morrisette, and Don and Joni Langevoort for helping with legal issues; Don Winslow for his help on matters of arson; Matthew Scott Hansen, Janine Smith, and Kendall Fitzhugh for their notes and for taking the time to listen to me jabber about plot points until I figured them out; Maureen O'Brien for saying the book was perfect, even if it's not; and James C. Vines, who agreed with her.

Author's Note

In writing a novel set in the world of radio, one finds it necessary to use call letters to identify different radio stations. The only problem is that call letters come and go like the wind. Had I used call letters that were not in use at the time I wrote this story, they might have come into use before we published. The ones I ended up using may be out of use by the time this gets into a book store. So here is my rationale for the call letters I used in the following tale:

Many stations select call letters to reflect the city they're in. I opted to do the same. I used KBND to refer to a station in Bismarck, North Dakota (as of the day I write this, a news-talk station in Bend, Oregon, uses these call letters). I used WVBR to refer to a station in Vicksburg, Mississippi (at this moment, these are the call letters for a rock station in Ithaca, New York).

Other stations select call letters to reflect their format. Many years ago there was a format known in the industry as AOR, which stood for Album Oriented Radio (as distinct from Top 40 radio, which was singles oriented). Over the next two decades, AOR evolved into what is now known as the Classic Rock format. Since this story is set at a classic rock station, I gave it the call letters WAOR-FM. As of this moment, WAOR-FM happens to be a classic rock station in South Bend, Indiana.

All of that is another way of saying this is a work of fiction. Names, characters, places, incidents, and radio station call letters are products of the author's imagination (as limited by FCC rules) or are used fictitiously and are not to be construed as real. Any resemblance to actual events, locales, organizations, radio stations, or persons, living or dead, is entirely coincidental.

RADIO ACTIVITY

1

It was hard to say which looked more depressed, the seventies-era shopping center or the man pulling into its parking lot. Both had seen brighter days, though in fairness it had to be said the man wore it better than the shopping center.

He called himself Rick Shannon and there was a semitragic, end-of-the-line aspect about him. Time had chipped the youthful cockiness off the outside, but some of his underlying swagger remained. There were men Rick's age who envied his thick head of hair; others envied his freedom. The two things Rick had plenty of, freedom and hair, the currency of the sixties. But, like the songwriter said, the former was just another word for nothing left to lose. The latter, well, Rick could still lose that.

There were more weeds than cars in the parking lot. Half the storefronts were boarded, the rest were just waiting for the other shoe to drop. Rick parked his truck. This was exactly what he swore he'd never do. But here he was. He killed the engine and sat there, staring at the dashboard. The gas gauge. Empty. Same as his wallet. He mumbled, "Fuck."

Rick was unemployed again. When he worked, he worked in radio. He'd grown up listening to AM, when "Yesterday" and "Satisfaction" were Top 40 hits, when radio was all about singles. But his first job was on FM, during album-oriented radio's heyday. He'd been the youngest jock at the station when *Imagine* and *Sticky Fingers* were new. A few decades later Rick was doing the night shift at KBND-FM, Bismarck, North Dakota. Rockin' the Sioux State at 99.9. The pay was adequate and Bismarck was, well, it was more like every other city these days. The same franchised fast food and twenty-screen cineplexes lining indistinguishable main drags, town after town. Rick had worked in dozens of cities. He'd seen it everywhere. Homogenization was just a sign of the times.

Especially in radio. More stations owned by fewer corporations. Consultants and music researchers conspiring to make everything sound the same. And they weren't even looking for songs people liked. The research was geared to find songs people didn't dislike. That's what they played to keep listeners until the next commercial break. That's what so much of radio had become.

So Rick had been playing all the rock radio clichés until Clean Signal Radio Corporation bought the station and broomed the staff. It was Clean Signal's fifth station in the market and it showed. All sense of community had vanished as the satellite feed bounced in voice-tracked jocks from Chicago and Florida.

As he had walked out of KBND's studios with his final check, Rick had thought about how media watchers in the fifties had predicted that television would be the ruin of radio. He wondered if anyone would appreciate the irony that radio had killed itself.

Rick mailed tapes and résumés all over the country and spread the word on the grapevine. He was available. A rock-steady pro with production skills, on-air talent, whatever. Rick tried not to dwell on the fact that he and all the other DJs of his era were like silent movie stars at the dawn of the talkies. By and large their skills didn't transfer to the new iteration of the medium and they would soon be forgotten and replaced as things changed.

And now Rick found himself parked outside a storefront under a sign that said: B-SIDE VINYL—WE BUY AND SELL USED TAPES, CDS, AND LPS. It was either this or start bouncing checks.

Rick looked down at his arm. He knew that big fat vein, blue and pulsing, was a potential source of revenue, a renewable resource he could tap again and again. But he also knew plasma didn't fetch much, and besides, that had always seemed to Rick like such a sure sign of having reached the last resort. He couldn't bring himself to check in there. Not yet anyway. So he had tapped his record collection instead.

Looking up and down the sidewalk in front of the shopping center, Rick saw only one person, a man who looked to be in his sixties. His shopping cart brimmed with indistinguishable bundles, folded cardboard boxes, a water jug, plastic bags filled with crushed cans. His face was sunburned and peeling as his cracked lips wrapped around the mouth of a bottle.

Rick took this as a reminder that things could be worse. He got out of his truck and walked around to the other side. He opened the passenger door and looked at the box filled with rare albums, including an original UK version of Pink Floyd's *The Piper at the Gates of Dawn,* signed by the entire band. Rick had promised himself that he wasn't going to part with that for less than two hundred. Of course, more than once he'd made the promise that he'd never sell any of his records, but things change.

Rick picked up the box and kicked the door shut. As he approached B-Side Vinyl, the homeless man made eye contact and extended a hand. "Help out a fellow record buff?"

Rick paused, a sympathetic look on his face. "Sorry," he said, shrugging with the heavy box in his hands. "Trying to get some together myself."

The old man gave a nod. "Don't sell 'em all," he said. "Hang on to something, you know, just in case."

Rick smiled and said, "Thanks for the advice." He pushed the door open and stepped inside. The bouquet of cardboard, dust, and vinyl welcomed him. Nothing else smelled quite like a room full of old albums. The cobwebs in the corners of the store spoke volumes. There were no other customers, just the owner sitting behind the counter reading a magazine. He lowered the magazine and looked over the top of his glasses. "Cleaning out your attic?"

Rick set the box on the counter and said, "Something like that."

The man put his hands on the box. "Cash or store credit?"

"Cash."

The guy slid the records from their sleeves. He held them at angles to look for scratches. Rick walked down an aisle rooting through the record bins out of habit, his fingers deft at flipping the albums, mostly dreck from the early 1980s: Whitney Houston, Frankie Goes to Hollywood, Flock of Seagulls.

The owner was about halfway through the box when he said, "You work in radio?"

Rick paused before answering. "Used to."

"Least you got out in time. Not like old J.J.," he said, nodding toward the sidewalk.

Rick looked up from the record bin and said, "J.J.?" His eyes went to the homeless man. "As in J.J. Maguire?"

"The very same." The man nodded. "Jukebox Johnny."

He was a Top 40 radio legend, one of the big boss jocks of the era. "He was huge," Rick said. "Had like a forty share in San Francisco."

"You believe it? Big as he was, and ends up on the sidewalk? Couldn't adapt, I guess. After the glory days he drank himself into a job at an oldies station here. By the time they went automated, he was a serious hooch hound, couldn't get work. Started showing up here with his 45s."

Rick saw Johnny's head tilting back. "Hate hearing stories like that." He didn't want to think about how they struck too close for comfort.

"J.J. sold me all but one of his records," the man

said. "No matter how bad he needs the money, he can't bring himself to sell that last one." The man waved Rick's original copy of Skynyrd's *Street Survivors* toward the door and said, "Somewhere in that pile of junk there's a clean copy of The Beatles' 'Please, Please Me' on Vee Jay. Probably worth four hundred bucks," he said. "You believe that?"

Rick shook his head and wondered what he would hang on to if it came down to that.

The man finished looking through Rick's box and said, "You got some great stuff here."

"Yeah, what're they worth?"

"Well, what they're worth is a different question," the guy said. "But I can only give you fifty for the lot."

Rick didn't hide his surprise. "Fifty? I figure they're worth a couple of thousand."

"Sure, to collectors, none of whom live in Bismarck as far as I been able to tell."

Rick looked at the guy. "Fifty's the best you can do?"

The guy shrugged and scratched his head. "Or a hundred store credit. Not much demand for this stuff anymore."

"Yeah." Rick nodded. "Not anymore."

"You probably do better selling them on-line."

"Except I need the money now."

"That's usually the case."

Rick slid the box toward himself and pulled out the Pink Floyd. "What can you give me for this?"

The man looked Rick up and down. "I tell you what," he said. "You're in a spot? I can give you, say, ten bucks."

Rick shook his head and explained the differences between the U.S. and the UK versions of the album.

"Okay," the guy said. "Twenty."

"It's signed by the entire band." Rick pointed at the album's psychedelic cover. "Look, that's Syd Barrett's signature."

The guy figured he could get fifty bucks selling it online. "All right," he said. "Thirty."

"It's the original pressing," Rick insisted. "There's not a scratch on it, and not only that—"

The guy reached into a drawer and pulled out some money. "You want the thirty or not?"

Rick looked at the cash for a moment. Then he reached out and took it. "Thanks." He grabbed his box and carried it outside.

Jukebox Johnny looked up from the sidewalk. "How'd you do?"

Rick's head rocked back and forth. "Coulda been worse," he said.

Johnny nodded at the box. "Glad to see you kept a few."

"Yeah, well, just in case, right?" Rick put the albums into the man's shopping cart and said, "See what you can get for 'em." Then he turned and headed for his truck.

Jack Carter was handcuffed to a fence in the backwoods of Deckern County, Mississippi. The fence was an old property line, rough hand-split cedar and barbed wire. Here, it was a tangent to a small clearing. Loblolly pines and a lone white oak tree surrounded Jack Carter, as if gathered to watch him die. There was a creek nearby, swollen by the rain. Things were muddy and bleak as Jack struggled and sobbed and sank slowly in the red clay muck.

He coughed and choked when a black cloud of diesel exhaust swallowed his face. The fumes came from the backhoe operating a few feet closer than safety regulations suggest. The backhoe, mounted on a big crawler, was digging a hole large enough for a man.

Jack Carter shouted over the machine noise, pleading for his life, offering bribes he had no hope of delivering, then apologizing for his misdeeds, then cursing his fate. A flash of lightning illuminated his doomed, rain-soaked face.

One-Mississippi. Two-Mississippi. Three-Mississippi. Thunder.

The backhoe operator finished the hole then climbed down from the idling tractor, a Smith & Wesson .45 in his hand. He approached the fence with an expression like putting down a bad dog. Grim but not sad, business that had to be done.

"You can't do this," Jack Carter shouted as he pulled against the fence. "Please! I won't tell anybody. Nobody has to know!"

The backhoe operator looked to the sky, waiting. It came a moment later. Another flash and he raised the gun. One-Mississippi. Two-Mississippi. No one heard the shot as the thunder rumbled through the woods.

For a moment, the rain and the rushing creek were the only things to hear. Then the sound of a boot sucking out of a wet hole and then another as the backhoe operator stepped closer to the fence. He removed the handcuffs then returned to the crawler. He climbed into the seat and laid his hands on the control sticks. The hydraulic arm jerked and the steel-toothed bucket shook as it reached down to drag the body into the hole.

* * *

When Rick got back to his apartment, his machine was flashing. He had one message. *Beep. "Yeah, Rick? Clay Stubblefield, WAOR, McRae, Miss'ippi. We're an FM rocker with an opening for someone with experience. I heard you were available. Now I need to move on this quick, so gimme a call if you're innersted."*

Rick thought about it. Mississippi. Oh, Lord. But it was a job, and not far from some decent markets—Memphis, New Orleans, parts of Florida. It didn't take him long to decide he was, in fact, "innersted." So he called Clay Stubblefield and struck a deal. The gig was seven to midnight plus the usual production duties. The pay wasn't great but Rick knew a little went a long way in a small Mississippi town. The job also came with a spacious apartment near the studios for only three hundred a month, so the next morning Rick loaded eighteen Peaches Record Store crates full of albums into the back of his truck and headed south.

Rick was returning to the Magnolia State after a long time gone. He'd grown up in Jackson, where he had his first radio gig, so he had a history with the place. He still had a few relatives there along with some friends from high school, and an old girlfriend or two.

Rick drove through Sioux Falls, Omaha, Kansas City, St. Louis, and Memphis. As he scanned the dial, finding each city indistinguishable from the last, Rick kept thinking about J. J. Maguire and wondering who was to blame for the old man's fate. Of course Rick knew the answer, he just didn't like it. He wanted to hold someone *else* accountable, preferably some faceless consultant. But he knew the truth was simpler than that. Things had changed and J. J. Maguire had refused to change with them. And now Rick was starting to ask himself if it was time for him to change, too, lest he end up on the sidewalk outside a used record store. But change how? Into what?

As he crossed the state line into Mississippi, Rick told himself not to worry. He didn't have to deal with that at the moment. He was on his way to a new job. Change could wait.

Rick crossed the Deckern County line just before three and tuned the radio to 102.9 FM. They were in a commercial break, a classic small-market radio spot, bad copy read at a machine-gun pace. *"Behind on your bills? Credit-card balances piling up? Tired of paying late fees? Need quick cash? We can help! Universal Financial Services has the solution to all your problems. Got bad credit? We don't believe it! Universal Financial Services wants to give you an advance on your next paycheck without embarrassing credit checks."* It was annoying but you'd remember Universal Financial Services. The spot ended with, *"UFS? It's the best!"*

The DJ came out of the spot break. "This is WAOR-FM, McRae, Mississippi. Classic rock for Deckern County!" When he heard the opening licks of "Whole Lotta Love" by Zeppelin, Rick had to groan. He thought, *So many good songs, so few of 'em played.*

Ten minutes later Rick hit the outskirts of McRae. He passed a billboard: HOME OF CENTRAL MISSISSIPPI UNIVERSITY—GO PANT   s! It was supposed to say, GO PANTHERS! but the HER had been painted over by some drunk frat boys. Rick drove past a lumberyard, an equipment rental place, a couple of motels. A few miles ahead, at the town's center, the highway crossed Bilbo Avenue, the town's main drag. Rick turned east. It looked the same as the main drag in Bismarck, all the same franchises. A few miles later, he pulled into a parking lot.

Rick stared at the building, his new office—an unpainted, T-shaped cinder-block structure. Mounted above the door in red blocks two feet tall were the call letters, WAOR-AM & FM. At the far end of the parking lot was a van with a fancy paint job, no doubt known as the WAOR Prize Patrol Van or something similar. Rick sat there, absorbing the glamour of the moment and wondering about his choice of professions. *Fifteen cities in twenty years,* he thought. *At least I get to travel.*

Rick got out of the truck and stretched for a minute before heading for the building. *Here we go again,* he thought. He opened the door and stepped into the station. The receptionist was on the phone. She didn't notice him at first. Rick guessed she was in her late twenties. She tore the message from the pad and said, "Mmm-hmm, buh-bye." She speared the message onto a brass spindle and looked up from underneath the shade and quantity of blue eye shadow that had thrilled Rick in his pubescence. He had believed it was an indication of a woman's willingness to sin, specifically with him. If only he had known what to say, which he never had. But he'd always had a thing for blue eye shadow, and lots of it.

The receptionist was about to speak to Rick when the phone rang again. She held up a finger then pushed a button on the switchboard. She was wearing one of those headsets, so she didn't have to pick up the receiver. "Dubya-ay-oh-ahhr," she said. "Mmm. Hold, please." She transferred the call then looked up at Rick with a sweet-tea smile and said, "Can I help you?"

He liked her already. "Yeah, hi, I'm Rick Shannon. Here to see Mr. Stubblefield."

"Oh." She pointed at him. "You're the new guy." She held her hand out. "Hi. I'm Traci, with an *i*." She tilted her head a bit and squinted. "Where're you from?"

"Jackson, originally."

She looked skeptical. "Sure don't sound like it."

"I've been out of the state for a while." Rick shrugged. "Guess I lost the accent."

"That's okay. You'll get it back." Traci held up an index finger. "Just a sec." She punched a button on the switchboard. "Mr. Stubblefield, Mr. Shannon is here." She looked back to Rick. "He'll be right with you." The phone rang again. Index finger in the air. "Dubya-ay-oh-ahhr. Mmm. Hold please."

Rick glanced around the lobby. The station's call letters were mounted on the wall behind Traci. The opposite wall sported a couple of framed gold records from the seventies and an aerial photograph of the radio station that looked to be at least thirty years old. A speaker in the ceiling piped in the FM signal. "Hair of the Dog" by Nazareth. *Funny how things change*, Rick thought. *You couldn't have played this in McRae, Mississippi, when it came out. Too vulgar. But after rap, I guess it's tame*. Rick absentmindedly sang along with the chorus in his head, *Now you're messin' with a son of a bitch*.

Clay Stubblefield came into the room like he was

approaching the line of scrimmage. A bull neck in a salesman's sports coat. "Rick? Clay Stubblefield." His big hand reached out. "Glad to meecha, buddy." After a handshake, he pointed at Traci. "This is Traci Foster, if you didn't already—"

"We did," Traci said, never taking her eyes off Rick.

"All right, good." Clay clapped his hands together once then pointed at Rick. "You sure made time gettin' here. It must be, what, eleven, twelve hundred miles?"

"About sixteen hundred," Rick said.

"Whoa!" Clay shook his head slowly. "Never been there myself." He folded his arms and continued by saying, "Played a game in Nebraska once, got our butts kicked, too, but never been to North Dakota. I think we mighta won there." He winked.

Rick guessed the obvious. "You played for CMU?"

"A few decades ago." Clay laughed a bit. "How fast the time goes. I tell you what." Clay gestured toward a door. "Hey, lemme show you around real quick." He pointed down a hallway at one end of the building. "Sales, traffic, bookkeeping, and all that's down there." He turned to lead Rick in the opposite direction. "Studios and staff offices are down here, c'mon."

Rick followed Clay but paused to look back at Traci. "Nice to meet you," he said.

She smiled. "You, too."

The station was exactly what Rick had expected. The equipment was a mix of analog and digital. There were old Collins rotary-pot control boards in the on-air and production studios. They were still using a single Ampex reel-to-reel for commercial production. The walls and ceiling were yellowed acoustic tile. The AM side, mostly syndicated news and talk programming, was directly across the hall from the FM. Large double-paned windows allowed you to see from one studio to the other.

Clay stopped at a cabinet at the far end of the hall. "Hey, listen," he said, reaching into the cabinet. "Somethin' came up." He pulled out a WAOR-FM T-shirt. "And it's good news for you." He handed the shirt to Rick.

Rick fingered the cheap fabric. The iron-on logo was curling off. He looked at Clay and said, "Why do I doubt that?"

Clay looked down at his shoes and scratched his head. "All right. You're right. Shoot." He hemmed and hawed for a moment before saying, "Here's the deal. The past twenty years we been the only rock radio game in town, right? Well, about a month ago the local beautiful music station went to some kinda damn adult contemporary pop-rock format that's squeezing our numbers. I talked to a consultant and we agreed the problem was we were too broad. Hell, we were playing stuff from 1970 to the present, just all over the damn road, you know, long as it was rock. So we gotta narrow it down to a stricter format for a little older demographic. Since we already got a pretty good library, I figured we'd go with classic rock. Then I lost my program director and you were on your way here and I figured with all your experience, you'd be the guy for the job. Think of it this way," Clay said. "You ain't been here a day and you already got a promotion."

Rick forced a diplomatic smile. "Well, Mr. Stubblefield, that's not what we agreed to."

Clay ducked his head then looked up at a boyish angle

for forgiveness. "I know and I'm real sorry. I am. But all that happened after we talked. I was gonna call but, well, hell, it's done and I swear I'm 'onna make it up to you." He straightened up to full size, pointing at Rick. "Anyway, look at the bright side, you get the morning show."

Rick's diplomatic smile dissolved. "I'm not what you'd call a morning person."

Clay chuckled, shook his head. "Shit, I know how you feel, but the other guy left and, well, it's what we got." He shrugged, looking a bit embarrassed. "You don't want it, I sure understand, since it ain't exactly what we talked about." Clay pointed back down the hall. "C'mon." He led the way back to the reception area. "I tell you what," he said. "You think about it. You decide it's not for you, you can be back in Bismarck by the weekend."

Funny guy, Rick thought. *Is he daring me? He knows I don't want to make that drive again. He knows he's the lesser of two evils. I suspect he's done this before and gotten his way. Probably why he hired me instead of someone who didn't have to drive so far. But the morning show? And programming on top of that? I don't think so.* "Look, I just want the night shift. Nothing else. I prefer to come and go in the dark."

"Awww, c'mon." Clay clapped a fraternal hand on Rick's arm. "Give yourself a little time to think about it. A PD job on the résumé looks good if you bring in a couple of nice books. Besides, it's classic rock, how much work can there be?"

"Uh-huh. And what tax bracket would this 'promotion' put me in?"

Clay snickered and ducked his head some more. "Oh yeah, we'll talk about that," he said. "No question we'll make it worth your while. You can count on that."

Rick shook his head. He'd been railroaded before, but never so soon after walking into a building. "Let's see this apartment," he said.

Clay clapped his hands once. "Good idea." He led the way out to the parking lot. "You're probably pretty tired after that drive." Clay checked his watch. "Tell you what, I gotta meet a client in a little while. Just sold him a big run of schedule, a six-month campaign." He pointed at Rick. "Maybe give you a shot at producing the spots. Pick up a little extra folding money, you know?" As was his habit, Clay paused and sucked some air through his teeth. "Tch. So. Why don't you follow me out to the place, get your shoes off, have a cold one, and think about it."

Rick followed Clay's Crown Victoria for six miles before they turned down a dirt road. A couple of hundred yards later they came to a stop in a clearing and got out of their respective vehicles. Clay was beaming. Rick wasn't. "There she is," Clay said with a sweeping Century 21 gesture. "Whaddya think?"

"Well, it's not an apartment so much as it's a trailer, is it?"

"Manufactured home," Clay said. "Double wide. Great floor plan, too."

"When you said it was close to the station?" Rick gestured at the dirt road. "I got the impression it was like walking distance."

"Hell," Clay said, "North Dakota's walking distance. It's just a long walk's all." Clay smiled and slapped Rick on the back. "C'mon, wait'll you see the inside."

Clay keyed the door and they entered. The place was filled with someone else's stuff. It was a mess, like the place had been ransacked then put back together by someone who didn't really care. "You didn't mention it was furnished."

Clay waved a hand at the living room. "Yeah, well, no, all this belonged to the guy you're replacing."

"Which one? The night-shift guy, the program director, or the morning-show guy?"

Clay ignored it, pointing instead at the massive record, tape, and CD collection. "That's a helluva record collection, iddnit?"

Rick nodded. "You don't think he's gonna miss it?"

"Shiddif I know," Clay said with a friendly shake of the head. "I figure if he wanted it, he'da taken it when he left."

"Where'd he go?"

"Shiddif I know," Clay said again with a little laugh. "Just didn't show up for work one day. Disappeared, left all his stuff behind. And me, high and dry."

"Cops?"

"Said they didn't find any foul play." Clay shrugged. "Not a clue."

Rick pointed around the room. "Looks like there was at least a little foul play in here, don't you think?"

"Yeah, no, Chief Dinkins and his boys poked around in here trying to find some clues, see if something mighta happened but said they didn't find nothin'." Clay looked at his watch. "Meanwhile I gotta fill this job." He poked a finger at Rick's chest. "And you da man. The place and the job are yours if you want 'em. And we'll talk about that money, too." Clay headed for the door, talking over his shoulder. "Guy's brother's supposed to come collect all this in a week or two, so don't think I'm gonna stick you with that."

"Who was it?"

"The jock?" Clay stopped at the door. "Guy named Jack Carter."

"As in Captain Jack?"

"You know him?"

"Sure, by reputation."

"Yeah, and he had one, too, didn't he?" Clay turned around and took a step toward Rick. "Listen, I'm sorry about all this. I hope you don't think it was intentional or anything. It all just kinda happened, outta my hands. And I swear"—Clay aimed a finger at Rick, his thumb up like a gun's hammer—"I'm gonna make it up to you. Tch." The hammer dropped.

Rick parked his truck under the fiberglass carport next to the trailer. He was too tired to unload anything but a suitcase. He found a couple of tall beers in the fridge and was working on the second one while he tried to decide his future.

He was sitting in Captain Jack's Barcalounger, possibly the most comfortable chair Rick had ever sat in. A joint was burning in the ashtray stand next to the chair. Rick wondered why anybody would abandon something this cozy, let alone this record collection. It seemed way past weird that a collector would just leave it. But there it was, staring at him. It was twice the size of what Rick had been dragging around the country for the past two decades.

Rick pushed himself out of the chair and moved

closer, looking at the spines of the albums, his head tilting to the right. The dark swirling colors of *Abraxas,* the green-and-silver *Hissing of Summer Lawns.* Rick had one of his bad impulses and looked for the tiny streak of rainbow on the spine of *Dark Side of the Moon.* Right next to it was a copy of *The Piper at the Gates of Dawn.* He took it to replace the one he'd sold in North Dakota. It wasn't signed by the band but at least it gave him his favorite Floyd tune, "Scarecrow."

Rick closed his eyes and reached for the shelf. He let his fingers thrum back and forth across the long row of albums. He stopped at random, his index finger on *Beggars Banquet. Brian Jones's last record,* Rick thought. *Except for the two cuts on* Let It Bleed. Rick put it on the turntable, a beautiful old Bang & Olufson 4004 with the linear tracking arm. A four-hundred-watt McIntosh amp pushed a pair of JBL studio monitors hanging in the corners. He turned it up halfway, then a little bit more. He pushed the button on the turntable and watched as the arm tracked over to the lip of the disc. He turned and tilted his head back to the angle of the speakers and closed his eyes. He loved that rich thump when the needle settled into the vinyl groove and made the woofers jump. *Thump.* Rick smiled and started moving with the congas and maracas. Decent rhythm for a white guy. He went, "Yoww!" along with Mick's echoed yelp. He turned it up a little more. "Yoww!" *Please allow me to introduce myself.* What a song. It was one of the rare songs that classic rock stations couldn't burn out, no matter how many times they played it. *Been around for a long, long year.*

Rick toked the joint and stood in front of the wall of

music. He started looking through the collection. Albums, 45s, 78s, CDs, DATs, a few eight-tracks, several boxes of reel-to-reel tapes, but no cassettes. *That's weird,* Rick thought.

There were a dozen boxes of reel-to-reel tapes, all labeled. Some were air checks, some were programs Captain Jack had produced, others were interviews he had done with rock legends during his own, storied career: DYLAN @ WNYW-FM 1971; TOWNSEND @ WRKK-FM, 1970; CLAPTON @ KMEL-FM, 1972.

Rick returned his attention to the albums. As he expected, they were arranged alphabetically by artist's last name or first letters of band's name. Jethro Tull was filed under *J* not *T.* Rick saw a record collection as a peek into the owner's mind. Was he a closet Abba fan? (Carefree, peppy, and chatty?) Did he have the entire Leonard Cohen oeuvre? (Morose, despairing, unstable?) Were blues mixed with rock or was the collection segregated? (Purist, fanatic, fence builder?) Was he devoted to complete artist catalogs or was he interested only in worthwhile output? (More interested in collector value than artistic value?) Of course the technique worked better with people who actually had to buy their records. Radio folk tended to have everything in their collections since the records were free.

The collection was dotted with box sets. Springsteen live, the Phil Spector collection, Clapton's history, *All Things Must Pass,* and a dozen others, including *Chicago IV,* the famously bloated four-record live set from Carnegie Hall, released in October 1971. Strange thing was, all the albums were filed right next to the box they came in. Rick thought that would make sense only if you listened to the records so often you didn't want to waste time pulling them from the box. But since Rick figured nobody had listened to *Chicago IV* since approximately November 1971, this piqued his curiosity.

He pulled the box from the collection and looked inside. There, he found something wrapped in a hand towel. Rick unfurled the towel. Inside was a standard seven-inch reel, unlabeled, with five or ten minutes' worth of tape on it, depending on the recording speed.

Rick put the tape on Captain Jack's old Crown SX-700 reel-to-reel machine. He switched the amp to auxiliary, cutting Mick off in the middle of shouting out about who killed the Kennedys. Then he started the tape deck. A moment later, Alvin the Chipmunk began chattering. The machine was set at seven and a half IPS. The tape had been recorded at three and three-fourths. Rick rewound it, corrected the speed setting, and started again.

A man began talking. His first words were these: *"And you know that bitch wanted me to come back to her motel room and piss on her?"*

Well.

Rick had to laugh at that. From the sound of the tape it was a phone conversation between two men. Rick listened to the whole thing. It was a six-minute forty-two-second litany of crimes and indiscretions, delivered in a smooth redneck swagger. One man did most of the talking while the other listened, giggling now and then, sometimes asking questions, almost like he was taking notes. The talkative man sounded vaguely familiar but neither voice belonged to Captain Jack Carter.

Rick listened to the tape three times. Now and then

he had to rewind it to figure out what the men were saying, they were so colloquial. After the third time through, some words triggered a thought. Rick rewound the tape. *"Wonk I fiddihs."* He listened again. *"Shiddif I know,"* the one man said, the man who did most of the talking. Rewind. *"Wonk I fiddihs."* Play. *"Shiddif I know."* Rick laughed again. No question. It was Clay Stubblefield.

Rick shook his head in amusement. *You just have to love the quality of people you meet in radio,* he thought. He switched back to the turntable and started *Beggars Banquet* over at the second track, "No Expectations." He sat down in the big soft chair and toked the joint, wondering what had happened.

Radio legend Captain Jack Carter had somehow ended up in McRae, Mississippi. Then he disappeared, leaving behind his possessions, chief among which was a record and tape collection worth many thousands of dollars. Okay, that was mysterious. Just as strange, in Rick's estimation, was the absence of cassettes from Carter's collection. He had 78s, 45s, LPs, reels, eight-tracks, DATs, and CDs—why wouldn't he have cassettes? Very odd indeed.

Granted, this wasn't exactly crop circles, but these facts begged for an explanation. The only fact that *had* been explained was a fourth anomaly, namely that Captain Jack's place had been ransacked. According to Clay Stubblefield, the cops had done that before declaring there were no signs of foul play in Carter's disappearance. But given Clay's extravagant credibility problem, Rick had no reason to believe that was true.

And what about a car? Rick thought. *Captain Jack*

Carter sure wasn't walking to work from here. So what happened to his car?

Rick rubbed his eyes. It didn't require much imagination to see how the tape might lead to trouble. Even without the tape, though, it looked like something unusual, and probably bad, had happened. But what and why? Rick toyed with various explanations.

Captain Jack had a reputation for an off-and-on cocaine habit. And in an industry famous for such, one had to work hard to get a reputation. Maybe he had ripped off the wrong dealer. Or maybe he'd slipped into the netherworld of crack and was in some godforsaken place sucking on a pipe. Maybe sold his car for some rock. Rick had seen it happen.

If it wasn't drugs, maybe it was sex. Perhaps he'd been caught with somebody's wife and had ended up sucking on the business end of the husband's gun. Or maybe he'd just met with some other form of bad luck. These things happened.

And while those were all viable avenues down which one might find an explanation for Jack's disappearance, none of them explained the tape. Had Captain Jack bugged Stubblefield's phone? Had he bought the tape from someone who had? A private investigator? Hired by whom and for what? And if it had been a PI, why did the tape start during the middle of the conversation instead of the beginning?

The last track on side one of *Beggars Banquet* started. "Jigsaw Puzzle." Rick smiled and thought, *Yeah. Might as well try to put it together.* The tape was the obvious place to start. In the course of the six and a half minutes, Stubblefield bragged about several of his own sexual escapades as well as those of a few other folks. And that wasn't the juiciest part. Clay went on to name a couple of people whom he described committing what sounded to Rick like felonies, though, since he wasn't a lawyer, he couldn't say for sure. Rick also wasn't an extortionist, but he felt the most likely use of this tape was obvious. And if Captain Jack had gone down that road, it might account for his scarcity.

"Jigsaw Puzzle" faded out. A second later, the tone arm lifted and tracked straight across the back to its starting position. Rick loved the design of this turntable with the tone arm that didn't come at the record from that weird angle all the others did. He didn't know if it produced a discernibly better sound, but it sure looked cool.

Rick sat there mulling his options. He was new in town. He didn't know anybody. He had no hobbies. He was single and without prospects, although he had hopes for Traci Foster, whom he had known for a grand total of six hours . . . something about that eye shadow. He figured looking into the disappearance of Captain Jack could prove to be an amusing diversion.

Suddenly hungry, Rick decided to see what Captain Jack had left in his cupboards. He pushed himself out of the chair, hoping for Oreos. But on his way to the kitchen Rick had a thought. He stopped in front of the wall of albums, his head tilted right. He squinted as if looking for something in his mind, then he reached for the wall. He pulled Robert Palmer's 1974 gem, *Sneakin' Sally Through the Alley*. He looked on the back and found the song that had come to mind. He thought for another moment, then pulled 10cc, *The Original Sound-*

track. It contained a song with the same title as the one on Palmer's album. *Was it the same song?* Rick had never thought about it until now. He looked at the writing credits. The first was by Palmer and the late Lowell George of Little Feat fame. The other was written by 10cc's Stewart and Gouldman. Different songs, but with the same potent one-word title: "Blackmail."

2

Rick woke up in the chair. The Robert Palmer album was in his lap along with what looked like a pair of small orange dice. These turned out to be carrot bits from the frozen dinner Rick had found in the freezer the night before. It wasn't in a box, just an aluminum tray covered in foil. The dessert had been pried out long ago. The meat substance was freezer-burn gray, but Rick had guessed Salisbury steak.

Rick squinted at a clock on the shelf. It was just after eight. He reached down for the handle on the chair and cranked it forward. He stretched and cracked his neck before getting up to shuffle into the kitchen. He found a can of Community Coffee with enough for about two decent cups. Rick knew he'd need more than that before he could decide his future. He drank what he had, then took a shower before heading back toward town. He'd seen a coffee-shop-cum-truck-stop about halfway between the station and the trailer.

It was called Kitty's Road Café. It looked like it had been there for half a century. It also looked like they'd retained the original waitresses, grizzled, stooped, and churlish. Depending on the food—and assuming they served cold beer—it was just the sort of place Rick looked for when he moved to a new town. It was his routine. One of the first things he did was find a locally owned and operated eatery. He couldn't eat at Chili's or Friday's or Applebee's or Ruby Tuesday or any of the others. He didn't want meals that had been conceived in test kitchens and given foolish names. And he didn't want to be subjected to pep-squad food servers belting out "Happy Birthday" while he tried to eat. He didn't want meals with a Hollywood theme or a Hard Rock theme or a NASCAR theme. He just wanted good food and genuine atmosphere.

Kitty's was just such a place. It smelled like pork fat, coffee, and pecan pie twenty-four hours a day and it was just clean enough not to be shut down by the health department. Rick sat at the counter and picked up a dog-eared menu that looked like it had been printed in 1967 and kept alive by the miracle of lamination. At the top it said: HOME OF KITTY'S BISCUITS AND THE ORIGINAL WORLD-FAMOUS TATER WADS. Without asking, the crusty waitress behind the counter slid a cup of coffee and a sweating glass of water in front of Rick and growled, "What can I getcha, hon?"

He looked up, pointing at the menu, and said, "What's a tater wad?"

The waitress snatched the menu from Rick and wedged it back behind the napkin dispenser. She turned and called back to the kitchen, "Number three!"

She looked down at Rick. "How you want the eggs?"

"Uh, scrambled." He didn't know what else to say.

"Scrambled!" Then she left.

Rick figured the woman was a professional, knew what she was doing, so he let her go. He figured the answer to his tater-wad question would show up with the number three. Meanwhile he sipped his coffee and resumed weighing his options. He didn't want the morning show and he didn't want to be a program director. But he didn't want to be unemployed either. A lawsuit was too much trouble and he didn't have enough of a financial cushion to go back to school so he could get something more akin to what his last girlfriend referred to as a grown-up job. So the path of least resistance called. He'd take the job, but try to negotiate something closer to the original offer. Worst case, he'd stick around long enough to put together a good tape and then move on.

"Here ya go, hon." The waitress slipped the plate onto the counter as she passed by. Four sausages that looked homemade, some scrambled eggs, toast, and a pile of what Rick assumed were Kitty's Original World-Famous Tater Wads. He speared one with his fork and popped it into his mouth. Cupped inside a crunchy crust was a preparation somewhere between hash browns and buttery mashed potatoes. He couldn't tell if they were deep-fried or browned in a skillet. There were some herbs, too, thyme and something else, he wasn't sure what. Rick's eyes closed involuntarily as he chewed. "That's a tater wad," the waitress said from the far end of the counter.

Rick looked at her. "What's in it?"

"Don't talk with your mouth full," she said, pointing at him.

Rick swallowed, wiped his mouth, and asked again.

"Ain't tellin'," the waitress said.

Rick didn't care. He'd found his place to eat. He took a bite of the sausage. Lamb, pork, and unknown spices, the best he'd ever tasted. And the location was as perfect as the tater wads. He grabbed the menu. "Hey, can I get a couple of Kitty's biscuits?"

"No," the waitress said as she pulled her order pad from her apron. "Them taters is all the starch you need for breakfast 'less you're fixin' to plow a field, which I bet you ain't." She yanked the top page off the pad and laid it by Rick's plate. "Come back and have the biscuits with yer dinner." Then she walked away.

Rick just said, "Okay."

Twenty minutes later Rick was at the radio station, sitting across the desk from Clay Stubblefield. "Next time try the tomato gravy on grits," Clay said. "Man, it's good." He pointed at Rick. "And get the fried grits, not the regular kind."

Rick nodded. "Uh-huh."

"Regular's fine but I like that crunch you get with the fried ones." Clay made a snapping movement with his hand.

"Sure," Rick said. "I'll do that." He glanced around Clay's office. Paneling from the seventies, photos from Clay's college football days, some local service-club plaques hanging on the walls, a thick glass ashtray, and a framed picture on his desk. "Now, Mr. Stubblefield—"

"Hey, do me a favor. Call me Clay." He rocked back in his chair, hands behind his head. "I'm not real big on formalities."

"Fine. Clay. So, let me ask you—"

Clay sat forward and slapped a hand on his desk. "Oh, hey, I heard a good one last night." He ducked his head and lowered his voice a bit. "This gal left work on a Friday after gettin' her paycheck, right? Went straight to the bank, cashed it, and stayed out the whole weekend partyin'. Spent her whole paycheck. Well, she staggered in late Sunday night and her husband's all pissed off 'cause he'd been stuck with the kids all weekend, right? He'd missed his tee time and a poker game, so he let her have it with both barrels. Finally he stopped yellin' and said, 'How'd you like it if you didn't see me for two or three days?' She said, 'That'd be fine with me.' So Monday went by and she didn't see her husband. Tuesday and Wednesday came and went with the same results. But on Thursday, the swelling went down just enough where she could see him a little out of the corner of her left eye." Clay delivered the punch line with a wink, then slapped the top of his desk.

Rick faked a laugh and thought, *Jesus, this guy's a serious Gomer*. He hoped Clay didn't have a million of 'em. *Then again, based on that tape, this is probably par for the course*. "That's a pretty good one," Rick said. He folded his hands together. "So, Clay. How are we going to work out our situation? Like I said—"

"Oh, yeah, listen. That meeting I had yesterday afternoon? Paid off. Gonna do a big station promotion to announce the new format, lots of on-air giveaways, T-shirts, hats, CDs, all that crap, plus a big cash prize at the end."

"That's great but—"

"But I'll tell ya the best part," Clay said. "Best part is, it's somebody else's cash. That's what that meetin' was about yesterday. That and their time buy." Clay grinned and pointed at Rick. "I mean it's not like we got a real big budget for promotions, right?" He waved dismissively. "You've worked in small markets. You know what I'm talkin' about. But I got that loan outfit to kick in the cash prize on a trade-out. So anyway, you need to get on the horn with all the record reps, local car stereo places, you know, anybody who might throw something in the kitty for a little advertising, get whatever they'll give ya. And start working up some spots, too. You know, something like . . ." Clay dropped into his idea of an FM announcer voice. "W-A-O-RRRRRReal rock. Real cash." Clay seemed surprised at how good that was. "That's not bad." He wrote it on a pad of paper. "You should use that. And use Pink Floyd's money song." He stabbed his pen at the note.

Rick leaned forward and said, "Soon as we get our business squared away."

"Oh, don't worry about that." Clay gave a reassuring chuckle. "I'm going to take care of you, like I said." Clay wrote something else on the pad. He looked up at Rick. "Makin' myself a note right now, talk to payroll about adjusting your situation." He finished his note with a flourish and jabbed a period on the page, then he picked up a spiral-bound document. "Here's your employee handbook." Clay wagged it as he said, "All the usual about insurance and all that." He handed it to Rick. "Read it, sign it, and get it back quick as you can so we can get you on the policy." He paused before saying, "You ain't got any dependents, do you?"

Rick shook his head. "Nope."

Clay winked and said, "At least none you know about, huh?" He picked up the framed photo from his desk. "Here's mine," he said, showing the standard-edition family portrait with the mottled gray backdrop. Mrs. Stubblefield was an angular beauty with dark hair in a soft flip. She was seated with one child in her lap and one sitting at her feet. Clay was lording over them from behind as if it were the late-nineteenth century. "'Course, that was taken a while ago." He pointed at the kids one at a time. "This one's in high school and this one's in seventh or eighth grade. It's hard to keep up."

"Very attractive woman," Rick said.

"Sure was." Clay set the photo back in its place.

Great. She's dead. "Oh. I'm sorry."

"No, nothing like that," Clay said with a smirk. "Shit, Lori's still around . . . my neck, if you know what I mean." He opened his Day-Timer and glanced at his schedule. "In fact you're bound to meet her sooner or later. She likes to drop by unannounced every now and then."

Rick nodded. At first he assumed that meant they were divorced and that the former Mrs. Stubblefield enjoyed picking up her alimony checks in person. Then he noticed the wedding band on Clay's finger. *So he's either remarried or he considers Lori his mill-stone,* Rick thought. *But if he remarried he'd be more likely to have a photo of the new wife on the desk, which he doesn't. And if Clay considers Lori his mill-stone, then those sexual entertainments he bragged about on the tape are more actionable indiscretions than mere escapades. And if that's the case, it ups the number of potential blackmail victims by one Clay Stubblefield, assuming he cares about his marriage. Hey, this amateur detective thing is kind of fun,* Rick thought.

"Anyway." Clay pointed at the speaker in the ceiling. Cream's "White Room." "I assume you been listening since you've been here?"

Rick shrugged. "What I heard on the drive into town and what I caught today. Sounds like you've already changed format."

"Yeah, I put a note in the control room, told every-body to start playing the old stuff. Told 'em the new PD would be here today to narrow it down for 'em." Clay jutted his chin out and rubbed under his neck for a moment, waiting for Rick to say something.

Rick listened as the DJ went from the Cream into a commercial. *"Thinking about a weekend trip to the casinos? Universal Financial Services is your ticket to the tables. If you own your car, get cash today and still drive away! Quick and confidential. Car title loans, payday advances. You need money and we've got it! Universal Financial Services . . ."*

"I get to decide the exact format," Rick said.

"Knock yourself out."

"No interference."

"Well, not until the next ratings book anyway." Another wink, then, "Tch."

Rick reached over and tapped Clay's notepad. "And you're gonna take care of that."

"Consider it done." Clay held his hand out to shake.

Rick knew he was going to regret doing so, but he did it anyway. *It's only rock 'n' roll,* Rick thought. *But I like it.* He shook Clay's hand. "Okay."

Clay looked at his watch. "Good. You need to get started promoting the new format with this contest. And hit that cash-giveaway real big. Folks love the cash giveaways. I don't care what your format is."

"How much?"

"You're gonna love this. Grand prize is one thousand twenty-nine dollars." Clay cocked his eyebrows. "As in one-oh-two-nine? FM? Get it?"

Oh boy, Rick thought. *Big-time Charlie.* "Yeah," he said. "I get it. So when's payday?"

Clay smiled and scratched the side of his head. "Two weeks from yesterday."

"Naturally." Rick and Clay both knew who had whom by the whats. Rick knew his only option was unemployment in a place where he lacked residency and could not, therefore, file for benefits. For that he'd have to drive back to North Dakota.

"Well, okay," Clay said with a glance at his watch. "I gotta get going." He walked Rick out of his office on his way to the parking lot. Stopping in the lobby, Clay reached a hand out to Traci. "Any calls?"

Traci held up a fist of pink message sheets. "Mr. Dribbling called," she said. "Wants you to call back." ·

Rick tried not to react when he heard the name. Bernie Dribbling was the main player Clay talked about on the tape. He wondered what the call was about but switched his attention instinctively to the overhead speaker when he heard the DJ segue to The Band from *Rock of Ages*. Rick nodded. This was the first interesting music selection he'd heard since he arrived. Allan Toussaint's horn arrangement on the Holland, Dozier, Holland classic "Don't Do It" had only improved over the decades. Rick imagined the guy in the control room was a balding sixties relic in tie-dye.

Clay took the phone messages from Traci then shook Rick's hand again and said, "Welcome aboard, buddy." Then he breezed out to the parking lot, the glass door closing slowly behind him.

Rick stood there, looking after Clay, shaking his head.

"We call it gettin' Stubbled," Traci said from her desk. She wrinkled her nose and said, "It's a little rough at first but you get used to it." She flashed a welcome-to-the-club smile.

"Guess I should've seen that coming," he said.

"As long as you've been in radio?" She nodded. "Yeah."

Rick smiled and sat on the corner of the reception desk. "You would've warned me if you'd had the chance, though, right?"

"Oh, if I knew then what I know now?"

"Yeah."

"Oh yeah, I'd've given you the heads-up."

"Appreciate it."

"It's nothing."

"True," Rick said. "But in theory you would've saved me some trouble."

Traci held her right hand out and looked at her fingernails. She said, "I don't care much for theories."

Rick gave a nod. "You're more practical."

"Exactly." She picked at a cuticle. "I prefer the concrete to the abstract."

"Concrete like, for example, dinner?"

She paused before saying, "Maybe." The phone rang. Traci held up her finger. "Dubya-ay-oh-ahhr." Her voice lapsed into Southern Belle every time she answered the phone. Rick wondered if she knew she did that. "Mmm. Hold, please." She connected the call then looked at Rick, more wary than anything else. "Where were we?"

"Maybe at dinner."

"Right," Traci said. "Now, what, exactly, did you have in mind?"

Rick conjured an innocent look. "I was just hoping you might be able to help me out since I'm new in town. You know, the whole kindness-of-strangers thing. Show me the local hot spots, help me with my accent, fill me in on who's who in McRae, that sort of stuff."

"Oh. And that's it?"

To Rick's dismay she still sounded more suspicious than disappointed. "I tell you what," he said. "Why don't you think about it?"

"Think about having dinner with you?"

Rick cocked his head and said, "What else would you think about doing with me?"

Traci smiled and adjusted her headset. "I guess I should've seen that coming."

Rick stood up. "Long as you've been beautiful?" He nodded. "Yeah."

When the phone rang again, Traci pointed down the hall. "Don't you have a job?" She punched a button. "Dubya-ay-oh-ahhr. Mmm. Hold please."

Rick turned and headed for his office, intrigued and infatuated. He liked how Traci switched from Southern Belle to screwball-comedy flirt and back at the drop of a hat. He knew about the dangers of office romance but some things are stronger than mere knowledge.

Rick walked into his new office. Mail was piled on the desk: *Radio & Records, Hitmaker* magazine, *Billboard*, and promotional CDs. He sat down and was about to start reading the charts when "Don't Do It" began to fade overhead. Rick wondered what the jock would play next. It turned out to be Clapton's "Lay Down Sally." Rick thought, *Could have been worse. Could have been "Cocaine."*

He tossed the *Billboard* onto his desk and headed for the studio. He stopped at the double-paned window and looked in. The guy in the chair was facing away, looking at the albums on the far wall. Rick tapped on the glass then walked in. The guy wheeled around to see who it was. To Rick's surprise, he wasn't a leftover hippie. He a wide-eyed kid, fifteen or sixteen, young enough to be Rick's son. He waved tentatively and said, "Hi. Can I help you?"

"I'm the new PD," Rick said. "Who are you?"

"Oh!" The kid jumped up and held out his hand. "Mr. Shannon. I'm Rob North." He pointed at the microphone. "Mr. Stubblefield said I could do the morning show till you got here." Rob started gathering his stuff.

"What are you doing?"

"Getting out of your way."

"Shouldn't you be in school or something?"

"Oh, I dropped out." He tried to say it in a way that sounded cool.

"So you could work here?"

He nodded. "Mr. Stubblefield said I could just get a GED. Said I didn't really need college if I was going to work in radio, which is what I want to do."

Rick pointed at the turntable. "Your record's running out."

"Oh!"

Rick figured the LP had about five revolutions before the song was finished. No way the kid was going to pull this off. Rob yanked an album from the wall. In one smooth motion he slipped the LP from the sleeve, eyeballed the song list, flipped to the other side, slipped it onto the spindle, dropped the needle perfectly in the groove between tracks two and three, and brought the level up to the applause leading into "Space Captain" from *Mad Dogs and Englishmen*. Rob looked at Rick. "Is that okay?"

Rick nodded, impressed. "Fine."

"Not too obscure?"

"No, in fact we're going to start playing more stuff like that." Rick reached for the album cover. "Where'd you learn the music?"

"My dad mostly. He had a pretty good collection. It's mine now." He paused for a moment before he said, "And I grew up listening to a New Orleans station that played all this stuff."

Rick gestured at the board. "Turn it up." Leon Russell, Rita Coolidge, and a dozen others attending Joe Cocker's finest moment. It was enough to make Rick forget for the moment that he'd been conned by Stubblefield. It sounded so good it reminded Rick of what he loved about radio and he suddenly saw the bright side of his circumstance. Someone had just given him the keys to a fifty-thousand-watt rock 'n' roll radio station. A laboratory to create the perfect "classic" format. True, you couldn't get a loan against that, but it was something.

Rob checked his program log and pulled the appropriate spot carts for the upcoming break. Then he grabbed *Goat's Head Soup* and cued "Dancing with Mr. D." "Listen, Mr. Shannon, uh, I know I'm not that experienced or anything but like I told Mr. Stubblefield—"

"How much is he paying you?"

"Paying?"

"Yeah, like minimum wage?"

Rob shook his head. "Mr. Stubblefield said he couldn't pay me but I could work for free, for the experience. For my résumé."

Rick narrowed his eyes. "You dropped out of high school to work for nothing? They didn't teach you much before you dropped out, did they? How long've you been doing this?"

"Working for free? About a year, but mostly overnights. I just dropped out a week ago so I could do mornings after Captain Jack stopped coming to work. This is the first time I've done a morning shift. Traci said I need to talk more, but I figured nobody's tuning in to hear me talk, so I've been concentrating more on music than the whole, you know, personality thing."

Rick folded his arms and looked at Rob. "You're

aware that Stubblefield is a USDA, grade-A weasel?"

Rob laughed nervously and glanced down at the turntable. "Traci calls it gettin' Stubbled, but he's okay, I guess. I get free CDs and stuff. Plus it's cool to work here. I mean I wanna work in radio for a career and all, so—"

"You want a paying job?"

"Yeah, but Mr. Stubblefield said nobody'd pay me since I don't have experience, so he—"

"Stubbled you."

"Well, I didn't think of it like that."

"You want a paying job now?"

"Here?"

"Right here."

"Yes, sir."

"You're hired."

"Really? Overnights?"

Rick shook his head. "Morning show."

Rob's eyes popped wide. "For money?"

"Yeah, but not enough to quit school for."

"Thanks, Mr. Shannon. The money's not important."

"Good," Rick said. "With that attitude, you'll go far in radio."

Rick returned to his office with a sense of satisfaction. Not only had he made Rob's day but he'd stuck it to Stubblefield, at least a little. He couldn't believe the moron had told Rob to drop out of high school. The kid had some talent and what he needed was someone to nurture it, someone to encourage him to pursue his education. What he didn't need was Stubblefield's advice.

Back in his office Rick looked at the employee files.

He found the name of Rob's high school and placed a call. The principal and the guidance counselor were both busy, so Rick left a message. He was about to start working on the spots for the big cash giveaway when he heard someone coming down the hall singing, "Meet the new boss! Dat-da-dah! Same as the old boss! Dun-du-duh!"

Rick looked to the door just as J. C. Whalen, the midday jock, entered playing air guitar.

"Hoodang howdy, y'all! J. C. Whalen reporting for duty." He gave a salute and said, "You must be Ricky Dicky Shannon." With a big drooping mustache and weathered face, J.C. looked like the cowboy on the cover of a Pure Prairie League record. He sat across the desk from Rick. "Got any do's and don'ts I should know about, Kemosabe?"

Rick smiled and shook his head. "I'm pretty easy to work for, J.C."

"That's what they all say, Ricky Dicky." J.C. fluttered his hands as he said, "But next thing you know, I've crossed some invisible line and then I'm working overnights for a beautiful music station in Tulsa wondering where I can get my hands on a gun and wondering if I should put it in my mouth or to my temple, so just go ahead and tell me now what I'm not allowed to do or say and everything'll be beautiful in its own way."

Rick grinned and said, "Okay." He leaned across the desk gravely. "Two rules."

"Name 'em."

"Okay, first rule. No dead air."

"I'm down with that," J.C. said. "What else?"

"Second rule is this. If I catch you playing anything by Yoko, I'll dock you a day's pay."

J.C. fussed with his mustache and said, "Shit, boss, if you catch me playing Yoko, you can hang my nekkid ass from the transmitter tower." He held out his hand to shake. "I think we'll get along just fine. Now, if you'll excuse me." J.C. stood and headed for the control room. "Won't get fooled agaaaaiiinnnnnnn!"

The phone rang. It was the principal from Rob's high school. Rick talked the guy into reenrolling Rob and turning his radio job into a work-study program for credit. The principal agreed and worked out a schedule for Rob's remaining requirements.

After that, Rick phoned the rest of his jocks to introduce himself and to call a staff meeting. He spent the rest of the day getting acquainted with station routines and paperwork. He also met the afternoon jock, a bubbly product of Central Mississippi University's radio, television, and film department. She called herself Autumn Browne and swore it was her real name. She was competent on the board and had a perky presence on the air, though she knew precious little about music before Duran Duran. But she was adventurous and willing to play anything requested, no matter how jarring the mix. Thus did Rick have to explain why she shouldn't follow the synthesized prog-rock of Yes's "Roundabout" with the southern boogie of the Marshall Tucker Band without something transitional to soften the blow.

All in all, though, Rick was pleased. Now that he'd hired Rob for mornings, he could take the gig he'd signed up for in the first place. He could start his day midafternoon and leave after his evening air shift, resulting in minimal contact with Stubblefield. The programming wouldn't take much time, and the extra money would be good. Of course that assumed Stubblefield would actually come through with the raise and wouldn't fire him for hiring Rob. *And if the prick does fire me,* Rick thought, *there's always the tape.*

On his way home from work, Rick was tempted to stop at Kitty's for some more tater wads or to try the biscuits or the tomato gravy on grits but he figured there would be plenty of time for that. Instead, he stopped at the grocery store, then drove back to the trailer to make dinner. Afterward he sat down to listen again to the tape of Clay's phone conversation.

"And you know that bitch wanted me to come back to her motel room and piss on her?" Rick was as interested in how Clay said this as he was in the words themselves. Rather than sounding offended at the suggestion, Stubblefield sounded like he was bragging, as if he was proud to possess whatever it was that made a woman invite a man to do such a thing in a Mississippi motel room.

The other man whispered, *"No kiddin'?"* He sounded impressed or jealous, one.

"Hell no, I ain't kiddin'," Clay said with a chuckle. *"And I was ready to go get it, too."*

"Oh yeah."

"You know."

"Sure. You bet."

Clay continued by saying, *"That's thing I love 'bout these pageants. These gals always trying to get ya to do all kinda stuff, which is fine, you know. But I tell you, it's something. Tch."*

"Oh, I bet it is."

"And she was just one of the gals I met at this last one."

"Yeah, what was the deal on that?" the other man wanted to know. *"You started tellin' me at the Booster Club meeting. This was down on the coast?"*

"Yeah, them promoters got damn pageants goin' all the time, you know, Miss Collard Green or Miss Central Jones County, or whatever. They all over, but this one was at that new casino in Biloxi, the Gold Coast? Anyway these promoters always need celebrity—so-called celebrity judges, you know, sit up there, make it look official." Clay sucked a little air through his front teeth. *"Tch."*

"Oh yeah, I gotcha."

"And lemme tell you what, those girls are the most ruthless, cutthroat bitches you've ever met in your life."

"Really?" The other man seemed surprised to hear this.

Clay sounded incredulous as he said, *"Ohhh, my God, they're just professional whores."* Then he lightened his tone a bit before continuing: *"When I say professional whores, I mean they just, they eat up with this beauty pageant shit. They just live, breathe, and eat it and would just do anything to win, you know. Anything. They didn't say, 'I'll fuck you,' you know, they—they just come over and they'd grab you and they'd just . . . your dick'd be harder'n anything you got and they'd be rubbin' all over you. They'd just flatter your ego. They'd say, 'I've heard so much about you. I am so thrilled to meet you. Damn, you're good-looking,' you know, and uh, 'There's nothing I like better than a sexy judge,' and shit like that."*

The man on the other end issued a strangled laugh. *"Oh, ho, ho, hoooo."*

Rick imagined this guy at his job, sitting behind his desk, hand cupped over the mouthpiece, trying to make it look and sound like he was on a business call. At the same time Rick pictured Clay in his office, feet up on his desk and his door shut, as he proudly told his tales.

"I mean just, like Tammy? She was one of the worst ones," Clay said. *"Just them girls all over you. Tch. Well, I went crazy and I had a piece of ass lined up and got drunk there and fucked around and finally left to go get this piece of ass and I was two hours late with this other gal and she got pissed off and stood me up and I came back and all the girls were done sacked up doubled together and I didn't get nothing but a hand job, you know."*

The other man said, *"Um-hmm."* Like it was the Gospel.

Rick stopped the tape. *This guy is a piece of work,* he thought. *Two hours late for a rendezvous and he accuses the girl of standing him up. And the claim about the hand job at the end of the night was pure bullshit. Had to be. Still, the dim bulb on the other end sounded like he was buying it. Stubblefield knows his audience,* Rick thought as he started the tape again.

Clay said, *"And then I had a judge, woman named Lisa Ramey, down there that was good-lookin' that I was takin' care of, so . . . but that's how I met Tammy."*

"Uh-huh."

"So that's the kind of girl she is."

"Ohhh yeah."

Rick thought it sounded like two goats talking.

"She could be had," Clay said, referring to Tammy.

"She just wouldn't meet you for a piece of ass. She'd go outta town with you, spend a little of your money."

"Yeah, you'd have to spend a little money on her." Suddenly the expert.

"Yeah," Clay said.

"Wouldn't be none of this wham, bam, thank you, ma'am. You'd have to spend a little money."

This part of the conversation was starting to dwindle when Clay either remembered or invented some more. *"That night, them girls, I mean, and braless in these loose tops?"* Clay was all but breathless. *"They'd come over and lean up and just . . . show you their titties, just turn that blouse around where you could look at 'em down there. And you'd just stare at 'em down there and they'd smile at you, you know. I'm tellin' you."*

"Where, down there at that pageant?"

"Yeah, it just drove me crazy. This was the Friday night before . . . the pageant was Saturday night, and this was a judges' reception cocktail party, held in a suite, and it's just the judges, and hell, the judges was—I was the only one coulda gotta hard."

"They were old?"

"Well, a buncha old women," Clay said. *"Director of the Hinds Highsteppers and the, some old lady that, uh, that was in charge of the Maids of Cotton for the Tourism Council or something, people like that, you know."*

"Uh-huh."

"Some old man, publisher of some newspaper up in the Delta and he was in his seventies, you know. And so, shit, them girls knew I'd compromise myself in a New York minute."

It was hard to tell whether Clay's chuckling tone was intended as a modestly shameful confession of his ethical shortcomings or was meant to convey pride in his lack of moral constraints in pursuit of pussy. In any event, the guy on the other end laughed before remarking, *"Say, your scruples are not that high, huh?"* He pronounced the word *skrreew-pulls*, emphasis on the *skrreew*.

"Shiiit no," Clay replied. *"Yours aren't either. I'da thowna vote for a piece of ass in a New York minute."*

The other guy got a big laugh out of that. *"Say, you coulda . . . you coulda been had, huh?"*

"Oh, I coulda been had," Clay said jovially before growing serious. *"You ain't never made a loan for a piece of ass, have ya?"*

The answer shot back. *"Newwwww! Uh-uh. Never have."* As if he were beyond reproach.

Clay jumped in with authority, saying, *"That's one criteria. I guess that's one thing when you're dealin' with money, you're dealin' with your morals or a little advertising or a damn T-shirt or something's a little different."*

"Oh yeah," the creep agreed.

Rick hit the stop button, thinking, *What?* He rewound it. *"That's one criteria,"* Clay said again. *"I guess that's one thing when you're dealin' with money, you're dealin' with your morals or a little advertising or a damn T-shirt or something's a little different."*

What the hell does that mean? Rick wondered. *Maybe he meant to say BUT a little advertising, not OR a little advertising. "When you're dealin' with money, you're dealin' with your morals, BUT a little advertising or a damn T-shirt or something's a little different."*

That made more sense but still didn't stack up as much of a philosophy.

Rick wondered about the other guy. Who was he? Clay's question about whether the guy had ever made a loan for sex narrowed it down to loan shark or regular banker. Clay narrowed it down even further at the end of the tape when he said, *"I tell you what, lemme run by tomorrow and pick up that damn thing, you still out at the branch?"*

"Yeah," the creepy guy said. *"It's out at the branch."*

"You, is that where you're at?"

"Yeah."

"Okay, I'll run by and talk to you and we'll see about that girl."

Creepy guy laughed and said, *"All right! We'll see ya."* Click.

In Rick's experience, there were only two things with branches: plants and banks. *You still out at the branch* implied this guy wasn't a bank president, otherwise he'd be at the main office. Rick figured he was a loan officer, perhaps a manager, at a branch of a local bank. Rick grabbed the Yellow Pages. There were about thirty listed. Not exactly a needle in a haystack, but still, a lot of legwork.

Rick laughed as he tossed the phone book to the floor. He was beginning to think he'd wandered down the wrong career path. So far this amateur detective thing was fun. Of course he remembered back to his first year in radio when it was still a thrill and not just an efficient way of going into debt without having anything to show for your troubles.

But he had to ask himself why. Why was he playing

Kojak? Just because Stubblefield had screwed him over? What was Rick going to do, blackmail Clay for cheating on his wife? And if so, in return for what? The lesser job he originally signed up for? No, he wasn't interested in blackmail. So what was he after?

The only motive that came to mind was finding out what had happened to Captain Jack. Rick was naturally curious. But why, beyond being nosy, would he care about what happened? It wasn't as if he'd taken a blood oath with the ancient fraternal order of disc jockeys, vowing to avenge the death of any fellow member. Besides, that assumed Jack Carter was dead. The only thing certain was that he had disappeared. But based on the rest of the tape, Rick couldn't escape his assumption that Captain Jack was as dead as Jerry Garcia and probably less grateful.

So that was it. Rick figured someone had killed Jack Carter. So why not just turn the tape over to the cops? Rick smirked while thinking you didn't have to be Sidney Poitier to suspect corruption in a small southern police department. Besides, that wouldn't be any fun.

So. Where would he start? His theory hinged on one or more irate blackmail victims, so Rick thought he'd start there. But which one? Clay was out since he knew where Rick lived and worked. And if it turned out that Clay was as dangerous as he was dishonest then revealing knowledge of the tape would just be plain stupid. So Rick would start with somebody who didn't know him.

The creepy banker guy seemed useless, nothing on the tape to blackmail him with. Ditto the women in charge of the Highsteppers and Maids of Cotton and the septuagenarian newspaper publisher whose only sin was erectile dysfunction. There was no dirt on the girl named Tammy but Rick thought she still might be worth talking to. But who was she? One of the beauty pageant contestants? How would he find her? *This private eye thing isn't as easy as it looks on TV,* Rick thought.

And what about the woman who wanted the golden shower? Rick figured that was at least minor blackmail material, more if it turned out she was in the choir. But Clay hadn't provided a name for her, just a predilection.

Then there was Lisa Ramey, the beauty pageant judge Clay said he was *takin' care of.* If it turned out she was married, she'd be open to blackmail. Rick decided to start by finding Lisa Ramey and seeing if she was married. If so, he'd start asking more questions.

Rick listened to the rest of the tape again. After the part about Lisa Ramey, the accusations graduated from fetishes to felonies, and Rick wasn't sure he was interested in crossing that line just yet. Not on his salary.

3

J. C. Whalen walked into Rick's office wearing sunglasses at two o'clock. He jerked to a stop when he saw the crowded room and said, "Bow me up like a cut worm on a cabbage leaf!" He lifted his glasses and looked around. "Nobody saved me a seat?"

Rob started to get up from the floor where he was sitting. "Here, take mine."

J.C. held him down. "Thanks, partner. I prefer the back of the class." He went to the far wall and leaned against it. J.C. looked around and said, "Where's the teacher?" When no one answered, he shrugged and started playing a drum riff on his stomach. *Pa-da-da-da-dapa-da-da*.

Rick walked in with a copy of Led Zeppelin's fourth album in one hand and a screwdriver in the other. He set them on his desk then nodded at the two weekend part-timers he'd met a few minutes earlier. He turned to Rob. "Did we hear from the overnight guy?"

"No, sir," Rob said. "He doesn't have a phone that we know of."

J.C. put a hand across one of his eyes and said, "Eyeeeee. Uncle Victor, the Midnight Pirate, doesn't attend staff meetin's. Arrrrrrrrgh."

"Anyway, he's probably still asleep," Rob said. "He told me once that he usually doesn't get up until four or five in the afternoon. I'll tell him everything, though, don't worry."

Autumn Browne bounced into the room. "Okay, we got fourteen minutes courtesy of Peter Frampton."

J.C. blurted out, "Dooooo yooouu, you! Feeeeel like . . . a midnight pirate?"

Rick held his hand up. "Okay, let's do this," he said. "I'm going to keep this short. As you know, I'm Rick Shannon, the new program and music director. As you've heard by now, we're switching from a very broad rock format to some version of classic rock." He turned and picked up the Zeppelin album. He slipped the record from its sleeve and said, "Now, I've worked in classic rock since before it was classic but this is the first time I've created my own version of the format. I haven't decided the exact parameters, but I can tell you one thing right now." Rick picked up the screwdriver and placed the tip into the groove at the start of "Stairway to Heaven." "We're not going to play the classic rock clichés." He gouged the screwdriver through the grooves of the song until he hit the label.

The jocks looked at one another.

"I want you to stop playing the same old shit and go to the deeper cuts on the albums," Rick said. "And I want you to play J. J. Cale and Ry Cooder and Frank

Zappa and Canned Heat. I want sets that are thoughtful and inspired. I don't want us to sound like every classic rock station in the country with a morning zoo crew and Two-for-Tuesdays and No-Repeat-Wednesdays and all that crap. I want us to sound so different that people will stop and listen. I want us to sound so unique that people talk about us. In the words of Joni Mitchell, I want to stand out like a ruby in a black man's ear." Rick tossed the record onto his desk and continued: "Rob's taking the morning shift. I'll do eight to midnight. Anybody interested in helping define our version of classic rock can meet here Sunday at noon. We'll eat some pizzas, have some pop, and argue about the music."

J.C. perked up. "Who's got some pot?"

"I said *pop*," Rick said. "But we need to talk later. Any other questions?" He looked around but no one had anything to say. "Nothing? Okay. One last thing, then. I want you to do every hour of your shift like it was mix tape for someone you love. All right? Let's rock and roll, guys. We've got some great music to work with, so let's do it. Thanks for your time." The staff scattered.

Rick went into the control room and started an inventory of the station's library. He pulled the obvious nonclassic rock discs, anything past '79 or so. When he was finished, there remained a basic foundation for Rick's idea of classic rock, though there were some holes to be plugged. Rick would provide from his collection (and Captain Jack's) and he'd ask staffers to provide what they could from their own collections until he got them for the station.

Among the records not in WAOR's library was the one Rick always played first when he started at a new station. Having anticipated this possibility, he had brought his personal copy. It was almost time for him to start his shift. He left the studio while Autumn was signing off the transmitter and program logs. When he came back with his record, she was on the phone taking a request. "Okay," Autumn said. "I'll tell the next guy. He probably knows." She hung up and turned to Rick. "Ever heard of Captain Beyond? The guy who just called wanted some song about . . . breathing or being short of breath or something. He couldn't remember the title. Oh, hang on." She started her last record, Robin Trower's "Day of the Eagle," then looked back at Rick. "Wasn't that, like, an old Elton John album? Like *Captain Beyond and the Dirty Brown Cowboys?*"

"*Captain Fantastic and the Brown Dirt Cowboy,*" Rick said. "He's looking for Captain Beyond's 'Sufficiently Breathless.' Band formed by some Deep Purple and Iron Butterfly guys. Did a couple of good records in the early seventies that we don't have."

Autumn unplugged her headphones and yielded the board to Rick. "It's all yours," she said as she went to file away her last couple of albums.

Rick sat down in front of the board. He pulled out his copy of *Johnny Winter and . . . Live* and cued up his song. "Of course you don't want to confuse Captain Beyond with Captain Beefheart." He stuck out his tongue and wiggled it around. "*Lick my decals off, baby.*"

Autumn said, "Excuse me?"

"Title of one of his albums."

"Captain Beyond?"

"Beefheart."

"Oh."

Autumn stopped at the door on her way out of the studio. "Know who I used to like? Captain and Tennille." She sang a line from the chorus of "Love Will Keep Us Together." "That's pretty old," she said. "Does that count as classic rock?"

Rick put his hands together and spoke in an exaggerated Master Po voice. "Glasshoppa, you have much to rearn." He gestured at the chair by the door. "Sit and I will show you tlue crassic lock."

"You know, when people talk about things being politically incorrect?" She pointed at Rick. "That's what they're talking about."

Rick feigned shock. "Porritcarry incollect? Sit and rearn."

Autumn looked at her watch. "Can I risten in my car? I've got to be somewhere in, rike, ten minutes."

Rick waved her off. "Go then, glasshoppa, but risten as you dlive about town."

"Okay, see you Sunday."

Robin Trower was winding down. Rick put on his headphones and cleared his throat a couple of times. At the top of the hour he opened his mike and said, "You're listening to WAOR-FM, McRae, Mississippi. I'm Rick Shannon and this . . . is classic rock." He slammed into Johnny Winter screaming *"ROCK 'N' ROOOOOOOLLLLLLLL!!!"* before Johnny and Rick Derringer tore the roof off the sucker with their version of "Johnny B. Goode."

Rick cranked the volume up until the windows shook and the jock in the AM studio looked over with concern. Rick waved, then sat back in his chair thinking, *Is this any way for a grown man to make a living?*

The phones were always active during a format change. The worst Rick had ever been through was in the midseventies. He was working at a rock station that switched to something known in the industry as "beautiful music." The venom and fury of the calls were astounding. "You pissant motherfuckers suck! You better watch your ass when you go to your car! Somebody's gonna kill you!" was typical. The reaction to WAOR's change was far less threatening. "Wow," one caller said. "I haven't heard that song in thirty years. Thanks, man." Of course there were some complaints, people wanting Metallica or Hootie and the Blowfish and other stuff that didn't fit the new format. Rick took it all in stride.

At eleven-fifty, the door to the studio opened. Rick looked up from the board to see an older man standing there, a worn leather satchel strapped over his shoulder. He had a blunt white goatee and pinched lips that brought to mind Dennis Hopper playing a rigid and discontented philosophy professor. He scanned the room before his eyes settled on Rick. "I'm Uncle Victor," he said in a voice like dark chocolate.

"How are ya?" Rick nodded. "I'm Rick Shannon, the new PD."

Uncle Victor squinted at him. "Do I still have a job?"

Rick smiled. "Yeah, no problem. But we're tweaking the format a little."

"Yes, I've been listening," Uncle Victor said. "I think I understand where you're going."

"Great." Rick started his final record for the night, the Blood, Sweat & Tears version of "God Bless the Child." "We're meeting here Sunday at noon to figure out the music."

Uncle Victor took the satchel from his shoulder. "That's good," he said.

Rick thought it was an unusual response until he realized Uncle Victor was referring to the old Billie Holiday song he was playing. Rick felt oddly pleased to receive this stranger's blessing on his music selection. As he started to gather his things, Rick said, "You really don't have a phone?"

"I don't like the noise."

Rick stepped aside and said, "Yeah, but makes it hard to order out for pizza."

Uncle Victor remained expressionless. He sat at the board and adjusted the master level downward the slightest bit. "I've never missed a shift," he said as he pulled a record from his satchel. It was a copy of *The Paul Butterfield Blues Band*. He cued Willie Dixon's "Mellow Down Easy." He put on his headphones and went about his work as if no one else were in the room.

"Well, great talking to you," Rick said. He filed his records then walked out of the studio thinking that anybody who came out of the gate with Paul Butterfield was going to be all right with the new format. He left the station confident that it was in good, if peculiar, hands.

Rick stopped at Kitty's for dinner. It was just past midnight and the place was quiet, only a few truckers having coffee. Rick ordered the tomato gravy on the fried grits along with a chicken-fried steak, two of Kitty's biscuits, and a beer.

He got back to his trailer a little before one. He turned on the radio to monitor the overnight show. Uncle Victor was in a commercial break. *"Universal Financial Services is the answer to your prayers. UFS? It's the best!"*

Uncle Victor came out of the spot break into Big Brother & the Holding Company. He followed that with the Velvet Underground. The man was obviously fluent with the new format but he never referred to himself as the Midnight Pirate as J.C. had led him to believe. Instead he called his show *Uncle Victor's Wax Museum.* Rick liked it.

He sat down in the Barcalounger and reached for his cigar box. Supply was running low. He'd talk to J.C. about that. He took a small hit on his pipe then started to think about how he was going to find this Lisa Ramey. He picked up the phone book with doubts that it could be as easy as that. But her number was listed, though it didn't show an address.

Rick went to his computer, which he had set up earlier in the day. He searched the Web and found forty or fifty hits on Lisa Ramey, the majority of which were associated with beauty pageants. She judged them. She promoted them. And she used to participate in them. Rick found a picture taken at the Deckern County Motor Speedway. It was Lisa Ramey being crowned Miss

Auto Tire & Parts 1995. No debutante, this girl. Sultry shoulders and misspent youth stacked on long legs sheathed in leather. Delta Burke meets Joan Jett.

Rick poked around on the other Web sites until he found what he needed. He hit the print button. It turned out that Lisa Ramey was judging a pageant the next afternoon, down in Biloxi. Rick returned to the Miss Auto Tire & Parts photo. It somehow reminded him of when he was a kid and he'd go to the Mississippi State Fair and he'd see the posters for the freak shows. And he was never sure if the seduction was fear or desire. But the next thing he'd know, he'd be digging in his pocket for coins.

Rick got up around eleven. He had some coffee and toast while he read what he had printed out the night before. The Junior Miss Magnolia Blossom Pageant was being held at the Convention Center in Biloxi at two that afternoon. *Just a five-minute drive from the Gold Coast Casino!* it promised. *Day care available!*

The Junior Miss Magnolia Blossom Pageant would be what was known in the industry as a one-day regional. There were two dozen categories, each of which promised three or four winners, each of whom would be looking at a rhinestone crown and a fifty-dollar savings bond for her trouble. The big winner would be ordained Overall Grand Supreme, which, to Rick, sounded more like a leadership position in the Klan than a beauty queen title. At the bottom of page two there was some specific—and rather pointed—language about how the judging at *this* pageant would be fair. Winners at *this* pageant would not be selected based on *who you know!* Rick couldn't help but snicker as he imagined some rabid pageant mom railing about how the integrity of these things must be maintained if anyone was going to take them seriously.

Rick filled a go-cup with coffee then turned to the refrigerator. On the front door, under a magnet, there was a photo of Captain Jack with his arm around a pretty brunette, somewhere in the French Quarter. Rick put the picture in his shirt pocket and left. It was just after noon.

Autumn Browne was working the noon-to-six shift. Rick called her from his truck. "Play me some Roxy Music," he said. "The song 'Beauty Queen.'"

Autumn came back a moment later and said, "Don't have the album. How about 'Miss America' by the Spin Doctors?"

"Fine song," Rick said. "Wrong decade. How about 'Biloxi' by Jesse Winchester?"

She came back a second later. "Got it."

"Gimme fifteen minutes." It would take about ninety to get to the coast and he wanted to be on the road when the song came on.

The drive to the coast was fast and easy, and for about forty minutes it gave Rick a chance to hear Autumn work. Rick had suggested she tone down her perkiness and try to sound more like an FM jock from the seventies. The result was a sweet and vaguely seductive persona that Rick thought suited the format. Autumn did a good job ad-libbing the cash-giveaway promo but she was still having problems with her segues. Rick almost drove off the road when she went straight from Don McLean's gentle, acoustic "Vincent" into Zeppelin's "Dancing Days."

When Rick was beyond the range of WAOR's signal he surfed for a rock station on the coast. He wanted to sample their playlist while he worked on his definition of classic rock. When he came across "Purple Haze" he shook his head. *So many great Hendrix songs but they only play six from* Smash Hits. It was the same for all the classic artists. This was what Rick and so many people hated about the format. The playlist was embarrassing. It patronized the audience and, in the process, alienated them from the music they once loved. Radio consultants had started this plague and Clean Signal had finished spreading it across the radioscape. But now that he had his own station, Rick could do something about it, in his own small way.

Rick stayed on Highway 49 until it T-boned into the coast highway at Gulfport, just at the Marine Life Oceanarium, where Donald Trump kissed a sea lion on the mouth while thinking about buying the property so he could build another money factory.

Rick had an early memory of a vacation in Gulfport. Two hours in the back of a Country Squire with rear-facing seats until they stopped at Stuckey's, where they sold fireworks and old black mammy salt-and-pepper shakers and license plates with a cartoon Confederate soldier declaring HELL NO, WE WON'T FORGET. Then another hour and a half down to the coast before emerging from the pine trees to a diamond-white beach and curling blue surf, or so it had seemed. He'd been to Marine Life and gawked at the dolphins' tricks. He'd run on the beach down to the salty water and he wanted to see it all again.

So he drove along the coast, past Marine Life and the

old yacht club. The blue curling surf he remembered was really just a flat, brown gulf, like tea with milk. But there was lots of sand. In fact, the stretch from Biloxi to Henderson Point was the largest man-made beach in the world. Rick remembered when Hurricane Camille hit in August of 1969. Winds over two hundred miles an hour blew in like it was clearing a path for the release of Blind Faith a week later. "Can't Find My Way Home" had always been one of Rick's favorites. After Camille a lot of folks just plain couldn't find their homes.

Rick drove slowly along the coast, marveling at a development plan that mixed garish casinos and tacky T-shirt shops with Beauvoir Plantation, where Jeff Davis had lived his last days.

A hundred and fifteen years since he died and there were still folks on the side of the road waving the Confederate battle flag, like maybe if they could win this one, all wouldn't be lost. Naturally there was a second group, on the far side of a barricade, demonstrating against the first group. They were all gathered near the display of the eight flags that had flown over the Gulf Coast at various points in history. *Too bad they can't put this to rest,* Rick thought.

The protest brought to mind some of the hopeful music of the sixties. Rick thought about the Youngbloods and the chorus of "Get Together." *C'mon, people, now.* And what about Sly and the Family Stone, the integrated San Francisco band that managed to sell racial harmony as it created an original soul, rock, funk sound that could still haul more freight than anything on contemporary "urban" radio? Rick caught a glimpse of the angry face of one of the protesters and was reminded of Sly's song "Don't Call Me Nigger, Whitey."

The nostalgic moment passed a mile later when Rick saw a sign for shrimp po'boys. He stopped and had one with fries and a cold beer and wondered how long it would take him to reach three hundred pounds, given his new diet. After lunch Rick continued down the coast to the Convention Center. He found a space in the far corner of the lot then walked to the ticket window and paid his admission.

Inside the vast Convention Center, Rick paused to get his bearings. The pageant was being held in Hall A, the largest room in the complex. Thirty-nine thousand four hundred and eighty-six square feet of plush carpeting, twenty-foot ceilings, and chandeliers, all divided into smaller areas for the various competitions. Rick saw a sign that said TRUE MAGIC AIRBRUSH TANNING IS AVAILABLE! BOOTH 119! Based on what he'd seen so far, he could imagine a fervent mother dragging her pale child into the booth for a quick spray painting for the George Hamilton competition.

Rick looked through a program to find out which event Lisa Ramey was scheduled to judge. It was sportswear, starting in five minutes. He wouldn't have a chance to talk to her beforehand. He recognized Lisa Ramey the moment he saw her, though she didn't look much like the girl in the 1995 Miss Auto Tire & Parts photo. She made Rick think of the Springsteen lyric about having skin like leather and the diamond-hard look of a cobra. Rick thought she might frighten some of the children.

The competition got under way, so Rick took a seat

and thought about what he'd say to her. Thirty minutes later, after the rhinestones and savings bonds had been doled out, Lisa packed up her stuff and made for the door. Rick followed. She paused now and then in the hallway to chat with people she knew from the pageant circuit. When she finally headed for the parking lot, Rick made his move. "Excuse me," he said from behind. "Miss Ramey?"

"Yes?" She turned around. She must have been expecting someone else because her expression changed from professional affability to something more lurid. "Well, hellooo." She said this in a tone that Rick interpreted as attempted enticement. "What can I *do* for *you?*"

Rick could imagine Stubblefield, a drink sloshing in one hand while he pawed at this woman's desperately enhanced breasts with the other. Rick tried to shake the image from his head. He had to stick to his plan, which was straightforward if rather flimsy. It revolved around a phony identity, a polite smile, and some obvious questions. "Miss Ramey, my name is Buddy Miles," he said. "I'm working a missing-persons case?"

She looked him up and down then smiled and said, "Are you asking me or telling me?"

"Telling," Rick said. He slipped into his deepest FM voice. "Can we speak privately for a moment?"

She touched her ear and said, "You have a *very* nice voice."

Rick gave a slow nod of appreciation. "Can we talk?"

"I take it you're not with the police, since it's not Officer Miles or Detective Miles."

"No," he said. "I'm not with the police." He almost said, *That would make me Stewart Copeland,* but what would be the point?

Simultaneously tilting her head and arching her eyebrows, she said, "So you're a private dick?" She smiled and seemed to glance down at his belt buckle.

He looked, too. "Not exactly."

She reached over and pretended to brush something from his shirt. "You mean you're not licensed to be dicking around?"

Rick smirked at that "No, I'll admit, I'm dicking around without the state's blessing."

"Well, good for you," she said. "Now. What do you want from me?" Again with the suggestive voice.

"Just a few questions."

"Awww, so disappointing, but"—she shrugged—"story of my life. Go ahead."

Rick pulled the photo from his shirt pocket and showed it to her. "Have you ever seen either of these people?" He didn't want to tip his hand by pointing at Captain Jack.

Lisa looked at the photo and said, "Uh, no." An obvious lie.

Rick took the photo back. "Do you know a man named Jack Carter?"

"No." An honest answer.

"Bernie Dribbling?"

She shook her head.

One lie and two answers that seemed on the up-and-up. Rick wondered if she was on to him. Maybe she'd picked up on the Buddy Miles thing. Was it too obvious a pseudonym? He decided to throw in some other names that might shed light on that theory. "How about Brian or Carl Wilson?"

"No, sorry." She shrugged.

Rick nodded slowly. *She wouldn't know the Beach Boys if they showed up in her driveway with a big woody.* He felt it was a safe bet she didn't recognize the name of Jimi Hendrix's onetime drummer, so he forged ahead. "You know anybody named Tammy?"

Lisa snorted a laugh. "Might as well ask if I can point you toward a casino."

"So that's a yes?"

"Sure it's a yes. You can't swing a dead cat around here without hitting a Tammy."

Rick flashed an appreciative grin and said, "How about Clay Stubblefield?"

Lisa reached into her purse for a cigarette and a lighter. "Uhhh, no." Another lie.

"Uhhh, no, you couldn't hit him by swinging a dead cat or you don't know him?" Rick took the lighter from Lisa and sparked it.

Lisa held his hand steady as she lit her cigarette. "The name doesn't ring a bell," she said, taking the lighter back.

"Hmm." Rick nodded. "That's interesting."

"How so?" Lisa turned her head and exhaled. She seemed nervous.

"Well, the reason I say that is Mr. Stubblefield has been overheard telling people that the two of you had, uhhh . . ." Rick looked around before making a subtle punching gesture with his right fist.

She looked at the gesture, then at Rick. "Really."

She took another drag on her cigarette then said, "Well, Mr. Stubblefield told *me* he was hung like a jack donkey."

Rick tried not to look surprised. "Did he?"

"Yeah, but that didn't make it true." She smiled.

Rick looked at her for a moment before he said, "Lemme buy you a drink?"

"Are you asking or telling?"

By the time they got to the Gold Coast Casino it was past four and the bar was crowded. They sat at the table farthest from the door, where the constant ding-ding-dinging of the slot machines was least annoying. They ordered drinks. Lisa pulled another cigarette from her purse. She tamped it down solid on the table. "So who's the missing guy?"

"Name's Jack Carter."

The waitress brought their drinks. A bottle of beer and a vodka rocks. Lisa poked at the lime in her glass. "What do you think happened to him?"

Rick sipped his beer then said, "I think he tried to blackmail somebody and it backfired."

"And you think I'm the blackmailee?" Rick lit her cigarette. "You think I made him a missing person?"

"Not really," Rick said. "I've got a couple better prospects. I was just hoping you might know something that would help."

Lisa cocked her head and blew a column of smoke toward the ceiling. "So what, was he a friend of yours, or are you hired help?"

Rick picked at the label on his beer bottle. "Let's say he was a friend."

"Good, 'cause I wouldn't want to go to bed with anyone who was doing this for money."

Rick thought that was pretty finicky for a woman who had slept with Clay Stubblefield. Still, she had his attention, despite her reptilian appearance. He said, "So has anyone approached you about—"

"The guy." She reached over and pulled the picture from Rick's shirt pocket. "He tried to get some money from me. But he didn't call himself Jack Carter. Didn't use a name at all."

"What happened?"

"He said he'd been hired by Clay's wife. Said he had a tape with Clay on it that implicated me . . . us." Lisa rolled her hand in a gesture intended to mean sex. "He said I'd get dragged into legal proceedings surrounding the divorce, and it wouldn't be worth it." She made a sour face. "But he said he could keep my name out of it."

"For money."

"A fee, yeah."

"And?"

"And I told him to fuck off."

Rick smiled. He liked her attitude. He waved at the waitress then looked at Lisa. "You want another?"

"Please."

Rick ordered another round then returned her attention to the photo. He tapped it with his finger. "So you told him to fuck off and that was the last you saw of him?"

"Yeah, until I took him out on a shrimp boat, chopped him up, and tossed him in the Gulf Stream." She finished her drink and started chewing on a piece of ice.

Rick looked mildly abashed before he said, "Sorry to have to ask this, but . . . you and Mr. Stubblefield. Really did . . . uhhhh?" He made the punching motion again.

"Yeah. Once." She stamped her cigarette out and looked at Rick, shrugging her eyebrows. "We met at one of these pageants. We had a few drinks. It was just one of those things."

"So he was telling the truth about that."

"Long as he didn't brag he was good in bed, he was telling the truth." She shook her head. "He's a sorry fuck. Strictly in it for himself. He's also a tightwad and a liar."

"You mean about his . . . manliness?"

"That plus he said he was divorced. And, obviously, I found out later he wasn't." Lisa leaned forward and said, "Has anyone ever told you you have beautiful hair?" She reached up and ran her fingers through it. "I hope you don't mind."

Rick sat there and let her do it. It felt nice. He tried to imagine what she looked like twenty years ago. The waitress brought the second round of drinks. Rick handed her his credit card and asked for the tab.

"What's your hurry?" Lisa squeezed the lime wedge, then sucked the last bit of juice from it before dropping it into her glass. "You interviewing a prettier girl later?"

Rick pointed vaguely north and said, "I've got a little drive ahead of me." He wanted to keep this strictly business, but he was a weak man. Despite her appearances, if she made one more suggestive remark, he might cave in. Rick waited until the waitress was out of earshot before he said, "You think he's capable of killing someone?"

"Clay?" Lisa shook her head. "I doubt it. My limited experience? He's a *lot* more talk than action. But he hinted around that he was connected, you know, all plugged in. 'Course, he might've just been trying to sound like a big shot, you know, to compensate." She wiggled her pinkie.

Rick paused and lowered his voice. "Connected like, what, Dixie Mafia?"

Lisa made a face. "Oh, I don't know about that. Maybe just some mean-ass people, but on the other hand, who knows? Could be. Guys like Clay know everybody who runs anything in and around Deckern County."

Rick sipped his beer. He hadn't considered that as a possibility, but why not? The Dixie Mafia wasn't a charity organization. They were serious, violent rednecks, and if Captain Jack had crossed them, well, his radio career wasn't the only thing that was over. Rick set his beer on the cardboard coaster. "Excuse me for a minute." He stood and looked around before stopping a waitress to ask directions to the rest room.

At the door to the bar, Rick had to step aside when a boisterous trio rambled in three abreast. Two women about the size of four with no business wearing shorts had left home wearing them anyway. They were flanking a guy who seemed excessively smug to be sporting a T-shirt that said WHO FARTED?

The woman on his left spoke with a cigarette bobbing on her lips. "Oooh, are we fixin' to have us some large fun now, or whuuut?"

"Hell pecker, yes," the man said. "It don't get no better'n this!"

Rick wondered if the man's optimism was buoyed more by the size of his escorts, his plastic cup full of nickels, or the fact he still had several teeth in his mouth. Rick made his way to the bathroom knowing this would remain one of life's mysteries.

When he returned, Lisa was gone but the plastic folder with the credit card receipt was on the table. He figured Lisa had gone to the ladies' room, so he sat down to sign the tab. When he opened the folder he saw his credit card was missing. In its place was a hotel-room key card. He thought for a moment. *Did she tell me her room number? I don't think so. Maybe if I don't show up, she'll come looking for me. Or maybe she's out running up my credit card. Fabulous.* Rick signed the tab and looked at the key card. He knew the front desk wouldn't tell him what room it was for. And going floor to floor trying it in every door would probably result in a meeting with the security staff.

"Sir?" It was the waitress. "You have a call at the bar."

Rick handed the check presenter to the waitress and followed her back to the phone. "Hello?"

"Hey, sugar, why don't you bring a bottle of something up to fifteen thirty-one?"

Rick hated himself for doing it. And he knew he'd regret it later. But he did it anyway. Still, two questions nagged. What did this sort of behavior say about his character? And when did he start worrying about that kind of crap? Rick wasn't a saint, didn't pretend to be. He was just a guy and sometimes guys did these sorts of things, right?

But this? It gave him doubts. Rick flipped open his cell phone and thumbed 411 as he drove. Information connected the call for an extra two dollars. After a few rings, a woman came on the line. "Yeah," Rick said. "I lost my credit card."

After canceling his card, Rick flipped his phone shut and kept driving north. It was another hour to McRae. He spent a few miles wondering why he hadn't gone up to Lisa Ramey's room. It wasn't as if he had so much jelly roll on his plate that he could afford to turn some down. So what did this say about him? Was he just getting old? Did he need a testosterone patch? Rick finally told himself it was a matter of taste and good judgment. He didn't want to go to bed with any woman who would have Clay Stubblefield even once. Still, Rick knew he'd regret not going up there.

Rick turned on the radio. The Biloxi station was playing Fleetwood Mac's "Over My Head," a pop-rock treasure by Christine McVie that Rick had always loved. It got him thinking about the next day's meeting. How was he going to define the classic rock format he had in mind? The term "classic rock" was virtually meaningless. Classic to whom? Buddy Holly, Elvis Presley, and Duane Eddy were classic to one generation. Van Halen, Motley Crüe, U2, and R.E.M. were classic to another.

That first generation of rockers was born in the 1930s, while David Lee Roth, Tommy Lee, Bono, and Michael Stipe were born in the 1950s and '60s. Rick was aiming at the generation in between, the rockers born in the 1940s. These were the people who were classic rock by Rick's definition. Lennon, 1940. McCartney and Hen-

drix, 1942. Jagger and Richards, 1943. Cocker, 1944.
Fogerty, 1945. Allman, 1946. Plant, 1948.

So that was one thing. Date of birth would carry
weight with his format. No classic rock station would
ever play both Buddy Holly and Jimi Hendrix, so why
would they play both Van Morrison and Van Halen?
Sure, they were all under the big rock umbrella, but
they each spoke to a different generation.

By the time he walked into the station at noon on
Sunday, Rick felt he had a basic set of criteria that
would allow them to define *his* version of classic rock.
The meeting was in the station's conference room. It
was Rick, Autumn, J.C., and Rob. They ordered pizza.
J.C. brought some beer, though he wouldn't let Rob
have any.

Rick stood in front of them and said, "I was in Los
Angeles not long ago and I heard the big classic rock
station there play 'White Wedding' every single damn
day I was there." He shook his head. "Now, Billy Idol's
music may be a lot of things, but it's not classic rock.
When he was born, John Lennon was already fifteen
years old. They are not of the same generation." Rick
sat on his desk and continued. "The biggest problem
with most classic rock stations is that they're after the
wrong demographic. They seem to think rock and roll
is only good for attracting a young audience, so they
jam new rockers in with old rockers hoping they'll ap-
peal to high school and college kids." Rick made a face
and shook his head. "Well, I'm here to tell you that the
people who grew up with the Moody Blues and Lou
Reed ain't so young anymore. In fact, here's a good
way to think about things," Rick said. "Every artist

who performed at Woodstock is now either dead or eligible to join AARP." He paused to let that little nugget sink in before he said, "Folks, classic rock is an oldies format. Let's embrace that instead of trying to hide it. What we need to do is figure out when true classic rock started and when it ended." He held his arms out wide. "Anybody want to suggest some dates?"

A few moments passed before Rob said, "How about '62 to '82? An even twenty years."

J.C. shook his head. "No way. Dylan doesn't show up until '63 and The Beatles and Stones hit in '64. And even then, their albums were just collections of singles. They didn't start making real FM albums until, like, *Rubber Soul* and *Revolver,* which was what,'65?"

"Sixty-six," Rick said.

J.C. thumped Rob on the head. "And '82 is waaaay too late. Jesus, next you're going to suggest Toto is classic rock."

"I like Toto," Autumn said.

"I like 'em, too," J.C. said. "Well, a few songs, but that's not the point. Toto was just a bunch of session guys trying to make pop-rock radio hits."

Rick said, "That's a little harsh, don't you think?"

J.C. shrugged. "No. Besides, you get the point. I mean, you think that's what Hendrix was trying to do?"

"Okay," Autumn said. "For the end? How about August first of '81, when MTV went on the air?" She nudged Rob. "Remember that?" She started singing "Video Killed the Radio Star."

Rob shook his head. "I wasn't even born then."

J.C. held a hand up. He said, "Okay, that's better but it's still too late. By '81 punk had come and nearly gone, so you know classic rock was way in the rearview." J.C. took a bite of pizza and kept talking. "I propose a test for any band we consider for the format. I call it the Fillmore East test." He looked askance at Autumn.

"Yes, I've heard of Fillmore East," she said.

"Okay, so if a band would fit on a bill at Fillmore East, they're in."

Autumn said, "Is that place still open?"

"Nope," Rick said. "Bill Graham shut her down in the summer of '71."

"I wonder whatever became of the Joshua Light Show?"

Rick said he had no idea. "Okay, moving on. How about 1963 to start, so we can play *The Freewheelin' Bob Dylan*?"

"What about his first album?" Rob asked.

"It was a folk record," J.C. said.

Rick held up *The Billboard Book of Top 40 Albums*. "Let's look at the charts," he said. "Okay, things were middle of the road until '63 and Top 40 until '67." He pointed at one of the charts. "The top albums of '66 include Barry Sadler's *Ballad of the Green Berets*, Sinatra's *Strangers in the Night*, the *Doctor Zhivago* soundtrack, and two by Herb Alpert."

"Oooooh, rock on, brother," J.C. said.

"Also three Beatles albums, Mamas and the Papas, and the Supremes, so we're starting to get to our music at that point. In '67, three of the top seven albums were by the Monkees, and one each by the Supremes, Bobbie Gentry, and Herb Alpert, not exactly classic rock."

Rob couldn't believe it. He said, "What about *Ser-*

geant Pepper and *The Doors* and the Byrds' *Younger Than Yesterday?*"

"*Pepper* was the only one to reach the top of the album chart," Rick said. "But you're right, there were plenty of classic rock albums that year." He thought of Pink Floyd's *Piper at the Gates of Dawn.* "The charts are just a rough guideline. Even though the *The Doors* isn't there, you can see that the charts changed radically between '66 and '68."

"Summer of love, baby," J.C. said, holding up a peace sign.

Rick traced a finger down a page. "In 1968," he said, "the charts show Cream, Hendrix, Doors, Big Brother, Rascals, plus two each by The Beatles and Simon and Garfunkel."

"No *Doctor Zhivago*s there," J.C. said.

They kept whittling it down. Rick suggested that the midpoint of classic rock could be mid-1970. "The optimism of the midsixties had faded," he said. "Think of it like a bell curve, the music ascends to the infamous Isle of Wight Festival in August 1970. In the next two months, Hendrix and Joplin both died. After that, I think it's fair to say, classic rock begins its descent to the end." Everyone agreed. Now they just had to figure out how many years on either side of 1970 the format would cover.

There was a contagious energy in the room. Rob continued to impress Rick with his knowledge of a body of music that was recorded decades before he was born. Autumn's strength was making points about the end of the era. J.C. played devil's advocate against their arguments and went off on tangents about his favorite obscure bands. "I can't believe you've never heard of Osibisa," he said to Autumn. "They were world music before anybody thought of the term. Sort of Santana meets Tower of Power with a whole Afro-Cuban jazz thing rumbling alongside."

As J.C. went down that road, Rick remembered that he'd seen six or seven Osibisa records in Captain Jack's collection. Next thing he knew, he was back to wondering what had happened to Jack Carter. He thought back on what Lisa Ramey had told him. Her admission that she'd slept with Stubblefield lent some credibility to Clay's other claims. The most interesting thing Lisa had revealed was the possibility that Clay had Dixie Mafia connections. *But what the hell IS the Dixie Mafia? Are they a real organization? Is it families like La Cosa Nostra or is it just a loose affiliation of mean-ass crackers, constables, and Southern politicians?*

"How about this," Autumn said, recapturing Rick's attention. "The classic rock era ended when Jefferson Airplane became Jefferson Starship?"

Rick thought about that for a moment. "That's not bad," he said. "Musically, it was true for the band, but I think that was around '73 and that's a little too early."

"Ohmigod," Autumn said. She pointed at Rick, suddenly getting it. "I see what you mean! This is a niche market." She slapped her thighs and wiggled like a cheerleader. "I mean, think about it. If you grew up in the sixties, like my dad, you probably don't care about Megadeth, right? And, like, vice versa? That's what makes us different from WWRK. So that's our unique selling proposition."

J.C. looked at her. "Our what?"

"Our USP," she said. "It's an advertising term."

"You're an evil corporate drone," J.C. said. "But you're okay on the air, so we're not going to kill you just yet."

"Hey, what about this?" Rob said. "You know how some stations say, 'Classic rock that really rocks'? How about 'Classic rock that's really classic'?"

"That's good," Rick said. "We need more stuff like that." He wrote it on his notepad, then looked up at the clock. It was nearly six, a good stopping point. "Okay, let's recap." He read from his notepad. "For now, we play nothing before '63 and nothing after, say, '79. Artists have to pass the Fillmore East test. The music has to have some sort of attitude that distinguishes it from pop. What else? Oh, an artist cannot have grown up *listening* to classic rock artists and also *be* a classic rock artist. And finally, just because a song is on a classic rock album doesn't mean you should play it. There's a lot of dreck out there, so be careful."

J.C. cupped his hands around his mouth and said, "Paging Iron Butterfly."

Rob raised his hand. "What about R and B?"

"Generally speaking, it's in. Otis was at Monterey with Jimi and personally I don't want to listen to a station if it's not going to play *James Brown at the Apollo* every now and again."

J.C. nodded. "Hoo-dang! Amen! And bow up!" He did a James Brown spin up on the ball of one foot, his arms tucked tight to his chest. When his other foot landed, he screamed, "Oww!" Then he snapped his head back and headed for the studio to do his shift. "I feel good! Da-ba da-ba da-ba da."

Autumn and Rob helped Rick clean up. Autumn said she had an idea she wanted to discuss with Rick, so they set a meeting for later in the week. They split the remaining pizza before going their separate ways.

As much as Rick had enjoyed talking about the music and homing in on the format, he was eager to get back to the trailer so he could listen again to the next part of the tape.

Rick laughed and thought about Osibisa. *Didn't they do a song . . .* He thought for a moment. *Yeahhh, on the* Happy Children *album.* He couldn't help but think of several other songs of the same title. The Robert Gordon version of Springsteen's song or the Pointer Sisters', or the one-hit wonder of Arthur Brown, or the classic by Hendrix. And, as fate would have it, just like Robert Palmer's "Blackmail," this also had a muscular one-word title: "Fire."

4

When Rick got back to the trailer, he tossed two slices of pizza on a cookie sheet and put them in the oven. He grabbed a beer and his little pipe and went outside, where a plastic chair leaned against a wooden cable spool turned on its side as a makeshift table. He took a hit and sat there, feet up, sipping his beer. It was warm out but pleasant and the mosquitoes weren't bad. Just over the top of the pine trees Rick could see the outline of a water tower against the dusky sky.

He closed his eyes and took a deep breath. The air reminded him of his youth. He could taste the green pines, and their sap, and the clay, and something sweet like honeysuckle in his nose. Rick told himself he should take a walk through the woods like he used to do when he was a kid. That was the kind of thing he had to remind himself to do anymore. As a kid, he did it by instinct. But it had been trained out of him. Now almost every waking hour was spent inside. *Note to self: Get out more.*

Rick tilted back in the chair and looked up. The sky was clear and it was quiet out, except for the drone of crickets and cicadas. Then, a deeper noise. A bullfrog. Rick figured there must be a creek nearby. *Yeah, I need to get out there and walk some.*

As he sat there with his feet propped up, Rick fell into the thing he frequently did when he got stoned. He got to thinking. *Let's say, for the sake of argument, that I'm halfway through my life. Now, on average, at my age, with my level of education and the number of years I've been paying into Social Security, I could be within shouting distance of retirement, yet all I've got to show for my life is an old cable spool and two pieces of left-over pizza. And the cable spool's not even mine. What the hell am I doing with my life?* Moments like this seemed to be coming more frequently for Rick these days, even though he tried to avoid them. It's not that he was against taking stock now and then, he believed a little self-reflection was worthwhile, but lately his conclusions were too depressing. *Why did I take this damn job? This one? Why am I still in radio at all? I mean, how humiliating is it that I make my living playing Wet Willie on the radio in a small town? Not that it would make any difference if I were playing Tchaikovsky in Chicago. I wonder, is it too late to switch to hate-talk radio? At least you can make a living and you don't have to think much. But, no, you can't fake that sort of narrow-mindedness. Maybe I should go back to school, get a degree. But in what? I'll never be a doctor or a lawyer. I don't want an M.B.A. Am I just lazy? Am I such a mediocre human being that I'm satisfied with this?* He paused for a moment. *Hey, I wonder if that pizza's hot.*

Rick finished his beer, went back inside without answering any of his questions. He found it was easier to carry on if he ignored them and just plowed ahead as if the questions might go away if he paid them no mind. He turned on the radio. A bunch of Brits were playing a song by a guy from Tippo, Mississippi. *"That's John Mayall with Eric Clapton from the* Blues Breakers *album, 1966,"* J.C. said. *"The Mose Allison standard, 'Parchman Farm.' Hey, speaking of ol' Mose, I ran into him down at the jazz festival in New Orleans a few years ago and . . ."* J.C. proceeded to tell the longest shaggy dog story Rick had ever heard. It was about neither Mose Allison nor the jazz festival nor John Mayall nor Eric Clapton. Rick finally concluded that the story had no point, other than to allow J.C. to talk about himself.

After his rambling monologue and a spot break, J.C. went into a set of Foghat, ZZ Top, and Aerosmith. Rick slid his pizza onto a plate, grabbed a paper towel, and sat in the Barcalounger. As he chewed to the chugging beat of Foghat, he kept looking over at the reel-to-reel player. Ever since Lisa Ramey suggested a possible connection to the Dixie Mafia, Rick had been rethinking his new hobby. He wasn't sure there was much to be gained by crossing the local thugs. Still, curiosity tugged.

After finishing his pizza, Rick went to the kitchen to wash his hands so he wouldn't get grease all over the gear or the tape. He kept the reel hidden on the off chance that whoever had come looking for it once (if, indeed, that's what had happened) might come back. Captain Jack's hiding place still tickled him. It really was a canny idea but Rick decided it could be improved. Instead of having the records right next to the box, which had triggered him to investigate in the first place, he seeded the records throughout the entire collection.

He was threading the tape onto the reel-to-reel when he heard car wheels crunching on the gravel outside. Rick stopped. Clay Stubblefield was the only person he could think of who knew he lived there. He couldn't imagine any reason for Clay to drop by on a Sunday night—or any other time, for that matter—but who else could it be? A spooky sensation passed over him. *Maybe it's Captain Jack.*

Rick pulled the tape off the machine and put it back in the Chicago box, which he slipped back into the record collection before crossing to the door. He was reaching for the knob when the door jerked open. A man stormed into the trailer yelling, "Where's the fuckin' money?" He was a big son of a bitch. Rick figured he was about the size of Meatloaf.

"What money?" Rick was backing up when he said this, trying to stay out of the guy's reach. "What are you talking about?"

The guy pointed at Rick. "You don't pay, I'm 'onna tie your asshole in a knot!"

Rick looked around as the intruder advanced on him. The record collection blocked a window he might otherwise have jumped through to escape. The only other way out was past the bull moose presently bearing down on him. Turning to face the man, Rick held out his hands and said, "Now, hang on a second." The next thing he saw was a fist. The blow knocked him across the trailer, into the kitchen. Rick's tongue found a loose tooth. Using the back of his hand, he wiped blood from his mouth and screamed, "You got the wrong guy!"

"'At's bullshit!" The intruder grabbed Rick by his shirt, yanked him to his feet. "Tell me where that money's at or I'm 'onna preach your funeral." He punched Rick in the gut.

Rick got a second taste of his pizza but managed to keep it down. The man let go of his shirt, dropping him to the kitchen floor.

The man leaned over and yelled, "Get up, you pissant, or I'm 'onna cut the blood outta you lyin' rat there on the floor!" He started rooting through drawers, looking for a knife.

Gasping, Rick lay there wondering why he had never really learned how to fight. How come no one had ever bothered to show him so much as the rudimentary aspects of boxing or kung fu or something? His father had refused to send him to the Boys Club to learn, saying that wasn't how you became a sophisticated and refined person. Just now, Rick could see the folly in that line of reasoning. A moment later he got his breath. He looked up and said, "Stop! I'm not the guy!"

"Bullshit!" The intruder kicked him in the ribs. "Them the clothes you wanna die in?" He kicked again. "Gimme the goddamn money!" The man grabbed one of Rick's feet and started to drag him out of the kitchen. Rick reached out for something to hold and found the handle to the storage drawer at the bottom of the range. He reached inside and came out with a Griswold number five. It was the smallest cast-iron skillet they made. It was easy to swing, and if it didn't actually break the man's shin, at least it broke his spirit for a moment.

The man howled and let go of Rick. "Son of a biiiitch!" He was up on one leg, holding on to the counter to support himself while he cursed and wailed and hopped around.

Rick took the opportunity to swing the skillet again. He hit anklebone this time, dropping the intruder. A third swing landed the Griswold flat against the side of the man's head and he went limp and silent.

Rick dropped the skillet, wondering if he had killed the guy. It didn't seem like he had hit him that hard. He checked for a pulse and was relieved to find one. He figured you'd have to hit this guy with a Griswold number fifteen, maybe even a Dutch oven, to do any real damage.

Rick found some clothesline to tie the guy's hands and feet. He was unconscious, facedown on the floor, tied like a salami at both ends. Rick pulled another beer from the fridge, then opened the freezer and grabbed a sack of frozen peas. He sat in the Barcalounger with the skillet in his lap. His heart was pounding. Between foamy gulps on the beer, he held the frozen peas to his mouth, hoping to keep his lips from swelling into Angelina Jolie proportions. After a few minutes, he calmed down. He went over to the intruder to look for a wallet. He had his hand in the man's back pocket when the guy stirred and said what sounded like, "Gedfuug offme."

Rick tapped the guy on the back of the head with the

skillet. "Shut the fuck up." He couldn't find a wallet or any ID. He frisked the man for weapons. Finding none, Rick stood and put his foot on the man's back, trying to figure what to do next. After a moment, he poked his toe in the man's ribs. "Turn over."

The guy wiggled and thrashed and seemed to be stuck on his belly, so Rick gave him another prod with his foot, helping him over. The guy rolled onto his back with a groan and said, "Why'd you hit me?"

Rick stared at him for a moment. "You ought to thank me for not hitting you harder."

The guy lifted his head so he could see Rick. He blinked a couple of times to clear his vision. "Hey, shit," the guy said, jutting his chin toward Rick. "You ain't him."

Rick leaned down, wagging the skillet like an admonishing finger, and said, "That's what I been telling you, you dumb fuck."

The guy lowered his head to the floor. "Well, where the hell is he, then?"

"Who?"

"That Carter guy. He owes for an eight ball."

"Owes you or somebody else?"

The guy hesitated before saying, "Somebody else."

"Who?" Rick wasn't expecting an answer but it wouldn't hurt to ask.

The guy shook his head. "Ain't sayin'." He laid his head on the floor for a second then lifted it back up and said, "Who're you?"

"I'm the guy who lives here now."

"Oh. Well, where's that Carter guy at?"

"That's the million-dollar question," Rick said.

"And you don't know?"

"I look like I got a million dollars?" Rick shrugged. "All I know is Carter's gone and I got his job and this place. And now I got a loose tooth and your big ass on my kitchen floor."

The guy lifted his head again, almost smiling this time. "You work at the radio station?"

"Yeah."

The guy stuck his chin out again and said, "Man, y'all oughta play more Ted Nugent. He rocks!"

Rick gave a noncommittal smile. There was no point in arguing with Nugent fans.

"Damn," the guy said. "My leg hurts like a sumbitch."

"You want me to call the cops, see if they can help?"

"Noooo." The guy shook his head. "That's all right."

Rick went to the kitchen and opened a drawer. He pulled out a steak knife and knelt at the guy's side.

His eyes got big. "What're you fixin' to do?"

"I'm fixin' to cut you loose and you're going to act nice after I do it." Rick poked the tip of the knife into the guy's chest. "Right?"

The guy nodded so Rick cut him loose. The man rubbed his shin and his ankle, both of which had knotted up and were turning a deep purple. "It wasn't personal," the guy said. "It's just business."

"Yeah, but not *my* business."

"Yeah, well," the man said. "Ain't my fault you live here."

"Ain't my fault either," Rick said.

The guy pulled himself up, teetering on his tender

sticks. "Well look, I can't leave without the three hundred." He looked around the trailer. "Or sumpin'."

Rick noticed he was starting to look at the stereo components. "All right," he said. "I understand. I mean, if the guy owed you, he owed you. So let's think on this for a second." A moment passed before he clapped his hands once, startling the guy. "Oh! Shit, you gave me a great idea." He walked over to the albums and started looking for something. He turned and pointed at the guy. "You're a Nugent fan, right? You'll appreciate this." He turned back to the records. "Carter said he didn't have the money? Hell, it's been right here all along." He pulled a record and held it out like a holy relic. "You know the Amboy Dukes, right?"

"Yeah, 'at was the Nuge's first group, wadn't it?"

"Exactly." Rick turned the album over and made like he was looking for a serial number or something. "Yep, what I thought. This is a first pressing," he said with authority. "We're talking serious collector's item here. *Journey to the Center of the Mind*, from 1968." He slipped the record out of the sleeve, balancing it perfectly with the spindle hole on his middle finger. He examined it under the light, flipping it over to check both sides. "Pristine," he said as he slipped it back in the sleeve. "This is worth at least five hundred bucks." Rick handed it to the guy. "I were you? I'd put this puppy on eBay or, hell, take it to one of those rare-record stores down in New Orleans. You can get the three hundred for whoever and make a couple hundred for yourself."

The guy's eyes lit up. "No shit?" The guy took the record from Rick. He looked at the cover and pointed at the first song title. " 'Mississippi Murderer,' " he said. "I bet that rocks."

"Oh hell yeah," Rick said as he urged the guy toward the door. "Rocks like a mother."

As the guy limped toward his car, he held up the album and said, "Thanks, dude." Then he got in his car and drove off.

Rick stood in his doorway watching the taillights disappear in the dust. "What a moron," he mumbled. The record wasn't worth more than about eight bucks. Rick figured the guy would take it to a used record store and get a low offer. Then, assuming the person behind the counter was trying to rip him off, the Motor City Madman fan would go off and, best-case scenario, end up in jail for assault. On the other hand, if and when he discovered Rick had lied to him, the guy would probably come back and attempt to inundate him with bodily harm. Rick started to think now might be a good time to become a gun owner since that took a lot less time than learning how to fight.

He locked the door and considered the implications of this recent visit. If Captain Jack had owed someone money for cocaine and that person had made Captain Jack disappear, they wouldn't then come crashing in here looking for him, would they? So what did that leave? Either Captain Jack owed money to a second coke dealer or, more likely, Rick was right that someone on the tape was responsible for his disappearance.

Rick pressed the sack of frozen peas to his throbbing mouth and thought for a moment about abandoning his nascent investigation. If he was going to get beat up every time he asked a few questions, he'd have to consider getting a new hobby. Then he realized tonight's attack had nothing to do with the tape. The debt collector would have shown up regardless, so that was no reason to quit.

Rick tossed the peas onto the kitchen counter and went back to the albums. He pulled *Chicago IV* from the collection and removed the tape. He threaded it onto the machine and hit fast-forward, watching the counter until it reached 3:20, the point where he had left off. He hit play then listened as Clay said, *"You ain't ever made a loan for a piece of ass, have ya?"*

The wormy little banker replied quickly. *"Newwwww! Uh-uh. Never have."* Rick could just see him shaking his head and making a face like he wasn't that kind of a guy.

"That's one criteria," Clay said. *"I guess that's one thing when you're dealin' with money, you're dealin' with your morals or a little advertising or a damn T-shirt or something's a little different."*

That got funnier every time Rick heard it. Clay Stubblefield was a marvel of moral engineering.

The banker tried a little bragging of his own but was undermined by his pinched and indecisive voice. *"Yeah, but I've, uh . . . I tried to . . . screw a girl I made a loan to . . . but I didn't make it to do that, you know."*

"Yeah," Clay said in a dismissive tone. *"Now, I tell you what I did one time."*

Rick stopped the tape and laughed. The moment Clay realized his banker buddy didn't have a pussy story, he charged straight into another one of his own sordid tales. *"Now, I tell you what I did one time,"* he said. *"There was a place called Moore Furniture. Burned down."*

"Here in town?"

"Yeah, it was over . . . Woman set it on fire, I think, over there in Three Pines Shopping Center."

"Mmmm-hmmm."

"Uhhh, I don't know what in the hell's . . . it's some kinda damn shoe-store-looking thing in there now. But there was uh old girl ran that thing that I was crackin'. Tch. I used to go over there and we'd shut the store down and put a sign in the window, 'Takin' Inventory,' 'n go back where the mattresses were at—"

"No kiddin'?" Amazed that such things happened.

"And we'd crack in there, you know."

"No kiddin'?" Like someone had found the cure to cancer.

"Well, she had this friend needed some money and there was an old—"

"Moore, uhhh, Furniture Company?"

"Yeah. Her name was Donna Moore. And she—"

"Donna Moore?"

"Yeah, so she had this friend, name of Holly Creel . . ."

Rick stopped the tape. This was where things started to take a turn for the dangerous. It was one thing to confront someone about infidelity. It was altogether something else to confront someone about arson and insurance fraud. Maybe Lisa Ramey was right. Maybe this was Dixie Mafia territory. Rick rewound the tape and played it again.

"Woman set it on fire, I think."

Casual as all hell. Stubblefield seemed to toss it off in a hurry so he could get to the crackin' part of his story. *The man's a lower primate*, Rick thought.

Did Stubblefield mean it? Was he joking? He didn't

just say the place burned down, which by itself might imply arson. He came right out and accused her of doing it, presumably for profit. Why else burn your business down? To kill someone? Maybe, but given Clay's casual attitude toward all this, he probably would have tossed in *killed some people* if it had happened.

And what about the banker? He's talking to a man who says he knows a woman who committed a major crime or two in their own community and he doesn't even seem to hear it, doesn't even seem to blink he so badly wants Clay to get to the part about the crackin'. And even after he hears that part he doesn't bother to go back and ask about these crimes, like arson and insurance fraud don't amount to much in Deckern County.

One thing did get Rick's attention, though. After Clay started naming names, the banker interrupted for clarification. *"Moore, uhhh, Furniture Company?"* Like he's writing it down.

Clay said, *"Yeah. Her name was Donna Moore. And she—"*

"Donna Moore?" You could almost hear his pencil scratching.

"Yeah, so she had this friend, name of Holly Creel . . ."

Rick's first thought had been that the banker was writing down her name as if thinking Donna Moore sounded like his kind of gal and maybe he'd just look her up and give her a call, 'cause hell, if she'd do it in a warehouse with Clay, maybe he could get some, too. But now Rick had another thought. What if the banker was writing down all the information so he could blackmail these people? Of course he wouldn't have any real evidence since he didn't know the conversation was being recorded. Or did he? Maybe he was in cahoots with Captain Jack. He could have conspired with Captain Jack and later double-crossed him. No, Rick didn't buy that. Anybody who would make a point of sounding offended at the notion that he'd make a loan in exchange for sex didn't have the testosterone for blackmail, conspiracy, and a double cross.

So he was back to his theory that Captain Jack had acted alone. So what did he do? Threaten to tell Miss Moore's husband about her affair, and threaten to go to the police about the arson? This line of reasoning involved at least two assumptions: first, that she was married; and second, that she had, in fact, committed arson.

Rick figured it would be easy enough to find out if the place had burned down. If it had, he'd look for newspaper articles to see if they mentioned arson. Alternatively, Rick realized he could just go to Donna Moore and ask if anyone had tried to blackmail her on these points. The problem with that was obvious. If Captain Jack had tried to blackmail her and she, in turn, was involved in his disappearance, she wasn't likely to admit any of that to a complete stranger. And worse, if she had something to do with one guy's disappearance, what would stop her from having something to do with another?

Rick rewound the tape and put it back in its hiding place. He turned the radio on.

"Need quick cash? We can help. Universal Financial Services has the solution to all your problems. Got

bad credit? We don't believe it! At Universal Financial Services . . ."

Rick sat in the Barcalounger and mulled things over. What kind of trouble was he flirting with? J.C. came out of the UFS spot and into Elton John's "My Father's Gun," which raised the question in Rick's mind of whether he needed a weapon. He also wondered if there were any state laws regulating private investigators. And what about the tape? What were the laws on recording phone conversations? If wiretapping was illegal, was there any penalty for merely being in possession of an illegally recorded tape? Did any of those potential legal matters compare to a run-in with the Dixie Mafia?

All this made Rick wonder why he was so keen to pursue the matter. Sure, he was curious about Captain Jack's fate. But at the same time it seemed likely that whatever had happened, the man had brought it on himself. Still, if it turned out Captain Jack had met with foul play, Rick would like to see justice done, especially if that justice were to come down on the head of Clay Stubblefield.

There was no question but that Stubblefield was a reprobate, cheating on his wife and bragging to his friends about it. But Rick wasn't interested in defending the honor of Lori Stubblefield. He wasn't that chivalrous. He just wanted to get back at Stubblefield for lying to him. After all, if it hadn't been for Clay, Rick wouldn't be sitting in a trailer in the backwoods of Mississippi with a fat lip and a loose tooth.

Rick decided he'd go ask Donna Moore some questions, see if her answers shed any light on the situation.

He wondered if he was crazy. The whole thing was starting to feel dangerous. His tongue pushed on his loose tooth. It wiggled, but it would heal. He smiled. Dangerous or not, Rick had to admit this was starting to get interesting.

The radio, television, and film department at Central Mississippi University required a research paper for seniors. Autumn planned to write hers on the format change at WAOR-FM. But first she had to get Rick's attention long enough for him to sign off on her idea before she could go to her adviser and get the final go-ahead.

A few minutes before the meeting was scheduled to start, J.C. strolled into Rick's office dancing like Carmen Miranda while singing, "Welcome to the Hotel Mississippi . . . such a lovely place." He spun and pointed both his index fingers at Rick. "Such a lovely face."

Rick demurred, saying, "You're too kind."

"Plenty of room at the Hotel Mississippi. Cha-cha-cha."

"Oh, hey," Rick said. "I just remembered. I want to talk to you about something."

"The warm smell of colitas?"

"No, actually. I heard you do a break last night, after Mose Allison," Rick said. "You might want to be a little more concise when you talk between sets. It was kind of long-winded."

J.C. looked betrayed by the suggestion. "Well, bow me up," he said. "I knew it! First day we met, I asked if you had any do's and don'ts I should know about and all you said was—and I'm quoting here—no dead air and no Yoko." His head bobbed as he spoke. "Now we come to find out the truth, don't we? It's like they say, boss, the truth'll out!" He pointed at Rick, this time with just one finger. "And out it comes." He made a dramatic sweeping gesture across the room as if the truth went thataway.

"J.C., it's not that big a deal. It's just that I heard you talk for three minutes without saying much of anything."

"No dead air and no Yoko," J.C. said. "You didn't say anything about suppressing my personality."

"I'm not trying to suppress your personality, J.C. I'd just like you to try to bring it into focus more quickly. That's all. And maybe try a little more variety in your music. I'm hearing a lot of Sabbath and Budgie and Cream but not so much at the other end of things."

"Oooooh, so that's what's crawled up your hole, huh? I'm just playing the classic rock, and none of the clichés, just like you said."

Autumn walked into the office waving a piece of paper at Rick. "Hey, can we do this?"

Rick gestured for her to sit. "In a minute," he said. "J.C., just mix in a little more of the acoustic stuff. Try to strike a balance."

This led to a five-minute discussion on the contributions of folk to classic rock during which Autumn looked like a spectator at a tennis match.

At one point, Rick said, "It depends on your definition."

"No, sir," J.C. replied. "It depends on *your* definition, seein' as how you're the PD. I'm just sayin' from the jump, Cat Stevens ain't rock 'n' roll." He strummed his acoustic air guitar and warbled a line from "Morning Has Broken."

"C'mon." Rick smiled. "What about 'Tuesday's Dead' and 'Bitterblue'? You saying they don't rock?"

"It's upbeat folk."

"Okay," Rick said. "So you're saying a song has to be electric, loud, and fast to be rock?"

J.C. shrugged. "You tell me."

"What about Dylan before he went electric?"

"Folk."

"After?"

"Folk rock."

"But it's *Dylan!*"

"Can't argue with that," J.C. said. "The question is, do we play it just because it's him?"

Autumn meekly raised a hand. "Excuse me?" She waved her piece of paper at Rick. "This won't take a second."

Rick looked at her, nodded, then returned his attention to J.C. and said, "What about the other singer-songwriters? James Taylor, Carole King, Neil Young, all that? You can't have a classic rock station without playing stuff from *Tapestry* and *After the Goldrush*, can you?"

"I don't know," J.C. said. " 'Smackwater Jack' is close. But 'Way Over Yonder'?" J.C. shook his head. "Now, on the other hand, 'Southern Man' rocks."

"I can't tell you how sick I am of that song," Rick said.

"But 'Till the Morning Comes'?" J.C. shook his head. "Doesn't rock."

"So you're back to your loud-and-fast argument." Rick pointed an accusing finger at J.C. and said, "Based on the loud-and-fast rule, we can't play half of *Déjà Vu.*"

"You're right," J.C. said. " 'Helpless' is a slow country song."

Rick held up both his hands as if pleading. "If every single track on *Déjà Vu* isn't classic rock, I don't know what is."

J.C. shrugged. "But it's not rock 'n' roll."

"So we can't play any Joni Mitchell?"

J.C.'s head rocked back and forth. "There's some stuff on *Miles of Isles* and *Court and Spark* that're maybes. But she's a folkie. Hell, she's one of their leaders."

Autumn cleared her throat and tapped the face of her watch.

Rick ignored her. "So, J.C., we can play 'Foxy Lady' but not 'Castles in the Sand'?"

J.C. paused a moment. "Well, now, Jimi's different, don't you think? He was a rocker."

"So if an artist plays enough songs loud and fast enough, you'd allow their slow and quiet stuff, too."

J.C. fussed with his mustache and said, "I see your point."

"That's right, otherwise you can't play 'Black Mountain Side.' "

"But that's Zeppelin!"

"And it's a fine song, too," Rick said. "But it's English folk mixed with a whole Middle Eastern–sounding thing, and it's not rock 'n' roll. All I'm saying is, too many classic rock stations have let the hard rockers hijack the format. Zeppelin and Cream and Black Sabbath and all that was only a *part* of the music and not always the best part. What we want is to find a good balance of the two."

Autumn rustled her piece of paper again. "Uh, Mr. Shannon?" She looked at him hopefully.

Rick looked at her and said, "The problem is with the word 'rock,' don't you think?" He leaned back in his chair and gestured vaguely around the room. "Maybe we shouldn't even call ourselves a 'classic rock' station. Maybe that's misleading if we're going to be playing John Prine and Jesse Winchester along with Savoy Brown and Black Oak Arkansas." Rick looked like he had a sudden notion. He pointed at J.C. "Speaking of Jesse Winchester? You remember the last track on side one of *Nothing But a Breeze*? That's me."

It took J.C. a few seconds to figure out what Rick meant. Then he said, "Ohhhhhhh. No problem. Gotcha covered."

Autumn, who had been following the conversation up to this point, lost them on that turn. Her patience wasn't far behind. She started tapping her foot and drumming her fingers on the desktop. She planned to start whistling soon.

J.C. said, "What're we gonna call it if we don't call it classic rock? Classic rock-pop-folk-psychedelic-soul?"

"I liked Rob's slogan," Rick said. "'Classic rock that's really classic.' But there's still the problem with the word 'rock.' I think it does imply loudness."

J.C. said, "How about, 'WAOR-FM, your classic music station' and let the listeners figure out what we mean by *classic music*?"

"That's it!" Autumn slammed her palm down on Rick's desktop. The two men jumped. "Jesus Christ Superstar!" she shouted. "Why don't we just call it the Shit Rick Likes and be done with it!"

J.C. and Rick looked at her for a moment as if considering the idea. Finally, Rick said, "Nahhh."

"What do you mean, 'nahhh'? It's perfect," Autumn said. "It describes the format and doesn't use the word 'rock.' And it brings to a conclusion this pointless conversation!" She looked at them both. They were momentarily stymied. "Good? Okay, fine. Moving on." She put the piece of paper in front of Rick. "Now would you please sign this?"

Rick was about to sign it but he stopped. He looked at J.C., then at Autumn, and said, "Well, it's not really true."

"What isn't?"

"We're not talking about playing only stuff I like," Rick said. "I've never been a huge fan of Rush or Wishbone Ash but we play their stuff."

Autumn issued an anguished sigh. "Okay." She sat on the corner of Rick's desk and looked around the office. "All right. Let's see. Old stuff, right? Not just fast and loud. Soft antiques, hard vinyl? No. How 'bout, loud dinosaurs and quiet ones, too? No. Uh, rockin' all over the road—no. How about 'WAOR, our rock's not just hard anymore . . .'" She paused to look at J.C. "I bet you already say that." Autumn winked at him, then, after a beat, she cracked a big smile and said, "I got it."

"You know, a little sarcasm goes a long way," J.C. said.

Autumn cleared her throat. "WAOR-FM. Redefining classic rock." She hopped off Rick's desk as if dismounting the balance beam.

Rick and J.C. looked at each other with surprise for a moment before J.C. said, "How about 'Classic rock, redefined.'"

"What-ever!" Autumn leaned across the desk. She

grabbed Rick's hand, clamped it around a pen, then put it on her paper. "Signing." After Rick scribbled his name, she snatched the paper from under the pen. "Thank you." She flashed an exaggerated smile, waved preciously, and said, "Buh-bye." Then she left.

J.C. turned and yelled, "Bow up!" as Autumn disappeared down the hallway. Then he wagged a finger at the empty doorway and said, "She's pretty good."

"Yeah, 'redefining classic rock' might work," Rick said.

J.C. stood and did a little dance toward the door while singing the chorus from Jesse Winchester's "Twigs and Seeds." He pinched a finger and thumb together and held them to his lips. "Uh, Ree-charrrd, is this an e-merrrr-gency?"

"No, whatever and whenever is fine, thanks."

"You got it." J.C. nodded and disappeared out the door singing "I want to take you higher."

Rick spent the next couple of hours writing commercials to promote the format change, including the thousand-dollar cash giveaway. He couldn't decide if he liked Rob's or Autumn's suggestion more. Both had something to recommend them. *Classic rock that's really classic. Redefining classic rock.* Rick decided they both had merit, so he wrote two different spots, each revolving around one of the phrases.

WAOR had two rivals in the market. One was an automated station billing itself as "rock hits of the seventies, eighties, nineties, and more!" The other was a Clean Signal station which ran the homogenized version of the classic rock format which consisted of a playlist of about fifty songs cycled over and over and over.

Meanwhile, those same fifty songs were also being played on the Automated Rock station, where they were jarringly mixed with a hundred other songs from different eras. Rick nearly bit off part of his tongue when he heard them go from Procol Harum to Quiet Riot one afternoon. He was confident his format would stand out.

After polishing the copy, Rick made a list of the potential music to cut into the spots. He wanted to use hooks and riffs and lines from tunes that would make people go, "Oh yeaaahh! I haven't heard that in ages," and reach to turn up the volume. He composed a list about twice as long as he would need and then he started to narrow them down. After a while, it started to get harder than trying to cut friends from a wedding party. Rick was also running out of gas. He needed a break before he started his air shift. His head slowly drooped until it thumped on the desktop. He lifted his head and dropped it. And again. After doing this a few more times Rick heard a knock at the door. He stopped with his head still on the desk and said, "Yes?" He turned his head sideways and saw Traci standing in the doorway. She was wearing a short sleeveless sweater that revealed an alluring pierced belly button.

She said, "When you're done banging your head against the desk, how'd you like to buy a hungry girl some tater wads?"

5

Rick tried not to stare too much as he drove, but something about Traci made him look. She had a teased blond mane that could have fronted a hair-metal band. But it was her bent for cosmetics that really appealed to a questionable aspect of Rick's character. And it wasn't just the blue eye shadow. She also had a heavy hand with eyeliner and mascara that Rick purely loved.

Traci looked over from time to time as she made small talk but she didn't seem to notice how Rick's eyes were always on her. Or maybe she did notice. Maybe she didn't want him to stop looking. Rick could never tell about these things.

When they arrived at Kitty's Road Café, there were several semis idling out front. Local long-haul drivers back for supper after trips to Texas and Illinois. Rick parked off to the side and they headed for the front door. Crossing the parking lot, he couldn't help but watch how Traci walked. Every time she got in front of him to squeeze between two cars it reminded him of a funky bass riff from a Brothers Johnson song.

Traci slowed in time for Rick to get past her to reach the door first. He held it open for her and she smiled like he'd passed a small but important test. They stopped at the hostess stand.

The hostess took them to a booth and gave them a couple of menus. Traci opened hers, glanced at it briefly, then looked over the top at Rick. "What do you recommend?"

"You've never eaten here?" It seemed weird, the place was so close to the station.

"Once." She shrugged. "But I like the Steak 'n Surf better."

"Really." He sounded more disappointed than disparaging.

"Oh yeah. Their Sizzling Shrimp Skillet Sensation's my favorite."

Rick pointed at her menu. "Yeah, well, these tater wads are so good they've got their own registered trademark," he said. "And Kitty's biscuits? They're little pillows of flour and lard. And the fried grits with tomato gravy is a singular gustatory event."

"Gustatory, huh?" Traci looked at the menu and said, "I like more vegetables than that."

Rick spoke from behind his menu. "Well, if you think about it, tomatoes are vegetables. And grits are corn. And I'm pretty sure potatoes are plants. This is almost vegan."

"Except for the lard."

A shadow drifted onto the tabletop. It belonged to

their waitress, who had shuffled up to their booth. Her name tag identified her as Ruth. She put down two glasses of water, looked straight at Rick, and said, "You again?" She sounded like two cartons of cigarettes.

"Yes, Ruthie dear. I have returned," Rick said. "This time with a guest."

The waitress never changed expression. She wiggled her order pad in Traci's direction. "He kidnap you or sumpin'?" She didn't smile, just stared for a second before turning back to Rick and saying, "We got a special on the softshell crabs." She leaned over and lowered her voice. "But they little bitties. Look more like softshell ticks, you ask me, lying there with those little legs startin' to crick up like 'at." She made her hand into a little softshell-tick puppet, upside down, with fingers curling toward her palm.

"Thanks for the tip," Rick said. He looked at Traci. "What'll you have?"

Traci closed her menu and handed it to the waitress. "Fried chicken salad with a side of tater wads, please."

"I'll have the fried grits, tomato gravy, side of sausages, and two biscuits. And ice tea." Rick wasn't sure if his loose tooth could handle sausage but he figured he could just chew on the other side.   •

"I'll have a coke," Traci said.

"What kind you want?"

"Uh, Mountain Dew."

As Ruth shuffled off, Traci pulled one leg under the other and leaned onto the table. "So," she said. "What do you think of McRae, Mississippi, so far?"

From her tone of voice, Rick gathered he was supposed to be unimpressed. "It's okay." He pulled a couple of napkins from the dispenser and handed one to Traci. "We used to drive through here on the way to the coast when I was a kid," he said. "So I had an idea what it was like. It's grown more than I expected, though. This where you're from?"

"Yep." Traci's eyes dropped to the table as she straightened out her knife and fork. "Been here all my life."

Rick was spinning his water glass in its circular puddle. "You make it sound like you were sentenced."

She shook her head, still looking at her flatware. "Oh, it's not that bad."

Ruth returned with their drinks and croaked, "Ya-food'll be out in a minute." She tossed a couple of straws onto the table and lumbered off.

Traci nodded at Rick and said, "Hold your hand up. Like this." She demonstrated how she wanted it done. Rick complied, holding his right hand out to the side of his head like he was swearing to something. Traci tore off one end of the paper sleeve and blew into the straw. The wrapper corkscrewed into the air, missing Rick's hand by several feet. "Damn," she said, plunging her straw into her soda. "So what about you? Clay showed me your résumé. You've been all over." She sipped her drink. "That must be great, moving around, living in different cities all the time."

Rick gave an ambiguous shrug. "I actually used to like it. Used to enjoy the change of scenery and a little sense of adventure, I guess. But it got old pretty quick and there's no real change of scenery anymore. Everywhere's pretty much the same now." He was hoping to steer the conversation seamlessly around to Stubble-field and Captain Jack and anything Traci might be able to tell him—however inadvertently—about the people mentioned on the tape. As he waited for the chance to change subjects, Rick fished the wedge of lemon out of his tea and gripped it for squeezing. "Once? Just after I'd moved to a new job? I woke up in the middle of the night and had no idea where I was," he said. "No idea what city or state. Nothing." He squeezed the lemon and a seed shot onto the floor.

Traci looked at where it had landed. "That must've been weird."

Rick kicked the seed underneath the next booth. "Yeah, I sat up in the bed for the longest time trying to remember where I was. But the apartment looked like the last twenty I'd lived in, you know? Cottage-cheese ceiling, thin walls, hollow doors. So I turned on the TV but the local newspeople looked like the local newspeople everywhere, like they're spit out of a factory or something."

"What'd you do?"

"I finally got up and found the phone book. I was in Fort Worth."

"Hmm." There was something wistful in the way Traci said, "But it has a good side, too, right? I mean, like every time you move you get to leave behind whatever you want. And when you get to the next place you can pick the best parts of the past to tell or you can make up something without worryin' that someone who knows different is going to make you a liar."

Rick touched his left hand to his chest. "Of course I don't have anything like that in *my* past."

Traci played along. "Oh no, not you. Of course. I was speaking theoretically."

Rick squinted at her in mock skepticism. "I thought you weren't real big on theory."

"Depends."

"On?"

"Depends on whose theory," Traci said. "Mine, for example, is fine." She batted her eyelashes.

Rick got lost momentarily in Traci's heavily made-up eyes. It looked like Liz Taylor had done them while drinking. Rick was examining the thick black lines along her lower lids when he said, "Well, I'd be lying if I told you I'd never left anything behind."

"Oh yeah? Like what?"

"Let's see." Rick started counting on his fingers. "A broken dishwasher, an unpaid cable bill or two, an ironing board that wouldn't stay up, lots of cheap-ass lawn furniture, and one really mean woman."

"Ewww, jackpot!" Traci bounced a bit in her seat. She could tell by the way Rick had said it, it wasn't a sore spot. So she said, "Wife or girlfriend?"

"We weren't married," Rick said. "And when all was said and done, she wasn't much of a friend either."

Traci rolled her eyes and said, "Been there."

Rick noticed Traci's mouth move as if she was about to say something else, but she stopped. He wondered what it was, and he thought about asking. It felt personal, the way she had looked, like she was about to tell him what she would leave behind if she ever had the chance. It was as though she had almost reached a certain level of trust with Rick, but not quite. And now there was an awkward silence that begged to be filled by a change of subject. Rick seized the moment and asked how long she'd been at the station.

Traci smiled her gratitude. "A couple of years. But it's not like I woke up one day thinking how much I wanted to answer phones for a living. I really want to work on the air."

"Really?"

"Yeah, I figured working at the front desk would be my best chance to get on the air without any experience. Besides, it can't pay any worse than being a receptionist."

Rick made a derisive snorting noise. "Did you know Clay had Rob working for free?"

"No."

Rick nodded. "And told him to drop outta high school for the honor."

Traci shook her head. "Gosh, there's a shocker. Clay did something shitty."

"Oh, reealllly?" Rick laughed. "How bad is he?"

Traci's expression became suddenly guarded. "Well, I'm not sure I wanna go there," she said. "You might . . . I dunno." She shrugged.

"I might what? You think I'm Clay's spy boy? You think I drove here from North Dakota to . . . wait a second." Rick stopped and sniffed the air. "I smell sausage."

"Here's yer food," Ruth said, setting the plates on the table. "Bone appetite," she said before dragging herself away.

Rick offered salt and pepper to Traci, then said, "Okay, let me ask you . . . who was the last program director here?"

"Guy named Wayne Summers, why?"

"When did he leave?" Rick cut his sausage into easy-to-chew pieces.

"I dunno." Traci popped a fried chicken nugget into

her mouth. "A few weeks before Captain Jack stopped showing up."

Rick speared one of his sausage bits with his fork and gestured with it as he spoke. "Clay told me the guy left while I was on my way here, leaving him in a jam. Ended up roping me into the job."

Traci seemed to think that was pretty funny. "Aww, is this the first time you've been lied to, little boy?"

"No, but it's the sort of thing, for example, that'll keep me from spying for him." Rick put the sausage in his mouth, careful to avoid his loose tooth. "That's my point."

"Yeah, well, I'm not going to burn any calories defending the guy," Traci said. "But that's just how bosses are, in my experience."

"Yeah, mine, too," Rick said. "And speaking of bosses. Who owns the station?"

"Old guy named Eugene Gentry, lives in Mobile," Traci said. "I've never met him. He calls and talks to Clay every now and then but he never comes here as far as I know. I think he owns two or three stations around the South and just lets his general managers run them."

They stopped talking for a minute while they ate. Rick used his biscuits to bulldoze gravy, grits, and sausage onto his fork. He seemed to lose interest in anything other than how fast he could shovel it all into his mouth.

Traci showed a little more reserve. She ate all the fried chicken pieces before starting on to the salad below. She jabbed her fork into the bowl and came up with a load of lettuce. Opening her mouth, she tried several angles of approach but none was sufficiently graceful. Finally she stuffed the whole thing into her mouth and chewed like a mule.

Rick noticed a dollop of the green onion dressing waiting at the corner of Traci's mouth. It was the first time he'd noticed the curves of her lips. He was studying their contours when her tongue darted out and hauled in the dollop, startling him slightly. Rick was so captivated by Traci's features that he didn't notice the guy at the hostess stand who was staring at him. Traci was facing the other way, so she didn't see him either. The guy seemed to be torn between attacking and retreating, large muscles pulling him in both directions. After a moment, he turned around and stormed back out to the parking lot, mumbling to himself.

Rick finished his second biscuit and waved at Ruth for the check. He had to be on the air in twenty minutes. He took out his wallet then looked at Traci. "By the way," he said. "What do you think happened to Captain Jack?" He tossed it off like it was no big deal.

"My guess?" Traci made a serious face and said, "Something really bad."

As they walked back to Rick's truck, neither of them noticed the black Trans Am parked on the far side of the lot. It had a busted taillight and a gold metal-flake firebird painted on the hood. The driver was slouched in his seat, packing a big dip of snuff behind his lower lip. The beer can between his legs was about a third full of slippery brown spit. The driver waited until Rick pulled out of the parking lot. He fired up the Pontiac and pulled onto the road behind them.

As they drove back to the station Traci admitted she had no evidence to support her feeling that something bad had happened to Captain Jack. "It just seems obvious to me," she said, "that if someone disappears and leaves all their stuff behind, and not just the broken ironing-board kind of stuff, but *every*thing, including a paycheck—then something bad must've happened."

Rick said he agreed and, without being too conspicuous, made it clear he was curious about the fate of Captain Jack. He left it at that. He was tempted to tell Traci about the tape, and tell her his theory, and engage her as a confidante who might be able to help him navigate whatever murky local waters he might encounter, but he didn't know her allegiances well enough. He didn't know if he could trust her, though his instincts said he could. Still, he felt it was safe to say, "You know I'm staying out at his old place."

"Out at the trailer?"

"I prefer manufactured home, but yeah. First time Clay took me out there it looked like the place had been ransacked. Clay said the cops had been there looking for clues."

"They find anything?"

"I guess not," Rick said. "From what I gathered, they don't even have a working theory on what happened. Did anybody at work tell the cops anything interesting?"

Traci shook her head. "They never even came to the station to talk to anybody as far as I know." She paused a moment as something occurred to her. "Don't you think that's weird?"

"Yeah," Rick agreed. "Seems weird to me." He

paused a moment, then said, "I think you're right that something bad happened to him."

"Really?" Traci turned to face Rick with sudden, curious animation. "Do you know something?"

"I know I had a visitor last night," Rick said. "A big one. He busted in looking for Captain Jack. Seems a coke dealer was owed some money."

"Oh my God, what happened?"

"He showed me his boot, I showed him my cast-iron skillet, then we talked a little about Ted Nugent. It was lovely."

"Did he hurt you?"

Rick turned his head slowly toward Traci. "This is a small point," he said. "But in the future? If such a circumstance should repeat itself? I'd appreciate it if the first question you asked was how bad did I hurt the other guy."

"Sorry. You said he was big."

"And he was. I'm just saying."

"I understand."

"But it's sweet that you care whether I got hurt." Rick reached up and pointed at his tooth. "He kinda loosened this one."

Traci shook her head. "Aww, poor baby." She reached over and gave Rick a pat on the leg. "Bless your heart."

As they pulled into the studio's parking lot, Rick thought about how Traci had seemed on the verge of telling him something while they were at Kitty's. He wondered if she knew more about Captain Jack than she was letting on. He was tempted to ask, but let it go. He figured she'd tell him sooner or later. As they pulled into a parking spot, the black Trans Am cruised past the station unnoticed.

Traci got out of the truck and said, "You better hurry. You've only got about five minutes." She walked over to her car and paused before getting in. "Hey, thanks for dinner."

Rick was at the door to the station. He stopped and said, "Do it again?"

"Sure. Next time, we'll go to Steak 'n Surf and talk about the Kennedy assassination." She pointed at the building. "Now go play me a song."

"Okay, but you'll have to guess which one is yours." Rick disappeared into the station.

He rushed into the studio and found Autumn dancing to "The Music Makers" from Donovan's *Cosmic Wheels* album. "Hey," she said as she writhed to the exotic rock groove. "This is such a great song! I can't believe I've never heard it before."

Rick went to the wall and pulled Lou Reed's *Transformer*. "You stumble across it or did somebody request it?"

"Request," Autumn said as she danced out from behind the control board like a newborn hippie. "I can't believe how much of this stuff I've never even heard. How come nobody plays this anymore?"

"Somebody does, now." Rick put his record on the turntable and cued his song. "You know the Donovan song 'Jennifer Juniper'?"

"Yeah."

"Do you know who it's about?" Autumn shook her head no. "Well, Jennifer was Jenny Boyd, who later married Mick Fleetwood."

"As in Fleetwood Mac?"

"Yeah, and long before Buckingham and Nicks joined the group. Anyway, Jenny had a sister named Patti, who had a bit part as the girl on the train in *A Hard Day's Night*. Her one line is, 'Prisoners?' Anyway, Eric Clapton fell in love with Patti."

Autumn stopped dancing and said, "Really?"

"Yes, unfortunately Patti was married to George Harrison at the time, which left Eric wallowing in despair and unrequited love and led him to write what famous song?"

"I have no idea."

" 'Layla.' "

"Are you making this up?"

Rick shook his head. "Patti eventually left Harrison and married Clapton."

"I don't believe it."

"It's true. Sadly, Eric and Patti divorced in '88." Rick signed on to the program log then turned back to Autumn. "Now, before she inspired 'Layla,' Patti was the muse behind several other songs, including Harrison's 'Something' and, later, Clapton's 'Wonderful Tonight.' You could probably do half an hour of songs on these girls. In fact, I just might."

Autumn resumed dancing as she moved toward the door. "Oh, before I forget? Stubblefield called, wants us to start running the cash-giveaway promo four times an hour." She held up four fingers, then smiled. "Have a good show." She waved good-bye and slipped out the door.

"See ya." Rick put on his headphones as Donovan faded out. He cleared his throat a couple of times then opened his mike and said, "You're listening to WAOR-

FM, McRae, Mississippi. Redefining classic rock."
Rick pictured Traci's eyes and said, "Here's Lou Reed
from 1972 with his ode to the proper use of cosmetics.
A little something he called, 'Makeup.' "

The phones were active all night—mostly positive
feedback from an audience starved for real rock clas-
sics—though there was one brain-dead metalhead who
wanted a double block of Queensryche. More often
than not Rick found himself trying to explain the format to bewildered children of the late seventies. As he
said to one caller, "It's not about whether Journey is as
good as the Allman Brothers. It's about the music from
a specific time period."

Rick used the final thirty minutes of his shift to test
the theory that you could do a half hour of songs re-
lated to the Boyd sisters. He started with "Jennifer Juniper" then went to George's early songs for Patti,
starting with "I Need You" from the *Help!* sound track.
He followed that with "Something" from *Abbey Road,*
noting on the air that Frank Sinatra considered it one
of the best love songs ever written. After that Rick
played "For You Blue" from *Let It Be*. He then
switched to Clapton's point of view, starting with
"Layla" and making a nice transition from its coda into
"Wonderful Tonight." Harrison's response followed in
the form of his spiteful rewrite of the Everly Brothers'
ditty "Bye Bye Love," which featured barbed refer-
ences to Patti running off with "old Clapper." After this
came Clapton's postdivorce tune, "Old Love," and finally, back to Harrison's *Dark Horse* album to wrap it
up with "So Sad."

Uncle Victor walked into the studio just as Rick was starting the last song. As always, he had his ancient leather bag strapped over his stooped shoulder. He pulled a copy of J. J. Cale's *Naturally* and ran his finger down the song list. Without looking up at Rick he said, "As inspired as this tribute to the romantic affairs of Slow Hand and the Quiet Beatle is, I believe 'Old Love' was released in 1989 on the *Journeyman* album and thus . . . violates the format." His pause was short but dramatic. Uncle Victor then stepped behind the board and cued "Call Me the Breeze" with an air of tranquil superiority.

"Busted," Rick said as he filed his records. "And if I hadn't heard you at about two-thirty yesterday morning playing something from *Swordfishtrombones,* I'd feel like a real hypocrite about it." He tried his own dramatic pause here before saying, "But, as you know, sometimes the music requires things the format doesn't allow." He glanced over his shoulder to gauge the response.

Uncle Victor grinned like a guy who was used to getting caught. He cleared his throat, turned on the mike, and said, "One-oh-two-point-nine-FM, WAOR, McRae. Here's J. J. Cale with something Lynyrd Skynyrd liked so much they did their own version three years later." He started the song and killed his mike. He removed his cans and said, "The Tom Waits was essential to my set."

"Yes, it was," Rick said. "And that's my point." He stepped closer to Uncle Victor. "This format is like a musical instrument," he said. "You have to know how to play it. Otherwise, it's like a monkey banging on a drum, a lot of noise and not much music. And, though you were *technically* outside the format, you played it like a maestro." Rick crossed to the door. "That's all I ask."

Uncle Victor took a small bow at the compliment. "You have to understand the rules before you can break them," he said.

"Exactly, like so many things in life."

"Well. I'm glad we had this talk." Uncle Victor went to the wall and pulled *Boogie with Canned Heat*. "Have a good night," he said.

Rick gave him a salute then opened the door. "I'm on the road again," he said on his way out. Rick locked his office and headed for the front door, stepping out of the station just after midnight feeling optimistic about all manner of things. He and Traci seemed to have made a connection over dinner. Rick could tell she was intrigued by Captain Jack's disappearance, and though he wasn't sure how, he thought she might be helpful in trying to find out what happened. Beyond that, the format was taking shape and so far they hadn't lost a single sponsor. Topping it off, he felt tonight's show had been his best in a long time.

He was so pleased about things that it wasn't until he was actually sitting in his truck that he noticed his windshield had been completely shattered. It looked like someone with a Louisville Slugger had taken batting practice on it. His anger rising, Rick moved in the seat and heard the pebbled safety glass crunching under his weight. He stepped out of the truck to check his tires. They were fine. He popped the hood. The plugs and belts and the few other things he knew about all seemed intact. He turned and looked to the end of the parking lot where the WAOR Prize Van was parked. Rick walked over and looked. It hadn't been touched. He returned to his truck and slammed the hood shut and wondered if this was the work of someone who didn't like the new format, perhaps the disgruntled metalhead. But if so, wouldn't it be more symbolic to bust the window from the van with WAOR painted on the side? Maybe symbolism was beyond the vandal's range. Or maybe it was the Nugent fan coming to get revenge for his cracked ankle. Rick hadn't been in town long enough to make many more enemies than that. Of course, it could have been run-of-the-mill mayhem, a little random violence that had nothing to do with Rick except that his truck happened to get in the way of someone's uncontrolled rage.

Rick looked around, trying to control his own. He saw himself standing in the parking lot of a small-town radio station in the middle of the night. Someone had smashed the windshield out of his old truck. And he couldn't shrug it off anymore. He was too old. He'd call the Auto Club if he made that kind of regular money. And he'd call a friend if he had one. But he was new in town and broke to boot. And this wasn't the first time. Maybe not this exactly, but like it. Worst of all, Rick knew there was no one to blame but himself. He wondered, *Is this the best I can manage? What the hell am I doing here? What can I do to change that? Or should I just lower my expectations?* He found himself asking more rhetorical questions the older he got.

He took a deep breath and waited for the moment to pass. Then he walked to the back of his truck, opened his toolbox, and grabbed his tire iron. He pried the busted windshield out in two pieces and tossed it in the Dumpster at the side of the building. He brushed the glass off the seat and hood and started the engine. While the truck idled, Rick put the tire iron back in the box and rooted around until he found an ill-fitting pair of plastic safety goggles. He figured he'd be pelted by all manner of insects drawn to his headlights on the ride home, and as unpleasant as it would be to take a few bugs in the teeth, a big one in the eye at forty miles an hour would probably blind him. Go right through to his brain. And who needs that?

Rick got back in the cab of the truck and was about to let off the brake when he had a notion. He got out again, reached back into his toolbox, and grabbed the tire iron. He tossed it on the seat next to him. Just in case the vandal was keen on following. He put on the safety goggles, pulled the straps tight, and put the truck in gear.

On the drive home, Rick made the mistake of yawning once without covering his mouth. He discovered that certain insects of the family Bibionidae had a nutty, almondlike flavor. He choked and coughed as he spit heads, thoraxes, and abdomens, not to mention all the legs. By the time he got back to the trailer, his goggles were smeared with a greenish-yellow goo. Rick climbed out of his truck fighting the urge to reflect any further on the state of his life. He brushed a couple of tenacious moths from his hair then went inside looking for his cigar box.

Rick woke up early the next morning and couldn't get back to sleep. *What the hell,* he thought. *Might as well start the day.* He poured a cup of coffee and went outside to sit at the big wooden spool. He glanced at his truck and wondered how much a new windshield was going to cost.

Rick sat back, propped his feet up, and surveyed his pastoral surroundings. Except for the driveway that cut a corridor through the trees, the trailer was surrounded by woods. It was mostly pine, with a few hardwoods here and there, black gums, oaks, poplars. Rick knew Mississippi had once been a magnificent virgin forest, but when the lumber reserves of the northeast ran out, the lumber industry moved south and worked feverishly to deflower her. Like a lot of small towns that popped up around the lumber mills in this part of the state, McRae was founded during the timber boom that started in the late 1800s.

Rick turned to look when he heard the tap-tap, tap-tap-tap of a woodpecker. He scanned the trees but never saw the bird. But he noticed some movement out of the corner of his eye. Looking closer, he realized it was a deer. In fact it was a large buck, eight points, maybe ten, which was unusual for this part of the state. The trophy bucks were up in the Delta and the Big Black River bottom. Still, Rick figured by this time next year, that bad boy's head would be stuck on somebody's rec-room wall with a New Orleans Saints baseball cap hanging off his rack.

Rick watched as the buck wandered leisurely into the woods and he thought he should do the same. He had told himself he needed to get outside more and this was a perfect opportunity. He had time before he had to be at work, so he finished his coffee, put on some boots, and took a hike.

As he crossed the tree line into the cool woods Rick took a deep breath. The air smelled like it had been scrubbed clean. Squirrels chattered and leaped overhead and he could still hear that woodpecker somewhere. Each step crunched beneath his feet as he walked over the bed of dry, brown needles. He stopped for a moment to take it in. The beauty and stillness reminded him why he had wanted to do this in the first place. It was like the woods near his house when he was young, when there were still all sorts of possibilities. Possibilities that were gone now. Rick and his friends had built forts and fought wars in those woods. They had blasted down paths on Stingrays with banana seats and sissy bars and five-speed gearshifts. They were daredevils then, wild and reckless and indestructible. And sometimes they stopped and laid the bikes on the ground and sat with their backs against the trees. And they talked about things they didn't understand and they tried to figure it all out and the memory of those days was sweeter remembered in a place like this.

The woodpecker was closer now. The tap-tap-tap pulled Rick back from his reverie and he moved on. A little deeper in the woods he came to an old forgotten fence. Sage-green lichens, ruffled and cracked, grew on hand-split cedar posts linked by weary barbed wire. It looked to be an old property line but, long neglected, its line was broken here and there. Rick noticed some hair snagged and dangling from a barb. Long, coarse, and black—he figured it was from a mule's tail or maybe a horse. But it could have been a wild boar. There were still some out here. Big Russian razorbacks.

Rick walked along the fence line until he came to a clearing. The contrast where the shade and shadow of the green trees gave way to direct light on the exposed red-orange clay was startling, like pop art in the middle of a Renaissance gallery. Rick ducked between the barbed wires to the other side. He looked down. The tracks of heavy machinery in the sandy clay brought to mind skidders and haulers and Rick figured someone was in the process of selling off a little timber. The clearing was surrounded mostly by long-leaf yellow pines, though there was one large white oak that stood near the banks of the creek Rick had been hearing.

Rick walked along the creek, following it back the way he had come. He eventually reached a bend near the tree line and he could see the trailer. He checked his watch and decided he might as well go to work. It was payday and he had to get his windshield fixed. And he was curious if Traci might tell him what she had come so close to saying last night.

He went back to the trailer and grabbed a few records. Then he got in his truck and strapped on his plastic goggles.

Rick walked into the station brushing something from his shirt. Traci looked up and said, "Hey. I listened until eleven last night, then I fell asleep, no offense."

"None taken," Rick said as he admired the devilish sweep of eye shadow Traci had applied that morning. "Did you hear your song?"

"I have no idea," she said. "Was it the Larry Raspberry song, 'Dixie Diner'? You know, since we ate at

Kitty's?" She handed him a couple of phone messages.
"That's my best guess."

"Mighta been." Rick glanced at the messages,
record reps returning his calls.

"Ohhh," Traci said. "So it's gonna be like that? An
international-man-of-mystery sort of thing."

"What do you want me to do, play 'Tracy' by the
Cuff Links? That's no fun. Besides, it doesn't fit the
format. Might as well play the Archies."

"So what did you—" Traci's eyes went wide and she
shrieked. She pushed back from her desk while pointing at Rick's head and saying, "Get, get, get, ooooooh!"

Rick ran his hands through his hair and quickly found
the problem. It was a bee. Rick made a noise that was less
masculine than he might have wanted. He shook his head
like a wet dog trying to get the thing out of his hair before
it stung him. After a moment the bee landed on the carpet, stunned and staggering. Rick bent over to look, but
he couldn't see where it was. He stomped blindly, all the
while saying, "Where is it? Where did it go?"

Traci came out from behind the desk. "Don't *step*
on it."

"What do you mean, don't step on it?"

"It didn't hurt you, why do you want to hurt it?"

"You're suddenly in the society to prevent cruelty to
venomous insects?"

She pushed Rick away then grabbed a sheet from a
memo pad and scooped the bee onto the paper. "I can't
believe you screamed like that," she said, barely hiding
her laugh.

"You screamed first," Rick said.

"That's different," she said, without explaining how

or why. Traci went to the door and tossed the bee outside. She was turning to come back in when she did a
double take on Rick's truck. "Ohmigod." Her hand
went to her mouth. "What happened to your windshield?" There was something about her expression
and the way she asked the question that went beyond
mere surprise. Rick detected a vague sense of responsibility in her tone. He got the feeling Traci wanted
him to say it wasn't what she thought it was.

"I came out after my shift last night and found the
windshield smashed," Rick said. "My first guess was a
beer-fueled miscreant who wanted some Billy Idol, but
then it occurred to me it could just as easily be a local
auto-glass replacement place out to drum up some business."

Traci's mouth opened with some reluctance. "I don't
think so," she said.

"What makes you say that?"

"Oh, jeez." Traci went back behind the reception
desk and pulled out the phone book. "I wanted to tell
you last night but . . . I didn't."

"Tell me what?"

Traci flipped through the phone book and said, "My
ex-boyfriend."

"Billy Idol fan?"

"Well, yeah, but he's also real jealous."

"Okay. So?"

"So, I don't know. Maybe he saw us at Kitty's."

"Did you see him?"

"No, but . . ." She pointed feebly at the phone book.
"I'll call these guys, they'll come out and replace your
windshield. And I'll pay for it, don't worry."

"Wait a second," Rick said. "How 'ex' is he?"

"We broke up about a month ago."

"You were the breaker and he was the breakee?"

She nodded. "He just, he's got a real bad temper and I'd had enough of it. I should've told you last night. And I thought about it, really, but, anyway, I'm real sorry he did that."

"Well, look, we don't know he did it," Rick said. "And even if he did, it's not your responsibility." He looked down at the calendar on Traci's desk. "Today's payday, right? It's my problem. I'll pay for it." Then he pointed at the phone book. "But if you'd call and have 'em come out I'd appreciate it."

"Are you sure? I'll split the cost because—"

"Traci?" He shook his head and said, "Forget about it." He turned and headed for his office. As he walked down the hall Rick wondered if Traci was right. A jealous ex-boyfriend was as good an explanation as any. The bad news was that they tended to hold a grudge longer than disgruntled headbangers, so if Traci was right, Rick had to wonder how many windshields he was going to have to replace.

6

Back in his office Rick spent some time on the phone calling the record reps, trying to get some back catalog to fill out the library. As he figured, a lot of what he wanted just wasn't available on CD. Fortunately between Captain Jack's and his own record collections, and a CD recorder, he could fill in the blanks. Rick was making a list of the albums he needed to burn onto disc when Clay stepped into the doorway and said, "Hey, those promo spots you did are pretty good."

Rick glanced up. "Glad you approve."

"Yeah, you bet. But listen, I thought you were gonna use that Pink Floyd money song we talked about, the one with that cash-register sound effect and all."

Rick gave a noncommittal nod. "Money" was one of those songs that had been so overplayed on classic rock radio during the last thirty years that it had become peeling aural wallpaper. It was exactly the sort of song Rick wanted to "rest" for a while as he recast the classic format. Instead of playing it two or three times a day, seven days a week, as most classic rock stations did, he would move it to an infrequent rotation, playing it no more than two or three times a month. "I thought about using Pink Floyd," Rick said. "But I decided that had been done so many times we should try something else."

Clay assumed the expression of a rather bright caveman and said, "Huh." He seemed caught off guard, as if he had expected Rick to apologize for not taking his suggestion and run to the production room to recut the spots. Clay chewed on the inside of his cheek for a second before he said, "So what was that damn song you used?"

Rick looked up from his list and said, "Grateful Dead song called 'Money, Money.'"

"Issat right?" Clay turned his head and softly spit whatever it was he'd chewed off his cheek. "So, anyway, I'm 'onna need you to go ahead 'n cut a new one."

Rick looked at him but didn't speak.

"Not just 'cause of the music," Clay said. "You need to add that the grand prize drawin's gone be done by the new Miss Loblolly Pine." He winked and said, "I'm 'onna see if I can get her to do it in a thong bikini or a wet T-shirt or some damn thing, but don't put that in the spot yet, 'cause I hadn't asked her yet. I'll let you know if she goes for it and you can just recut 'em then." Clay turned to leave but stopped and said, "Oh yeah, and as long as you're cuttin' new spots you might as well put that Pink Floyd song in. And don't forget my idea about saying, 'Rrrrrreal rock, rrrrreal cash.' That's good stuff." There was a pause before he did his "Tch." Clay turned and rapped his knuckles on the door on his way out. "Cash and titties," he said as he walked down the hall. "I'm telling ya, that'll sell anything."

By the time Rick finished recutting the promo spots— without Clay's clichéd tag line or the Pink Floyd—it was nearly five. It dawned on him that he still hadn't received his paycheck. He asked Traci what the procedure was and she told him to check his employee mail slot in the break room. He did, but it was empty. So he went to see the bookkeeper.

His office was just down the hall. When Rick walked in, the man was locking the gray metal file cabinet that served as a credenza behind his desk. He had oddly indistinguishable features, like he could stand in a police lineup with no fear of being picked.

"Hi, I'm Rick Shannon. I'm trying to track down my paycheck. I hear you're the man to see."

The man looked up submissively and said, "I was just leaving."

"Well, I won't keep you any longer than it takes to hand over an envelope." Rick smiled.

The bookkeeper didn't. He stood there for a moment before he took his keys from his pocket. He sat down and reopened the cabinet, fingering through to a specific file. He turned back toward Rick and said, "Shelton?"

"Shannon. Rick. I'm the new PD for the FM."

The man closed his eyes for a moment like he knew what was coming and didn't want to see it. He said, "Uhhh, exactly how new?"

"Two weeks," Rick said. "About as long as the new format, that you may or may not have noticed."

The bookkeeper let the file slip back into the drawer. He shut the cabinet and sighed.

Rick narrowed his eyes and said, "Is there a problem?"

"It's the employee handbook." He pulled a copy from the credenza and turned to a well-thumbed page. "A lot of people don't read it, so they're surprised." He pushed the document halfway across the desk. Then, with a weak gesture toward one of the pages, he said, "It's right there." His eyes stayed on the words.

Rick looked around for a moment, thinking about how he hadn't read an employee handbook since his third job. He scanned the paragraph. It said the station would hold his first two weeks' pay in "reserve." This money would be held until the end of his employment, without interest. When his employment was terminated they'd give him his first two weeks' pay and call it severance. Solid policy. For the station.

Rick pushed the manual back across the desk. He took a deep breath. *Stubbled again,* he thought. *Get to work a whole month for nothing.* "Let me ask you," he said. "When I do get paid, how much will I be getting?"

The bookkeeper pulled out a ledger and looked up the number. He wrote it on a piece of paper and seemed ashamed as he handed it over. Rick looked at it for a good moment, his mood growing hostile. He could see Stubblefield in his mind, that first day, saying, *No question we'll make it worth your while. You can count on that.*

Rick pointed at the piece of paper with the number on it. "This was the original salary I was supposed to get just for the night shift. Stubblefield was supposed to talk to you about this."

The bookkeeper shook his head. "He never said anything to me."

After all of his years in radio, Rick had grown accustomed to being lied to, but he still didn't like it. In fact, he'd just about had it with this kind of crap. Every single bit of it. He'd never been in the business to get rich—he wasn't that naive—but as corporate ownership increasingly sucked the air out of the lungs of a job that once required creativity, turning something he loved into a miserable grind with little to no future, Rick felt he was at least entitled to being treated like a professional.

As he stalked down the hallway to Clay's office, Rick rehearsed a thundering sermon that opened with a litany of Stubblefield's managerial shortcomings, moved on to threats of legal action, and ended with the promise to tear him a new asshole.

When he got to Clay's office and found it dark, a salesman in the next office said, "You just missed him. Probably headed for happy hour." Rick made a beeline for the parking lot and caught Clay as he was getting into his car.

"I just left the bookkeeper's office," Rick said, obviously agitated. "We have a problem."

Clay tossed his briefcase into the passenger seat then checked his watch and said, "Is it the kind that can wait?"

"Not if you expect me to keep working here."

Clay propped an arm on the roof of his car and put his foot on the running board. "Hell, sounds pretty serious," he said. "What's up?"

Rick was ready to let go with both barrels when he

thought better of it. As he stood in the parking lot, it occurred to him that if he really wanted to stick it to Stubblefield, his best bet was to keep his job. He might be able to find out all he needed by following the leads on the tape, but you never knew when proximity, the ability to poke through files and computers, would come in handy. With that in mind he lightened up and said, "I, uh, hadn't had time to read my employee manual, so I just found out I'm not gettin' paid for two more weeks."

Clay's head rocked back in a quick laugh and he slapped the top of the car. "Oh shit, that's right. I hadn't even thought of that. You need me to float you a loan, tide you over?" He stabbed a hand into his pocket and pulled out some folding money.

"Well, you know, I was gonna squeeze by all right until somebody saw fit to bust the window out of my truck."

Clay reflexively thumbed the edge of his bills like it was a deck of cards and he was about to do a trick. "Oh yeah, heard about that," he said with no evidence of real concern. "You think it's somebody's gonna come back?"

"I doubt it, but it's hard to say. That kinda shit just happens sometimes."

"'Cause if it is, you might wanna park down the road somewhere and walk here since we ain't exactly got secure parking."

"I might do that," Rick said.

"Hey, hey, hey." Clay thumped his folded bills with a finger. "Just had a brainstorm that'll put some cash in your pocket and help me out, too, a regular win-win deal." He peeled five twenties off his stack. "Got a little thing coming up next weekend and we need a DJ for the dance afterward." He held the hundred out toward Rick. "I can advance you this and pay you the rest, night of the show. A hundred tide you over?"

"I'll make it stretch." Rick, playing bashful, reluctantly took the cash and said, " 'Preciate it." He pushed the bills into his front pocket. "Been a while since I emceed a party. How long's the gig?"

"Just be a couple of hours," Clay said. "And I already got the gear lined up, so you ain't gotta worry about that."

"Who's dancing? Kids? Adults?"

"The Bob Seeger crowd," Clay said. "Just get them old records off the shelf." He rapped his knuckles on the roof of his car. "All right, then, glad this worked out."

"Oh, by the way," Rick said, gesturing at the building. "I forgot to ask while I was in there. You had a chance to talk to the bookkeeper yet, about adjusting my pay?"

"You bet," Clay said as he got into his car. "All taken care of. You can count on that. Tch."

Rick used a credit card to pay for the replacement windshield and gave J.C. fifty bucks to replenish his cigar box. He figured if he cooked his own meals instead of eating at Kitty's every day he could hold out for two more weeks without a paycheck, maybe even lose a couple of pounds in the process.

In lieu of being blindsided by additional station policy, Rick took the time to read his employee handbook. Among other things, he found out that the company's meager dental plan didn't go into effect until he'd been employed at the station for six months, so it was a good thing his tooth had firmed up in his jaw on its own.

Over the next few days Rick used his free time to look into various matters. It turned out that Mississippi had no state laws regulating private investigators, no license requirement or anything, though there was an association of PIs lobbying to change that. In the meanwhile he was free to hold himself out as a professional shamus.

The issues surrounding the tape were more complicated. Poking around the Internet, Rick found what looked like legitimate citations of Mississippi law regarding "the interception and acquisition of the contents of wire, oral, or other communications with a mechanical or electronic device." Rick's best interpretation was that it was illegal to record a conversation if none of the parties involved knew it was being taped. However, "if a person is a party to a communication, or has obtained consent from any one of the parties, no civil liability can be imposed unless the interception was accompanied by a criminal or tortious intent."

Not that it mattered particularly, but Rick wondered if the law protected conversations about illegal activities, and if it did, why? He was pretty sure contract law didn't apply to contracts for something illegal. But maybe his problem was in applying logic to legislative matters. Regardless, in his reading of the law, Rick was unable to ascertain if being in possession of an illegally recorded tape was a crime in and of itself. But he suspected that absent criminal or tortious intent, it wasn't.

It was a felony, however, for anyone "who is not a law enforcement officer to disclose the contents of intercepted communications for any reason other than testifying under oath in a governmental or court proceeding, and the penalty for such disclosure can be up to five years imprisonment and up to a $10,000 fine." Rick wondered what constituted "disclosure of the contents." Had he violated this already by telling Lisa Ramey what he had? He made a mental note to keep this in mind as he moved forward. As much as he wanted to yank Clay's chain, he sure as hell didn't consider it worth five years or ten thousand dollars.

All this got Rick thinking again. It seemed obvious that Clay didn't know he was being recorded; even someone as possum-brained as he was had better sense than to say such things knowingly on tape. The banker, on the other hand, hadn't said anything incriminating. This meant either that he had nothing incriminating to say or that he had been careful not to say it, while at the same time he had encouraged Clay to dig a deeper and deeper hole for himself and for others. If the latter was true, it seemed to suggest once again that the banker might have been involved. Since he was a party to the conversation, it wouldn't have been illegal for him to record it, unless he had criminal or tortious intent, which would be the case if he was the blackmailer.

Of course blackmailers, by definition, aren't particularly concerned with the law. That and several other points seemed to mitigate against the banker's involvement: the tape starting in the middle of the conversation instead of the beginning; the tape being in Captain Jack's possession, not the banker's; and the fact that the banker came across as too much of a weak sister to be involved in a crime.

Everything came back to Rick's original theory. The

problem was, he was no closer to proving it now than he was the day he found the tape.

Rick looked online but couldn't find anything about the furniture-store fire. He had visited the Web site for the local newspaper, the *McRae Monitor,* but there was no search engine for archives. He called the paper and the local library and was told by both that there was no index to back issues. Hoping to narrow his search, Rick asked if anyone recalled the fire. No one did.

Rick thought back to the tape, hoping for a clue as to time frame. After casually mentioning that he thought the woman had set the place on fire, Clay had said, *"I don't know what in the hell's . . . it's some kinda damn hardware-store-looking thing in there now."* That helped a little. It meant the fire must have occurred at least a few months ago, time enough to rebuild and open a new business in the same space. Based on that, Rick decided he'd start looking at issues of the *Monitor* from three months ago and work backward from there, one issue at a time.

But first he had to get to a staff meeting.

Autumn was standing in the doorway to Rick's office, dressed like she was on her way to Woodstock— bell-bottom jeans, tie-dyed T-shirt, and blue-tinted granny glasses. J.C. was sitting on the floor with a cowboy hat tilted down over his face. Rick propped his feet on his desk and said, "You sure it wasn't Lester Bangs?"

"Yep." J.C.'s hat bobbed up and down.

"And it wasn't Greil Marcus or Christgau or somebody like that?"

J.C. pushed the hat out of his eyes and said, "Bow up and listen! It was Roy Plomley in 1942 at the BBC.

They still do the show, but with a different host. And it's eight, not ten. It was never ten."

"I always heard ten," Autumn said. "That's how we always played it."

Rick glanced at the clock on the wall and wondered where Rob was.

"Obviously, you can do it with any number," J.C. said. "But the original was eight, so that's what we're doing. And no greatest hits or career retrospective box sets. That's cheating."

"What about, like, *Woodstock,*" Autumn asked. "Is that one or three records?"

"One," J.C. said. "And not a very good one at that, except in terms of quantity of crowd noise." He sat back and pointed at Rick. "So what're your eight?"

"I can't do it with eight *or* ten," Rick said. "There's just no way." He thought for a moment before he said, "What about doing it with artist catalogs instead of albums?"

J.C. shook his head. "Why do it at all if you're not going to do it right?" He threw up his hands. "All right, fine. Desert-island *catalogs*. But only five, not eight."

"Here's what I always wanted to know," Autumn said. "If you're on a deserted island, how are you supposed to play these?"

J.C. ignored her and pointed at Rick. "Go."

"Okay. Five artists. Everything they recorded? Is this limited to—"

"Not limited to anything."

"We gotta limit it to something," Rick said with a mock whine. "How about pop rock? 'Cause if I can take jazz I'm not going to be able to do this. That's just too much to choose from."

"Christ, it's not supposed to be easy." J.C. stood up, waving his hands. "Oh, just forget it. Where the hell's Rob? Let's get this show on the road."

"No," Rick said. "Don't be like that. How about this? What if we get a different island for different types of music? You got rock island, jazz island, reggae island, like that."

J.C. lifted his hat with one hand and rubbed his head with the other while saying, "How 'bout we just forget I brought it up and you just call this dang staff meetin' to order?" He put his hat back on and said, "I swear. You're more irritating than those damn UFS spots."

"No, hang on. I'm gonna do this," Rick said. "If I was stuck on a desert island and I could have the catalogs of five pop-rock artists, I'd take Bob Dylan, Van Morrison, Paul Simon, Bruce Springsteen, and Steve—"

"Oh, hey, Rob," Autumn said. "We're doing desert-island discs."

"—Earle."

Rob stepped into the room like he was sorry he took up space. "Sorry I'm late," he said. He had the expression of a boy whose dog had just died. "Mr. Stubblefield stopped me on the way in. Said he had to let me go."

Simultaneously the others said, "Whhhhaat?"

"I just wanted to say good-bye."

"What're you talking about?" Rick sat there, shaking his head. "That's crazy."

Autumn knew how much Rob loved his job. The poor kid looked like he might start crying. She went over and put an arm around his shoulder. "What'd he say?"

Rob twisted an angry look onto his face, trying to overcome his dejection, trying not to cry. "He said he couldn't afford to pay me. I told him I'd go back to working for free but he said it was probably better if he let me go, so I could concentrate on school." He shrugged like it was the sort of reasoning only adults could understand.

"That rat bastard!" Rick was furious. He slammed a fist on his desk as he stood. "This is the same guy who told you to drop out of school so you could work for free. That's how concerned he is about your education. This is bullshit, Rob, don't worry about it. Stubblefield did this to get back at me for putting you on the payroll without consulting him." He slammed his fist on the desk again. "Goddammit! Not only are you *not* fired, I'm giving you a raise."

Rick took his time with the meeting. He figured if he charged down to Stubblefield's office before he cooled off he'd find himself directly behind Rob in the unemployment line. If this had happened on his first or second day on the job, he wouldn't have hesitated, but as things were, he was too invested in his format. He had the feeling it was starting to work and he had to get at least one good ratings book before he could leave the station on an upward career trajectory. Plus he wanted to stay and be a thorn in Stubblefield's side.

Rick started the meeting with some cheerleading, complimenting everybody about something he'd heard them do, a good segue, a good set, a good improv on the station promos, whatever. He talked up the positive feedback he'd heard about from the sales staff, then he touched briefly on format issues. "New rule," he said. "Let's avoid anything over ten minutes between seven A and seven P," he said. "There's very little at that length that's worth playing."

J.C. raised a hand and said, " 'Funeral for a Friend/ Love Lies Bleeding' is eleven-oh-five."

"Thank heaven for small favors," Rick said.

"But I love playing that," J.C. said.

"Play it at home. It's a cliché and it's too long for the day part."

"Oh, that's right, and you want me playing Judy Collins and Buffy Sainte-Marie."

Rick shot him a glance. "That's right, and I'm considering a Joan Baez hour, so don't push me. Now, between seven to ten at night, try to keep tracks under fifteen. After ten you can play "Mountain Jam," "Foreigner Suite," "Thick as a Brick," or whatever you want. If there's something you can edit for day play, fine, but let me hear it first." He finished the meeting by selling the importance of the cash-giveaway promotion that was ten days away. "Remember, try to get people out to meet us. We want to connect to the community face-to-face, okay?" Everyone nodded. "All right. We're sounding good," Rick said in closing. "Keep it up."

As the jocks went their different ways, Rick stopped Rob and pointed toward the control room. "You're going to be in that seat tomorrow morning, right?"

Rob smiled and tried to act cool and grateful at the same time. He said, "Oh yeah, no problem, Mr. Shannon. If you say so." He looked at the carpet, then at Rick and said, "Thanks."

* * *

Clay was going over some sales contracts when Rick walked into his office and asked why he had fired Rob. For the first time since Rick had been at WAOR Clay dropped his aw-shucks-how-can-I-help-you routine and said, "Hell, you shouldn'ta gone behind my back and hired him in the first place. Bet you thought you were bein' pretty cute with that little move, huh? Gettin' outta doin' mornin's and givin' me a jab at the same time." Clay tossed the contracts into a file. "We gotta control costs, here. These're budget considerations." He made an angry gesture toward the studios. "That shift was pure profit, and then you give the kid a damn salary."

"I'd hardly call minimum wage a salary. Besides, Rob does a good job, he never misses a shift, and he knows the music inside and out."

"That's right, Professor. And he was doin' all that without costing us a dime until you started givin' away my money."

"You're the one who made me the program director," Rick said. "And traditionally that's who hires and fires air staff."

"Yeah, well, we got different traditions," Clay said, jabbing himself in the chest with his thumb. "I'm the big swinging dick around here. It all comes through me, you got it?" He gave Rick his best intimidating stare.

Rick stood his ground despite the obvious dismissal. "I hired him back."

Clay blinked. "Bullshit."

"Gave him a raise, too."

Clay's expression turned into the sort of thing that tended to foreshadow unemployment, but after a moment, he smirked. "What kinda damn raise'd you give him?"

"It was unspecified," Rick said. "How much do you think it should be?"

"Shiddif I know." Clay leaned back in his executive chair, hands behind his head. He almost chuckled. "Tell you what," he said. "You give him whatever raise you want. I'll just take it out of that adjustment I was gonna make in your pay. How's 'at? That's pretty clever, don't you think?" He sat forward and snatched the phone off its cradle. "Hope that's gonna work for you." He punched a number then wagged the handset toward the door and said, "Excuse me. This is a private call."

Rick walked into the reception area and sat in one of the chairs. He looked at Traci, who was reading a *Billboard* magazine, and said, "I believe I've been Stubbled again."

A hint of amusement crossed her face. Traci kept reading but nodded her lack of surprise. "What'd he do this time?"

"Well, first he fired Rob."

Traci looked up darkly, the amusement gone from her face, replaced by anger. "That sorry son of a bitch." She thrust an incensed middle finger toward Clay's office and shook it for good measure. "The one thing that kid's got and he takes it away?" She glanced to see if Clay was coming down the hall, then lowered her voice and said, "Somebody oughta kick his big fat sorry stupid ass."

"Yeah, well, I did the next best thing," Rick said. "I hired Rob back and gave him a raise."

"Well, good for you," Traci said, still indignant. "I'm glad somebody's willing to stand up to that asshole, if you'll pardon my language." She paused to answer a phone. "Dubya-ay-oh-ahhr," she said. "Mmm. Hold please." Traci transferred the call then turned her attention back to Rick. "You probably didn't know, unless he told you, maybe he did, I don't know, but Rob's dad died about six months ago." She shook her head sadly. "Threw the poor kid for a loop."

Rick shook his head. "I didn't know."

"At his age you're confused enough," Traci said. "Lord knows I was. Then his dad . . . you know? He really reacted, like it confirmed all those negative thoughts you have as a teenager. You know, everything's pointless, the future's hopeless, all that? He was seriously depressed." Her eyes drifted into the middle distance for a moment before she looked back at Rick. "I think Captain Jack and J.C. knew he needed something, so they kept giving him things to do at the station. He started spending all his free time just hanging out in the studio talking to the jocks. He really looks forward to being here. He needs it."

Rick nodded. He'd seen the excitement in Rob's eyes, and he hated the idea of Clay cutting that out. He said, "You know it takes most general managers about a month to make me actually taste bile, but Stubblefield . . . He seems to go out of his way to piss me off."

"Oh, that's right," Traci said. "You didn't tell me how he Stubbled you this time."

"Huh?" Rick stood up and waved a hand when he figured out what she meant. "Oh, doesn't matter," he said. "Listen. Don't worry, Rob's gonna be fine. I'll make that a personal project."

Traci smiled and said, "Bless your heart."

Rick started toward the door. "I've got to run some errands but I'll be—" A thought interrupted him. "Hey, maybe you know this." He crossed back to Traci's desk and, lowering his voice, said, "You know Three Pines Shopping Center?" She nodded. "Do you remember a fire at a place called Moore Furniture that used to be over there?"

Traci squinted as if trying to bring her memory into focus. "Yeah, it was about—" As she thought back, trying to pin down the date, she grew suspicious. "What's that got to do with anything?"

"Nothing," Rick said. "I heard about it and wondered when it was, that's all." Unable to leave bad enough alone, Rick gestured toward the studios and said, "It came up somehow in a conversation with a caller last night. He requested the Hendrix version of "Fire" and in the course of things he said something about that store burning down."

Traci wagged a sly finger at him. "But even then, why do you want to know about *when* it was?" She looked at Rick like he was a shifty character. "There's something you're not telling me."

Rick smiled and said, "Yeah, well, maybe I'm getting back at you for not telling me about your ex-boyfriend until I needed a new windshield." He smirked at her and she smirked back. "You don't want to tell me about this, that's fine," Rick said. "I'm going to the library anyway.

I can look it up. No big deal. You need any books? *The Complete Idiot's Guide to Answering Simple Questions* maybe? No? Okay, I'm outta here."

As soon as Rick put his hand on the door Traci said, "This isn't about Rob, is it?" She paused a moment. "It's about Captain Jack."

Rick stopped, wondering if he could trust her. He went back to the reception desk. "You first. When was the fire?"

"About six months ago." She folded her arms, waiting for Rick to reciprocate.

Rick hesitated before he said, "How about dinner at Kitty's?"

"Nope." Traci shook her head and said, "Steak 'n Surf."

When the librarian asked Rick for the date range of his search, something new occurred to him. Had Captain Jack's disappearance been treated as a news story? Had anyone filed a missing-persons report? Clay had made it sound as if he had contacted the police about the mysterious disappearance of an employee. This, according to Clay, went to explain why the trailer had been ransacked. But if Rick's blackmail theory was correct, it seemed more likely that someone involved in Jack Carter's disappearance had been at the trailer looking for the tape. If that was true, it meant Clay had lied about the police and was, therefore, involved.

So maybe the cops didn't even know about Captain Jack's disappearance. Since he didn't have any local family, it was possible no one had contacted them about it. Rick remembered something else. Clay had said that Captain Jack's brother was coming to collect his personal effects, so clearly someone in the family knew he had gone AWOL.

Rick was standing at the reference desk trying to sort through all this when the librarian said, "Sir? What dates do you want?"

Rick made two requests. One for the month following Captain Jack's disappearance and one beginning six months earlier and going back two months. The good news for Rick was that the *McRae Monitor* was a small-town paper. World and national news stories were secondary to headlines like DECKERN ELEMENTARY PLANS FALL FESTIVAL and SAFE DRIVING FOR SENIORS MEETING RESCHEDULED. Obviously it didn't take much to make the front page, so he figured a missing media personality or a fire destroying a local business would merit banner consideration.

Rick found no mention of Jack Carter but he did find a headline from seven months earlier: SUNDAY FIRE DAMAGES FURNITURE OUTLET. The story was short and sweet: "McRae City and Deckern County firefighters responded to a call early Sunday morning at the Three Pines Shopping Center at Bilbo Avenue and Broadway. The fire was contained to Moore Furniture, a retail business at the east end of the center, said Captain Virgil Boggs of the McRae Fire Department. The cause of the fire had not been determined, Boggs said."

Rick wondered if "the cause of the fire had not been determined" was fire chief code for "it looks like arson but I ain't gonna tip my hand in the press!" Rick figured there were a couple of ways to find out. One was to call Virgil Boggs and ask. At worst Virgil would say

he couldn't comment on the investigation. Another
way would be to ask someone at the insurance company. But how would he find out who the insurer was?
The only way he could imagine was if there was a
mortgage on the property. If there was, that information would be on a deed of trust at the county court-
house. And while the insurer probably wouldn't be
named on a deed of trust, the lender would be, so
maybe he could get them to say who insured it. Then it
dawned on Rick that Moore Furniture was in a shopping center, so they probably had a lease, not a mortgage. And with that, he was back where he started.

He went to the library's computer and looked for
The Complete Idiot's Guide to Being a Private Detec-
tive but didn't find anything. So he did a periodical
search on arson and found a couple of magazine articles on arson investigations, including a useful list of
arson-for-profit indicators. Phony or missing recipts
for big-ticket inventory, insurance policy about to ex-
pire, financial distress indicated (bankruptcy or other
legal problems), and several more. He compared the
newspaper article with the list of indicators and found
two matches; (A) the fire happened in the early morning hours and (B) during a three-day weekend.

The library was about to close. Rick was supposed
to meet Traci at the Steak 'n Surf in fifteen minutes. He
had time for one last bit of research. He pulled the
phone book off the shelf and looked up Donna
Moore's address.

7

The Steak 'n Surf was everything Rick feared it would be. It started in the parking lot. He was greeted by a guy in a cow costume. Following a script that must have been deemed hysterical when it was adopted at the Steak 'n Surf Restaurant Image Committee meeting, the cow opened the door for Rick and—big cow tongue in cheek—urged him to order the seafood platter.

At the hostess stand Rick encountered a woman wearing Steak'n Surf's trademarked big red lobster mittens, which she snapped playfully at whoever approached. Kids loved it. Rick stood out of reach as he looked for Traci. He saw her and managed to slip past the hostess, unpinched.

Traci had changed from work clothes into black jeans, cowboy boots, and a soft blue denim shirt. She was seated in a booth between two delightful families. A man at one of the tables was shoveling fried shrimp, drowned in ketchup, into his mouth at an astonishing rate while saying, "I swaaare. I'm 'onna be there for ya, baby, forever. You know that." He wiped his greasy fingers on the front of his shirt then reached across the table to hold her hand. "I just got this thing, see? I met this guy. And we gonna do this deal." Like that explained everything. He cast his eyes down, as if he was about to invite the woman to pray over the matter with him. Then he said, "You gunna finish them onion rings?"

A woman at the other table was ignoring her two screaming babies while she wagged a slippery beef rib at the man with the hangdog face sitting across from her. "You go near 'at bitch again and I will tear the hair RIGHT outta your skull! You hear me?"

The man shrugged in defeat as he tried to suck some meat out of an anemic king crab leg.

Traci looked at Rick and said, "Isn't this great?"

"Truly fabulous," Rick said as he looked around at the red Naugahyde and fake brass railings.

Traci used her menu to pop Rick on the head. "Stop acting so damn superior and tell me what you think that fire's got to do with Captain Jack."

Rick looked at Traci for a moment before he said, "I love your eyes." He pointed toward her and made small circles in the air with his finger. "The way you do your makeup, it's sexy as hell. I hope you don't mind."

Traci smiled, flattered. "I don't mind at all." She leaned forward, batting her lashes. "Now spill me an earful," she said. "I am *dying* to know what you're up to."

Rick told her about the tape, describing it as "Clay talking to some guy at a bank, bragging about his infidelities and talking about other people committing some serious crimes."

"Like what?"

"Well, like a woman named Donna Moore, who Clay accuses—well, more or less accuses—of committing arson for profit."

Traci stopped him and said, "That's the fire at Moore Furniture? Oh my God, they used to advertise on the AM," she said. "And I think it was Clay's account." She gave Rick's arm a flirty nudge. "This is great. Go on."

Rick gave a few more specifics. Traci treasured every word. "Ohhhh, maaannnn," she said, keeping her voice down. "This is unbelievable." She rubbed her hands together like a mad scientist. "When do I get to hear it? You know what she should do—" She paused a moment before she said, "Wait, what's it got to do with Captain Jack?"

Rick was about to explain his theory when the waitress arrived singing the Sizzling Shrimp Skillet Sensation song, which was mercifully brief. When it was over she said, "Whooo's hungry?" She put the food on the table. "Plates are hot, hot, hot. So don't touch 'em." She handed Rick a faux steer's horn, then pointed to the mouthpiece at the small end. "If you need anything, just toot your horn and I'll come a-runnin'!"

Rick had another idea about what they could do with the horn but he kept it to himself. After the waitress was gone he said, "Captain Jack tried to blackmail the people on the tape. My bet is, somebody took exception to that and made him disappear."

Traci said, "Are you guessing all this? I mean, how do you know?"

"I'm only guessing about what happened to Captain Jack. I know for a fact he tried to blackmail one of the people on the tape. Seems fair to assume he tried the others, too." Rick told Traci about his chat with Lisa Ramey, adding that he didn't think she had anything to do with whatever happened to Captain Jack. "But if Donna Moore committed arson for profit and got away with it, Captain Jack could've threatened her. She could be looking at twenty years, along with whatever civil judgment the insurance company might win."

Traci swallowed a shrimp and said, "But women don't usually commit violent crimes, do they?" Rick glanced over her shoulder at the woman in the next booth who had threatened to snatch bald-headed her wandering mate. "Okay," Traci said. "Let me rephrase that. I don't think women kill men who ain't currently cheatin' on 'em. Besides, Captain Jack wasn't a small guy. It'd take some work to stuff him in the trunk of a car, if that's what you'd do."

"I think you're right," Rick said. "If Donna Moore had something to do with it, she probably had help." He pulled a piece of paper from his shirt pocket. "That's her address. You know where it is?"

Traci looked. "Yeah," she said, pointing east. "Go down Bilbo about two miles. Right on Lynwood, and I think it's the second street on the left." She handed it back to Rick and said, "So what're you gonna do, knock on her door and ask if she torched the place?"

"I haven't figured that out yet," Rick admitted. "The newspaper article didn't mention arson, just said the cause was under investigation."

"So at least it's a possibility."

"Yeah," Rick said. "But she'd have to own the place, right? I mean, she wouldn't benefit otherwise." He looked up at the ceiling. "I'm trying to remember what Clay said. I think he said she ran the place, like she was a manager, not the owner."

"She coulda been in cahoots with the owner or been pissed off at him, either one," Traci said. "Or maybe both—I mean, maybe she'd been sleeping with the owner and that went sour. You know he coulda been making her all kinds of promises about leaving his wife, buying a boat, and headin' off to the islands, and who knows what all? Then maybe he tells her one day that all bets are off and they've got to stop seein' each other. And her sense of betrayal gets to her and next thing you know she's dropping cigarettes in the waste-paper basket. I could see that."

Rick took a bite of his dry nine-dollar hamburger and said, "Viable as that scenario is, it brings in too many new variables. Let's just assume Clay was telling the truth about what he and Miss Moore were doing back in the mattress warehouse. Now, if Captain Jack had tried to blackmail her, she might have turned to Clay for help. And if Clay was also being blackmailed, well . . ." He shrugged. "There's your cahoots right there."

"Yeah, Clay's strong enough to stuff somebody in the trunk and that Crown Victoria is big enough, too."

Rick nodded slowly, thinking. He remembered that he hadn't talked about the last part of the tape. He said, "You know a woman named Holly Creel?" Traci shook her head. "Okay, what can you tell me about Bernie Dribbling?"

Traci's mouth dropped open and the words "Bernie Dribbling" fell onto the table and lay there for a moment before she said his name again. "Bernie Dribbling is mentioned on the tape? Accused of something?"

"Yeah, Clay pretty much accuses him of—I don't know what you'd call it—maybe bank fraud . . . among other things. You know him?"

"What does that mean, 'among other things'?"

Rick shook his head as if embarrassed on Bernie's behalf. "Wait'll you hear the tape," he said. "What do you know about him other than he buys lots of airtime for Universal Financial Services?"

Traci lanced a sizzling shrimp with her fork. "I've met him," she said in a tone that didn't speak well of the man. "He's one of those guys who'd probably be recruitin' for the Citizens' Council if it was still around." She dragged the shrimp through the butter that had pooled on her plate. "You know, he's probably just like Clay." She went down the grocery list: "Trustee at his church, active in the service organizations, huntin' buddies with the businessmen and midlevel politicians around the state. So he's one of those guys, very old school." Traci thought about him for a moment, wrinkling her nose in the process. "And he's a creepy old shit. Always makes really crude sexual comments when he comes to the station. You know, I don't mind a little flirting, even with older guys, but this one? A truly sorry example of your gender."

"You think he's . . . I don't know . . . violent?"

Traci watched the butter drip off her shrimp for a moment before saying, "I could see him *hiring* someone to do it but I don't think he could do anything like that by himself—I mean physically." She scrunched her nose and shook her head. "He's old and fat. But he's got money," she said. "And I bet he could be a pretty mean old cracker, so, I could see it happening that way." She was about to put the shrimp in her mouth when she stopped and said, "And you know what else? I just realized this." She waved the shrimp at Rick as she spoke. "He's always advertised on both stations, you know, for his finance company? But he just bought a huge run-of-schedule. Way more than usual. He spent a lot of money."

"Just recently?"

"Yeah, I remember because Clay came in bragging about his big commission on the deal." Traci looked at the buttery shrimp glistening on the end of her fork. She smiled and said, "I just love these things."

Rick was captivated watching Traci eat, her teeth and tongue provocative as they drew the pink crustacean into her mouth. He unconsciously licked his lips and he wondered if her kiss was as soft as powdered sugar or if it just looked like it would be. His mind was starting to wander in more erotic directions when the waitress dropped by with their bill. They both reached for it but Rick was quicker. "I'll get it next time," Traci said.

"Fine," Rick said. "But next time we're going back to Kitty's."

"I got a better idea," Traci said. "How about I pick something up and bring it over to your place?"

After his shift that night, Rick walked out to the parking lot and glanced at the sky. There was a quarter moon struggling behind thick clouds. A perfect night to drive over to Donna Moore's and sneak up to her house. *And do what?* he asked himself. *Peep in her windows?* Suddenly realizing the flaw in his plan, Rick went back inside the station.

He sat at Traci's desk and turned on a small lamp. He hummed along with "Theme from an Imaginary Western," which Uncle Victor was playing as part of a Youngbloods, Mountain, and Cream set that Rick was trying to figure out. It finally struck him that the connective tissue was songwriter Gail Collins. The Youngbloods had recorded a few of her songs. She was also cowriter of Cream's "Strange Brew" as well as another on the *Disraeli Gears* album, which was produced by her songwriting partner and husband, Felix Pappalardi, who formed Mountain in 1969 with Leslie West and whom she shot in the neck and killed on the night of April 17, 1983.

It turned out that Felix had been having a long-standing affair with a younger woman and that Gail knew about it. The jury bought her story that it was an accident and they convicted her of criminally negligent homicide instead of second-degree murder. Rick was doing mornings at a station in Texas when he got the news. He remembered thinking, *What a drag to have to pay your taxes and, two days later, get killed by your wife.* As he sat there, he entertained a thought: *What would Lori Stubblefield do if she heard Clay on that tape?*

Rick got up and walked down the hall to Stubblefield's office. The door was locked. He went back to the front desk and picked up the phone. He called

Traci, waking her up. "Sorry," he said. "I need to get into Clay's office, is there a key somewhere?"

She was groggy. "Uhhhh, no." She cleared her throat and said, "But do you see the letter opener on my desk?"

"Yeah." Rick could see how you might use it to pick the lock.

"What you need to do is take that and stick it somewhere that hurts really bad, like an eye or something. What time is it?"

"I said I was sorry at the top."

She cleared her throat again. "What do you need in his office?"

"I want to look at his Rolodex."

"Where are you?"

"At your desk."

"Then it's right in front of you." She made a sleepy moaning noise that Rick liked. She said, "You think the lazy bastard makes his own calls?" Then she hung up.

Rick flipped to the M's and found Donna Moore. Under her name, "Moore Furniture Store" had been scratched out and replaced by "McRae Tool and Equipment Rental."

Rick woke up at nine the next morning and had coffee while listening to Rob. "... *Thinking about a weekend trip to the casinos? Universal Financial Services is your ticket to the tables.*"

Rob came out of the spot set and did a live station promo pushing the thousand-dollar giveaway. *"There's still plenty of time to enter,"* he said. *"Just send your name, address, and phone number on a postcard or drop by T-Bone Records on Bilbo Avenue, or any Steak 'n Surf location in greater McRae and enter in person. You don't have to be present to win but we'd sure like to see you there. We're gonna be rockin' Riverside Park next Sunday starting at noon. Come on out and meet the WAOR staff,"* he said. *"Drawing's at three with the beee-you-tee-ful Miss Loblolly Pine, Joni Lang. We'll also have lots of giveaways, so come on out to Riverside Park, next Sunday. All that cash just might be yours from WAOR-FM, where we're gettin' at the roots of classic rock."*

Rob went into Gram Parsons and Emmylou Harris singing "Cash on the Barrelhead" from *Grievous Angel*, followed by Poco's "You Better Think Twice" from *Deliverin'* and Loggins and Messina's "Back to Georgia" from *On Stage*. It was a good set of live upbeat country rock, songs Rick hadn't heard in a long time and which he knew would make the right listeners smile like they'd run into a friend they hadn't seen in years.

Rick picked up the phone and hit speed dial. "Rob," he said. "It's me. I like that line. 'Gettin' at the roots of classic rock.' It's perfect. Put it on the card with the other tag lines." He listened to Rob for a moment then said, "Don't worry about it. I'll go to bat for anyone who's reliable and does good work."

Around ten-thirty Rick put on a suit for the first time since his father's funeral. He drove over to meet Captain Virgil Boggs of the McRae Fire Department. "I'm a private investigator," Rick said for the first time. He was still in his truck when he said it, alone, parked out-side the fire station. He wanted to practice it a couple of times before trying it on a stranger. He looked in his rearview mirror, all serious, and said it again. "Hi, I'm Buddy Miles, private investigator." He thought the name fit the job. It had more gravitas than Rick Shan-non. He lowered his voice and repeated it. "Buddy Miles, PI."

Rick checked his tie then headed for the building. A jittery little wirehaired mutt rushed out from the station to greet him on his way inside, demanding some atten-tion. Rick gave him a scratch behind the ears then went in, introduced himself, and started asking questions.

Captain Boggs was friendly and as helpful as regula-tions would allow. He said he couldn't give any particu-lars about the case but acknowledged that the fire at Moore Furniture was, in fact, suspicious. "But the prob-lem with arson isn't figuring out if a fire was set on pur-pose," Captain Boggs said. "The problem is figuring out who set it. We only close about fifteen percent of arson cases by arrest and only two percent close by conviction."

"Can you tell me if the insurance paid?"

"Nope."

"Can't tell me or don't know?"

Captain Boggs smiled and said, "Both."

"Fair enough. I'll get that from the carrier," Rick said. While at the library, he'd read about a database that recorded insurance coverage by property. It al-lowed insurers to see if an applicant has had a pattern of claims. "What can you tell me about motives?"

"Well now, motive's a little slippery," Captain Boggs said. "Insurance industry says about forty percent of arson fires are set for revenge." He made a skeptical face before saying, "And that gets us back to the problem of proving who set the fire. People who burn their own home or business tend to say things like, 'Oh, yeah, I gotta lotta enemies,' you know? And if we can't prove otherwise, even if we know the owner did it, those fires get filed under 'revenge.' So my point is, you need to take that forty percent with a grain of salt. Other'n that, about thirty percent are set for the thrill of it, twenty percent are attempts to conceal another crime, and about seven percent are just pure vandalism."

"What about arson for profit?"

"Only about five percent, as far as get proved anyway."

"But you think it's higher?"

"Oh, it's higher all right, just can't prove it. I'd say it could be as high as thirty percent, maybe more."

"And they're just going for a straightforward collection of insurance money for lost property?"

"Usually," Captain Boggs said. "Though you'll find some done to terminate an unprofitable lease or to get out of a business that's losing money, things like that."

"Makes sense," Rick said. "So who's your typical arsonist?"

"Typical is white male, under twenty-one, middle class, absent or abusive father, some learning problems, and childhood sexual abuse or incest. But like I said, arson for profit is atypical. The profile there's an older white male, say midthirties to midfifties. A lot of times they're ex-firemen or fire investigators, since they've got on-the-job training, so to speak."

Rick thought for a second. What did Stubblefield say? *Woman set it on fire, I think.* Now, given that the odds were against any arson being for profit, and that most arsonists were male, Rick wondered if Clay had just said that to spice up his story. "Let me ask you one more question," Rick said. "When an arson's committed to cover up another crime, what're they usually trying to cover up?"

"In my personal experience?" Captain Boggs smiled and said, "Murder." He paused to let that sink in before he said, "But statistically, theft by the owner's probably more common." He tapped a fingernail on his desktop then pointed at Rick. "We had a case not too long ago, owner of a travel agency went out and bought a bunch of junked computers for nothin' and used 'em to replace the computers in his office. Then he burned the place down and claimed the loss for his real computers that he had the receipts for. Now, we knew it was arson, the insurance guy knew it was arson, but we couldn't prove who did it, so they had to pay. A month later, the agent went to deliver the check, right? Well, he's sittin' there in the lobby waiting for the owner and he can see the serial number on the back of the receptionist's monitor. He didn't have anything else to do, so he called it in." Captain Boggs grinned and pointed north. "Sent that boy right up to Parchman Farm." He looked at his watch. "Got another eight years to go."

Rick said, "What about Moore Furniture? Y'all find a body?"

"One of my guys found a dog tied up inside." Captain Boggs looked past Rick. "He's around here somewhere. Cute little thing." He looked at Rick and said, "The dog, I mean."

"Yeah, I met him on my way in."

"That was another thing made that one suspicious. Woman who owned the place said she didn't have a dog. Professional arson, lotta times they'll get a stray and burn it with the building, tryin' to make it look like something that could only happen by accident."

"But as far as you know the fire wasn't meant to cover a murder?"

Captain Boggs held up his hands. "Well, I can't go into that," he said. "But I think if we had found a body, you'd've read about it in the paper." He gave Rick a little wink and said, "Sorry I can't narrow it down more for you."

Rick thanked the captain for his time and they walked out to the parking lot, followed by the dog. As they shook hands at the door Rick said, "Thanks for your help. I'll let you know if I find anything."

"I'd appreciate that," Captain Boggs said. They stopped at Rick's truck. "This sort of thing can look pretty confusing if you give equal weight to all the possibilities."

"Amen to that," Rick said.

"You want my advice? It ain't original, but it don't cost nothin'," he said. "Follow the money."

As Rick drove out to McRae Tool and Equipment Rental he mulled over his conversation with Captain Boggs. He figured the wink meant they'd found no body, so he could eliminate covering up a murder as the reason for the fire. And while he was glad he wouldn't have to factor that into his increasingly complicated investigation, his meeting with the fire chief still left him with more motives to consider than he had when he started. But Boggs's last comment, *Follow the money,* seemed to narrow it back down. Virgil Boggs seemed to be telling Rick not to worry about revenge, thrill seekers, or vandals. It's usually about greed.

McRae Tool and Equipment Rental was on the service road by the highway just inside the city limits. The office was a small prefab unit sitting on the better part of an acre, all surrounded by chain link topped with razor wire. Rick parked and made his way through the compressors, steam cleaners, lift mules, and pressure washers. At the back of the lot, sitting under a shed, he saw a cherry picker, a small dump truck, and a big crawler with a backhoe on it.

The only person Rick could see was a guy who appeared to be a mechanic working on a diesel jumping-jack tamper. Rick had arrived during a lull between the frantic morning pickups and the testy end-of-the-day returns. He walked into the office. It smelled like machine grease and burned coffee. The walls were covered with coiled extension cords, band-saw belts and blades, bolt cutters, and all kinds of tools and accessories. There was a tall bar stool behind the counter with no one sitting on it, least of all Donna Moore. Rick directed his voice toward the back office. "Anybody home?"

A woman's voice came in reply. "Be right with you." It was neither friendly nor cordial, just business. A moment later she came into the room like a gas-powered drop hammer. Nearly six feet tall and attractive despite apparent attempts to play it down, she wore painter's pants and a dark short-sleeved shirt with MCRAE TOOL AND EQUIPMENT RENTAL over the pocket in bright yellow stitching. In a tone meant to discourage small talk she said, "What do you need?"

Rick smiled and said, "How're you today?"

The woman nodded just enough to be polite. "You call about the arc welder?"

Rick glanced around the room. "No, actually, I didn't." He held out his hand and said, "My name's Buddy Miles. I'm looking for Donna Moore."

Her face iced over. "You found her," she said. "Now what?" Donna folded her arms and looked at Rick as if daring him to do something, anything.

Rick noticed an ugly scar on her forearm, about the size of a fifty-cent piece. He figured she'd burned herself on a hot exhaust pipe or some other equipment. "I'm a private investigator," he said, dropping his unshaken hand. "I was hoping I could ask you some questions, if you're not too busy."

"Questions about what?" She seemed both defiant and defensive.

"A missing-persons case." The words caused a distinct change in Donna's demeanor. She suddenly seemed more interested, as if she were looking for someone, too. Rick pulled out the photo of Captain Jack and the pretty brunette in the French Quarter and handed it to her. "Do you know either of these people?"

She looked at the picture longer than she needed to to answer the question. Her attitude hardened again. She looked at Rick severely and said, "Who're you working for?"

Rick thought that was an interesting question. Like

there was a right and a wrong answer, one that would allow her to talk and one that would make her shut up. He said, "To tell you the truth, I'm working for myself."

"And what if I don't believe you?"

"Well, I could start telling lies until you find one you like," Rick said with half a smile. "And we could go from there."

"Huh." Donna didn't exactly smile but she seemed to ease up a bit. She tossed the photo on the counter and said, "Is one of these the missing person?"

Rick tapped the picture. "This guy. His name's Jack Carter."

Donna didn't look at it this time. She kept her wary eyes on Rick. "So if you're working for yourself, I have to assume you're a friend of his."

Rick gave an understanding nod. "That would make sense," he said. "But no." Now shaking his head. "I never met him."

"Interesting." Donna reached under the counter and pulled out a gleaming steel drywall hammer. It had a wedge-shaped blade like a small, keen axe opposite the hammer's head. "So," she said. "If you've never met him, I have to believe you're either working for some-body else or there's something you haven't told me." She adjusted her grip on the tool's hickory handle and said, "Take your pick, but either way, I think you should just go." She nodded toward the door. "I've got a business to run."

Rick backed away from the counter, keeping his eyes on the hammer. He took a deep breath and let it out slowly, puffing his cheeks in a sign of defeat. "You're right," he said. "I haven't been completely honest."

Donna tapped the hammer on the counter and said, "Yet you're still standing in my office."

"Look," Rick said, pointing at the photo. "I'm just trying to find out what happened to that guy."

"So you said. But I don't know anything about it, so . . ." She aimed the hammer at the door.

"I know, but, see, the thing is, I don't think you're being completely honest with me either."

"You can think whatever you damn well please," Donna said. "But you best go think it somewhere else."

"All right, look, I'm just gonna put my cards on the table," Rick said. "When I'm done you can tell me to leave and I'll go. Or we can talk. But I think we might be able to help each other."

Donna tensed at the suggestion. For a moment, it looked as if she might swing the hammer. "I have gotten this far in my life without any of *your* help," she said. "I suspect I can go on just fine without it."

"I'm sure you can," Rick said. "But at least hear me out." He picked up the photo of Captain Jack. "I think this man's been killed." He paused before he said, "And I think there might be a connection between that and your fire at Moore Furniture."

"You son of a bitch." Donna raised the hammer and shook it at Rick, leading with the blade. "I did not burn down my store! You hear me?" She brought the hammer down on the counter, startling Rick. "Who the *hell* you think you are?" She raised the hammer, threatening Rick as she carried on. "That big redneck set the fire. And as far as I'm concerned, your friend's just as much a criminal as the other one. So I not only hope that bastard is dead, I hope he suffered along the way!"

"Whoa," Rick said. "Back up! I didn't say *you* burned it down."

"Oh." This took her by surprise.

"In fact, I'd bet you didn't."

Donna paused, the hammer still raised by the side of her head. "Oh yeah?" She lowered it a bit. "Really?"

"Yeah, really. But you might want to know that Clay Stubblefield is telling a different story."

Donna looked at her grip on the hickory handle and said, "Clay Stubblefield." She started smacking the side of the blade into her palm, like an irritated cop with a nightstick. "I shoulda known." She exhaled the way people do when they're about to let go of something they've been holding too long. "It's that goddamn tape, isn't it? Now *you've* got it." There was defeat in her voice when she said, "Christ A'mighty." She tossed the hammer onto the counter and threw her hands in the air. "What do you want? Huh? There's nothing left in the kitty. Your *friend* cleaned me out already." She gave a rueful shake of the head. "I gave at the office."

"First of all," Rick said, "the guy wasn't my friend, okay? Second, I'm not trying to shake you down, so relax."

"Well, you'd be the first." Donna gave up on her tough gal routine. She dragged the bar stool over and sat on it. "So what do you want?"

"Information." .

"Like what? You want the details of my sex life? You want pictures or something?"

"No. I really don't care who you have sex with or where you have it. Unless it's got something to do with Jack Carter's disappearance."

"It doesn't."

"Fine. So that brings us to the part about Clay Stubblefield telling people he thinks you burned down your business."

"Which I didn't."

"I believe you," Rick said. "But Captain Boggs said the fire was arson. So if you didn't set the fire, I'm thinking you know who did."

"Maybe I do," Donna said. "But how is that supposed to help me?"

"I don't know," Rick admitted.

"Can I trust you?"

"You don't seem like the kind of woman who'd believe a man if he said you could."

She nodded and said, "So where does that leave us?"

"Just tell me what happened."

Donna's husband said she was crazy, said she didn't need to work, said he made plenty of money and why did she need to go out and embarrass him that way, making it look like he couldn't take care of his family? But that missed the point as far as Donna was concerned. She had to make something for herself. So, armed with ambition and nineteen years of retail sales and management experience, Donna Moore put together her own business plan and took out a loan. She found the perfect space in the Three Pines Shopping Center, redesigned and decorated the interior, and opened Moore Furniture.

As with all retail businesses, the first year was a struggle. Donna frequently put in eighty-hour weeks, sometimes without pay, and rarely with her husband's moral support. But things worked out. Business picked up during the first quarter of her second year. Still, Donna thought she could do better. She realized she needed to advertise, but she couldn't afford TV. So she tried radio. She called different stations and got their rate cards and claims of demographic superiority.

Donna was trying to decide where to put her money when Clay Stubblefield walked into her life. He was the first salesman to show up in person, and sell he did. Clay told Donna they could make Moore Furniture a household name in Deckern County and he sold her a run on both the AM and the FM sides. After a few weeks, Donna began to see positive results. So she started to buy more time and Clay started taking her to lunch to thank her for being one of his best accounts.

And Clay kept selling. In addition to ad time, he also sold Donna on how attractive she was and how her husband didn't seem to appreciate what a fine, smart, independent, and—pardon me for saying so—sexy woman he had on his hands. Donna bought it all and they started having an affair. It started off with a weekend at a fancy hotel in New Orleans but that didn't last. After a few months, Clay started dropping by the store to tear off nooners and sell a little more ad time. Not long after that, he broke things off and a junior member of the sales staff started making the monthly calls. Donna chalked it up as the inevitable conclusion to an affair with a good old boy like Clay. She had to admit, though, he had made it easy to say good-bye. At the start of their affair Clay would say things like, "I want to make love to you all night." Four months later his idea of amour was saying, "Just bend over, I only need a minute."

After the affair, Donna was racked with guilt. She could hardly think of anything else and it was driving her crazy. In an attempt to keep from obsessing on it, she threw herself back into her work. She found that the busier she was, the less she dwelled on her bad judgment.

One night, just before closing, Donna was putting up a new window display. When she turned to lean a mannequin against the glass she saw a man standing on the sidewalk watching her. She wondered how long he'd been there. He had a fat, stubby cigar in one hand but it wasn't lit. Donna gave a slight smile, which the man acknowledged with a nod before sauntering into the store. She couldn't say what, but something about the guy put her ill at ease.

He was wearing casual clothes and a houndstooth check hat like he was Bear Bryant, though he was a smaller man and slightly more narrow between the eyes. When Donna climbed out of the window she found the man sitting in a leather wing chair. To her surprise, he gestured at the chair opposite him and said, "Miss Moore, why doan-cha take a load off?"

She tilted her head slightly. "Do I know you?" Friendly but cautious.

"Well, not yet," the man said. "That's why you oughta siddown and pass some time."

Donna glanced around the showroom and said, "Much as I'd like to, I've got stuff to do before I can close up."

The man pushed back the brim of his hat and said, "Awww, now, don't be lack 'at." He pointed at Donna. "You know what they say, no ham and all hominy . . ." He gestured again for her to sit.

Donna said, "Are you interested in the wing chairs?"

The man's smile faded. He said, "I'm innersted in you takin' a seat, Miss Moore. Now, c'mon, you're wastin' my time."

This got Donna's hackles up. "Excuse me? You obviously know who I am, but you haven't introduced yourself properly."

The man showed a few yellowed teeth and said, "Well what'll my mama thank? I tell you what, you just call me Boss, or hell, Shirley Temple, I don't much care." He pointed at the chair again. "Now sit yer ass down," he said. "We got a business proposition to discuss."

Donna's stomach churned into a knot at the way he said it. She sat down thinking it might be the best and quickest way to get rid of this guy. "What sort of proposition?" She was beginning to think he was running a protection scheme.

"Real simple," Boss said. "I represent a, well, what would you call it? A group of businessmen, let's say, who know a good investment opportunity when they see it."

Donna shook her head. "I'm not following you. You got friends who want to invest in Moore Furniture?"

The man pointed his stubby cigar in Donna's direction. "Exactly."

"I don't need any investors."

The man gave an avuncular chuckle and said, "Well, now, Miss Moore, we ain't too concerned about what *you* need." He sat forward in the chair. "Lemme just tell you how it's gonna be, save us some time. My associates are going to invest in a whole mess of inventory for the store here, lotsa big-ticket stuff, you know? Prob'ly some real expensive antiques outta New Orleans. Big old French arm-whars and chase lounges and stuff lack 'at, you know. Primo stuff. We talkin' in the neighborhood of fitty thousand dollars. Uh-course you gonna need to insure all this fine furniture. In fact, my associates will insist on that, you know, just to protect their investment in case something should happen."

Donna gestured around the store. "Well, first of all, as you can see, I don't have the space for that," she said. "And secondly—"

"Shhhhhhh." The man put a finger to his lips. "All you need to do is getcha some more *in*surance to cover that fitty thousand of new inventory. We'll take care of the rest." He pulled his cigar lighter out of his pocket and continued talking, though Donna didn't really hear what he said. She realized this was neither a protection scheme nor was it a clumsy attempt to launder money, which had been her second thought. It was plain old garden-variety insurance fraud with her as the unwitting go-between.

With this in mind, Donna just sat there imagining the worst. All her hard work? Down the drain. Sacrifices? Wasted. Bright future? Dimmed. She'd be ruined. And she wondered why. How had this come to be visited upon her? Was her husband so threatened by her growing success that he had arranged this? Had he found out about her affair with Clay? Maybe both those birds had come home to roost at the same time.

In any event, it seemed to leave Donna with only two choices. Surrender or fight.

Donna said, "I think you should leave. I'm going to call the police." She started to stand but the man reached over and grabbed her arm, pulling her down violently. He gave her arm a terrible twist and pinned it on the table that was between the two chairs.

"Now, you need to learn to cooperate," the man said. With his free hand he snapped his cigar lighter to life. It shot a blue flame like a NASA rocket. The man leaned into Donna's face and spoke with gamy breath. He said, "You know how, when you're fixin' to whup your kids and you say, 'This is gonna hurt me a lot more'n it's gonna hurt you'?" He shook his head. "This is different."

8

"I guess I passed out," Donna said, touching the scar. "When I woke up, the son of a bitch was gone and he'd taken that wing chair with him. All I found was a card with a phone number on it, said to call when the insurance was in place."

"What'd you do?"

"What could I do? I called my insurance agent and told him to increase my policy limits. Of course he said he couldn't do it on the phone, said he had to come see the inventory, get it appraised. So I called the number on the card and told 'em. A couple of days later this big-ass truck pulled up to the loading dock and they unloaded all these expensive antiques. God knows where they came from. My insurance guy came over with an appraiser and they put the value around sixty thousand. Two days later the truck came back, they loaded the antiques and left a bunch of crap behind, old chairs and desks and tables not worth a hundred bucks. Then I was told I oughta go spend the next three-day weekend down on the coast. So that's what I did."

"And they torched it while you were gone," Rick said.

She nodded. "What could I do?" She held up her arm. "He said it'd be easy to make my face look just like this." She put her arm down and said, "About a month later a cassette comes in the mail addressed to me. No note with it. No explanation about what it is, so I listened to it." Donna shook her head. "Crackin'," she said with a shake of her head. "First time I've heard it called that. Anyway, I figured whoever sent it wasn't far behind. And sure enough, the next day, this man knocks on my front door not five minutes after my husband left to work."

"Jack Carter?"

She nodded. "Asked if I'd listened to the tape. I think he could tell from my reaction that I had. He stood there on my front porch and laughed at me. Said he figured I'd gotten the check from the insurance company and he wanted a thousand dollars or he was going to let Mr. Moore hear the tape."

"Did you pay?"

"I didn't know what else to do," Donna said. "I know it was stupid but . . ." She shrugged. "The son of a bitch came back a week later for more. That's when I knew I was screwed. I figured he'd keep coming back as long as I paid him, so I refused. I told him that I'd already told my husband about the affair with Clay and he didn't have anything on me."

"And he called your bluff?"

"Yeah." Donna looked past Rick as if searching for her past out in the parking lot. "Two days later my husband came home from work and put the tape on the stereo real loud while he packed his bags."

"Ewwww."

Donna smiled sardonically and shrugged. "It wasn't much of a marriage anyway. Not by then."

"He left you?"

"Yeah, made a clean getaway, too. Didn't cost him a dime. Took the tape with him, said he was gonna play it for his new girlfriend."

"You think Clay had anything to do with the fire?"

"I don't know why he would," Donna said. "I was a good account, you know?"

"Yeah, but Clay's a short-term thinker," Rick said. "Maybe he got a cut of the insurance proceeds."

"You got a reason to think he was involved?"

"Just the timing, I guess. The fact that the guy with the cigar lighter didn't show up until after Clay had broken things off with you." Upon hearing himself say the words, Rick realized how thin his reasoning was.

"Yeah, well, all I know is, the day after I got the check from the insurance company, I called the number on that card. The guy had me meet him at the bank and get him a cashier's check for fifty thousand dollars. Then he thanked me for doing business with 'em and told me not to worry, said I'd never see him again. And I haven't."

Rick thought about that for a moment, then said, "They probably don't want any patterns in who's collecting insurance money on their scams."

"They?" Donna gave him a look. "They who?"

Rick shrugged. "They who organize crimes like insurance fraud involving unwitting third parties."

It took her a second but then, in a surprised voice, Donna said, "You mean organized like the Mafia?"

"Well, I haven't looked in the phone book," Rick said. "But I'd bet there ain't no Gambinos in Deckern County. You know anything about the Dixie Mafia?"

"Oh, I know people talk about it like it's real," Donna said. "But I don't think it's like *The Godfather* or anything as grand as all that. I think it's usually just the local powers that be, you know? Politicians, cops, prominent businessmen, people like that. They all know each other, go to deer camp together, belong to the same clubs and churches and so forth."

Rick nodded. "What about the girl named Tammy that Clay talks about on the tape? Do you know who she is?"

Donna looked genuinely confused by the question. She shook her head. "What Tammy? There's no Tammy on the tape I got. It's just Clay braggin' about puttin' the 'Takin' Inventory' sign in the window and goin' to the back where the mattresses were and crackin' back there, as he so romantically puts it."

"How long is the tape you got?"

"I don't know, about thirty seconds, I guess. Like a snippet from a longer conversation."

"Yeah, he sent you an edited version," Rick said. "The original's six or seven minutes. And it mentions quite a few other names."

"Well, I mean, I know a girl named Tammy, but who doesn't?"

Rick wondered why Captain Jack didn't send the whole tape. He thought of a couple of reasons. First of all, it kept the blackmail victim focused on his or her

problem. And second, it would keep the blackmail victims from knowing about one another and possibly
joining forces and conspiring against him. Rick didn't
see any point in asking if Donna knew Lisa Ramey,
and he'd only asked about Tammy in hopes of getting a
last name. But given what Clay said on the last part of
the tape, he knew the next two names would ring a bell.
"What about Holly Creel and Bernie Dribbling?"

Donna blanched. "Oh my God." She put a hand over
her mouth. "What happened?" She grabbed Rick's arm
and said, "Does he say what happened to Holly?"

Her reaction surprised Rick. He was expecting a bit
of shame, maybe, or regret, but not this. "Well, he talks
about the loan and the, uh, the collateral," Rick said.
"But from what's on the tape, it sounds like whatever
happened to Holly is still going on."

"No." Donna shook her head. "She's missing. That's
who I thought you were talking about when you came
in here talking about a missing person. I haven't talked
to Holly in over a month," Donna said. "I think she's
dead."

Donna didn't have any evidence that her friend
Holly had been killed, only a bad feeling in her stomach. "She gambled," Donna said. "A lot. After she
maxed out her credit cards, she borrowed some money
from a guy she shouldn't have. When he started to
threaten her, she came to me. Of course I didn't have
anything to lend, but, anyway, that's why she needed
the money. So I said something to Clay and he put her
in touch with Bernie Dribbling." She shook her head.
"I talked to Holly after the first time she met him at the

hotel and she said it wasn't that bad. But after that she said things started getting really weird. A couple of weeks later she stopped returning my calls," Donna said. "At first I figured it was because she was ashamed about it or maybe she was mad and blamed me for getting her into it, but then I called her job and they said she didn't work there anymore. So I went by her apartment but she was never there, day or night. That's when I started to get worried."

"She paid back the first guy?"

"I think so. That's what she used Dribbling's money for."

"Did you say anything to Clay about her disappearing?"

"Hell no," Donna said. "I figured if something bad had happened to Holly, he probably knew about it, and if I brought it up, I don't know, same thing could happen to me. Besides, after hearing that tape, I don't plan to talk to that son of a bitch again except to testify in court about his lack of character or to go cuss him at his funeral." She wrote down Holly's address and gave it to Rick. She asked him to let her know if he found out what had happened to her.

After he left McRae Tool and Equipment Rental, Rick drove by Holly's apartment complex to see what he could. There was an eviction notice stuck on her door. The curtains were drawn. He went to the manager's office. The guy there just said that after three years of paying her rent on time, she'd stopped. After the required amount of time passed, he submitted the necessary paperwork and got the eviction notice. The guy started to complain about having to put Holly's

stuff in storage but Rick cut him off. He had to get back
to work.

Back at the station, Rick found a stack of production
sheets warming his in-box. There were a few national
spots that needed to be localized. They came with pre-
produced jingles, some on CD; others still came to the
small-market stations on reel-to-reel tapes. The in-
structions from sales told Rick to use the thirty-second
donuts on most of them, which meant he just read fifteen seconds of copy over the music bed in the middle
of the commercial.

Next came Rick's favorite type of small-market radio spot. The supermarket ad, a staple of radio advertising since the 1950s. Such spots had been rendered
antiquated jokes by the 1970s. Their continued use in
the twenty-first century proved only that there was still
one being born every minute.

"This week only, Florida pink grapefruit four for a
dollar," Rick said as if Florida was a shade of pink and
his life depended on it. "Shasta sodas, twelve-ounce re-
turnable bottles, regular or diet, just two ninety-nine.
Russet potatoes, five-pound sack, just three forty-
nine." He wondered if there was someone out there in
the piney woods of south-central Mississippi listening
to their rock 'n' roll radio station who would hear this
and think, *Russet potatoes, huh? Hell, I might just have
to get up from here and run down to the store and get
me summa them.* But who wouldn't budge if it was
long whites. "Iceberg lettuce," Rick said. "Cello-
wrapped, ninety-nine cents a head. Extra-lean ground
beef in the five-pound chub, just six dollars . . ." The

chub, Rick's all-time favorite unit of meat measurement. The spot went on and on, ticking off so many products and prices and store times and phone numbers and sale dates and store addresses that you'd have to be a court reporter to get half of it.

Rick was dubbing one of the spots for the AM when he noticed the yellow light on the wall flashing. He picked up the phone and said, "Production."

"Hey." It was Traci calling from her desk in the front.

"Hey," Rick said. "Let me ask you a question. What's a chub?"

Traci paused. "A what?"

"Never mind," Rick said. "What's up?"

"I just called to say, if you don't let me hear the tape soon, I'm just gonna have to ask Clay if he remembers what he said in that conversation."

"Wait until you hear what Donna Moore had to say."

"You talked to her?"

"Yeah," Rick said, cradling the phone in the crook of his neck. "The plot thickens. But I can't go into it now."

"Sure you can. You have to. You can't tease me like that and not give details."

"No, there's too much to tell and I've got a dozen spots to cut before I can get some dinner."

"You mean supper," Traci said. "Dinner is lunch."

"Whatever. You can join me if you'd like but I'm going to Kitty's."

"Can't, I've got exercise class. How about tomorrow night?"

"I'm doing that Booster Club party for Stubblefield. You wanna be my assistant?"

"Love to, but I'm"—she paused before saying—"baby-sitting for my sister. How about after the dance?"

"Goin' home, goin' to bed."

"Oh, don't be such an old fart," Traci said. "I'm coming over after the dance. And if you're in bed . . . I'll just deal with it."

Rick was standing in front of the music library thinking about Traci's last comment. Would she wake him up and make him play the tape or would she slip under the sheets and get her information that way? Assuming she meant the latter, Rick wondered if should let her. He knew that he *would* let her, but he wondered if he *should*. He'd gotten involved with coworkers before and the end was always some degree of ugly. He figured the easiest way to avoid the problem was not to go to bed before she showed up. But how much fun was that?

He turned his attention back to the task at hand and began to pull music for the Booster Club party. Based on Clay's description of the crowd, he was gathering some seventies pop-rock dance stuff. He was reading the song list from an Average White Band album when Autumn breezed into the room and posed. She was wearing a flowery headband, a white cotton blouse with billowy sleeves, hip-hugger bell-bottoms, and a peace medallion. She said, "Am I a groovy, far-out chick or what?"

Rick looked at her slim college-age hips and said, "Lord, am I getting old."

Autumn looked down at her exposed belly button. "What, this doesn't do it for you?"

"Well . . ." Rick smiled with a little lust in his eyes.

"I'm not allowed to say on account of sexual harass-ment laws, not to mention my inherent gentlemanly comportment. But my point was simply that if you live long enough to see a fashion come and go . . . and come back? You're old," he said.

Autumn looked at him skeptically and said, "I think you were trying to work a compliment in there some-where, so thanks."

"You're welcome. How's your paper coming?"

"Oh, fine," Autumn said. "Work-in-progress, you know. But listen, I wanted to tell you something real quick." She nodded back toward the studio where she was on the air. "I've only got a minute."

"What're you playing?"

" 'Dear Mr. Fantasy.' "

"Original or *Welcome to the Canteen*?"

"The original. Anyway, I wanted to tell you about this idea I had last night," she said. "I was listening to Uncle Victor's show and he played the most amaaaaaazing set of stuff. It was this whole woozy alt country thing with the Grateful Dead and I don't even know who all, but the harmonies on 'Till the Morning Comes' were *so* great. And there was a song by some other group about going to the country, got to leave right away? That sound familiar?"

Rick thought about it for a second then said, "Steve Miller Band from *Number 5*. A great record."

"Anyway, the whole set is just jammin', okay? And I was driving home and I stopped at a light and I pulled up next to this, like, Lexus or something and there's this guy, he's like an older business guy, right? And he's singing and his head's bobbin' and my head's bobbing and then I realized we were listening to the same thing and it was like, whoa! Uncle Victor's bridged a generation gap with this stuff. I mean, I'm groovin', *he's* groovin', and I thought we gotta do something about it. So I had this idea about a co-op deal with T-Bone Record Shop, since they already do a lot of advertising with us, right? I was thinking we approach them about putting up a WAOR classic rock corner in the store."

"A corner?"

"Yeah, like literally build a thing in the back corner of the store. Make it like one of those old head shops with black lights and all the old posters, like the *Easy Rider* poster where they're flipping the bird and the *Keep on Truckin'* poster and the Dylan poster and lava lamps and beads, and incense, all that stuff. And only the music we play, with lots of the more obscure stuff because I really think—"

J.C. walked in and said, "Hey, toots, your record's running out." Autumn shrieked and ran back to the studio. The two men looked after her as she raced down the hall. J.C. said, "She wears those pants pretty well."

"What's up, J.C.?"

"Oh. I've been thinking about it and I've figured out what the last record is in classic rock."

Rick put the Average White Band record into his box and said, "Do tell."

J.C. held his hands up like a director framing a shot. "Picture it. Winterland Arena. November 1976. The backdrop from San Francisco Opera's *La Traviata* on the stage and those *Gone With the Wind* chandeliers overhead." J.C. lowered his hands and looked at Rick,

who was nodding his head at what now seemed obvious. "It has everything," J.C. said. "The title alone, I
mean, c'mon . . . *The Last Waltz* declares the end of the
era. And who's there to say good-bye with The Band?"

Rick, still nodding, said, "Dylan, Joni Mitchell, Neil
Young, Paul Butterfield, Van Morrison, Muddy Waters,
Ronnie Hawkins, Dr. John, Eric Clapton . . ." He started
shaking his head, embarrassed he hadn't thought of it.

"And don't forget Ringo, Ron Wood, and Steve
Stills," J.C. said. "Hell, that's The Beatles, the Stones,
and Buffalo Springfield right there. *That's* classic rock."

"I agree," Rick said, "it just sounds funny coming
from you."

"Hey, I never said heavy metal was the only kind of
rock. I just happen to like it more. But I was over at T-
Bone Records yesterday and they were playing it.
Damn thing rocks, except for 'Helpless' and a couple
of other songs. Anyway, it seemed like the answer to
the question."

Rick could've kicked himself. Of course, *The Last
Waltz*. Not only a knockout record, but thanks to Mar-
tin Scorsese's direction, probably the best rock concert
film ever made. "I think that's it," he said, suddenly
thinking of the girl he'd taken to see the movie when it
came out. "When was that released,'77?"

"Film and the sound track came out in April '78,"
J.C. said.

"So are you proposing the recording date or the release date as the end of the era?"

J.C. paused. "Hadn't thought about it," he said. "Anything essential come out after November '76?"

"Fleetwood Mac's *Rumours* is early '77."

"That's a great album," J.C. said. "But, honestly, can you see that incarnation of Meetwood Flac on the Fillmore stage? Green and Spencer were long gone and the rest of 'em had forsaken blues-based rock for pure pop."

"Yeah," Rick said, "and for what? Multiplatinum success? A few zillion dollars?" He pretended to spit on the floor.

"I'm not saying they weren't popular. They just weren't a classic rock band at that point."

"Well, now 'Sands of Time' wasn't exactly based on an Elmore James riff," Rick said. "But it's a pure classic FM song."

"I'll grant you that."

Rick turned and looked at the wall of music. "Hey, do we have the Buckingham-Nicks record in here? That was a fine little album."

"Uh, we're losing our focus here," J.C. said. "Do we agree that *The Last Waltz* marks the end?"

"Yeah," Rick said. "I just wish we had such a clearcut record for the start date."

"Workin' on it," J.C. said as he turned to leave. "I'll get back to you."

The McRae Booster Club held all its functions in one of the banquet rooms at the Magnolia Motor Inn. Saturday afternoon, a couple of hours before the event, Rick went to check the sound system Clay had arranged for him to use. As he passed through the lobby and down a dim hallway, Rick was struck by how much the place smelled like the early seventies. Maybe it was the old carpeting or something collecting in the ducts.

The Dogwood Room was at the end of the hall. Rick was surprised to find the gear already set up on a table on the far side of the room. There was a mixing board, two turntables, two CD players, an amp, an equalizer, and two speakers mounted on stands off to the sides. Rick went over and powered the system up. He put on a record and started to adjust the sound.

As he toyed with the equalizer, a couple of motel employees walked into the room carrying a podium. They stopped and looked at Rick for a moment before continuing to the dais at the front of the room. After securing the podium in the center of the platform, they reached down and picked up what turned out to be a banner that had been lying on the floor. They mounted it on the wall. It said: CONGRATULATIONS BOOSTER CLUB BUSINESSMAN OF THE YEAR!

The two men left momentarily before returning with a folding metal easel and something set in a large wooden frame that they installed on the right side of the stage. After mixing the sound, Rick went over to the easel for a closer look. It was a statement of the Booster Club philosophy. It called for members to help one another in all business endeavors by sharing information, making introductions, and facilitating deals among fellow members, lobbying against government interference in all business practices, and maintaining an image of high ethical standards. Rick thought about Clay and smirked.

He left to get a bite to eat and returned an hour later

as the first Booster Club members and their wives were arriving. When he walked in, the first thing he saw was Clay talking to a group of cops from the McRae Police Department, all of whom looked to be contemporaries of Clay. From the way their heads were all ducked together, Rick figured they were either in prayer or, more likely, listening to Stubblefield tell one of his stylish jokes. As Rick crossed the room he passed close enough to hear the words, "So the guy turns to his buddy and says, 'Are you kiddin'? I thought she'd opened a goddamn can of tuna!'" All at once, their heads heaved back in laughter. There was a great deal of backslapping, snickering, and repeating of the punch line. "Goddamn can of tuna!"

When the laughter finally subsided, Clay glanced around the room and saw Rick behind the table with the audio equipment. He nudged one of the cops, pointed at Rick, and said, "That's him."

Now, Rick had always had a healthy fear of small-town cops—a fear informed by more than a couple of personal experiences, and not all of them in the South—so when three big boys in blue made a beeline in his direction, he almost panicked. The fact that he hadn't done anything illegal had no bearing on his fear. He hadn't done much the other times either, but that hadn't stopped anybody from swinging that billy club.

Officer Bobby Higdon grabbed Rick and spun him around, saying, "Hands on the wall." Officer Higdon started to pat him down while everyone in the room stopped to watch. "Where they at?" Officer Higdon said.

Rick looked over his shoulder and said, "What're you talking about?"

Just then Clay and the older cop, who turned out to be the chief of police, ambled over. "Well," Chief Dinkins said. "Did ya find 'em?"

Officer Higdon shook his head. "Not on him."

Clay put his arm around Chief Dinkins's shoulder. "Do me a favor, Chief. Let my man slide on this here, otherwise we ain't got a DJ tonight."

"Well, Clay, I don't want to look like I'm soft on crime."

"What crime?" Rick asked.

Officer Higdon got in Rick's face and said, "Boy, we ain't heard no Grinderswitch or Iron Maiden since you got to town," he said, all serious.

The second cop stepped up and said, "We figured you musta stole all 'em records since we don't hear 'em on the station anymore."

Rick's expression must have been priceless. Clay and the cops tried to keep stone-faced but they all started laughing. Clay gave Rick a hardy clap on the back. "Had you goin' there, Rick! Whew! Shoulda seen your face, like you were in the middle of doin' somethin' bad and the lights come on."

Chief Dinkins shook his head. "Fish in a barrel," he said as he turned to walk away. "That was a good one, boys." He headed for the bar.

Rick figured he should go along and play the good sport. He held up his hands and said, "You got me, all right." He managed a smile. "I swallowed it whole."

"Hey," Officer Higdon said. "Hope I wasn't too rough there, putting you against the wall and all that. Just having some fun."

The words seemed to get under Clay's skin. "Christ,

Bobby," he said with contempt. "Ain't no need to get all queer about it," he said, soliciting a laugh from the other two cops. "You ain't never hurt anything in your whole life." He made it sound like an accusation, the sort of thing one should be ashamed of. Clay leaned toward Rick while pointing at Bobby. "Careful he don't try to kiss and make up with you. Tch." As Clay turned and headed toward the bar, the other cops nudged each other and sniggered at Bobby Higdon's expense.

The moment passed quickly but before it did Rick tried to measure it. *What was the point of that?* he wondered. Then he realized Clay hadn't done it to make a point. He simply enjoyed inflicting small, needless humiliations. *You ain't never hurt anything in your whole life.* Given the cultural imperative of violence among certain men, this taunt might have sprung from any number of events. Perhaps a failure in a boyhood fight over neighborhood honor, or maybe a missed opportunity on a football field, or possibly a show of humanity on a hunting trip. Whatever it was, Officer Bobby Higdon was stuck with it. He turned and walked away without saying another word.

As the two other cops drifted off in Higdon's wake, one of them said, "I thought she'd opened a goddamn can of tuna!"

Rick marveled at the caliber of personnel deemed acceptable for local law enforcement.

The room was filling up fast with people and noise. Boosters were three deep at the bar calling their orders. Rick checked his watch. The official presentation of the award was an hour away. In the meanwhile he played a steady stream of pop jazz and watched the crowd, mostly couples in the thirty-to-sixty range in standard business attire. He wondered if the pigeon-hearted banker from the tape was among the crowd. Rick decided to keep an eye on Clay to see whom he talked to during the event.

Out of the corner of one eye, Rick noticed a pink glow when the heat lamps came on over the roast beef station, signaling the opening of the buffet.

Over by the entrance to the Dogwood Room, Clay was shaking hands with Chief Dinkins, who was apparently done for the night. The two men were, by all appearances, old buddies. And if that was true, it fit with Rick's theory that the local cops weren't looking for clues when they tossed Captain Jack's trailer. He thought about his chat with Donna Moore. *What did she say? A cassette came in the mail. That might explain why there were no cassettes in Captain Jack's collection. They probably assumed the master tape was a cassette and, just to be safe, took every one of them. Then again, it was possible the cops hadn't been to the trailer at all. Maybe Clay had taken the cassettes.* In any event, assuming he managed to find some admissible evidence against Clay or whoever was involved in Captain Jack's disappearance, Rick figured he'd have to find someone other than Chief Dinkins to tell about it.

Right now, however, Rick had to find his next record. He bent over and looked at the crate of albums that was under the table. He pulled out an old Crusaders LP and went to cue "Way Back Home." He had the headphone pressed to his ear when he noticed a woman on the far side of the room. Her sense of fashion caught his eye.

She stood out in a revealing black pantsuit with a back-less halter top by Giancarlo Proli and four-inch black stiletto heels with tapering gold straps crossing over exquisite tanned feet. She looked like the kind of woman who could reward a man's curiosity.

As the Crusaders grooved into the room, Rick kept watching her. Remarkable as her outfit was, he was more intrigued by the way she carried herself. Her strides were smooth and assured as she dodged and weaved through people like poles on a slalom course. A genuine smile here, a whispered aside there, a snide glance in another direction. She dealt them like cards. Rick wondered who she was. A city council member? Old lumber money? Whoever she was, her combination of style and attitude made her look like she'd be in charge of the military wing of the Junior League if such a thing existed.

She eventually made her way across the floor to where Rick was. She stood next to his table for a moment, drinking deeply from a frosted Collins glass. She gazed at the crowd and then, without ever looking at Rick, said, "You wouldn't happen to have a gun, would you?"

9

Rick played it cool. He gave a secret-agent smile and said, "No. Sorry." Like "you wouldn't happen to have a gun" was the most common request he got.

She let out a sigh and said, "Damn. I was hoping you might put me out of my mis'ry." She looked at her drink and said, "I guess this'll have to do."

Rick gave a perceptive nod. "I know the feeling," he said.

"Noooo, you don't." She shook her head but kept smiling all the while.

"You can't possibly know the feeling until you've lived in McRae, Mississippi, for at least thirty years. Enduring these *elegant* functions month in, month out, acting like you're just so pleeeeased to meet them and aren't those the cutest shoes and yes, it's a pure shame what's happened to property values in the older neighborhoods, but that's what happens when *they* move in." She stopped a passing waiter and put her glass on his tray. "Bring me another one of those, would you, sugar?"

"Yes, ma'am." The waiter looked at the glass. "Is that a gin and tonic?"

"Yes, please, without the tonic if you would." She looked at Rick. "Something for you? A little personality, as they say?"

"No, thanks," Rick said. "I don't start drinking until the last hour of a gig." After the waiter left, he held out his hand. "By the way, I'm Rick."

"Hello, Rick." The woman shook his hand. "I'm a bitter, unfulfilled, and somewhat tipsy housewife. It's so nice to meet you."

Rick figured if she didn't want to tell him her name, that was her business. Maybe she was some sort of local celebrity and she assumed he knew her name. Whoever she was, he liked her mordant sense of humor, not to mention the occasional glimpse she was allowing into her loose-fitting halter top. And given the way she was inhaling the gin, he figured she was well on her way to drunk, after which point she might say who she was. He gestured at the crowd and said, "So you know all of these folks?"

"Oh, I know everything," she said. "Who they are, what they do, who they're sleeping with, where the bodies are buried." She rolled her eyes and said, "It's all deathly boring after a while." The waiter returned with a fresh drink. She took the glass and made a sweeping gesture with it. "Most of these fine, upstanding citizens are . . . well, how shall I put it?" She took a long swallow of gin and said, "Let's just *say* they're all fine and upstanding . . . until they get caught at whatever they do. At which point we're all asked to summon our compassion and forgive them so that there's very little negative consequence for any sort of bad behavior."

Rick's song was starting to fade, so he bent over and pulled a record at random from the crate. It was George Benson's *Breezin'*. Rick dropped the needle on the Leon Russell ballad "This Masquerade" and segued straight into it. "So," he said as he put the Crusaders back in their sleeve, "which one of these respectable citizens are we honoring tonight?"

"Are you kidding? That's a secret," she said, wagging her finger. "Not revealed until the announcement itself." She leaned forward intimately and motioned for Rick to do the same. He met her halfway across the table. She whispered in his ear, "A toad named Bernie Dribbling." Then she stood up straight and held out her hands as if to apologize. "Oh, I shouldn't say that. Toads aren't all that bad, really."

"Which one is he?"

The woman raised up on her toes and scanned the crowd. Rick couldn't help but look down and notice the fine bones in her feet and her sleek, pedicured nails painted pink as the inside of a conch shell. "He's over there," she said, tipping the rim of her glass toward the dais. "Sixty-ish? Salt and pepper with the chamber-of-commerce cut? Suit by Sears?"

Rick saw him. An unremarkable man by appearance, though his behavior, at least as described by Clay Stubblefield, lent him an inescapable ugliness. "What're the criteria for this award?" Rick asked.

"Truth be told, I think it just rotates among the members of the club," she said. "Far as I can tell, it's got nothing to do with how well you run your business or how much you give back to the community. Of course conventional wisdom says that it helps not to be the subject of a grand-jury investigation, even though last year's winner was technically under indictment when he picked up his plaque."

Rick laughed and said, "You're kidding. Is he here?"

"No, he's currently appealing the conviction." She shook an ice cube into her mouth and crunched it between her teeth while looking around the room. "Where is that damn waiter?"

"Excuse me," Rick said as he bent down to grab another record from the crate. *Grover Washington? No. Hubert Laws? Nah. Ahhh, The Late Herbie Mann.* When he stood up he was surprised to see Clay wresting the glass from the woman's hand. Stubblefield forced a smile and said, "I see you've met my wife."

In Rick's defense, it had to be pointed out that Lori Stubblefield didn't look anything like the photo on Clay's desk, which had been taken eight years earlier. Her Mary Tyler Moore flip was now a Parisian blunt cut and a different color to boot. And the Suzy Home-maker personality he had projected onto her photo bore no resemblance to the slinky tart in the halter top.

She was seated on the dais now, sullen and brooding without her drink, as Clay stood proudly at the podium addressing his fellow Booster Clubbers. Rick found it hard to imagine her ever being attracted to someone like Clay, but then it was hard to imagine the woman in the photo turning into the one he'd just met. But regardless of what had drawn her to Clay in the first place, Rick wondered what made her stay. Financial security? The kids? Inertia?

"Before I present this award, I hope you don't mind if I take a moment to talk about all the good work that the McRae Booster Club does in our community." Clay proceeded to talk about the Little League team the radio station sponsored. The way he told it, Clay had paid for new uniforms out of his own pocket and the goodness of his heart and had put in thirty hours a week as a volunteer coach last year. "And enjoyed every minute of it," he said with a slap to the podium.

Rick saw Lori Stubblefield rolling her eyes and he figured it was more likely that Clay had done an advertising trade-out with a local sporting-goods store for some slightly irregular uniforms and had dropped by two practices for a total of about twenty minutes over the course of the previous season. In fact, assuming he ever received it, Rick would bet his first paycheck that the kids on the team couldn't have picked their alleged benefactor out of a lineup.

Clay's introduction of Bernie Dribbling was nothing less than fantastic. Winner of several awards similar in nature to the one he was about to receive, Mr. Dribbling was on the board of directors of three local charities, and of course he was deeply involved in pastoral activities in his church. "Ladies and gentlemen," Clay said. "The McRae Booster Club's Businessman of the Year . . . Bernie Dribbling!"

Bernie sat there for a moment grinning like a pickled possum. Then he lurched to the podium and accepted the plaque, slurring only a few words while thanking everyone for their votes. He tried to make a joke about how expensive some of those votes were, but he botched the punch line. Finally, after an obligatory, if synthetic, nod to God and country, Bernie pointed at Rick and said, "Now play that funky music, white boy!"

After the dance, Rick couldn't stop singing the chorus to "Boogie Oogie Oogie." He wanted to stop, he just couldn't. He wondered if that phenomenon had been studied, if there was a name for when you can't get a song out of your head. And why was it always goofy stuff? The theme to a sitcom or "Boogie Oogie Oogie"?

Rick needed some head Drano to purge the Taste of Honey from his mind. So he turned on *Uncle Victor's Wax Museum* for his drive home. The first thing he heard was the Yardbirds followed by Badfinger, Meatloaf, Grand Funk, and the New York Dolls. Rick was searching for the wild card because he knew Uncle Victor wasn't just randomly playing these songs; that wasn't how the *Wax Museum* worked. Next came a George Harrison tune followed by Patti Smith's "Dancing Barefoot," and Rick finally saw the light. The answer was the Runt.

In 1967 Todd Rundgren formed a band he called Nazz from the Yardbird song "Nazz Are Blue." Todd also recorded a version of the Yardbirds hit "Happenings Ten Years Time Ago" on his *Faithful* album. George Harrison's connection was that he'd been the first producer on the Badfinger album *Straight Up* but left the project before completion. Todd stepped in to produce the record and had the hit "Baby Blue," which is the song Uncle Victor had played. Todd had also produced the Meatloaf, New York Dolls, Grand Funk and Patti Smith albums.

When "We Gotta Get You a Woman" came on, Rick smiled and started thinking about Traci's comment that she would just "deal with it" if she got to his place and found him in bed. He entertained a fantasy wherein he was tucked warmly in the sack when she arrived. The door would be unlocked and she'd come inside to find a path to his bedroom lighted by candles. In the background, the erotic strains of Marvin Gaye's "Let's Get It On" would set the mood. Traci wouldn't say a word as she undressed and slipped under the covers and started to move to the slow, relentless rhythms of the music.

It was a nice fantasy but Rick couldn't help but project ahead to the days at work that might follow. He'd be maintaining a professional demeanor and she'd take it as a slight. She'd retaliate with stares and silence until she couldn't stand it anymore and she'd finally storm into the production room and give it to him with both barrels. Rick took a moment to examine why, in this projected future, he assumed Traci would be the cause of the problem. He wondered if he should seek counseling to deal with his unswerving pessimism about relationships, even the ones he didn't actually have.

The Todd Rundgren ended as Rick pulled onto the dirt driveway leading to his trailer. Uncle Victor did a backsell before going into a spot set, which, at this time of night, consisted solely of the Universal Financial Services commercial. *"Are you behind on your bills?"*

To his surprise, Traci was already there when he arrived, forcing Rick to rechoreograph his fantasy. She was sitting on the steps to the trailer wearing sweatpants and a T-shirt. As he approached from the carport, she stood and scratched at her armpit and spoke in her best white-trash accent. "Hey, Billy Rae," she said. "D'jew 'member tuh get that carton of Salem Liiights I sent you for? These kids're drivin' me crazy 'round here, and if I don't get me a smoke soon, I tell you what, I'monna cut yer water off and take yer meter out!"

Rick gave her a sideways glance. "That seems to come pretty natural for you," he said.

Traci aimed a finger at him. "You better hush or I won't share." She held up a paper sack with a bottle inside.

"Eww, malt liquor or Night Train?" Rick keyed the door and they went inside.

"You don't hush your mouth you're gonna find yourself in a tight fight with a short stick," Traci said as she pulled the bottle from the bag. "I'll have you know this is a rugged little Australian Shiraz blend with an exceptionally long finish and notes of raspberry jam." She looked at the label. "Or at least that's what they said down at the Pick 'n Pack. Supposed to go good with potted meat."

"Allow me." Rick popped the cork and pulled a couple of tumblers from the drain rack by the sink. "How was baby-sitting?" He filled the glasses and handed one to Traci.

"It was fun. My niece is four and just adores me, so what's not to like?" She held her glass out. "Cheers," she said, moving toward the sofa, where she sat down cross-legged. "So how was the Boosterville dance?"

"A little more intellectual than I'm used to," Rick said. "I never know what to say when someone asks, 'How 'bout them Panthers?' But I'll give 'em this. They were serving some fine roast beef." He went on to summarize the evening's events, from his introduction to the McRae Police Department to meeting Clay's wife and seeing Bernie Dribbling.

Halfway through his narration, Traci refilled their glasses. When he got to the part about having to play "Boogie Oogie Oogie," she interrupted him to say, "Okay, enough about that. What about Donna Moore? What did she have to say for herself? And tell it fast," Traci said. "'Cause I wanna hear that tape you used to lure me over here."

"Well, first of all, she didn't burn her place down," Rick said. "I'm pretty sure that was somebody else, maybe even the fabled Dixie Mafia."

"For real?" Traci seemed genuinely surprised by this.

"So it seems. I don't think there's any connection between the fire and Captain Jack's disappearance. But Captain Jack *did* blackmail her. Got a little of her money and broke up her marriage, too, before he disappeared."

"So she has a motive to be involved in that?"

Rick shook his head. "No, sounded like her marriage was already on the rocks. She wasn't nearly as upset about that as she was about losing her business. And setting aside for a moment whatever character flaw is revealed in her choice of paramour, and the cheating itself, she struck me as more or less honest."

He walked over to the record collection and pulled the box for *Chicago IV*. "But here's where the plot thickens," he said as he took the reel from the box. "Donna had a friend named Holly Creel."

"Yeah, I remember you asking me about her."

Rick threaded the tape onto the reel-to-reel, then turned to look at Traci. "Well, she's missing, too." He turned on the amp and switched it to auxiliary. "And the circumstances are at least suspicious."

"Suspicious how?"

Rick just grinned and said, "You ready?"

When Clay said, *"And you know that bitch wanted me to come back to her motel room and piss on her?"* a spray of wine shot out of Traci's nose. She couldn't help it. Her reflex was too strong. She sputtered and coughed and waved her hands and said, "Whoa! Play that again!"

Rick stopped the tape then went to the kitchen and tossed her a towel. "You might not want to have any beverages in your mouth as we go forward," he said.

"Thanks for the warning." She wiped her face then gestured for him to start the tape over. So he did. Traci listened with dismal amusement as Clay bragged about his sexcapades. Traci wasn't surprised to hear him say any of it. They were exactly the kinds of things she suspected Clay of saying all the time to his good-old-boy friends. And she found that actually hearing him say the words was engrossing, in a loathsome sort of way.

They eventually reached the point where Clay said,

"Yeah, so she had this friend, name of Holly Creel, who needed some money, right? So there's this old guy I know name Bernie Dribbling at Universal Financial Services. D'jew ever know him?"

The banker on the other end of the line giggled a bit and said, *"Un-uh,"* indicating no.

"Oh, weird old sumbitch," Clay said. *"About fifty-eight, fifty-nine, sixty years old, just talked about pussy all the time, you know. Ol' Bernie lives up in Jackson but comes down here and spends like three days each week running this business. He stays in the Knights Inn, over there, the Budget Six motel, something like that. And the clerks would give him a room next to couples checked in who were crackin', you know, 'cause he told 'em what he want. And he'd get in there at night and fix him a drink, lean up against the wall, listen to 'em crack, and beat his meat, you know."*

This caused the banker to let go with a big laugh, but not enough to stop Clay from talking. *"Sumbitch invited me over there for a drink one night, wanted me to lie on the floor, you know, and stick my ear up to the wall and hear them people gettin' it next door."*

"Are you kiddin' me?" The banker giggled a bit more.

"Hell no, I ain't kiddin'," Clay said. *"So anyway this Holly Creel needed some money, right? And so I told Donna, I said, 'Look, I might know somebody'll make a loan to your friend but she's gonna have to come across for him any way he wants to. And she said, 'No sweat.' Tch. So I went to Bernie and told him, you*

*know, about this deal. And she wanted ten thousand
dolla's now. This ain't like a damn hunn-ed-dollar,
ninety-day note, you know."*

The banker didn't say anything, he just kept giggling
in an encouraging way.

*"Tch. And Bernie worked the damn loan out for her.
For a piece of ass, or it was a series of pieces of ass,"*
Clay explained. *"She was going to take care of him for
a while and do all sorts of strange things for him, you
know, all kinda weird shit."*

"Uh-huh." Please, just tell me some more, he
seemed to be saying.

*"So anyway I lined that up for him and he made that
damn loan to her,"* Clay said. *"Tch. And I saw him two
or three days later, he was comin' to get it, you know,
an' he says, uh, 'I got something,' he says, 'You don't
think she'll mind if I wear this, do ya?' And that sumbitch had him a strap-on penis extension."*

The banker belly-laughed at this and said, *"No kiddin'!"*

*"Uh big ol' monster-looking motherfucker you wear
like a damn garter around you or somethin'."*

"Oh, I ain't believin' this."

*"And he said, 'You think she'll mind if I wear this
thing?' And I said, 'Shiddif I know, man. Go get it,
tiger.' "* Here, Clay giggled a bit himself before saying,
*"But I bet you Universal Financial Services has either
written that loan off or still got it on the books."*

"You reckon?"

*" 'Cause I know damn well that bitch couldn't pay
that."*

"He ain't with 'em anymore?"

"Hell, he's president of the company or somethin'."

"Is he?"

"He's one of the high moguls. Him and the may— him and Buddy Alford are partners in it."

The banker made a noise that sounded approximately like, *"Izzaahryyye?"* which Traci's trained southern ear knew meant, "Is that right?"

"You know Buddy Alford the ag commissioner?"

"Yeah."

"Okay, well, Alford and Dribbling and Dicky Crumly in Laurel, who's in the real estate business, shit, I think Wally Thigpen, three or four of 'em formed this. Started in Jackson, then in Hartsboro and McRae, now they've opened one up down in Biloxi."

"Dang," the banker said. He paused here, presumably waiting for more gossip. When none was forthcoming, he said, *"Well, uh . . ."*

"I tell you what," Clay said. *"Lemme run by tomorrow and pick up that damn thing, you still out at the branch?"*

"Yeah, it's out at the branch."

"You, is that where you're at?"

"Yeah."

"Okay, I'll run by and talk to you and we'll see about that girl."

The banker gave a quick laugh. *"All right!"*

"Okay."

"See ya later."

"Later."

"Bye." Click.

Rick stopped the tape and looked at Traci. "Whaddya think?"

"Wow." Traci finished her glass of wine, then she said, "Talk about your predatory lending practices." She looked over at the tape machine as if it had told her a crazy story. "It's hard to know where to start," she said. "I mean, you're definitely gonna have to play it again so we can dissect it better, but for starters, what was that part about when you're dealing with your money you're dealing with your morals? What in the world was that supposed to mean?"

"That's one of my favorite parts." Rick gave Traci his interpretation, then looked at her to see if that cleared it up.

Traci studied it for a moment. "No, I don't see how that helps any."

"No, not really," Rick agreed. He pushed the button to rewind the tape.

Traci took the wine and refilled both their glasses. Then she stood and walked over to the Barcalounger and plopped down in it. "I'm ready when you are," she said.

Rick pulled a footstool over to the tape deck and perched on it so he could stop and start the deck when they wanted to scrutinize a particular part of the conversation.

Finally they got to where Clay said, *"And the clerks would give him a room next to couples checked in who were crackin', you know, 'cause he told 'em what he want."*

"Whoa!" Traci raised her hand as if to testify. "Stop it

right there!" Incredulous, she said, " 'He told 'em what he want'? How do you ask for that? Ewww!" She gave an exaggerated shiver. "Makes me want to shower." She waved at the deck and said, "But keep going."

Rick started the tape again, and as it played, he watched Traci's reaction. Her expressions went from disgust to dismay but never to surprise. He figured she'd spent her whole life around good old boys like this. Rick could see the gears spinning in her head. She had the look of someone eager to embark on an adventure. When it was over, he rewound the tape.

"Well, he's slimier than I thought, which is no small deal," Traci said. "And he might've set a new indoor record for moral bankruptcy. But does it help us any?"

"What do you mean?"

"Well, is any of it illegal?" She tipped back in the big soft chair, sporting a boozy smile. "I mean using sex as collateral. Right? Wasn't that the deal? Or wait, is she using sex to pay back the loan or just to get it?"

"I wondered about that," Rick said, pointing at the tape deck. "Clay said he thinks Universal has either written the loan off or still has it on its books. So it sounds like the sex is what secured the loan but that she had to pay back the principal, presumably with interest."

"Okay, so what's the crime? Prostitution? Soliciting?"

"I'm not sure, but—"

"You know, now that I think about it? I wonder if it *is* prostitution." Traci reached down and pushed the seat lever. Her feet hit the carpet and she leaned forward, resting her elbows on her knees. "I mean, look, a hooker standing on the street is approached by a guy, right? He offers money in exchange for sex. The money only goes one way. He gives her money. She gives him . . . well, you know."

"Yes, I like to think so."

"But with *this* deal, the money is returned, with interest. The sex is just collateral, like you said."

Rick squinted at her. "I think you're splitting pubic hairs here."

"All right, try this," Traci said. "If I offer to have sex with you in return for money, I'm a prostitute and can probably be arrested. But if I offer to have sex with you for free, I'm just a slut." She smiled.

Rick smiled, too. "No, you'd be doing charity work," he said. "But remember, this wasn't for free. Dribbling had to give her money before she'd have sex with him."

"But she had to give the money back with interest. So, if you look at it that way she actually had to *pay* for the sex with *him*. If anyone's guilty of prostitution, it's Dribbling!"

"And as much as I'd like to see someone sell that to a jury, it misses the point, which is this: There were three serious crimes committed here, none of which is prostitution. The first was extortion. We know Captain Jack tried to blackmail Lisa Ramey and Donna Moore, and they really weren't guilty of all that much, given the topsy-turvy little world we live in."

"And you figure if he was willing to try it on them, there's reason to think he'd try it on the bigger fish as well."

"Deeper pockets and more to lose," Rick said.

"Which leads us to the second and third crimes. Kidnapping and murder."

"And maybe two of each. Maybe more."

"Captain Jack and Holly Creel."

"Right."

"So we have to find out what happened to Captain Jack or Holly Creel, one."

"That's the first thing," Rick said. "Then, assuming we find them on the wrong side of the grass somewhere, we have to connect Clay and Bernie to it. We need evidence. But even if we find some, we can't just go to the cops since Clay, and probably Bernie, are buddies with Chief Dinkins."

Traci said, "We could try to blackmail them." She seemed serious. Rick paused, considering the merits of the idea. "I'm kidding," Traci said. "It'd be more fun to visit 'em up at Parchman."

Rick put the tape back in its hiding place then sat on the sofa, where Traci joined him. They talked for a while about different points raised by the tape. It turned out that Traci recognized the other voice as that of Kenny Owens, the manager of a branch of Pine Belt Savings and Loan. Traci was less sure, but thought that the Tammy mentioned at the start of the tape could be Tammy Callaway, who worked briefly in sales at WAOR and who had competed in some local beauty pageants but who didn't have that win-at-any-cost attitude.

It was pushing toward two in the morning and the wine was running out. Traci excused herself to the bathroom and Rick reached over and put Uncle Victor on the stereo. He caught the very end of Ballin' Jack's "Try to Relax" as it segued into something by the Sons of Champlin. He pulled out his cigar box and loaded his pipe. He lit two candles on the coffee table and then took a hit. When Traci returned and saw the pipe, she looked pleasantly surprised. She took a small puff before she plopped back down on the sofa. Rick couldn't help but notice she'd taken off her bra while she was gone. She was beautiful in the candlelight. Traci said, "Let's talk some more about what I'd be if I offered to have sex with you for free."

Rick weighed his options and then shook his head. He stood up and said, "I've got a better idea." He held out his hand. "Let's not talk."

There was nothing particularly romantic about it, which wasn't to disparage any of the acts that followed. It was more athletic, more like a contest than something from the archives of true romance. Each tried to outdo the other. Faster, slower, longer, harder, more. There were shows of strength and there were weaknesses for certain sensations and it wasn't long before they were making jokes about qualifying for different events in the mattress Olympics. At one point Traci hopped out of bed and raced out of the room. A moment later she came running back shouting "Broad jump!" and leaped into the bed. They laughed as much as they moaned and they eventually ran out of breath and steam and they fell sound asleep.

The next morning they picked up where they left off. They were in an unusual position and engaged in a rather vigorous deed when Rick thought he pulled a hamstring. "Shake it off," Traci said. And he did. It was just a cramp.

Afterward they showered, dressed, and went to Kitty's for breakfast. Rick had the chicken-fried steak and egg special while Traci had a mushroom-and-sausage omelette. "Now, you can't be acting all mushy and lovey-dovey at work," Traci said. "We don't want to let on."

"I think I can control myself," Rick said.

"Uh-huh. Some control." She pointed her fork at him. "You told me you had a rule about not getting involved with coworkers."

Rick shrugged and said, "Yeah, well, maybe I'll do something to get myself fired."

"All right, but just so you know, I can't make you a kept man on my salary."

"Maybe you oughta get-chu a better job," Rick said.

Traci laughed at the way he said it. "I think you got yer accent back," she said, shaking her head. " 'Get-chu a better job.' " She looked at her watch and sort of giggled. "You better get-chure butt on over to Riverside Park for the thing. Who's setting up over there?"

"Supposed to be Rob and J.C. But you're right. I oughta get on over there." Rick pulled his wallet and paid the tab. "You comin' with?"

"I think I'll go home and change," Traci said. "It's too warm for these sweats." Then she winked at him and said, "But I'm comin' with later."

10

On his way to Riverside Park, Rick stopped at a florist. He handed a note to the woman behind the counter and asked her to send a dozen yellow roses to the address he gave her. Then he headed to the park. To his surprise the weather was cooperating. The forecast had called for a 60 percent chance of rain, so Rick was expecting cloudy skies. But it was a clear blue Mississippi day.

Riverside Park was on the western edge of town on a small rise not far from the Strong River. The park had nature trails, a swimming pool, and playgrounds spread over a couple of hundred acres. In the center of the park there was a stand of eight Italian cypresses that formed a tall backdrop to a large concrete platform that was used as a stage for everything from graduation ceremonies to theater-in-the-park productions.

The WAOR Prize Patrol Van was parked on the grass nearby. Rick parked next to it. The Allman Brothers were booming from a pair of big speakers standing next to the van. J.C. and Rob stretched a banner across the back of the stage. WAOR-FM—REDEFINING CLASSIC ROCK!

After setting the speakers on the stage, the three of them set up the WAOR Prize Barrel, which would hold all the contest entries. The size of an oil drum, it was made from a metal mesh you could see through. Mounted on a stand, the barrel had a Z-shaped handle to spin it on its axis. There was a small hatch in the middle allowing you to reach in to draw the winning name.

Rick was eager to see the turnout. The next ratings book was two months away and he wanted to get a sense of how the format was doing before that. One of the good things about live promotional events was that you could meet your audience and talk to them. It gave you a qualitative measurement of the real audience as compared to the contrived quantitative audience measurement you got with the the conventional ratings system, which Rick considered inherently flawed since it forced stations to employ programming that was proven successful in getting *ratings* as compared to actually building an audience.

Rick felt he could objectively argue that programming based on the ratings methodology tended to serve the station owner more than the audience, and he was one of those finicky guys who considered that a violation of the FCC license and a betrayal to the local citizens to whom the airwaves belonged.

Anybody with a big budget could give away sweaty wads of cash at seven-fifteen every Thursday morning during a ratings period. It was called "forced listening" and usually resulted in a document that said you had the largest measured audience for morning drive time. Of course those people probably listened only for a total of twenty minutes, spread out over four days, and not every day from six to ten in the morning as the sales staff would suggest. But what happened when you *weren't* giving away money? Were those same people listening then?

Rick knew that if you had the highest ratings in a time period the price for ad time would soar beyond what local businesses could afford. And that was fine with the sales manager since national franchises with regional co-op subsidies would swoop in and buy all that pricey time. The problem from a local perspective was that late in the afternoon, when the audience was hungry and driving home from work, they'd hear ads for McDonald's and Pizza Hut instead of locally owned businesses, which could only afford to buy time between midnight and six, when they weren't even open.

Of course, when you're trying to earn a living on commission, you can't reasonably be expected to concern yourself with the idea that Mom and Pop put money back into the community and that their businesses give the community its unique identity. And if you work in sales you certainly can't worry that those who profit most from the franchises by and large take money from the community in exchange for a bunch of minimum-wage jobs.

With all that in mind, Rick wondered why Clay wasn't giving the thousand dollars away in smaller parts, say, two-fifty a week for four weeks. But he didn't think about it for long. The contest had been put in motion before Rick arrived and the whole thing was out of his control.

People started showing up around eleven with ice chests and picnic baskets and barbecue grills. Rick and the other jocks mingled with the crowd and talked about the music. On the whole it was a fan fest. One guy in his late forties said to Rick, "Man, when I heard you go from Clapton's 'Easy Now' to Van Morrison's 'Wild Night,' I thought I'd died and gone to heaven. You never hear that kinda thing on the radio anymore." Of course some came to complain but they did so reasonably and not without dropping their name in the barrel for a shot at the thousand bucks.

The weekend DJ back at the studio was having a good shift, mixing a steady stream of rollicking, good-time, blues-based boogie from J. Geils and Wet Willie to Black Oak Arkansas and Brownsville Station. It took Rick back to the seventies when carefree, bare-foot teens with long hair and cutoff jeans tossed footballs and Frisbees and smoked a little pot and had some hot fun in the summertime.

Rick was caught off guard when a woman snuck up behind him and grabbed him in a bear hug. She started kissing his neck and whispering in his ear, "You are the sweetest man I have ever met."

Tight in the woman's grip, Rick couldn't turn around. He said, "Sorry. I didn't get your name."

Traci gave him a squeeze. "You can call me whatever you want," she said. "Long as you keep calling." She let

Rick turn around. "I don't know if I liked your note or the roses better. My heart just felt like it swole up."

"Don't worry," he said. "I know a good cardiologist." He kissed her then looked around. "We're not supposed to be doing this in public. I thought you said you could control yourself."

"No, that was you," Traci said. "I know better than to say stuff like that." After kissing him again, she saw something over his shoulder. She said, "Sorry, but you'll understand later." Then she slapped him, spun around, and left in a huff.

Rick was still rubbing his cheek trying to figure out what had happened when he heard someone sniggering behind him. He turned around and Clay said, "Yeah, she's a hard nut to crack, all right. Tch. I give it a shot every now and then but that girl can wiggle out of a corner." Before Rick could say anything, Clay gestured at the crowd. "Pretty good turnout," he said. "Just think how many mighta showed up if you'd used that Pink Floyd song like I told you." He gave a little wink, then said, "You seen our beauty queen? She's s'posed to be here by—" He looked past Rick and waved at someone. "Air she is. C'mon, lemme introduce ya."

Rick turned to see Joni Lang, the newly crowned Miss Loblolly Pine, walking toward them in a designer sweatsuit. She wasn't the tallest beauty pageant winner Rick had ever seen but the pinkish-red, spike-heeled, open-toed pumps she was perched on gave her the allure of a six-foot strumpet. Clay introduced her to Rick then gave her a lingering pat on the ass, which she obviously didn't appreciate. They made small talk before Rick excused himself to get ready for the drawing.

A little before three, they took the stage. Rick had planned to emcee the actual drawing but Clay pushed him toward the prize barrel and grabbed the mike himself. "Hey, all right, how's everybody doin'? I'm Clay Stubblefield, general manager at WAOR, the station with rrrreal rrrrock, rrreeeaalll cash!" He thrust a fist in the air to punctuate the line and the crowd responded with a tepid round of golf applause that gave Rick perhaps more satisfaction than it should have. "Okay, before we do the drawing I'd like to introduce somebody who probably doesn't need an introduction, but what the heck. She's a McRae native, folks, so let's give a big WAOR Classic Rock welcome to the newly crowned Miss Loblolly Pine, Joni Lang!" He turned and offered his open palm to the side of the stage and Joni sashayed out sporting a big tiara and doing the beauty queen wave. She stopped midway across the stage and, in one deft motion, yanked off her sweatsuit to reveal a thong bikini. Clay flashed the okay sign and said, "All right! Joni Lang! Let's hear it!" He waved a fist in a circle over his head while making a *whoop, whoop, whoop* sound as Joni crossed the stage to where Rick was standing next to the barrel.

"Well, okay," Clay said. "Let's get this show on the road. Rick, why don't you give it a spin and let Joni draw the name for third prize?" He held up a stack of CDs. "The folks over at T-Bone Records put together a collection of their top ten classic rock discs, and man, are they good ones!" Rick cranked the big barrel around half a dozen times then opened the hatch. Joni drew a name and handed it to Clay. He called out the name and a young woman in the crowd let out a happy scream and came running up to collect her prize. They repeated this process and gave away dinner for two at Steak 'n Surf.

"All right," Clay said. "Everybody ready? It's time for the moment of truth. Can I have a drumroll please?" The DJ back at the station played the sound effect. Rick popped open the hatch. Joni reached in and pulled a name then handed it to Clay. He fumbled it a bit then looked at the entry form and said, "WAOR's grand-prize winner is . . . Ken Stigler!" He shaded his eyes, looking out over the audience. "Ken Stigler! You out there?"

A big guy in the back of the crowd let out with, "Yo! Right here!"

"We have a winner," Clay said, pointing at the guy, who—based on his muttonchop sideburns and worn leather coat—Rick figured for a Steppenwolf fan.

The DJ back at the studio went into The Beatles singing "Money (That's What I Want)" as Ken made his way to the stage. People clapped him on the back and gave him the thumbs-up for his good fortune. Clay made a big gesture and said, "C'mon up here, Ken. Get your one thousand twenty-nine dollars from WAOR-FM, the station with rrrreal rrrrock, rrreeaalll cash!"

Ken whooped and hollered and gave high fives to everybody with a hand in the air. A photographer from the *McRae Monitor* came onstage and took some pictures of the winner accepting the poster-size check from Clay with Joni Lang and Rick standing alongside.

After the photos, the party continued. The Beatles segued improbably into a flashy set of Bowie, Mott the

Hoople, and Roxy Music. Rick was standing over by the WAOR van talking to J.C. when he noticed Joni Lang still on the stage putting her sweatsuit back on. He thought about asking her if Clay had ever judged any of the pageants she had competed in and, more to the point, if there had been any contestants named Tammy. But that got sidetracked when he noticed Joni looking around as if to see if anyone was watching her. She walked over to the edge of the stage and looked into a cardboard box that had become an impromptu trash can. Joni quickly reached into the box and pulled something out. Then she stuck it in her pocket and hurried off the stage.

After the event, Rick and Traci went back to his place. "That's a nasty burn," Rick said as he untied the knot on Traci's halter top. "You should've let me put some sunscreen on you."

"I know," Traci said. "I was bad. But I was having so much fun."

Rick squeezed a dollop of aloe vera into his hand and said, "Brace yourself."

She tensed when Rick brought the cold gel to her skin, but as he slowly rubbed it in she began to relax. "I think the backs of my legs got burned, and maybe my feet, too," Traci said. "You better just rub everything, and not necessarily with that goo."

The last light of the summer sun bathed the room in gold, and as happens in situations like this, Rick and Traci made love. They started on the sofa, then moved to the floor and the Barcalounger. Afterward they moved back to the sofa, where they drifted to sleep, spooned in the advancing darkness.

A few hours later Rick woke to the patter of a steady rain. He opened his eyes. It was pitch-black in the trailer. Traci was pressed against him, breathing deeply and lost in a dream. It was as close to a scene of domestic bliss as Rick could recall being part of, and he liked it. He thought about how it would be nice to have this, or something like it. Really *have* it. He touched Traci's hair and wondered if she would go with him when he went to his next station, because there was always a next station. And would she follow him to the next and the next after that? Was it fair to ask someone to do that? And if it was, and if she would, Rick wondered if they would still *have it* each time or would it disappear and leave them disappointed?

Rick smirked at his gloomy musings. Probably just his mood. He was in that displaced zone he got in whenever he fell asleep in the afternoon and woke up in the dark. He turned his head and listened. The rain had finally come but only a drizzle. It was quiet. Peaceful. Rick draped his arm over Traci and figured that if it was possible for good things to fall away and disappoint, it was also possible they could evolve into something better. After a moment's reflection he thought, *Yeah, but what are the odds?*

A distant light passed through the windows and Rick watched as shadows moved across the walls. He figured it was the moon finding a break in the clouds. But a moment later a pair of headlights switched to bright and lit the room like a fuse.

Rick sat up, waking Traci. "What's going on?" She was still half-asleep.

A car pulled up outside and the lights went out, leaving them in the dark with dilated pupils. Traci was dazed and sleepy. "What time is it?"

"I don't know," Rick said as he got up and put on his jeans.

"Is someone here?" Traci sat up and looked at the clock on the wall. "It's nine o'clock."

"Yeah, and the last time somebody dropped by this time of night I ended up with dental problems." Rick pointed toward the bedroom. "Go to the back and lock the door. And don't turn on the lights. If it sounds like I'm getting the shit kicked out of me, call the cops. And a dentist." Traci grabbed her clothes and did what he said.

Rick went to the kitchen and grabbed his cast-iron skillet, then crossed to the door. It was unlocked. He expected the Ted Nugent fan would just let himself in again. Only this time Rick would get the first shot. He took his backswing and held it, waiting.

There was a small knock at the door followed by a woman's voice. "Hello? Jack?" The knob rattled and turned and the door opened and she stepped inside.

"Hold it right there," Rick said in his deepest voice. "I've got a gun."

The lights came on and virtually blinded Rick, who hit himself in the head with the skillet when he went to shade his eyes. "Oww!"

The woman stood there with her hand on the switch and said, "You lied."

Rick blinked a couple of times before he said, "I felt

entitled, what with you breaking into my place in the middle of the night and all." He lowered the skillet to his side. "Who *are* you?"

"The door was unlocked," the woman said.

Rick shook his head. "Just because someone leaves their door unlocked doesn't mean you're invited in," he said. "I mean, what if my zipper was down?"

The woman didn't respond. She was tired and she looked it. She took off her coat and laid it across the back of a chair. "I was under the impression that my brother lived here," she said. "At least until he disappeared."

Rick opened his mouth to speak but was interrupted when Traci entered the room and said, "You're Carol?" Traci gestured back and forth between them. "We've talked on the phone. My name's Traci. I'm the receptionist. That's Rick, the program director. Rick, this is Captain Jack's sister, Carol."

"Oh. Hi." It was all Rick could think to say. He handed her a clean kitchen towel so she could dry herself.

They stood there for a moment looking at one another before Carol said, "I came to get Jack's stuff." She made a weak gesture to the west. "I just drove from New Mexico."

Rick nodded sympathetically and said, "Sorry. I wasn't expecting anyone and—" He looked at Traci then back at Carol. "Stubblefield told me Jack's *brother* was coming to get his stuff."

"Yeah. He was supposed to," Carol said. "But here I am." She pointed at Rick. "And there you are." She gestured around the trailer. "But Jack's nowhere to be found," she said as she reached into her purse and pulled out a cassette. "And I think I know why."

* * *

Rick made some coffee and they went into the living room to talk about Jack Carter and the infamous tape. Rick told Carol everything he had learned since he'd been looking into it. He tried to keep the litany from sounding too grim but the facts weren't open to a lot of happy spin. Carol allowed that Rick's theory was more or less what she suspected. "Jack had a problem and everybody knew it," she said. "Frankly, we're surprised it took him this long to self-destruct." She sounded both disappointed and fed up. "We got him into rehab a couple of times but he never took responsibility for his actions, never exercised a bit of self-control." She looked around the trailer. "That's why he ended up here." Carol looked at Rick and Traci and said, "No offense. But Jack was good. He worked New York, L.A., Chicago. He was a major-market talent." She looked at the floor. "With a major-market nose."

A lightning strike cracked thunder and turned everyone's head. Traci cocked her ear toward an open window. She could hear the raindrops starting to get fat.

Rick asked Carol about the tape's origins.

"A couple of months ago?" Carol waved a hand in the air to imply the passage of time. "He calls and tells me this story. Says he went to work one day after the engineer had installed a new phone, uhhh, thing, a connection . . ."

"A phone patch?" Rick asked.

"Yeah, a phone patch in the production room. Well, apparently the engineer left the phone line feeding through the board when he was done, and when Jack's boss took this call, it happened to be on that line, right? Jack was walking past the production room a little later and heard his boss talking about things he might not ought to have been." She cocked her eyebrows as she said the last part. "As soon as Jack realized what was happening, he put a tape on the machine and recorded the rest of the conversation, just for the fun of it."

Traci looked at Rick and said, "That's why it starts in the middle of the conversation."

"So I said, 'Well, that's interesting, Jack,' and he says, 'Yeah, well, the reason I'm telling you is that I need to borrow some money.' Of course I knew it was for coke, so I told him I couldn't do it. I wouldn't," Carol said. "He tells me he understands but he wants me to know about the tape because he figures if I won't loan him some money he can make some using the tape. I guess he figured I'd loan him the money if I knew the alternative was him using that tape like that, but I told him he was crazy and that he was going to get in trouble. He just laughs and says he's gonna send me a copy of the tape, you know, so if something happened to him, I could give it to the cops. So I figured I'd do that before I left town."

"At least two problems there," Rick said. "Based on that story, the tape was made illegally, so even if it got the cops to investigate and it led to something, it would probably all be tossed out since the underlying evidence probably isn't admissible in court." He noticed Traci eyeing him skeptically. "I watch a lot of *Law & Order*," he said. "The second problem is the cops. They're Clay's pals. There are some other possibilities, though, like the county sheriff or maybe the district attorney who might look into it, but I think we need to know who knows who before we just hand the tape over to anybody. If we hand it over."

"What do mean 'if'?"

"I'm just not sure if it makes sense, that's all." Rick looked to Carol. "You should hang on to that one in case . . . well, just in case."

Carol didn't argue the point. She said she was curious about what had happened to her brother but that even if someone had killed him, they'd only finished what Jack had started and seemed bound and determined to do to himself. She seemed more resigned about his fate than angry. They talked some more about Rick's investigation. "So this Dribbling guy is the only one you haven't spoken to?"

"Well, him and our boss."

"The guy on the tape?"

"Yeah. I haven't figured out how to handle that yet. But I'll think of something."

"*We'll* think of something," Traci said. "Hey!" She sat forward on the sofa and pointed at Rick. "What happened to his car?"

"That's right," Rick said, having wondered the same thing. "You know what he drove?"

"Corvette," Carol said. "Like a '95 or '96."

"Torch red," Traci said. "It was beautiful."

"The ultimate midlife-crisis car, I suppose. Bought it in his last major market, the last time he had a chunky paycheck. I told him he should sell the thing if he needed money, but he said he'd start selling body parts before he got rid of his Vette." Carol sipped her coffee and said, "Know what I think? I think he was a depressed, self-medicating, middle-aged man in a business that no longer needed him. He didn't like change and he had a habit to support, and given his reputation, he was looking at the rest of his life going from one small market to the next. Who wouldn't be depressed?" She shook her head. "God bless him, but he was a mess."

Rick squirmed as her description of Jack's life brushed too close to his own. He gestured toward the back of the trailer. "I boxed up his clothes and personal stuff. But you're going to need a truck and some strong backs to move all these records."

Carol shook her head. "I don't want 'em."

"They're probably worth ten or twenty thousand dollars," Rick said. "Maybe more."

"Not to me. I don't care about music. You keep 'em. I just came to get the stuff out of here like they asked." There was another crack of thunder but more distant this time and Carol stood to leave. "I'll just take the stuff you boxed up. And if you find out what happened to Jack, I'd appreciate it if you'd let me know." She stopped at the door to put on her coat. She turned back to Rick. "Oh, and if you find the car, you can give me a call, too."

Rick and Traci talked for a while after Carol left. They agreed that finding out what had happened to Captain Jack's car might give them clues to his fate, but they had no idea how to do this. Had it been abandoned somewhere, burned up on some back road with Jack in the trunk? Or perhaps driven into a lake with a cinder block on the accelerator and Jack strapped into the driver's seat?

Rick and Traci also realized that they needed to find out what they could about the Deckern County Sheriff's Department in case they found some real evidence and needed some cops who were unburdened by a conflict of interests.

Traci left a little before midnight. She needed to go back to her place so she could be ready for work the next day.

After she left, Rick stayed up for a while, listening to Uncle Victor, who was working a weather-themed set that went from Traffic's "Coloured Rain" to Dylan's "Shelter From the Storm," followed by Chi Coltrane's "Thunder and Lightning" and James Taylor's "Fire and Rain." Rick went to bed around two and eventually fell asleep to the sound of a steady thundershower.

He woke up around nine the next morning to ominous gray skies. He made some coffee and turned on the radio. The Allman Brothers were wrapping up their version of "Stormy Monday."

"Now, I know T-Bone Walker said Tuesday's just as bad," Rob said. "But according to the National Weather Service, it'll actually be a little better because right now we're officially under a tornado watch." Rob said this over storm sound effects playing in the background. "We've got some unstable conditions with warm, moist air colliding with cooler, dry air blowing down from up north. Remember," Rob said. "This is just a watch, which means the conditions are right for tornadoes to develop but none have been sighted. This watch is in effect until eleven o'clock for all of Deckern County, along with parts of Lamar, Forrest, Jones, and Jefferson Davis Counties. For the latest weather information, keep it tuned to one-oh-two-point-nine FM, WAOR." A swelling synthesizer washed up and over the howling wind sound effects as Rob launched REO Speedwagon's "Ridin' the Storm Out."

Rick looked out a window to see how bad it was. It was raining again and the gray clouds were growing black. He had some grim thoughts about living in a tornado magnet such as he did and he suddenly wondered if his was tied down. He was about to step outside to investigate when REO Speedwagon faded abruptly halfway through the second verse.

"Sorry to interrupt," Rob said. "But the National Weather Service has just issued a tornado *warning* for Deckern County. This is a *warning,* not a watch. This means a funnel cloud has been picked up on radar or was visually sighted. Be prepared to go to a basement or an interior room or hall in the lowest level of the building you're in. Stay away from windows. If you're in a low-lying area, be aware of possible flash flooding." Rob continued reading the standard tornado warning tips that Rick had read a thousand times.

Rick started to open the windows of the trailer to equalize the pressure in case one touched down nearby. He was trying to remember if the atmospheric pressure increased or decreased in a tornado when he realized that it didn't much matter if you were killed by an implosion or an explosion. *Wait a second,* he thought. *That's a myth.* By the time a tornado is centered over your trailer, the place has been subjected to 150-mile-an-hour winds loaded with lumber, livestock, and telephone poles. After that, the trailer's got all the ventilation holes it needs to equalize any pressure difference. With this in mind Rick moved away from the windows.

The wind was picking up serious velocity and it made Rick think about a station he worked at once, somewhere in the middle of Kansas. Out in the prairie states, you had the advantage of being able to see a tornado coming. In the middle of a pine forest, you can't see like that. They just drop out of the sky and you better not be in the way.

Rick had seen a lot of storms in his life but never anything like this. For a moment he thought he felt the trailer move. Maybe shifting on the foundation or—no, it was something else. The attached carport started vibrating as it strained against the wind, the fiberglass and thin aluminum struggling to survive the onslaught of all this energy. There was a tremulous, keening screech reminiscent of a Yoko record just before the carport detached from the trailer and started cartwheeling toward the woods.

Rick glanced outside and saw the tall pines bending in the gale. He knew if the winds grew strong enough the softwoods would snap and the hardwoods would come up roots and all. A moment later it sounded like rivets hitting the walls and the roof. Rick looked out the window and saw hail like jawbreakers stripping the paint off his unprotected truck. "Oh shit!" This was a bad sign. Large hail usually precedes a tornado. That was one of the axioms he remembered.

Rick knew he was supposed to get out of the trailer and go lie in a ditch but the nearest one he knew of was several hundred yards away. He'd be dead before he got there, beaten to death by the hail or impaled by something carried on the winds. Still, he had to do something. Problem was, he was too scared to move.

Whatever fear had been triggered by the hailstorm was dwarfed by the sound of the freight train that followed. It was a horrible rumbling sound that promised death in a deep clear voice. It was the unearthly roar of fifteen tons of pressure moving across the land. A window shattered and something hit the wall inside. Rick turned in a jerk and saw movement on the floor. It was a fox squirrel, shaking its head like a cartoon character before running to hide under the sofa.

For some reason this launched Rick out the door like a shot. Pelted by the hail and stung by flying debris, he ran in a straight line toward a shallow ravine, his arms covering his head. When he was close enough he dove and slid into the ditch, where he sank his fingers into the wet clay and started praying.

It was over before Rick got to "Amen." The National Weather Service would later classify it as a Category F-2 tornado with top winds of 150 miles per hour. It was on the ground for roughly half a mile with a track width of about fifty yards. The freight train rumbling lasted ten or fifteen seconds then disappeared faster than Sopwith Camel. Then it was just the sound of the rain and the noise a wet disc jockey makes when pulling himself out of a muddy ditch in south-central Mississippi.

Rick had some minor cuts and bruises but was otherwise all right. He stood outside the trailer and undressed, leaving his clothes in the rain to rinse off the mud. Before he went inside he got down on his knees to look under the trailer. It was tied down.

Rick put on some sweats and chased the squirrel out the door. Then he rigged a makeshift patch for his broken window. He put on a raincoat then went out to his truck to assess the damage. He shook his head when he saw what the hail had done to his new windshield. He reached into his toolbox and grabbed his tire iron, then pried the busted glass out and tossed it by the side of the trailer. After that he strapped on his trusty goggles and headed for work.

Traci was at the reception desk looking through a file when Rick walked in and asked her to call the windshield replacement people again. Without looking up, she said, "Is the other one leaking in all this rain?"

"Yeah," Rick said. "Pretty bad, too."

"Oh!" She looked up from what she was doing and said, "Did you know we had a tornado warning about an hour ago?"

"Yeah, I got wind of it."

"Apparently a couple of them touched down but no reports of injuries so far."

Rick feigned immediate indignation. "Whaddya mean no injuries!" He touched a scratch on his cheek. "What does this look like?"

Traci leaned forward, squinting. "Shaving accident?"

"Oh fine, trivialize my trauma. I'm lucky I didn't end up in Munchkinland."

It took her a second but Traci leaned forward, a shocked look on her face. "You mean it was out at your place? Ohmigod, what happened?"

Rick waved her off like it was nothing. "Oh, no big deal really. Peeled the carport off the end of the trailer but I rode it out."

Traci looked at him skeptically. "Did it really or you just jerkin' my chain?"

Rick smiled as he gestured at the file on her desk. "What's that?"

"Oh, yeah. I decided to do some poking around while Clay was out." Traci tapped her finger on the file. "Guess who bought a huge run-of-schedule about a week before Captain Jack stopped coming to work?"

Rick pointed at Traci. "Universal Financial Services is the answer to your prayers."

"You bet. And at drive-time rates," Traci said. "Before that they'd never spent more than five hundred a month buying seven to midnight."

"What's the commission?"

"Doesn't say."

"Does it usually?"

"Yep."

Rick sat on the corner of her desk. "Okay, so maybe it's a payoff. Bernie paying Clay for getting rid of Captain Jack? Something like that?"

Traci shrugged and said, "Seems like a clumsy way to do it. But then again, he's not exactly Rico Suave." Her eyes looked past Rick when she saw Clay's Crown Victoria pull into the lot. "Uh-oh. Salesman of the decade's back," Traci said as she slipped the file back into the drawer.

A moment later Clay blustered through the front door and crossed to where Rick was pretending to look at phone messages. Rick looked up. "Oh, hey, what's going on?"

Clay tossed a copy of the *McRae Monitor* on Traci's desk. "Ya'll see this yet?" The paper was folded open to a picture of Clay handing the big check to Ken Stigler at the park. Rick and Joni Lang were standing behind the check. "That's some good publicity there," Clay said.

Rick picked it up and looked. "Not bad." He handed it to Traci.

Clay nudged Rick and nodded toward the parking lot. "The hell happened to your truck?"

"Same thing that happened to your trailer," Rick said. "Big-ass hailstorm and a little twister. I was just telling Traci. It snatched off the carport."

"Aww, shit," Clay said as he grabbed his messages and started for his office. "I got like a damn five-hundred-dolla deductible on that." He disappeared down the hall for a moment then came back. "Is it like . . . gone? Or is it just bent up or pushed across the field there or what?"

Rick gestured to infinity and said, "Way gone."

"Well, damn. Tch." Clay seemed to struggle with a small thought for a moment before he looked at Rick and said, "Hey, do me a favor. Take a walk around and see if you can't find it out there. Maybe we can haul the thing back and put it up good as new." He rapped his knuckles on the door frame then headed down the hall.

Traci said, "I'm glad you didn't get hurt."

Rick acted like a wounded schoolboy, touching his cheek lightly. "I did get hurt a little."

"Well, I'll kiss your boo-boos later," Traci said. "Meanwhile I'll get the windshield guys out here then I'll call around and see if I can find out what happens

to abandoned cars in Deckern County." She reached
for the phone book. "What're you gonna do?"

"Me? I've got a regular job."

Rick was playing Supertramp's "Crime of the Century" and thinking about what Traci had learned that
afternoon. According to her source, cars abandoned in
Deckern County were towed and the owner-of-record
notified. If the owner failed to respond in sixty days,
the car was sold at auction. Traci had a friend in the
used car business who frequented the monthly auction.
She was going to check with him to see if he remembered any torch-red Corvettes on the block since Captain Jack's disappearance.

As Rick went into Thin Lizzy's "Call the Police," he
realized he didn't hold out much hope on finding the
Corvette. Since the car, or lack thereof, seemed unlikely to provide any leads, Rick wondered who or
what might provide some. There was still the Lady of
the Golden Shower and there was also Tammy Callaway. Rick didn't think either of them knew what had
happened to Captain Jack but he still wanted to talk to
them.

As "Call the Police" circled the turntable, Rick had a
sudden inspiration that sent him deep into the archives
looking for an obscure version of a song that had made
Bobby Fuller a star back in 1966. Rick found the
Ducks Deluxe album *Don't Mind Rockin' Tonight,* cued
their raucous version of "I Fought the Law," and let it
fly. His inspiration for playing the song had come from
the suspicious circumstances of Bobby Fuller's death
in Los Angeles in July 1966.

According to the L.A. County Coroner's Office, Bobby Fuller was found lying facedown in the front seat of an Oldsmobile, covered in gasoline. The windows and doors were shut but not locked and there was an open can of gas in the backseat. The autopsy said there was extensive bruising on Fuller's chest and shoulders and a witness testified that his right index finger was broken, as if it had been bent back until it snapped. Naturally, the Los Angeles Police Department said there was no evidence of foul play and ruled the death a suicide.

Rick considered suicide for a moment. Not for himself but for Captain Jack. His sister had said he was depressed. Serious drug users had been known to do themselves in. Put the two together and . . . paging Kurt Cobain . . . but, no, it didn't add up. Suicides don't usually hide themselves. You just find 'em with their heads in the oven or wherever they were at the time. That Captain Jack had been engaged in blackmail just prior to his demise also pointed to murder instead of suicide. So while Bobby Fuller's story hadn't shed any light on Rick's investigation, it had led to a good song for his Crime and Punishment set. As "I Fought the Law" neared its end, Rick cued Clapton's version of "I Shot the Sheriff."

Dismissing suicide, Rick was back to murder. Who had he not talked to? He felt a sudden pang of disappointment. On the day of the radio station promotion he had meant to ask Joni Lang if she knew any Tammys on the local pageant circuit. It was a long shot but that's all he had. He made a note to call her later, then turned his mind back to his show.

He came out of a spot break singing the praises of Al

Kooper. "He's one of those guys whose music you remember but whose name you don't," Rick said. "In 1965 he had a hit when Gary Lewis and the Playboys recorded his song 'This Diamond Ring.' That same year he played on Dylan's 'Like a Rolling Stone.' He went on to play with and produce a few bands you loved but never realized he had anything to do with. So let's start in 1966 with a song he wrote for the Blues Project, one of those underground radio chestnuts. Here's 'Flute Thing' on WAOR-FM."

Rick followed that with "I Love You More Than You'll Know" from Blood, Sweat and Tears and then went on to Kooper and Bloomfield's version of the Ray Charles standard "Mary Ann." About halfway through the song Rick took a call from an irate listener who complained about Al Kooper's lack of relevance to rock 'n' roll. "You oughta play some damn 'Freebird' or somethin'," he said.

"Ahhh," Rick said, "a Skynyrd fan."

"Hell yeah!"

"Me, too. Loved their first album."

"That's what I'm talking about! That thing rocks!"

"You know those guys started playing together in '65? Called themselves My Backyard."

"Yeah, but then they named themselves after that gym teacher who was always givin' 'em shit about their long hair."

"Yeah, and they played all over the South for years without a single record company tryin' to sign 'em up."

"Yeah, but somebody finally did, man."

"And it was the same guy that produced their first album."

"Hell yeah," the caller said. "Sumbitch knew what he was doin', too!"

"Damn right," Rick said. "You know who that was?"

"Uhhh, I dunno, like Duane Allman?"

"It doesn't matter," Rick said. "I tell you what. I'll play you something off Skynyrd's first record. How's that?"

"Hell yeah," the caller said before hanging up.

A few minutes later Rick came on the air and said, "That's a little somethin' sweet from Lynyrd Skynyrd's first album. A song called 'Mississippi Kid,' cowritten by the guy who discovered them. The same guy who produced their first three albums. He also played on the Stones' *Let It Bleed* and Hendrix's *Electric Ladyland,* sometimes under the pseudonym Roosevelt Gook. Of course his real name was . . . Al Kooper." He let that sink in for a second before he started the next record and said, "You're listening to WAOR-FM. I'm Rick Shannon and we're gettin' at the roots of classic rock. Here's Neil Young from *Tonight's the Night.*"

Rick took his headphones off and looked at the blinking request line. He was off the air in ten minutes, so there was no way he could play any requests but he figured he could leave a note for Uncle Victor. He picked up the phone and said, "AOR."

"Hello." It was a woman.

"Howdy," Rick said. "What can I do for you?"

"I saw your picture in the paper today," she said.

Rick thought he recognized her voice. "Yes, well, unfortunately they didn't get my good side."

"They didn't get your name right either." She paused. "Or did they?"

Rick hesitated, trying to figure out who she was. "Okay," he said. "I'll bite. What is my real name?"

"You told me it was Buddy Miles." That narrowed it down. It was Donna Moore. "And I'll tell you what else," she said. "The guy who won the thousand dollars? His name's not Ken Stigler."

11

Rick and Donna agreed to meet after he got off the air. On his way out of the station, he grabbed the newspaper off Traci's desk. He got in his truck and headed for Kitty's Road Café wondering what was going through Donna's mind. She had used a vaguely threatening tone during their brief conversation. What was she trying to insinuate? It obviously had something to do with the fact that he'd lied about his name.

It hadn't occurred to Rick that anyone who knew him as Buddy Miles would see his picture in the paper. But he wasn't inordinately worried about Donna's discovery of his dual identity since it had no bearing on the thing she was most concerned about. Holly Creel was still missing and Rick was still Donna's best bet to find out what had happened. The thing Rick was most curious about was why the contest winner had two names.

Donna was sitting in a booth waiting for him. He slid into the seat opposite her and tossed the paper onto the table just as a waitress arrived with a piece of pecan pie and a cup of coffee. Rick ordered tater wads and a beer.

After the waitress left, Donna looked at the photo in the newspaper and then at Rick.

"So," she said. "Who is Buddy Miles?"

"It's my nom de private eye," Rick said. "Took the name from a drummer who played with Jimi Hendrix. Remember *Them Changes*?" Donna shook her head. "It's a great album," Rick said. "In fact it's one of the best from 1970, which was a pretty good year. I mean, *Layla, Cosmos Factory, Moondance, John Barleycorn—*"

Donna held up a hand to interrupt. "Listen, if I said something to make you think I'm even vaguely interested in knowing this, I apologize."

"Oh, right, sorry," Rick said. "Anyway, I figured since I was using Rick Shannon on the air, I'd better use a different name for my private investigation persona."

"Uh-huh. And who is Rick Shannon?"

"That would be me."

"Is that your real name?"

Rick pointed at the caption under the newspaper photo. "That's what it says there."

"That might just be your radio name."

Rick smiled and said, "Well, yeah. But enough about me." He tapped the picture of the contest winner. "Let's talk about *this* guy's real name. He's a friend of yours?"

Donna shook her head. "Rents equipment from me now and then." She nodded at the newspaper. "When I saw that, it caught my eye 'cause I usually don't know anybody whose picture is in the paper. So when I saw *two* faces I recognized, well, it got my attention. And then I saw that the two names in the caption didn't match the names in my head. So I thought, this is interesting." She leaned toward Rick. "Now *I* get to put the squeeze on somebody."

"I don't follow you," Rick said, genuinely confused.

"Come off it," Donna, said. "You rigged the contest."

"What?"

"Did you split it fifty-fifty? I suspect DeWayne mighta gone for seventy-thirty." Donna's eyes darted side to side, gauging Rick's reaction to her accusation. "But then maybe Clay's in on it, too," she said. "'Cause I'm not sure you've been here long enough to find somebody as back in the woods as DeWayne without some local help, and hell, who knows, maybe that girl's in on it, too." Donna forked a piece of pie and held it up. "You know, everybody gets a little piece." She slowly put the pie into her mouth and chewed for a moment, staring at Rick all the while. Then she picked up her coffee mug and gestured with it, saying, "It doesn't matter. What's important is, I'm the one that gets to do the blackmailing now." She sipped her coffee.

"You're not serious," Rick said.

"No?" She put her coffee cup down. "Tell me there's not something suspicious about two people using bogus names involved in a contest where one of 'em's givin' money away and the other one's winnin' it."

Rick had never considered the possibility that the contest was rigged. But he was thinking about it now. "Okay," he said, "from that perspective, I see your point. But the fact is, I only used the bogus name when I came to see you the other day. But this guy, Duane?"

"DeWayne," Donna said. "DeWayne Ragsdale."

"He's the one using the bogus name at the contest, not me."

"And why should I believe you? Isn't that exactly what I should expect you to say if you *did* rig the contest?"

"I guess it is, but think about it. I wasn't in a position to fix it. Joni Lang pulled the name from the barrel and Stubblefield announced it. If anybody fixed the contest, it was your old buddy Clay, or maybe the girl, but I don't think so. She didn't strike me as the type. Besides," Rick said, "if I ever go to rig a contest, it's going to be for more than a thousand bucks." The waitress slid Rick's plate of tater wads and his beer onto the table. When she left he said, "So if you wanna blackmail somebody, you better go for DeWayne and Clay." He popped one of the hot tater wads into his mouth in a sort of punctuation to the end of his argument. Unfortunately, the thing was still about 350 degrees. It shot out of his mouth like a musket ball. "Yaowww!"

Donna had to laugh at Rick's pained expression. He grabbed his glass of beer and stuck his tongue into it, hoping to relieve the sting. After a moment he looked up at her and said, "You know, you need to keep more of a straight face if you want to look like a serious blackmailer."

She shook her head. "I don't wanna blackmail anybody. I just wanted to see your reaction when I said it. Wanted to see if I was right about you." She shrugged.

"And maybe I wanted to see how it felt at the other end of the stick."

"And?"

"It's pretty scummy." Donna picked up the knife from her flatware set and tilted it back and forth, looking at her reflection in the blade. She looked tired. "I don't think I'm cut out for that line of work." She pointed the knife at Rick and said, "How about you?"

Rick seemed to consider it for a moment. "Well, a couple of things come to mind. First of all, the risk-to-reward ratio is no good, just ask Captain Jack." Rick picked up another tater wad and blew on it, trying to cool it down. "And second, it's not enough."

"What's not enough?"

"It's not enough to prove that Clay fixed a two-bit radio contest, though you're probably right about that. But proving it doesn't give us any leverage against him. He's not likely to confess to murder in order to keep from being charged with rigging a contest for a thousand bucks."

"No, I guess not," Donna said. "But maybe De-Wayne knows something about Clay's other activities." She gave Rick a coy look and said, "Maybe I should hire a private detective to look into that."

Rick smiled. "Maybe you should."

"You recommend anybody?"

"I know a guy named Buddy Miles."

"Is he any good?"

"He's cheap. And he's motivated."

"That's a good combination."

Rick nodded and looked down at his beer for a moment before he said, "Do you happen to know where Mr. DeWayne Ragsdale lives?"

Donna smiled and pulled a piece of paper from a pocket. "I thought you'd never ask."

Eight hours later, Rick's radio alarm woke him up to the chiming finger cymbals and jangly strings of bouzouki and balalaika of Jethro Tull's "Fat Man." As that led into the halting backbeat of Little Feat's "Fat Man in the Bathtub," Rick dragged himself into his kitchen to make breakfast. He was about to butter his toast when Randy Newman came on singing about "Davy the Fat Boy." Rick looked down and put his hand on his stomach. Maybe it was time to adjust his diet.

Rick put the butter away and had his toast dry with some black coffee. He looked out to the woods and thought about taking a walk for some much-needed exercise, and as long as he was out there, he'd look for the carport that had blown off in the storm. Unfortunately he had to get to work. He wanted to tell Traci about his chat with Donna Moore and find out if she'd heard from her friend in the used car business. The exercise would have to wait.

"You've outdone yourself," Rick said when he saw Traci. She'd created a sexy sort of Cat Woman effect with her eyeliner and mascara.

Traci made a suggestive cat noise and said, "Kitty needs some love."

"I could make a scratching-post joke," Rick said. "But I think you'd rather hear about my meeting with Donna Moore late last night."

"What? Why didn't you—" Traci held up a finger when the phone rang. She pushed a button on the switchboard. "Dubya-ay-oh-ahhr," she said. "Mmm. Hold please." She directed the call then looked back at Rick. "Ohmigod, what'd she say?"

Rick told her about DeWayne Ragsdale and how it looked like Clay had fixed the contest. He handed her the newspaper he'd taken from her desk the night before. She looked at the photo but said she didn't recognize the guy. "You think he knows something?"

"Bound to know something," Rick said. "Question is, does he know something useful? And would he tell me if he did?"

"You gonna talk to him?"

"Not yet," Rick said. "I wanna talk to Joni Lang first. I think she might have seen something." He picked up the Rolodex and found her number.

"Oh, by the way," Traci said. "My friend said there hasn't been a Corvette up for auction in over a year. He said he'd know, too, 'cause he'd have bought it."

Rick gave that a moment's thought. "Well, that's too bad. Woulda been nice to find it."

Traci glanced over her shoulder to see if anyone was coming down the hall before she said, "Also, I called Tammy Callaway to ask her if she knows anything about . . ." She lowered her voice here. ". . . about the woman Clay said wanted him to pee on her. But she wasn't there, so I left a message for her to call me back."

"I'd love to know how you're gonna phrase that question."

Traci waved a hand, dismissing his concern. "Oh, me and Tammy got to be pretty good friends while she was here. She quit because Clay wouldn't stop playing grab-ass with her. If she's got any dirt on him, she'll shovel it my way."

Rick's expression changed abruptly. "Hey, today's payday, right?"

"Yeah, but not till after three."

"That's okay, I'm not looking for the check." Rick headed for the hallway.

The bookkeeper wasn't in. Rick went over to the gray metal filing cabinet and opened a drawer. He read the file labels until he came across one that said: CON-TEST W-9S. He pulled the file and looked inside. There were several W-9 forms from earlier cash giveaways but nothing for Ken Stigler or DeWayne Ragsdale.

"Lookin' for something?" It was the bookkeeper, standing in the doorway.

"Yeah," Rick said. "My paycheck." He shoved the file back in the drawer and closed it.

"You're not going to find it in there." The book-keeper crossed the room and opened the drawer, forcing Rick to step aside. The bookkeeper saw the W-9 file out of place. He pulled it out, then filed it properly before shutting and locking the cabinet. "Your check'll be in your employee mail slot after three. Meanwhile I'd appreciate it if you'd keep your nose outta my drawers." The two men looked at each other briefly before the bookkeeper said, "You know what I mean."

Rick went back to his office to do an air-check review with Autumn before she started her shift. He hit the play button on the cassette player and said, "Just listen." James Taylor's "Mud Slide Slim" was shuffling toward its end when David Bowie and Mick Ronson came roaring in with "Star" from *Ziggy Stardust*. Rick stopped the tape. "See now, that's a bit jarring," he said. "You might have found something a little softer to follow JT."

Autumn held her hands up in defense. "Somebody requested Bowie," she said. "I'm just trying to give folks what they want."

"I understand." Rick held up copies of the two albums. "Come with me." He led her to the production room. "Not that you usually want to follow JT with the thin White Duke, but if you do, you might try something like this." He put the needle near the end of *Mud Slide Slim* then cued "Rock and Roll Suicide" by Bowie. As James Taylor faded out, Rick started the Bowie. A slowly strummed acoustic guitar took over from JT, making a nice transition from one to the other.

"Hey, that's pretty good," Autumn said. "I just went with a song I knew off of *Ziggy*."

"If you're not familiar with a record, just drop the needle at the start of all the tracks and listen for something that sort of matches the end of what you're playing."

After Autumn went on the air, Rick met with J.C. They had their usual arguments. J.C. once again accused Rick of trying to stifle his on-air personality. Rick reminded him that the format was more about music than personality. "And speaking of the music," he said. "I'm still hearing a lot more metal than I'd like."

"Well, you know, sometimes I feel like it's my job to keep the station from sounding like a twenty-four-hour-a-day folk festival. But I'll work on it."

Afterward Rick called Joni Lang. His pretext was

wanting to discuss the possibility of Joni participating in another station promotion. He asked if they could meet that afternoon but she said she was busy until seven. For a minute Rick thought she was giving him the runaround but then she offered to come down to the station while he was on the air that night. "But only if your general manager isn't going to be there," she said.

Rick remembered how Clay had palmed Joni's ass at the park that day and figured she didn't want any more of that. He assured Joni that Clay wouldn't be at the station after five.

He started his shift at eight. Autumn stayed for a few minutes while she filed her CDs and records before she said good night. On her way out the door, Rick asked her to kill the overhead lights. There were several light configurations that helped create different moods in the on-air studio. Different jocks preferred different lighting. Autumn liked to work under full brights, in this case a row of fluorescent tubes overhead. Rick had always favored a darker room. He switched on the cool blue and red spotlights over the control board. Off to the side was a desk lamp on a dimmer that he brought up to the glow of a few candles. It soothed him and put him in the right mood for the music.

Rick started the nine o'clock hour with Gino Vanelli's "Storm at Sunup." Joni arrived a few minutes later. She was wearing jeans and a Hard Rock Café (Las Vegas) T-shirt. It was late enough for Rick to start playing longer songs, which would give them an opportunity to talk with fewer interruptions. Hearing the end of "Storm at Sunup" in his mind, he pulled *Quadrophenia* and cued side four.

They made small talk for a few minutes while Rick waited to get into The Who. Joni allowed as how her last name was really Langevoort. "I shortened it to Lang for entertainment industry purposes," she said.

Rick went into The Who, overlapping the storm sound effects for the easy segue. "Doctor Jimmy," "The Rock," and "Love Reign O'er Me" would play for twenty-one minutes. He turned the monitors down and spun around in his chair. He spoke matter-of-factly, going for a lawyerly tone. "Joni? I have to tell you. I lied about why I wanted to talk to you."

"Don't worry about it," Joni said, point-blank. "I lied when I said I'd be interested in doing another promotion with your station."

"Oh?"

"Yeah." She looked at him skeptically. "I hope you didn't invite me down here to hit on me."

"Uhh, no." Rick shook his head and assumed a severe countenance. "I wanted to talk to you about a possible legal matter." He leaned forward and dropped his voice. "In fact, there may be an investigation by the Federal Communications Commission and I wanted to—"

"Is it about the contest?"

"Yes, it is."

"Good, because I saw something and I wanted to tell somebody but I didn't know who. I thought about going to the police but I saw Stubblefield talking with the cops at the park that day and it looked like they were pretty friendly. So I thought about getting a lawyer, but, well, here's what happened," she said. "I drew the first two names and he read 'em, and then I drew the third name and I handed it to him. But he did a switch."

Joni mimicked Clay's awkward hand movements. "He had another one of the entry forms in his other hand. That's the name he called out. Later, I saw him toss something in the trash and I pulled it out and looked at it to make sure I wasn't imagining things."

"Do you still have it?"

She nodded. "Yeah, I just didn't know what to do with it."

Rick told Joni to keep the winning entry form in a secure place, a safe-deposit box if she had one. "The FCC will be in touch about your testimony when the time comes," he said with far more authority than he had.

Of course the FCC didn't know anything about the contest, at least not yet. But Rick knew there was a rule requiring broadcast stations to fully disclose the material terms of any contest or promotion they conducted. Failure to disclose that the contest was fixed was an obvious violation. He wondered if basic fraud statutes might also apply. In any event, Rick would contact the feds when the time was right. Meanwhile Joni seemed to be growing anxious about things and Rick thought that invoking a federal bureaucracy would be comforting in some way.

"Am I in any danger?"

"Nooooo." Rick gave an exaggerated frown and shook his head. "Don't worry about that. He has no idea he's under investigation." He wrote something on a piece of paper and handed it to her. "Here's my cell number. Call if you need me."

Joni took the number and said she would make herself available to federal authorities when the time came and that she'd keep the evidence in a safe place in the meanwhile. "But there's something I don't understand," she said. "Are you, like, an undercover cop or something? I don't get why you're the one telling me this instead of the FCC people."

"My reputation's at stake," Rick said. "I'm the program director, and when it hits the trade papers that this station ran a fixed contest, it's also going to say that I'm the one who brought it to the attention of the authorities. Otherwise I'm out of the radio business and there's precious little else I'm qualified to do." This was the first time he had bothered to look at it this way and there was more than a little truth in his appraisal. The trade papers would certainly give bigger play to the murder plot if it was proved in court, but the rigged contest on Rick's watch would be in there, too, so he actually did need to cover himself.

"That makes sense," Joni said. "It's sorta like if people found out a girl won a scholarship pageant because she curried favor with the judges." She shook her head. "She'd never qualify for another pageant."

"Yeah," Rick said, thinking back to some of the opportunities Clay talked about when he was a pageant judge. "It's sorta like that."

Joni stood. "Listen, thanks for your help," she said. "It's good to know there are still a few honest people out there." Rick demurred at the comment, since he'd been less than honest with her. Joni looked around the studio for a moment. A look of delight sparkled in her eyes and she said, "Hey, could you play a request for me, while I'm driving home?"

"Sure. What?"

"Could you play that Steve Miller song about Billy

Joe and Bobby Sue who shot a man while robbin' his castle? I love that song."

Rick found himself comforted knowing that radio still had the power to make people smile that way.

After playing Joni's request, Rick veered off in the direction of "Boogie Chillen" and the guitar riff that he figured was the jumping-off point for more "classic rock" songs than any other. John Lee Hooker ended up with most of the credit but the riff had been around since at least Charlie Patton or Blind Blake and the turn of the twentieth century. Rick started with ZZ Top's "La Grange." At the break two-thirds through the song he segued into "Shake Your Hips" from *Exile on Main Street*, then, at the break in that one, Rick went back to the ZZ Top without missing a beat. He came out of that into Canned Heat's "Woodstock Boogie" and went on from there.

The phones had been pretty slow for the past hour but around eleven the request line started blinking. Rick picked up the handset and said, "AOR."

"Kitty still needs some love," Traci said before making the suggestive cat sound again.

Rick felt a surge of blood and he said, "Hubba hubba. Meet me at my place?"

"Can't," Traci said. "I'm baby-sitting."

"Okay, how 'bout I come over there?"

"Can't, I'm—"

"You're baby-sitting, I know, but it's not like I'm proposing that we do anything in front of the child."

"Kitty's gonna need some love tomorrow night, too."

"Yes, but will Kitty be baby-sitting?"

"Nope."

"Then it's a date." Rick paused before he said, "Is that why you called?"

"Nope."

He waited for her to continue. When she didn't he said, "Do I have to put on a really long record and come over there and pull this out of you with a pair of needle-nose pliers?"

"I hope not."

"Then what's it gonna take?"

"Play me a song."

"Name it."

"No. You pick one."

A record came to mind and he snickered. "You sure?"

"I'll call you back after you play it."

Rick finished the "Boogie Chillen" set before playing Traci's song. Then he cleared his throat, turned on his mike, and said, "Tommy Bolin with the title track from his 1975 album, *Teaser*. And you know who you are." The request line started blinking immediately. "Well, the phone lines are lighting up now," Rick said. "So let's get back to the music. This next little gem was produced by Jimi Hendrix, though he doesn't play on it, which is a pure shame. Here's Cat Mother and the All Night News Boys with 'Good Old Rock and Roll' on WAOR-FM." He pulled off his head phones and picked up the phone. "AOR."

"Bet you think you're pretty funny," Traci said.

"Hey, you told me to pick, so I picked. Now, what were you going to tell me?"

"Would it have killed you to play something romantic?"

"I'll do that after you tell me whatever it is."

"Okay, you're gonna love this," Traci said. "I heard back from Tammy Callaway."

"What'd you tell her?"

"That somebody told me that they overheard Clay telling somebody else about some girl that wanted him to come back to her motel room and pee on her. And she knew exactly what I was talking about."

"Get out."

"Picture this," Traci said. "It was that beauty pageant down on the coast, right? All the girls and judges and promoters were havin' this prepageant reception and cocktail party. So, Tammy and this girl named Melinda something or other, Tammy couldn't remember the girl's last name, but the two of them were talking to Clay and a couple other men who were going to judge the thing. They were talking about fitness and makeup and Botox and all that kinda stuff when this Melinda girl mentioned a news story she'd heard about how there's a chemical in urine that doctors said helped reduce wrinkles. Well, Clay just jumped all over that, Tammy said. He wouldn't shut up makin' all these dumb comments. He started nudgin' the other judges and winkin' at 'em and sayin' stuff like how he'd be glad to go on back to Melinda's room and piss on her if that was the sort of thing she was into. Two hours later Tammy heard him tellin' the story to somebody else, just like he does on the tape."

"Boy's got an overactive imagination."

"That'd be a charitable way of lookin' at it, I guess."

"And that's it?"

"That's it, except that Tammy and Melinda lost to some girl named Mitzi."

"Didn't say anything about blackmail?"

"Well, since Clay was makin' the whole story up, I couldn't see there was anything to blackmail her with, so I didn't ask."

"Good point," Rick said. "So where does that leave us?"

"Leaves us trying to figure out what to do with Bernie and Clay. And leaves you playing me something romantic."

"Coming up," Rick said. "By the way, did you like the "Boogie Chillen" set?"

"I did," Traci said. "But right now I'm more interested in a hoochie-coochie man."

Rick decided to make Traci's the last song of his show. But what would he play? Over the years, he had shown a tendency, when smitten, to play fabulous, if sappy, old nuggets like Jim Croce's "I'll Have to Say I Love You in a Song." Its melody and lyrics had an undeniable romanticism, at least to some ears. But Rick's experience had taught him that one woman's romantic was another's puerile sentimentalism. He knew if he went too sweet, he'd come across as a dewy-eyed schoolboy, not exactly the image he wanted to convey. So he decided to avoid that school of song altogether.

Next he considered playing something tender but ambiguous. A pretty song with vague lyrics, open to interpretation. Something that wouldn't make him sound like a stalker if read in open court. Not that such things were likely to happen, but as Rick liked to say, it was a funny world and one just never knew. After thinking on it for a minute, Crosby, Stills and Nash's "Helplessly Hoping" came to mind with its exquisite harmonies, sweet melody, and harmlessly hopeful lyrics. But when he looked at the clock he realized that from where he was, the 2:38 of the CSN would leave him two minutes shy of midnight, which was one of those things he just couldn't do.

He needed something in the five-minute range and he needed it quick. The song he was playing was thirty seconds from its cold ending. Rick didn't have time to weigh the possible impact of any lyrics of a song that fit his time requirements, so he took the easy way out. He grabbed *Abraxas* and cued the sensual "Samba Pa Ti."

Rick walked into the station the next day and stopped dead in his tracks. Traci was sitting at her desk with the most elaborately made-up eyes he had seen since the last Kiss tour. She tilted her head just so and said, "How did you know I love that song?"

"I'm a professional," he said. "I just know these things." Privately, he was thinking, *Phew*.

"That was the song that was playing the first time I . . ." Traci decided not to say the words, instead she made a happy thrusting motion in her chair that made the point. "Anyway—"

Both of them jumped when they heard a violent thud against the common wall shared by Clay's office and the reception area. Rick imagined the dent Clay's thick glass ashtray must've put in that old paneling. This was followed by the sound of muffled yelling, but not so muffled that you couldn't understand Clay saying, "Goddammit, Lori! Look at what you did! I am so tired of this shit, I can't tell you!"

Mrs. Stubblefield's voice pitched to high indignation. "*You're* tired? I don't doubt it, all the 'business' trips you take! You think you're so damn slick, but you're not. Don't think for a minute I don't know what's going on. And don't think I won't call that lawyer either!"

"Go on then, call," Clay said. "You need a dime? Here's a handful. But you ain't gonna call nobody and we both know it, so just go on, get outta here. I got work to do. Jesus!"

Traci grabbed at the stack of mail on her desk and slapped a copy of *Billboard* into Rick's hands. "Read!" He buried his face in the charts while Traci feigned a phone conversation. "Yes, of course," she said. "I can fax a rate card right away. If you can hold while I get . . ."

Lori Stubblefield stormed through the lobby and hit the door at full speed, rattling the glass. A moment later Rick and Traci heard squealing tires. Rick went to the door to watch as she fishtailed onto the street. He turned and gave Traci a look of concern. Traci said, "Don't worry about it. They do this every month or so."

"*Do* they?" Rick looked back and forth between the hallway leading to Clay's office and the front door. "Interesting," he said, almost to himself.

Traci held up her hands. "It's not my problem and I don't ask." She started separating the mail into different stacks. "Some people just think that's a normal way to behave."

Rick shook his head at that before saying, "By the way, there's no W-9 on file for the contest winner."

"Is that good or bad?"

"Anytime you give away over six hundred dollars, you're required to get a signed W-9, and issue a 1099 at year's end. I don't think you're required to get the W-9 immediately, but it's usually done when you hand over the money, so it looks suspicious."

"But it doesn't prove the contest was fixed."

"No, it doesn't. That's why I wanted to talk to Joni Lang, who, it just so happens, paid me a little visit last night."

Traci dropped the stack of mail and looked sharply at Rick. "She did? When?"

"Just before you called."

"Why didn't you tell me last night?"

"I was trying to get laid last night," Rick said.

Traci fixed him with deadly eyes. "Trying to get laid by whom?"

"By youm," he said, mocking her tone. "All that talk about kitty still needs some love and that sexy little cat noise you make . . . had me distracted or I'd've told you."

"Did Miss Loblolly Pine have anything useful to say?"

"Better than that. She has some evidence." Rick recounted Joni's story about Clay palming the entry form. "She's keeping it in a safe—" He stopped when he heard Clay's voice. He was in the hall talking to one of the salesmen and it sounded like he was heading toward the lobby. "Film at eleven," Rick said as he grabbed his mail. "I'll be in production if anybody needs me." He went down the hall toward his office and the studios.

There was a short stack of national spots to dub, some of which required local voice tags. As Rick prepped his work, something occurred to him, and for the first time since Captain Jack's sister visited, he thought to look for a phone patch in the production-room board. None of the pots were labeled PHONE, so he lifted the cover and looked at the guts. There were a couple of wires that had the distressed look of having been yanked out with no small amount of fury. He traced them back and, sure enough, they led to the phone.

It was more evidence but not the kind Rick thought he needed. What he needed was to find Captain Jack's body stuffed inside the board with a note in his pocket explaining where to find the rest of the evidence. Then he'd have something to work with. A couple of frayed wires in a ratty old mixing board weren't going to prove anything.

Rick did the first three spots and was about to lay down a voice track on a fourth when the phone line for the production room started blinking. He paused everything, pulled off his headphones, and picked up the phone. "Production."

"Rick? It's Donna Moore," she said in an urgent whisper. "Have you been out there yet?"

"You mean DeWayne's house? No, not yet. I was thinking about—"

"Stop thinking and go," she said. "He's here right now. Renting equipment for a job he's doing this afternoon."

Rick threw all the production orders back in his in-box and said, "I'm on my way." He was out of the station in five minutes. Ten minutes later he was barreling down a county road looking for a landmark that Donna mentioned in her directions, specifically a double-wide trailer with a front door awning fashioned from the hood of a truck. That's where he was supposed to turn right. Down that road three miles was the driveway Rick was looking for. He stopped at the mailbox. There was no name on it. He stepped out of his truck and looked inside. A handful of junk mail and an electric bill addressed to Mr. DeWayne Ragsdale.

Rick pulled in. He didn't know if there was a Mrs. Ragsdale or a pack of junkyard dogs to deal with or perhaps both. He parked next to a rusting Plymouth Duster mounted on the traditional cinder blocks. As he sat in his truck looking at the property, he couldn't help but think he'd been lied to. On more than one occasion, people born and raised right here in Mississippi had told him that nobody in the Magnolia State really lived in a place like this. "That's all just negative stereotyping," they said. But here he was, looking at it. Rick came to the conclusion that if anybody was guilty of perpetuating this sort of cliché, it was the likes of DeWayne Ragsdale.

It was a single wide, white with rusting trim. There were several tires on the roof and more strewn about the ... *What would you call it?* Rick wondered. It wasn't a lawn or a yard, it was just dirt, weeds, and trash under a canopy of pine trees. Mostly fast-food containers, beer cans, and cigarette cartons. There was also a cheap bench press with 120 pounds on the bar and an olive-green washing machine that had been tilted against a tree and used for frequent target practice.

Rick got out of his truck and went to the door. He figured if there were dogs they'd've been on him by now and if a woman answered the door he'd just act surprised, put on his best *Hee Haw* accent, and ask for Billy Bob. When no one answered his knock, Rick tried the door. It was locked.

He looked through the front window. The nicotine film coating the other side of the glass lent the living room an old-fashioned sepia-tone appearance. Rick could see an old sofa in front of a big-screen television. There was also a rack of expensive-looking stereo gear and a tall stack of DVDs and CDs, all of which Rick suspected DeWayne had acquired for less than the full retail price. Or maybe he'd used his cash prize for some of it.

Rick circled around the side of the trailer, checking each window, but they were all locked. Peeking inside the various rooms, he thought of Neil Young and he began to sing one from the *Harvest* album. *A man needs a maid.*

He came around to the rear of the place and saw an aluminum toolshed and a big lump of camouflage in the backyard, which turned out to be a car under an ill-fitting boat cover. He lifted the camouflage and found himself looking at a Corvette. As best he could tell, it was a 1996. Jet black. Rick checked the doors. They were locked. The windows were tinted but he could still see inside. There was a shoe box on the passenger seat, full of cassettes. Rick thought, *Who listens to cassettes anymore?* Then he had another thought. He pulled out the keys to his truck and scraped at the Corvette's paint job. Underneath the jet black, it was torch red.

12

Rick handed Traci a piece of paper and said, "This is the VIN number. See if your friend can find out if it matches the number of Captain Jack's car."

"Sure," Traci said. "I'll call him."

"Thanks, I've got to go finish up in production."

Traci pointed down the hall. "You gotta go talk to Clay first. He said he wanted to see you when you got back."

"About what?"

Traci shrugged. "Didn't say." She picked up the phone as Rick headed down the hall. "Dubya-ay-oh-ahhr," she said. "Mmm. Hold please."

When Rick walked into Clay's office he was surprised to find himself staring down the barrel of a Remington 870 Wingmaster shotgun. Clay pumped it once. "Jesus!" Rick backed up holding his hands palm out at his chest.

"Oh hey, didn't see you there," Clay said as he rubbed the barrel up and down with a soft, oily rag.

Rick approached Clay's desk from a safe angle,

pointing all the while. "What the hell're you doing with that thing?"

"Gettin' ready for coon season, man, whaddya think?"

Rick looked closer. "With a twelve-gauge? Ain't gonna be much coon left if you shoot it with that."

Clay smiled and said, "Ain't that the truth?" He set the gun across his desk and looked at Rick like he was the one who'd called the meeting.

Rick waited a moment before he said, "So . . . what? You wanted to invite me on the hunt? Ask if you could borrow my coon squaller?"

"Huh? Oh, no, nothing like that." It looked like Clay was about to say something but then he seemed to change his mind about it. He said, "Hey, you find that carport yet? Thing can't've blown that damn far."

"Not yet," Rick said. "But if I can get my production finished in time I'll go out and look around this afternoon." He noticed the dent in the paneling where Lori Stubblefield had thrown the glass ashtray, probably right past Clay's head. "I'll let you know if I find it."

"Good." Clay kept looking at Rick as if waiting for him to say something.

"Is that it?"

"No, there's one other thing." He gestured toward the bookkeeper's office. "I heard you were looking in the W-9 file the other day."

"I was looking for my paycheck," Rick said.

"Yeah, well, don't worry about that W-9. That's not your problem."

"Didn't think it was," Rick said.

"Good. 'Cause I'd hate to have to start programming the FM."

"I'd hate that, too," Rick said. "But I don't see how one follows from the other."

"I'm just saying, the programmin's your business. The other stuff's my business. I don't mess with yours, you don't mess with mine. That's all."

"Wouldn't have it any other way," Rick said.

"Thing is," Clay said. "There wasn't a W-9 in there 'cause that old boy that won didn't know his Social Security number, so I just sent him home with the form. He's gone mail it back."

"Great. Anything else?"

Clay picked up the shotgun and looked down the sight. "Nahhh. Just wanted to get that straight. Tch."

Rick walked to the production room with the not-so-vague feeling he'd been threatened. He took it as a sign that he was barking up the right tree. At the same time, staring into the black hole that is a shotgun barrel made Rick realize he had to either rethink his hobby or find some solid evidence to nail Clay.

After finishing his work, Rick went back to his trailer. It was around five when he stepped down from his truck. He looked toward the woods in the direction where his carport was last seen cartwheeling. *What the hell,* he thought. *Take a short run, get some exercise, and see if I can find the thing.* He changed into shorts and put on an old pair of running shoes and then stretched for a few minutes before starting a slow jog toward the tree line.

Rick followed roughly the same path he had taken the day he went for his walk. The pine trees ahead of him had suffered some storm damage but nothing dramatic, broken branches and some stripped bark was all. But once he was past the tree line, things changed. About fifty yards into the woods Rick stopped and looked up. The tops of several pines had snapped off. One had landed on a section of that old split-rail fence, laying it to the ground. He guessed the tornado had touched down here.

Rick had never seen destruction such as this. He had once cut down a pine tree with an ax, took him an hour and it wasn't much of a tree compared to the big ones here. Rick knew that a humbling amount of force had moved through this space.

He found where the fence was still intact and he followed it toward the clearing he had seen the other day, where someone had been harvesting lumber. When he got there, he stopped and said, "Wow." And he meant it. That big white oak near the creek was gone. And not to the lumberyard. Its hard wood had refused to snap like the pines, so the storm had taken it whole. Ripped it out like a molar, roots dangling as it was carried off in a swirl.

There was a hole fifteen feet across where most of the oak's root system had been, near the bank of the creek. When the flash flood came down that gully afterward, the embankment couldn't take the pressure. It gave out and a torrent of debris burst through the gap, eroding tons of the reddish soil in a matter of minutes.

After eight hours the waters had returned to a level below the break in the bank.

Now, as Rick squeezed between the barbed wires into the clearing, the ground was still soft. He saw where large branches had been picked up by the torrent and pushed to the trees, where they formed brief dams and caught all sorts of rubble. A child's bicycle with training wheels was bent around a small trunk. He looked down and saw the prints of racoons and possums and birds but no deer or big Russian pigs. And no sign of the carport.

Rick walked over to the breach in the creek bank where the erosion was deepest. He looked at the color and striations in the wall created by the erosion. It was like a blank slate waiting to be marked and something about it reminded Rick of that place between Jackson and Vicksburg where they cut I-20 through those hills and you'd drive between the big dirt walls left behind. People stopped and carved things like BB LUVS CH 4EVER in six-inch letters but you couldn't read them at sixty-five miles an hour, so the only one anybody remembered was the only one you could read no matter how fast you were going. It appeared at some point after that motorcycle crash in October of 1971. Someone had carved, in neat square letters eight feet tall, the words REMEMBER DUANE ALLMAN. It was famous for a while and became a Mecca of sorts, standing for decades before the elements finally washed it away.

Rick was looking at the layers of earth revealed by the erosion when he came across a smooth white surface where everything else was rusty brown. It was hard to say with any certainty but it looked to be four or five feet below the original ground level. He looked closer and brushed away a little dirt. He leaned in and noticed a fine jagged line that sent a shiver up his spine. He picked up a stick and, with some trepidation, pried and scraped away more dirt until he was sure. It was the top of a human skull.

It took Rick's breath for a moment and he stepped back. He imagined the hollow eye sockets and the mouth gaping in its last scream. Rick gathered himself and got back to it. As he pried more dirt away he began to see hair and gray flesh and he realized this wasn't a skeleton. It was a body that hadn't been in the ground for too long. He assumed scavengers had cleaned the skin off the parietal bones that had been exposed by the erosion. The thin jagged line was where the plates of bone met at the crown of the skull. Scraping away a little more dirt, he saw what he assumed was a bullet hole. Rick stopped digging and thought for a moment. This had to be Captain Jack. What're the odds that someone else's dead body would be on this property?

Rick didn't want anyone to find this before he was ready. If the killer or whoever was clearing timber off this property came back, they might see it. He went to the edge of the creek and scooped up two hands of muddy clay, then went back to the exposed skull and covered it.

Rick got back to the trailer just before six. He called Traci and Donna then he grabbed a bite to eat before heading for work.

Traci arrived around eight-thirty and waited in the lobby for Donna, who got there a little before nine. The two of them knew each other from when Donna was buying ad time on a regular basis. They talked for a little while before going down to the studio. The ON AIR sign above the door was illuminated, so they waited there as Rick gave the station ID. When the light went off, they went into the control room and sat in the chairs underneath the big double-paned window.

Rick had just started Traffic's "Low Spark of High Heeled Boys." He had War's "City, Country, City" cued up, which would give them about twenty-five minutes to talk. Rick turned down the monitors, looked at Donna, and said, "You were right about the contest. It was fixed."

Donna flashed a satisfied grin. "Told you," she said. "What'd you find?"

Before Rick could answer, Traci said, "Well, first of all, Clay didn't get a W-9 form from the winner."

"However, he did say that he'd given one to De-Wayne to mail back to us."

This was news to Traci. "When did he say that?"

"This afternoon," Rick said. "Just after he pointed a shotgun at me and told me I should mind my own business."

Traci's jaw dropped. "What? Here at the station? Are you kidding?"

Rick shook his head. "Said he was getting ready for coon season and, oh, by the way, there's no need for me to worry about the W-9 form that we don't have on file."

Donna seemed skeptical. She said, "Is the missing tax form all you have? 'Cause he's got till the end of the year to fix that."

"There's more," Traci said. "You know that little short girl who pulled the names out of the barrel?"

"Also known as Joni Lang," Rick said.

"Well, she's not tall, is she?"

Rick held up his hands, surrendering the point.

Traci continued by saying, "Well, little Miss Loblolly Pine said she saw Clay palm the name she handed him and then call out that other name. After that, she saw Clay throw out the real winner's name and she went and got it out of the trash."

"Okay, so he's probably not declaring the money," Donna said. "What's that, tax fraud?"

"That's what the IRS is gonna call it," Rick said. "Add to that his failure to fully disclose material terms of the contest—"

"Like the fact that Clay fixed it?"

"That's the kind of thing the FCC will be interested in."

"Okay, so we've got two federal agencies interested in Clay's shenanigans," Donna said. "How does that help us find out what happened to Holly?"

"Well, I've got a theory," Rick said. "It occurred to me after I went out to DeWayne's house and found a red Corvette that had been painted black." He looked at Traci. "Did your friend call?"

"Not yet."

"Well, when he does, I bet the VIN number has Jack Carter's name attached to it."

Donna looked confused and sounded frustrated. "Which has what to do with Holly?"

"According to my theory, it's part of the payoff," Rick said. "Actually two payoffs, one for killing your friend and one for killing Captain Jack."

"Wait a second," Donna said. "All you can prove is the contest was fixed and that DeWayne Ragsdale got a car improperly."

"Not just any car," Rick said. "Captain Jack's car."

"Is that it?"

"Yeah, until this afternoon when I found a body buried in the woods."

"I only saw the top of the skull," Rick said. "I couldn't tell if it was a man or a woman."

"So we don't know if it's either one of them," Donna said.

"True, but the body's a thousand yards from where Captain Jack lived, so I think the odds are good it's him."

"Well, I hope it is," Donna said. "Bastard deserved whatever he got."

"What he got was one in the hat," Rick said. "I'm not sure how you measure what that's worth."

"If it is Captain Jack," Traci said, "it makes you wonder if, I mean, if they did kill Holly? It makes you wonder if she's buried out there, too."

"I can rent you a backhoe if you wanna go digging around," Donna said.

"I don't think that's our best idea," Rick said. "The body and whatever's around it is likely to have the only evidence we're gonna find. We've got to bring in somebody who knows what they're doing. And it has to be somebody who's not drinking buddies with the suspects."

Donna said, "Yeah, Clay used to brag that no matter how hard he tried, he couldn't get into any trouble in this town. I think they played football together or something." She shook her head. "What is it about guys bonding over violence and showering together?"

"We'll be sure to have the prosecutor ask that at trial," Rick said. "Meanwhile, we need to find out if the

Deckern County sheriff is part of the good old boys' club. And if he is, we'll have to go elsewhere, like a DA's office or—"

"The MBI," Donna said. "Mississippi Bureau of Investigation." Rick and Traci looked at her. Donna just shrugged. "I looked into it after that son of a bitch burned down my store, but I never called."

Rick mixed from the Traffic to the War as the three of them discussed how to proceed. Traci would follow up on the VIN number and Donna would find out what she could about the Deckern County sheriff's politics and affiliations. Rick would research the DA and the MBI.

Donna and Traci left the studio around ten. Rick finished up his shift with an unlikely mix of Nazz and Manassas. "Hello It's Me" flowed nicely into "Bound to Lose," which in turn went well into "Couldn't I Just Tell You," which ended cold with a flurry of drum licks that matched with the drum and cowbell intro of "It Doesn't Matter." Anyone who knew the Manassas record had the natural expectation that "Johnny's Garden" would come automatically after "It Doesn't Matter" in a whoosh of cymbals, guitars, and percussion. Trading on that expectation, Rick went into "Letters Don't Count" by Nazz, which he started at the last break in the song's glass harp intro.

At about five minutes before midnight, Uncle Victor walked into the studio with more verve than Rick had ever seen. "What are you playing next?" He seemed insistent and agitated as he moved to the wall of albums, searching for something.

"No idea," Rick said. "I was thinking—"

Uncle Victor found the record he wanted and pulled it. "Please," he said. "I have an idea."

Rick stepped from behind the board and made a sweeping doorman's gesture. "After you," he said.

At the end of "Letters Don't Count," Uncle Victor went to the Rascals, mixing the glass harp close of the Nazz song into the chirping-bird sound effects intro of "It's a Beautiful Morning." It was perfect.

Rick gave him a round of applause. "Very nice," he said.

"It was the least I could do," Uncle Victor said as he cued up his next song. "Had someone told me I could do such a set mixing Stills and Rundgren, I would have heaped scorn upon them. But I would have been wrong." He turned and put his hands together like a monk, then bowed in Rick's direction. "You are a master."

Under normal circumstances, this rare compliment from the proprietor of the *Wax Museum* might have sent Rick home with a satisfied grin. But after being threatened with a shotgun and stumbling across a dead body, he just shrugged and said thanks.

Rick found out there were twenty-two district attorneys spread throughout the state, each with a criminal investigator on staff. Under the department of public safety, the Mississippi Bureau of Investigation divided the state into three sectors, each with a regional supervisor. These regions were further broken down into nine districts, each run by a district lieutenant. The MBI ran the special operations and major crimes unit, running covert operations and providing surveillance for themselves and other agencies. Most important to Rick, the MBI was authorized to initiate investigations concerning any type of criminal activity.

He called Donna Moore. "The Deckern County sheriff is an elected position," she said. "Whereas the head of the McRae Police Department is appointed."

"Ahhh," Rick said. "So Chief Dinkins has a loyalty issue beyond Clay Stubblefield."

"Yeah, to the extent that he owes his job to Clay's friend the mayor, instead of the citizens of McRae. But Sheriff Terry Jackson might have loyalty issues as well," Donna said, "having once been in the employ of Chief Dinkins."

"Hmmm." So what's your sense of it? Can we trust the sheriff?"

"Don't know," Donna said. "People I talked to didn't tell me anything to indicate we couldn't, nobody remembers if Dinkins endorsed Jackson's campaign or not, but you know how the old boy network operates with all that back-scratching. I guess I'd be more inclined to go with a DA or the MBI or anybody not directly tied into the local scene."

"I think you're right," Rick said. "I'll let you know who I talk to."

When he got to the station, Traci told him that she'd heard from her friend. As expected, the VIN numbers matched. The car at DeWayne's house was Captain Jack's. "He also said somebody went to the trouble of making it look like DeWayne had bought the car at auction, even though it was never on the block."

Just then, they heard the door to Clay's office close, followed by the jingle of his keys as he locked it. He came into the lobby and saw Rick. "Hey, did you ever find that damn carport?"

"Nope," Rick said. "And I looked all over those woods, too."

"Damn." Clay scratched the back of his neck and shook his head. "Well, if it's gone it's gone." He crossed to Traci's desk and looked at his phone messages but didn't take any of them as he headed for the door. "All right, I'm outta here," he said. "Got a meetin' on the coast. Be back tomorrow afternoon."

Rick watched Clay get into his car and drive off. He turned to Traci. "How often does he go out of town for these little meetings?"

"More often than his lovely wife approves of," Traci said. "Why?"

The Stubblefields lived in a five-thousand-square-foot colonial in the Big Pine Lake subdivision. Rick drove past the house a couple of times before calling. It was a little after six and one of the kids answered. "Hi," Rick said. "Is your dad home?"

"No sir. But my mom is," the kid said.

"Hello? I think I'm losing . . . my cell . . . I'm just . . . try back . . . closer." Rick ended the call, drove around the corner, and pulled into their driveway. As he approached the front door, he realized that his truck, with half the paint stripped off by the hailstorm, looked like it might belong to someone wanting yardwork. After ringing the bell, Rick stood there gazing at the front lawn, wondering what Clay paid for maintenance. A few moments passed before he heard the click of high heels crossing the foyer.

Lori Stubblefield answered the door wearing a two-piece outfit of cream-colored linen and innuendo. She had a drink in her hand, and based on her expression, Rick figured it wasn't her first of the evening.

"Well, well, well." She leaned against the doorjamb and sipped her drink before tipping her glass toward him, saying, "Rick, isn't it?"

"Yes, it is." He smiled. "You wouldn't happen to have a gun, would you?"

She snickered at that. "What, now you wanna be put out of *your* misery? You haven't been in this town long enough." She hoisted her drink. "But I can offer you one of these." Rick shook his head and she lowered her glass. "No, that's right," she said. "You don't drink until the last hour of your show." Lori stepped aside, gesturing for Rick to come in. "I'm afraid Clay's not here," she said, closing the door behind him.

"I know. He's on one of his *business* trips." Rick said "business" in the same dubious tone he'd heard Lori use the other day. "That's why I'm here."

"Oh my," she said. "That sort of comment could mean so many things." She waved for him to follow her into the living room. "You sure I can't get you a drink? Maybe a small one?"

Rick hesitated before he said, "Got a cold beer?" He thought she might be more inclined to talk if he joined her in her hobby.

Lori smiled. "You want a glass with that?"

"No, bottle's fine. Or can, whatever."

Rick's cell phone started to ring as Lori disappeared into the kitchen. He looked at the screen and saw the call was from Traci. He decided to let it go to voice mail. A moment later, Lori returned with a cold Dixie in a bottle. "I must say I am intrigued by your visit," she said. "I don't get a lot of men callers these days. Certainly not as many as I'd like." She sipped her drink. "To what do I owe the pleasure?"

"Mrs. Stubblefield—"

"Please, call me Lori."

"Fine. Lori. I'm not sure it's going to be much of a pleasure. So I hope you don't mind if I just get right to the point."

"By all means. The intrigue is about to kill me."

Rick shifted in his seat, uncomfortable with himself and what he had in mind. He never would have considered doing this except that he could hear the clock ticking. He was afraid someone would discover the body and contact the McRae Police Department and the whole thing would be swept under the rug. There was also the matter of Rick not being able to think of anyone else who might know anything useful about Clay. "Listen," he said, "I wouldn't want your children to hear any of this. Are they"—he made a gesture to inquire as to their location—"around?"

Lori's expression changed as she sensed Rick's seriousness. "They're upstairs," she said as she put down her drink. "Would this by chance have anything to do with my philandering husband?" Rick must have blushed or done something equally telling because Lori suddenly seemed amused. "Oh, don't worry about trying to spare my feelings." She ran her hand over her hair. "I know I married poorly. I know Clay sleeps around and I suspect he's involved in all sorts of things he shouldn't be." She gestured around the spacious

room. "I'm not so naive as to think the general manager of a pissant radio station could afford this home."

Rick took a big swallow of the Dixie, hoping to
wash the bad taste from his mouth. He wasn't looking
forward to this but he didn't see any good options. He
took a moment to choose his words before he said, "I
know this private investigator, name of Buddy Miles. A
series of events not worth reciting led him to a tape
recording of a phone conversation, which put him onto
a missing-persons case. After some investigation, he
concluded that Clay might be involved."

Lori looked down at her empty glass for a moment
before she said, "And how is it I can help your friend?"

Lori fixed herself another drink and asked what was
on the tape.

Rick pulled a cassette from his pocket. "You want to
hear it?"

"No, a summary will suffice."

Rick told her about the whole story. He didn't mention Lisa's or Donna's names and Lori didn't ask. She
sat there listening as if she were too polite to tell Rick
that this was a story she'd already heard. If her expression changed at all, it was to make her seem less
burdened.

But her face darkened as Rick told her about Bernie
Dribbling and how Captain Jack mysteriously disappeared. It darkened further when he told her about
Holly Creel's loan and how she was missing, too. Rick
ticked off the evidence one piece after another. Lori
couldn't see the whole thing but she seemed pretty
good at making inferences and drawing conclusions.

After a moment she asked Rick what he thought had happened and he told her.

Lori sat there for a moment after Rick finished. She stared into the middle distance as she considered her future in light of her past. After a little while she stood and crossed the room. She fixed herself another drink and came back to the sofa. "Do you happen to know the law on tape recordings like that?"

"I know a little," Rick said. "Just what I picked up from Buddy."

"Do you know if a tape like that is . . . admissible?"

"Like in divorce court?"

"Like that."

Rick thought about it for a moment then said, "Well, one part of the statute said it was a felony for anyone other than law enforcement to disclose the contents for any reason other than testifying under oath in a court proceeding." He shrugged. "I'm not a lawyer, but that last part makes it sound like it would be admissible."

Lori nodded her head slowly. "I tell you what," she said. "For a copy of that tape? I can fill in a couple of your blanks."

Rick gave her a cassette. Lori held it in her palm, her fingers closing around it as if it were the key to a magic kingdom. Then she said, "Let me show you where Clay keeps his guns."

13

Rick didn't know if it was the liquor, the relief of confession, or a combination of the two, but once Lori Stubblefield started talking she found it hard to stop. Rick believed her when she said that the things she'd seen and heard were so removed from their context that they didn't mean anything to her. In her next breath she admitted that she must have known they were up to no good, but what was she going to do, ask for details? But after four drinks and some context, Lori told Rick what she knew. It was more than he could reasonably have expected, though it didn't answer all the questions and there were still things that had to be proved.

Rick left the Stubblefield residence about twenty minutes to eight. He figured that was enough time to make it to the station. He took the back route to avoid university traffic. But he didn't count on a freight train and there was no way around it. He sat there for a few moments before he killed his engine. There was no telling how long he'd be there. Rick watched the piggybacks creeping down the track and after a while he realized he was counting them. *Forty-two, forty-three, forty-four . . .* He glanced at his watch and picked up his cell phone. He called Autumn on the hot line and said, "Freight train got me. I'll be there as soon as the Illinois Central lets me."

"Don't worry," she said. "I'll start playing train songs."

He hung up then called Traci. When she answered he said, "Here, kitty, kitty, kitty."

She made a sexy little cat noise, then said, "Hey, where've you been? I tried calling and I got your voice mail."

"Yeah, well, I was having a drink with Lori Stubblefield when you called."

There was a moment of silence before Traci said, "What?"

"I thought she might know something, so I went over and—"

"You played her the tape? That's awful," Traci said.

"As compared to killing people?"

"Granted. But still . . ."

"Trust me," Rick said. "That woman holds no illusions about Clay. In fact, she was rather eager to get her hands on the tape."

"You gave it to her?"

"Just a copy. I think it'll get some play in their divorce proceedings. But don't worry, I got plenty in return. Matter of fact, with what she told me, I think I've got the whole thing figured out. All that's left is to prove it."

"Where are you?" Traci asked.

"In my truck at the railroad crossing about a mile from the station."

"Oh. So tell me what she said."

"Can't," Rick said. "I can see the caboose."

"So?"

"I don't have time. Come over to my place after work and I'll tell you all about it."

"How about you come to my place, and bring some of that catnip of yours."

"Deal."

Rick got to the station about a minute before he was supposed to go on the air. He raced down the hall and burst into the studio. "What do you have cued up?"

" 'Train Kept A-Rollin'.' "

"Take it off," he said as he grabbed *The Beatles* album. Autumn did as Rick said, then moved from behind the board.

Rick plugged in his headphones and cued his song. He cleared his throat, opened the mike, and said, "This is WAOR-FM, McRae, Mississippi. I'm Rick Shannon and I can't wait to feel your finger on my trigger. 'Cause you know what they say: Happiness is . . . a warm gun."

Rick got to Traci's apartment around twelve-thirty. She was wearing sweatpants, a CMU football jersey, and fuzzy slippers. "I made you a sandwich," she said.

"Thanks. You didn't have to do that."

"Is turkey okay?" She went to the refrigerator.

"Turkey's great." Rick smiled as he listened to Traci shuffle around the kitchen in her slippers. He was surprised and touched that she'd gone to the trouble, not that it was a great undertaking, but it was sweet and he wasn't used to being treated that way. He sat down at the table in the dining nook and told her about how he met Lori Stubblefield at the Booster Club party. "At one point she actually said she knew where all the bodies were buried."

"Yeah, but that's just a figure of speech," Traci said as she cut the sandwich on the angle and put it on a plate. "You want a beer with this?"

"Yeah, please," Rick said. "I know she wasn't being literal, but there was something about *the way* she said it. She's nobody's fool," he said. "She knows what goes on."

Traci brought the sandwich, a beer, and a bag of chips. She sat down across from Rick. "Okay, keep goin'."

"After their fight the other day, I figured Lori might be willing to talk, if she knew anything, so I took a chance and went over there." Between bites of his sandwich he told her what Lori had said.

Traci seemed surprised by one thing. "They just talked about all this in front of her?"

"I don't think she was in the room taking notes," Rick said. "But she wasn't locked up in the tower either. She was expected to serve drinks and cook dinner and be selectively deaf. As long as Clay sent her off to Dallas or Miami on shopping sprees now and again, she did what she was supposed to. Anyway, they never said anything obvious. It was always, 'We've got a problem and I need you to take care of it' sort of stuff."

"Then she's *somebody's* fool."

"I don't know," Rick said. "I guess she just found a

way to tell herself that Clay and his cronies were talking about legitimate business."

"So why would she talk now? She still gets to go shopping. You think she just wants to get back at him for cheating on her?"

"No, she could've done that a long time ago. I think it has more to do with the fact that she now knows real people are getting hurt. She couldn't tell herself it was legitimate business anymore after I told her about Holly Creel and Captain Jack and the body I found. By the way," Rick said as he brushed the crumbs from his hands. "Great sandwich."

"Glad you liked it."

He pulled a piece of paper from his shirt pocket. "She gave me this." It was a thin yellow duplicate page from a multipage form. He handed it to Traci.

She read the form, then said, "What's this?"

"A police report."

She looked at Rick and said, "Oh! You must be the guy from the Department of Duh. I was hoping for a little bit more of that context you've become so famous for." Rick explained how the police report fit into his theory. Traci thought about it for a moment and agreed it made as much sense as anything she could muster. "So," she said. "Now what?"

Rick wiggled his eyebrows and cast a suggestive glance toward the bedroom.

Traci had gone to work by the time Rick woke up the next morning. On the drive home, he stopped at Kitty's. They were between the breakfast and lunch rush, so he took a booth by himself instead of sitting at the counter. His favorite waitress approached in her charismatic shamble. "How you doin', Ruthie?" Rick asked.

"Feelin' wormy," she said. "You want mora them tater wads?"

"No, ma'am. I'll have coffee, grits, and sausage. If that's okay."

She poured Rick his coffee and said, "Makes me no never mind." Then she shuffled off.

Rick huddled over his coffee and thought about whom he should call and what he should say. He figured it made more sense to speak to one of the district lieutenants rather than one of the regional supervisors since the supervisor would just turn around and delegate to one of the lieutenants anyway. Rick thought it best to avoid those in the districts closest to McRae for obvious reasons, and the ones in the northern part of the state were too far away. This narrowed it down to the one on the coast or the one up in Jackson. He pulled a coin from his pocket and flipped it. It was heads, the guy on the coast.

The waitress returned with his breakfast and some more coffee. "Bone appetite," she said before grousing away. Rick savored the grits and sausage and considered what he might say to whomever he got on the phone. After eating, he went back to his trailer and made the call.

A woman answered. "Mississippi Bureau of Investigation. How may I direct your call?"

"Lieutenant Smith, please."

"Will he know what this is in regard to?"

"No, ma'am."

She paused. "Well, can I tell him what this is in regard to?"

"Sure," Rick said. "A dead body."

"Hold please."

While on hold, Rick was subjected to a Muzak version of a Janis Ian song. Why would you do that? he wondered. Was the original too raucous?

The music stopped when a very serious-sounding man came on the line. He said, "This is Lieutenant Smith. Who am I speaking with?"

It hadn't occurred to Rick that he might have to identify himself and now, suddenly pressured to give up his name, he wasn't sure if he should go with the truth or not. "Uh, Buddy Miles," he said. "Thanks for taking—"

"You don't sound too sure of yourself, Mr. Miles. You wanna try again or you wanna stick with that?"

Rick was startled by the lieutenant's confrontational approach. "Uhhh, I'll stick with that if you don't mind."

"I tell you what I mind, Mr. Miles. It's people wasting my time. Now, my assistant said you called to report a dead body. Is that right?"

"Yes, sir, that's correct. Maybe two."

"Maybe two? You don't sound too sure about that either."

"Well, I've only seen the one."

"Uh-huh. And have you called your local police?"

"No, sir. And I'll tell you why."

"Well, that'd be nice."

"The main suspect is friendly with the local police."

"Isssaat right? The main suspect, you say. And how is it you have a suspect in mind?"

"It's a long story."

"Wouldn't you know it? And what about your local sheriff, you called him?"

"No, sir. I don't know, but the sheriff might be friendly with the suspect, too."

"So you're sayin' all the police up in your neck of the woods're corrupt?"

"I can't say, but I didn't think it was worth taking the risk. That's why I called you."

"Uh-huh. Where you calling from, Mr. Miles?"

"Deckern County," Rick said.

"That where the body's at?"

"Yes, sir. And I was hoping you might be able to get up here tomorrow to start an investigation."

"Did you now?"

"Yes, sir."

"Like all I'm dealing with down here is bad checks at the casinos and I'll just drop everything and scoot up your way based on your, 'Uhhhhh, I think there might be two bodies'?"

"That's not what I meant," Rick said in frustration.

"Well, just put it out on the porch, son, I ain't got all day."

"All right, here's the deal. I'm a private investigator. I'm reporting the discovery of a dead body. I have other evidence and a theory. I believe there are at least three men involved and there's probably another body to be found. If you're not interested, fine, just say so. I'll call someone else, maybe your regional supervisor, maybe the press, and when the story breaks—and it *will* break—I will be sure to mention your name and your keen lack of interest in the matter."

* * *

"What did he say to that?" Traci asked.

"At that point, Lieutenant Smith made a little grousing noise and said he'd get somebody up here when he could."

A look of disbelief crossed Traci's face. "That seems kinda casual, don't you think? I mean—" The phone started ringing. She held up her index finger, then pushed a button on the switchboard. "Dubya-ay-oh-ahhr," she said. "Mmm. Hold please." She transferred the call, then said, "I mean, a guy calls to report a dead body, you'd think there'd be a little more urgency."

"You'd think," Rick said. "I figure I'll give him a day before calling one of the regional supervisors. It's either that or just call the sheriff and cross our fingers."

"Give it a day," Traci said.

Rick nodded then said, "You want to come over tonight after my shift?"

"Yeah, I do," Traci said. "But I can't. My niece is spending the night."

"My luck. Tomorrow?"

"Tomorrow's good."

Rick headed for the production room but stopped at the hallway door. "By the way, I meant to tell you last night. You're remarkably flexible."

Traci smiled. "Oh, that was nothing." She gave him a little wink. "Just you wait."

Rick blew her a kiss then walked down the hall, wondering how flexible a person could be. He was almost glad he had to wait a night. Rick savored the expectation of events. He believed that one of the most important things in life was having something to look forward to.

Rick walked into the production room and saw a stack of production orders, about two hours of work. He grabbed the first one and said, "This week only. Florida pink grapefruit!"

Afterward he grabbed a burger and brought it back to the station. It was seven-thirty. There was no one in the building except Rick and the two jocks in the studios at the other end of the hall. The place was quiet, dark, and depressing.

Rick went down to the employees' lounge, a grim little space with fluorescent bulbs that shed too much light on the futures of the people likely to be sitting below. Anyway, that's how it seemed to Rick as he sat at the messy table in the middle of the room. A red plastic stir stick, chewed at both ends, lay next to a container of powdered nondairy creamer that had been spilled but not cleaned up. Rick leaned down and blew the gritty white granules off the table. Some stuck. The refrigerator in the corner hummed. The overhead speaker was playing the AM side at a low volume. A syndicated financial adviser whispered investment strategies as Rick ate his hamburger and again wondered, *What am I doing here? Here? Hell, why am I still in radio? It's over. It's been over for a long time, at least as far as my skills and interests are concerned. I might as well be in the quill-pen business.*

The overhead financial adviser went to a commercial break. *"Are you behind on your bills? Credit-card balances piling up? Tired of paying late fees?"* Rick tuned it out.

He thought back to Jukebox Johnny Maguire sitting on the sidewalk outside B-Side Vinyl, looking like a

sad old gunslinger after law and order had come to
town. Rick thought about his years in the business.
He'd seen all the changes, from the days when it was
still about the music and the community to the moment
the consultants knocked down the doors with their
reams of research proving that the audience wanted radio to sound more like crap. Rick had watched, wide-
eyed, as management bought it, as research squeezed
the juicy life out of the thing, and as deregulation
pissed on the grave. Rick had been a witness to the car
crash that was FM rock radio and now . . . now he was
sitting in a depressing little employees' lounge thinking, *That's the way it goes. 'Tain't a bit of mercy in the
world and I can't expect market forces to yield to my
nostalgia.* He thought of the lyrics to a favorite old Top
40 hit. *"Bye-bye, so long, farewell."*

Rick considered his format for a moment. It wasn't
too long ago that he had had high hopes, even genuine
enthusiasm, for what he was trying to do. But now he
had to admit it wasn't going to work. It was a combination of things. Gaping holes in the music library. Bush-
league ad copy for the local spots. And his air
staff—well intentioned and hardworking as they were—
lacked the experience or polish necessary to succeed
without an abundance of personality, which they also
lacked. Rob, for all his enthusiasm and knowledge of the
music, sounded like someone's kid acting like he knew
what he was talking about. He lacked credibility with
the core audience. J.C. talked too much and played more
heavy metal than a stoned sixties audience would toler-
ate. And despite all the tutoring sessions, Autumn's
segues remained so jarring that Rick got calls from peo-

ple asking if he'd hired the deaf girl for equal opportunity reasons.

Could be better, Rick thought. *But then again, could be worse.* He smiled and took a bite of his burger. *On the bright side, I've got a date with a very flexible girl tomorrow night and I may be on the verge of sending Clay Stubblefield to prison. So at least there's something to look forward to.*

Rick finished his show that night with a three-song set starting with Spirit from *The Twelve Dreams of Dr. Sardonicus*. Over the end of "Nature's Way" he cross-faded the droning Indian sarod that led to the opening drum licks of "On the Road Again." Five minutes later, as the Hookeresque groove gave way to the sarod's irregular thrum, Rick started his next record. A few halting solo electric guitar licks laid over the end of the long fade of Canned Heat. Then an acoustic piano and rhythm guitar joined the electric and then drums, and before anyone knew what had happened, Donovan was singing "Barabajagle."

Uncle Victor entered the studio with more praise for Rick's music selection. "B. Mitchell Reed would've been proud," he said, referencing one of free-form radio's originators.

"You're too kind," Rick said as he filed his records.

Uncle Victor cued his first song and put on his headphones. He cleared his throat then opened the mike. "The Jeff Beck Group with Donovan wrapping up the eleven o'clock hour here on WAOR-FM, McRae, Mississippi. Redefining classic rock." He opened with Blind Faith's "Sleeping in the Ground."

Rick walked out to the parking lot and was pleased to find his windshield intact. As always, he listened to the *Wax Museum* on the drive home. Uncle Victor went from the Blind Faith to Derek and the Dominos' "Why Does Love Got to Be So Sad?"

Rick drove home the same way he always did. Since he usually had the county roads to himself at this time of night, he couldn't help but notice the headlights a quarter mile behind him that made the same two turns he did. Dylan's "Isis" came on just as he pulled onto the dirt driveway that led to his trailer. He stopped and killed his lights, waiting with his eyes in the mirror. A few moments later he saw a car pass, going well below the speed limit.

Rick shrugged it off and continued to the trailer. Inside he turned on the radio and went to the refrigerator for a beer. He sat down in the Barcalounger just as Uncle Victor went from Dylan into Phil Ochs's "Outside a Small Circle of Friends." Rick grabbed his cigar box and loaded his little pipe. He smiled when Phil sang the line about how smoking marijuana was more fun than drinking beer. "Yes," he said to the stereo. "But it's a close call." He took a hit off his pipe, chased it with a gulp, and raised the can to the speakers. He leaned back in the chair and listened to the music.

That's when he saw the white beams of headlights bouncing through the window. Rick brought the chair to the upright position, wondering who was coming to his place at one in the morning. Traci would've called if her plans had changed and he didn't think Captain Jack's sister would have come back from New Mexico. Clay seemed an unlikely candidate, so the Ted Nugent fan came to mind. Maybe he'd finally discovered that that Amboy Dukes record wasn't worth five hundred bucks after all.

Rick slid out of the Barcalounger. He went to the kitchen to grab his trusty skillet. He stationed himself by the door and waited. A few seconds later there was a hard knock. It didn't sound like knuckles, sounded more like a bat. Rick thought about throwing the door open into the face of whoever was out there, hoping to stun them long enough to land a few wallops with his Griswold number five. The doorknob wiggled as the interloper checked to see if it was locked. Rick said, "Who's there?"

A woman answered, "Sheriff's department."

"Really?"

"Yes, really," the woman said. "Are you Buddy Miles?"

"Uhhh, yes and no," Rick mumbled as he crossed to where his cigar box was, shoving it under the Barcalounger with his foot.

"What?" The woman banged on the door again. "Sir? Open the door now."

"Could you maybe come back during regular business hours?" It was feeble but it was all Rick could come up with.

"Sir, I've been out here eight times already," the woman said. "You ain't here a lot during regular business hours. We're gonna talk now."

"Okay, hang on." Rick opened the door and found himself looking at a solidly built black woman in her forties with a nightstick in her hands. "What's this all about, Officer?" He looked at his watch. "It's one in the morning." He smiled, trying to charm. "Not that I mind attractive women with big sticks dropping by at this time of night."

She glanced professionally at Rick's pupils, then, without entering the premises, she looked inside, checking for others. "I got a call from a Lieutenant Smith with the Mississippi Bureau of Investigation, said a man identifying himself as Buddy Miles had called to report a dead body. Did you make that call?"

Rick didn't think she'd be here if she didn't already know the answer to the question. He figured she was just giving him the opportunity to produce enough rope to hang himself with. Rick poked his lower lip out, tilted his head, and otherwise tried to look as confused as he could. "A dead body?" He scratched at the back of his head.

The woman wasn't buying it. "Sir?" She shook her head. "Would you rather tell me about the body or the distinct smell of marijuana coming from your trailer?"

Rick gave a resigned nod. "I see your point," he said. "Okay, c'mon in." He turned and walked into the kitchen as the woman entered behind him. As she moved, her leather-and-chrome accoutrements creaked and clacked.

Rick was pretty sure that possession of a small amount of pot in Mississippi was a misdemeanor, so he wasn't in a black panic about being busted, but on the other hand, it was always a good idea to avoid that first offense whenever possible. "Out of curiosity," he said. "Does Lieutenant Smith trace all his incoming phone calls?"

The woman looked like she felt sorry for people as

dim as Rick. "Caller ID," she said. "And a reverse phone directory. Now, about this body?"

"Right," he said. "Well, Officer. Is it Officer or Deputy?"

"It's Sheriff," she said. "Sheriff Terry Jackson." Rick's expression led her to say, "That's right, a black woman elected sheriff in rural Mississippi. What's this world coming to?"

Rick shook his head. "Actually that's not what I was thinking. I'm just surprised you're working the overnight shift if you're the boss."

"It rotates," she said. "Now if you can try to focus on—"

"But since you brought it up," Rick said. "How many black women have been elected sheriff in Mississippi counties?"

"You're looking at her."

"So you see? My surprise wasn't—"

"Sir? I can still smell the marijuana."

"Right, the body." Rick leaned against the kitchen counter. "Before I tell you about that, I have to ask, didn't you used to work for the McRae Police Department?"

Sheriff Jackson nodded. "Lieutenant Smith told me about your concerns," she said.

"Yeah? What'd you tell him?"

"I told him I'd worked for Chief Dinkins, and that based on my experience with his department, your concerns were well founded."

"No kidding."

"Sir, I was in the U.S. Army for four years as an MP," she said. "I came back here and earned a degree in criminal justice. I went to work for the McRae Police Department. Didn't take long to figure out they'd hired me for window dressing and weren't about to let me advance. Well, I worked too damn hard to let a bunch of wool-hatted hillbillies tell me what I couldn't do with my life. So I left the department and ran for sheriff. And damned if I didn't win." Sheriff Jackson turned and walked into the living room. She pointed at the Barcalounger. "Now, you wanna sit down and tell me about what you found?"

Rick looked at the Barcalounger, then he looked over at the record collection and said, "Have you ever heard Chicago's fourth album?"

"You're probably familiar with the laws on inter-cepted wire communications," Rick said as he threaded the tape onto the reel-to-reel.

"Generally," Sheriff Jackson said, looking at the tape. She was dying to hear it.

"I don't think I can be arrested on the illegal taping felony since Captain Jack made the tape," Rick said as he powered the amp. "But the other part of the law is about revealing the contents. That's also a felony, ex-cept in *certain circumstances,* if you get my drift." He gestured weakly toward Sheriff Jackson with his hands as if to suggest he needed some help.

Sheriff Jackson eyed the reel-to-reel for a moment. She was in its sway. She wanted to hear what was on the tape. She thought about the statute for a moment then stood up and motioned for Rick to do the same. When they were standing face-to-face, Sheriff Jackson looked at him with that level expression they must teach in cop school and said, "Raise your right hand and repeat after me." She held up her own hand, thinking it looked more official. Rick followed suit. "I do solemnly swear," the sheriff said.

"I do solemnly swear."

"That the testimony given here today is . . . true and accurate and . . . given without coercion of any sort." Rick managed a solemn expression as he repeated the words, after which Sheriff Jackson said, "You can put your hand down now. That concludes the swearing-in for the official testimony in a government proceeding." She sat down on the sofa, pointed at the tape, and said, "You may proceed."

Assuming that got him off the hook, Rick pushed the play button. The reels began to turn and a moment later Clay said, *"And you know that bitch wanted me to come back to her motel room and piss on her?"* Proud as a peacock.

Sheriff Jackson's reaction was priceless. Her flat expression vanished, replaced by one of pure guilty pleasure. But she regained her professional demeanor quickly and listened to the rest of the tape, all the while making notes and stifling giggles.

When it was over, Rick explained his theory. "I ended up with lots of parts of the story," he said. "But it was only after I talked to Lori Stubblefield that things started coming into focus. Now, I'm not sure about the time frame of this, but it all probably took place within the span of a month or two. And it started with Donna Moore and Clay Stubblefield having an affair."

"Wait," Sheriff Jackson said, glancing at her notes. "Is this before or after Moore Furniture burned down?"

"Before. Their affair was before the store burned down."

"Okay, so Donna and Clay were having an affair."

"And Holly Creel told Donna that she needed a big loan to pay off her gambling debts and that if Donna knew anybody who could help her, she'd *do anything*. Donna mentioned it to Clay, who mentioned it to Bernie Dribbling at Universal Financial Services. Bernie said he'd loan her the money in exchange for sex," Rick said. "But I think she was still obliged to repay the loan. So that got me wondering how Bernie Dribbling planned to get away with making such a conspicuously bad loan."

Sheriff Jackson glanced up at Rick. "Some of that fancy Worldcom accounting?"

Rick shook his head. "I don't think so. From what Clay says on the tape, Universal Financial Services is a partnership, the partners being Buddy Alford, Dicky Crumly, Wally Thigpen, and Dribbling. Apparently the board of directors made the strategic error of putting Bernie in charge of the money and he made this loan," Rick said. "For all I know, he's made a bunch of them. At any rate, Holly eventually told Donna Moore that the appointments with Dribbling were getting weird and violent and that she, Holly, planned to tell Dribbling that she wasn't going to do it anymore and she wasn't paying the loan back, and if he said anything, she'd go to the press and the cops and tell 'em about the deal."

"So you think he killed her and that's the body you found?"

"No. I don't think Dribbling actually killed anybody. I assumed he hired someone. But I wasn't sure until I talked to Lori Stubblefield. She said that one night, a month or so before Captain Jack disappeared, Bernie Dribbling showed up at their house all agitated and needing to talk with Clay. Lori heard him tell Clay that he had a big problem and that he needed help with it. More specifically she heard him say, 'The little bitch is going to ruin me.' Clay calmed Bernie down with a few drinks and told him he could take care of the matter but it wouldn't be cheap if he wanted it done right."

"So he hired somebody?"

"A guy named DeWayne Ragsdale."

Sheriff Jackson nodded knowingly. "Good old De-Wayne. At least he got out of the meth-making business."

"After Dribbling left that night, Clay made a call. About an hour later, DeWayne was in their kitchen talking to Clay. According to Lori, they talked for about half an hour before going to Clay's gun closet. After DeWayne left and Clay went to bed, Lori looked in the closet and saw that one of the guns was missing."

Sheriff Jackson looked up from making notes. "Did she know which one, what kind it was? Caliber, anything?"

"She said she wouldn't know a four-ten from a two-by-four," Rick said. "But all is not lost." He went to the wall of albums and pulled Roy Buchanan's *That's What I Am Here For,* which includes the song "Hey Joe," as in "where you goin' with that gun in your hand?" He reached into the sleeve and pulled out the yellow duplicate page from the police report Lori had given him. "The next day," Rick said, "Clay called his friends at McRae PD and reported his gun stolen."

"In case DeWayne got caught by someone like me?" Sheriff Jackson took the report and looked at it. "A forty-five," she said. "That'll kill ya, all right."

"Of course DeWayne doesn't work for free," Rick said. "And, dumb as Clay is, at least he tried to hide the payoff. My guess is that Clay got Bernie to put up the thousand dollars that the station would give away in a contest that DeWayne would win for killing Holly Creel. I assume he collected the prize under the name Ken Stigler for tax evasion purposes." Rick told Sheriff Jackson about Joni Lang's evidence and the W-9 and how Clay had threatened him not to look into the matter.

"What did Stubblefield get out of the deal?"

"He sold Dribbling an advertising schedule that would curl the hair in your nose. And I can't prove it yet, but I bet Clay commissioned it at around ninety percent."

"Good work if you can get it," Sheriff Jackson said. "So DeWayne killed Holly Creel for a thousand bucks and Clay got paid with the commissions. You ever figure out how Dribbling planned to get this past his partners?"

Rick made a waffling gesture. "I'm guessing," he said. "But I suspect that at the next Universal Financial Services board meeting, when his partners asked about the defaulted ten-thousand-dollar loan, Bernie was going to be sad to report that this young woman had disappeared. Just stopped showing up at work one day according to the police, he'll say. He'll report that the car title or whatever she gave for collateral turned out to be bogus. Of course there never was any collateral but he'll have to tell them something. He'll probably say it looks like she was a con artist and the local cops don't have high hopes of finding her. But the good news is, they can chalk it up to errors and omissions and cash in the insurance policy."

After a moment Sheriff Jackson said, "I guess that's plausible."

"Okay, so a few weeks pass," Rick said. "And one day Captain Jack is walking down the hall at the radio station when he hears Clay on the phone talking about Bernie Dribbling and his strap-on manhood extension." He gestured at the stereo. "That's when he made the tape. Then, after trying to extort Lisa Ramey and Donna Moore, he showed up on Dribbling's doorstep. Now, based on what Lori Stubblefield told me, it was probably later that night that Dribbling came over to their house again. She said he was furious and that it was clear that Clay had fucked up royally and it was causing Bernie bad trouble. He kept screaming, 'You dumb son of a bitch, what're you doin' tellin' people my business? This is yer damn fault and you damn well better fix it fast!'

"Clay said he'd take care of it, and according to Lori Stubblefield, the minute Dribbling left, Clay made a phone call. Thirty minutes later DeWayne showed up."

"What did DeWayne get for killing Carter?"

"A torch-red '96 Corvette, which I found sitting on DeWayne's property, painted black."

"What about Stubblefield?" the sheriff asked. "Did Carter try to blackmail him?"

"I don't know," Rick said. "But I doubt it. He probably figured that was too dangerous since Clay knew him."

Sheriff Jackson flipped her notepad shut. "So what

we need to do now is to dig up this body and get some forensics," she said as she stood. "So let's go have a look."

Rick looked up at her from the Barcalounger and said, "What, now?"

14

As they made their way through the woods, Rick was thinking that one of the good things about cops was that they always had great flashlights. Sheriff Jackson had two. Rick led her into the pine trees, following the path he'd been on before. He found the old fence line and followed it to the clearing. They scooted on their haunches down into the shallow ravine created by the flash flood. "It's down here," he said. It took them a few minutes to find where he'd put the mud patch. Then, using a stick, they pried and scraped until they exposed the parietal bones.

Sheriff Jackson shined her light on the spot and leaned in for a close look. "Well," she said. "That ain't no possum." She stepped back and shined her light around, trying to get a wider view of the area. "You know whose property this is?"

"No idea," Rick said. "I think the trailer's on station-owned property. Clay told me they bought it as a potential site for a new antennae. There's that old fence back there but I don't know if it's still a property line."

Sheriff Jackson shined her light around the clearing some more. "I don't suspect there's going to be any evidence left aboveground after all that wind and water came through here," she said. "I'll get the crime lab down here first thing and see what they dig up."

Around seven the next morning there was a loud knock on Rick's door. He rolled over in his bed and peered out the window. Sheriff Jackson was there with half a dozen employees from the state crime lab. He watched her step to the door and knock again. Rick grudgingly put on his sweats and some cheap sunglasses and went to the door. He stepped outside and Sheriff Jackson handed him a large Styrofoam cup of coffee. "Thought you might want this."

"Thanks," Rick said. "Did you call Donna Moore?"

The sheriff gave a nod. "Yep. Backhoe's on the way."

Sheriff Jackson introduced everybody then left Rick to lead the expedition into the trees. The parade of technicians in identical jumpsuits tromping through the trees in single file toting chrome equipment cases made Rick think of a Devo video. They reached the fence and then followed it to the edge of the clearing, where they stopped. Rick pointed to the spot and said, "Thar she blows."

The lead investigator turned around and said something that set his team in motion. Rick sat on a log, sipping his coffee, and watched.

After a consultation with his boss that included lots of finger-pointing around the area, the first guy set out to mark a wide perimeter, looping the yellow crime-scene tape around one tree trunk after another. Two others quickly set up an aluminum-framed canopy for the command post, under which they installed an array of computer and communications equipment. Rick was impressed. It looked like a well-coordinated military operation. A woman took photographs while a man took video, recording the scene from every possible angle. The photographer even shinnied up a tree for some aerial views. By the time Rick finished his coffee they were all standing around waiting for the backhoe to arrive.

Rick went back to the trailer, had breakfast, and got ready for work. Later, he went back to see if the tractor had arrived. He knew the answer before he got to the site. He could hear the diesel engine growling as it pulled something human from the earth.

Traci was on the phone when Rick walked into the station that afternoon.

She hung up and flashed Rick a smile. "Oh, hey," she said. "I've got a surprise for you."

Rick held out his hands and said, "What is it?"

Traci made a face. "Now, if I told you, what would it be?"

"Not a surprise?"

"Not so much. So that'll come later when you least expect it."

"Okay," Rick said. "I'm glad you brought it up."

"So. Did you miss me last night?"

"Not so much," Rick said, glancing at his finger-nails. "I had a lady visitor, kept me kinda preoccupied."

Traci stiffened. "You better hurry up and tell me it was your sister and ha-ha-ha wasn't that funny?"

"Sorry." Rick shook his head. He sat on the edge of Traci's desk. "I don't have a sister."

"And you're not gonna have a date tonight if you don't hurry up and tell me who it was instead of who it wasn't." The phone rang. She snatched it. "Dubya-ay-oh-ahhr. Mmm. Hold please." She transferred the call then looked back at Rick. "Your time and my patience are runnin' out, buster."

"Endearing as this exhibition is, there's really no point," Rick said. "Nothing *physical* happened. We just talked. Oh, and we took a walk in the woods around two in the morning."

"What?" Traci's torso wagged side to side as she said, "You did not go into those woods with another woman at two this morning."

It made Rick laugh. "I did so," he said, wagging his own torso. "And her name was Terry Jackson." He paused. "Sheriff Terry Jackson."

Traci's eyes widened. "The sheriff is a woman?"

"And black to boot," Rick said. "And if she's to be believed, she's no fan of Chief Dinkins either."

Rick told Traci about Sheriff Jackson's visit and what he had seen them pull from the ground before coming to work. "Two bodies," he said. "A man and a woman."

"Oh my God." Traci took a breath. Rick saw her lips moving as she made a small gesture, crossing herself.

"They're looking for the slugs now," Rick said. "Of course, if they find any, then they have to find the gun and match the things and who knows what all? I'm supposed to talk to Sheriff Jackson later, find out what's next."

The phone rang again. "Dubya-ay-oh-ahhr. Uhh, could you hold, please? I'll see if he's in." Traci put the call on hold and looked at Rick. "It's for you. Some guy from WVBR."

"Isn't that the rocker in Vicksburg?" He looked at Traci. "Did he say what he wanted?" Traci shook her head. "Well, okay," Rick said. "Put him through to my office."

The guy from WVBR was an old radio pro who knew a lot of the same people Rick did. In fact it was their mutual friend Marc Neiderhauser, a record rep for one of the major labels, who had mentioned Rick's name. The guy said he'd heard Rick's show a few nights earlier as he was driving back from Gulfport and was he interested in a job? They left it with Rick saying he'd give the guy a call in a few days to talk some more.

Rick weighed his options. There was no question that things were about to change at WAOR. He doubted that the station would shut down just because the GM was in jail but that fact would certainly bring the absentee owner out of the woodwork and that might lead to something entirely different from the status quo. Maybe he'd sell the station, maybe he'd change the format. And who could tell what might happen when the FCC found out about the rigged contest? Would they yank the owner's license and pull the transmitter's plug? Rick wondered when he should tell the jocks they should get their tapes and résumés in order.

Regardless of the answer to any of those questions, Rick had to consider the move. Vicksburg was a step up from McRae, improving his chances of leapfrogging to Baton Rouge or New Orleans or Mobile. Maybe, if he could get a contract and if he got a guarantee of a certain amount of control over— He stopped and shook his head, amazed that he was trying to talk himself into another radio job. He thought about J. J. Maguire pushing that shopping cart around Bismarck, North Dakota. Rick didn't think he'd end up like that but it raised the question of how he would end up. And he started to wonder what he should do with the rest of his life. Last night it had been merely a rhetorical question. But now he could see the fork in the road and he had to make a decision. Which would it be, the path of least resistance or the road less traveled?

Rick wondered what had kept him in the business all these years. What had prevented him from letting go of the past and embracing the future or at least the present? Maybe he was too lazy to learn something new. Or maybe he was just afraid that he'd fallen so far behind that he could never catch up. One thing was certain; there was no point in blaming the business. He could hate what radio had become, but he couldn't change it. He just had to deal with it.

But how? At his age? With his temperament? What could he do? Who would hire him and for what? The guy at WVBR would hire him to keep doing what he did, but that just delayed the inevitable. Then what? Rick could hear someone from the unemployment office saying that RadioShack was looking for salespeople. Such a fate was repulsive on so many levels that

Rick couldn't entertain it. Still, he had to try something. And soon. But what?

Then—*bang! bang!*—it hit him like Maxwell's silver hammer. Rick almost laughed out loud when it finally dawned on him. He'd already found his new profession. He even had a dba. He was Buddy Miles, Private Investigator. *What a moron,* Rick thought. *I can't believe it took me this long to figure that out.* He slapped his desktop and began to imagine how much press he could generate for having solved a double murder for hire as his first case. *What better way to launch a PI business?*

Of course Rick knew it wasn't that simple. It would take a while before he could support himself as a PI. He'd need something to tide him over. The job at WVBR was perfect. Rick figured any town with a bunch of casinos in it would be chock-full of seedy characters and shady goings-on. A good place for a PI to make a living.

But he didn't want to try to do it alone. He was tired of the solo act. He'd need an able assistant. He pushed back from his desk and went to the lobby.

Traci looked up from reading *Radio & Records.* "What'd that guy want?"

"Oh, he just said he'd heard my shift one night, driving through, and that he liked it."

"And you talked about that for twenty minutes?"

"That and some other stuff," Rick said.

"Like what?"

"Like my becoming his program director," Rick said.

"In Vicksburg?"

"Yeah."

She put down the *R&R*. "Wow. Are you going to take it?"

"I'm not sure," Rick said. "I've been thinking about getting out of radio."

"Oh," Traci said. "I didn't know that." Something in her voice surprised him, a small sadness maybe, or disappointment, he couldn't tell. "What would you do?"

"I was thinking about being a private investigator."

Traci looked at him like she was expecting a punch line to follow. Then she said, "Are you serious?"

"Why not?"

"Here?"

"No, in Vicksburg. But I'd need an assistant."

Traci looked at him like she was following—but at a distance. "Huh," she said.

"What do you think?"

"You'd probably be good at it."

"I mean, would you come with me?"

"To be your assistant?" Traci shook her head. "No." Then she smiled and said, "But I tell you what, if you ever go looking for a partner? You call me first."

Rick didn't press Traci about moving to Vicksburg to join him in his new venture. He'd planted the seed and that was all he could do. He hoped she would come but he knew it was a lot to ask.

Despite being disappointed by Traci's ambiguous response, Rick had a good show that night. He was enthused by the job offer and his decision finally to make a change in his life. His last set of the night started with "Drowned" from The Who's *Quadrophenia*. Near the end of the song, there is a break that turns into a barrel-house piano riff that Rick matched with the opening piano riff of Joe Cocker's "Hitchcock Railway." At the end of "Hitchcock Railway," he returned to the piano riff in "Drowned" and let the song finish. As it faded, he brought up the train sound effects at the beginning of Bowie's "Station to Station." And at the end of "Station to Station," Rick went into Dylan's "It Takes a Lot to Laugh, It Takes a Train to Cry."

After work, Rick drove home listening to Uncle Victor, who had decided to continue Rick's theme. He started with Lord Buckley's "The Train" and "Train Song" by the Flying Burrito Brothers. He pulled off the road onto his dirt drive near the end of Tull's "Locomotive Breath." He turned off the radio when Uncle Victor went into another UFS spot. When the trailer came into view, Rick noticed a car parked off to the side. As he got closer he could see someone sitting in the chair by the cable spool. He stopped and wondered if he should back out but then the person stood up and waved. It was Traci.

Rick drove up and parked where the carport used to be. He got out of his truck and said, "What're you doing here?"

Traci held up a white pastry box and said, "Surprise!" She started singing the "Happy Birthday" song.

Rick seemed a bit embarrassed by the display but let her finish. "How'd you know?" He opened the door to the trailer and let Traci in.

"I'm dating a private investigator," she said, putting the box on the table. "Plus I looked in the employee files."

"You shouldn't have."

"Looked into the files?"

"Gone to this trouble." Rick turned on the radio. Uncle Victor was playing Tom Paxton's "One Million Lawyers." "But thanks for doing it."

As Traci went to get plates from the cupboard she gestured at the piece of wood covering the window. "What happened there?"

"Flying squirrel," Rick said as he took the milk from the refrigerator.

Just then, a car pulled off the county road. The headlights were off. It sat there for a moment before it began creeping up the dirt road toward Rick's.

Traci opened the white pastry box and pulled out a pecan pie. "It's from Kitty's," she said. She pulled a small blue candle from her shirt pocket and stuck it in the middle of the pie. "Got any matches?"

Rick pointed. "Look in the drawer."

The car stopped about twenty yards from the trailer. A man got out, leaving the engine running and the driver's door open. He could see shadows and light in the trailer.

Traci lit the candle and started singing the Lennon and McCartney version of "Birthday." "Yes, we're going to a party party . . ." She stepped back to present the pie to Rick. "Make a wish," she said.

Rick thought for a second before leaning down to blow out the candle. That's when the shotgun blast ripped through the window. Glass and lead exploded everywhere. Traci screamed as Rick tackled her to the floor. The second shot blew a hole in the wood covering the broken window. Rick and Traci were scrambling down the hall on all fours when the third shot blasted through the front door. A moment later there was a fourth shot somewhere outside. Then they heard a car door slam and wheels tearing out on gravel. A final shotgun blast came from a distance as the car hit the county road and disappeared.

Rick and Traci stayed on the floor holding each other for a minute. The only sound was the radio, Uncle Victor playing Zevon's "Lawyers, Guns, and Money." When he felt it was safe, Rick looked at Traci and said, "Did you bring me a birthday present?"

She seemed surprised and said, "You mean, other than the pie?"

Rick smiled. "Don't get me wrong," he said. "I love pie."

"I did bring my birthday suit."

"Oh, I'd like to see that." He craned his neck to look outside. It was dark and quiet. "I think they're gone." He helped Traci up. "You okay?"

"Yeah, I think so."

Rick walked over to the splintered piece of wood and looked at the buckshot pattern. "You know anybody with a shotgun?"

"You mean besides Clay?"

"Yeah, I've seen his." Rick looked through the hole in the front door, then opened it and stepped outside.

Traci followed him, saying, "DeWayne Ragsdale probably has one."

"Probably."

"Then there's my ex-boyfriend."

Rick looked at her car. It was untouched.

"Should we call the cops?"

"I'll call Sheriff Jackson tomorrow," Rick said as he stopped in front of his truck. "Right after I call the windshield repair people."

* * *

Rick went to Sheriff Jackson's office the next morning. He told her about the shotgun attack but admitted they hadn't seen anything. "Well, it couldn't have been DeWayne," Sheriff Jackson said.

"Why not?"

" 'Cause we had him in custody."

"Since when?"

Sheriff Jackson said the coroner had identified the disinterred bodies as those of Jack Carter and Holly Creel. Both had been shot multiple times, including one each in the head. The slugs had come from a Smith & Wesson .45.

Based on Rick's statements to Sheriff Jackson, along with sworn affidavits from Donna Moore and Joni Lang, plus the police report Lori Stubblefield provided and DeWayne's prior convictions on drug, assault, and firearms charges, the Mississippi Bureau of Investigation obtained a search warrant for Mr. Ragsdale's residence.

The way Sheriff Jackson told it, DeWayne had been sitting on the weight bench outside his trailer in broad daylight. He was drinking a beer, taking the occasional shot at the washing machine propped against the tree. A Molly Hatchet CD was blasting on the stereo, so DeWayne never heard the two dozen law enforcement officers as they surrounded his trailer. The police watched from a distance as DeWayne fired his SW1911 .45 auto at the helpless appliance.

A man with the highway patrol was counting the shots. After the final round he keyed his radio. "That's nine," he said. "Go." On that signal someone tossed a couple of flash-bang grenades under the trailer right behind DeWayne. Each of the aluminum and potassium perchlorate explosions delivered a pressure wave of about thirty thousand pounds per square inch, which was quite a bit more than they really needed to disorient a drunk, unarmed man. Nonetheless, it made a for a dynamic entry.

DeWayne scrambled around in the dirt on all fours trying to figure out what the hell had happened. His first thought was that his propane tank had exploded. His second thought, which he cobbled together as he was being handcuffed and tossed in the back of the sheriff's car, was that he was going to need a lawyer.

After they matched the slugs to the bodies, DeWayne was taken to a small room in the sheriff's station. It was cold. He was in there alone for half an hour before two men from the Mississippi Bureau of Investigation walked in. Nice haircuts, dark suits, new shoes. "DeWayne, it's real simple," the first man said. "You were arrested in possession of the gun that killed these people. The rightful owner of that gun reported it stolen long before either one of them was killed. On top of that, you had one of the victims' cars on your property. So ipso facto, my seriously inbred hillbilly defective friend, those murders belong to you."

"He told you he bought the car at that auction," DeWayne's lawyer said. "And there's no call for the verbal abuse."

"Sorry. I'll send flowers."

It went on like this for about an hour. The interrogators made a series of accusations. DeWayne issued a string of weak denials. Rick and Sheriff Jackson stood watching on the other side of the glass.

At one point, the second interrogator pulled a small box from his pocket and set it on the table in front of DeWayne. He tapped the box top a couple of times then he said, "Your mama and daddy still alive, DeWayne?"

DeWayne scratched at his muttonchop sideburns and stared at the box. "Yeah. So?"

The second interrogator leaned down and started working the top off the box with one hand, slowly, holding the bottom down with his other hand. He said, "Are you afraid of needles, DeWayne?" He finally pulled the top off of the box to reveal a hypodermic. A big one, lying on a bed of cotton. "I mean, you'd want to be able to at least see your mama and daddy as they get on in their years, wouldn't you? Even if it was through all that thick glass with the handprints all over it. And you wouldn't wanna deprive them of seeing your pretty face for a few more, right?"

DeWayne gave an ambivalent nod and shrugged at the same time.

The first interrogator blew a low wolf whistle, then said, "Would you look at the bore on that needle?" his voice thick with awe. "Looks like a damn sewer pipe it's so wide. I hear that's the biggest gauge they make." Everyone was staring at the needle. DeWayne. DeWayne's lawyer. Both of the interrogators.

Everyone stared at it until the second man said, "They stick that needle up that big ol' vein in your right leg." He reached down to the inseam of his pants and did a grotesque pantomime of sticking the needle in his own leg. It hurt to watch.

Rick turned to Sheriff Jackson and said, "Is that really the kind of hypodermic they use for executions?"

Sheriff Jackson shook her head and pointed through the glass at the first interrogator. "He told me he got that from a large-animal vet he knows. I think they use that thing on horses and cows. But he thought it might be good for illustration purposes, you know? Help De-Wayne make a more fully informed decision," she said with a sly smile.

"You'd think his lawyer might object to something like this," Rick said.

Sheriff Jackson's head bobbed back and forth. "Like they say, you get what you pay for." She nodded at the room. "That one was free."

Back in the interrogation room, the first man said, "After they get that thing up in there, they give you a big load of that so-dium thi-o-pent-al." He said it in syllables for effect, then he pointed at DeWayne. "Now, of course, you being a drug user, you'll probably like the way it feels right up until it knocks you out. That's when they give you the pan-cur-o-nium bromide." He made a sudden fist in front of DeWayne and said, "Paralyzes your diaphragm so you can't breathe." He squeezed his fist tight, until it trembled. "Then comes the pièce de résistance. The po-tassium chloride. You know what that does, don'cha, DeWayne?"

DeWayne nodded slightly; his eyes were vacant.

"Takes 'em about five minutes to inject all that stuff into ya," the first man said. "Of course your mama and daddy can watch if they want. It's their right. But, De-Wayne, is that really how you want 'em to remember you? Splayed out on a gurney that way? That needle stuck up in your vein like that?"

DeWayne finally pulled his eyes off the hypodermic.

"I tolt you already," he said. "That old Stubblefield hired me. Why don'cha stick a needle in his leg?"

"I know, I know, you sang that song earlier," the first man said. "But see, the problem is, we just can't take your word on that, DeWayne. There's a little bit of a conflict of interest. And we gotta take something better'n that to the grand jury. 'Specially since you never had any contact with Bernie Dribbling."

"Well, that ain't my fault," DeWayne said. "You gone ess-cute me for that? That ain't right."

"DeWayne, ain't but one way out," the second man said. "We're holding it open for you. All you gotta do is just walk right on out that door, son."

The lawyer looked up and said, "What did you have in mind?"

The first man folded his arms and tilted his head toward the lawyer. "Your client is gonna set up a meeting with Clay and he's gonna wear a wire, and he's gonna get Clay to implicate himself and Bernie Dribbling in this whole thing."

"In exchange for what?"

"Visiting hours instead of a visitation."

The lawyer turned to his client. "Well, whaddya say? I think it's your best option."

DeWayne sat there for a while, stewing. These were some bad choices. Just like always. DeWayne never seemed to get any good choices to pick from, only crappy ones like these. It'd been like this ever since he was little, and there never seemed to be anything he could do to change it. But he didn't think he oughta let his mama see him die with that big old needle stuck up in his leg that way, so he said, "When you want me to set it up?"

"Tomorrow night," the first man said. "We'll get you a room at the Magnolia Motor Inn. Have him meet you there."

"What'm I s'posed to say?"

"Tell him you want another five or—no, ten thousand dollars for what you did. When he starts to squawk about it, tell him you have the master copy of that tape. Tell him you found it at the trailer when he sent you over there to look for it and that you kept it. And now you've decided that Clay and Bernie need to come up with a little more to square things away."

Rick turned to Sheriff Jackson. "I'd sure like to be there to hear what Clay has to say."

"I bet you would," she said. "I'll talk to 'em."

Rick left the sheriff's office and headed back to the station. He was in a good mood. He'd nailed this case and had fun doing it. The PI thing was an opportunity he'd hate himself for not taking, so he was going to take it along with the job in Vicksburg. He just hoped Traci would join him.

He got back to the station a little before five. Traci wasn't at her desk and Rick silently prayed she was in the ladies' room applying more blue eye shadow. He went to the production room and found a stack of spots he had to produce before he went on the air.

By five-thirty, just about everybody was gone for the weekend. Traci locked the front door then went down the hall to the production studio to find out what Rick had learned from Sheriff Jackson. He told her about the forensics while he dubbed the spots. Then he told her about the plan to have DeWayne wear a wire. "Unfortunately Sheriff Jackson said they won't let me or you or anybody else be there," he said.

"She say why?"

"Against MBI policy," he said with obvious disappointment.

Traci looked at Rick, a little disappointed herself. She crossed her arms and said, "So you're just going to sit around and wait to read about it in Sunday's paper?"

Rick could hear the derision in her voice. He said, "I assume you've got a better idea."

Traci stood and went to the door. "Come here," she said.

Rick gestured at the production orders in front of him. "I'm kind of—"

"Now," she said.

He got up and followed her down the hall. "Where are we going?"

"Just follow." She led him into the newsroom and past the old Teletype machine that still worked but was no longer used since the wire services now delivered news online. Traci stopped in front of a shelf on the far side of the room. She pointed at it and said, "What is that?"

Rick looked at it and shook his head. "I'll be a son of a . . . son of a sailor." He looked at Traci. "You know, if I ever do go looking for a partner, you're the first person I'm going to call."

"Partner?" Traci picked up the police scanner and said, "How about a supervisor?"

15

Saturday afternoon Sheriff Jackson told Rick that the MBI had tried to set the meeting up earlier in the evening, but Clay had told DeWayne he couldn't meet until ten and that was that. Stubblefield had seemed irritated that DeWayne was demanding to meet but he didn't seem suspicious about anything. The sheriff said she'd call Rick as soon as Clay was under arrest. Rick said he'd be sitting by the phone.

Around eight-thirty, Rick and Traci were sitting in a booth at Kitty's. After dinner they split a piece of pecan pie, then they drove over to the Magnolia Motor Inn. Rick pulled into the Denny's parking lot next door and backed his truck into a spot where they could see the doors to the motel rooms.

The Magnolia was a McRae landmark, a classic 1960s roadside motel, a two-story L-shaped building with a pool out front and a huge neon sign that gave off the sort of otherworldly nighttime glow that incandescent bulbs behind colored plastic could never achieve. The sign's animated features included an enormous swooping arrow with rows of yellow neon tubes lighting in sequence as if it were plunging toward the pool. At the top of the sign an immense magnolia blossom pulsed off and on as though it were a heartbeat. This electric sculpture lured beleaguered travelers with promises of air-conditioning and cocktails. Most of the citizens of McRae had never known this stretch of Bilbo Avenue without this flashing shrine. It was one of the town's last distinctive artifacts, its final morsel of identity, stubbornly refusing to yield to the homogenizing forces.

Traci looked at the Magnolia fondly and said, "You know, my dad used to take us there for summer vacation when we were kids."

Rick, who was fiddling with the police scanner, gave her a sideways glance. "Not exactly Six Flags," he said.

"It was to us. Just getting to pack our little suitcases and come over here was like going to Disney World or something. We were so excited. Dad let my sister and me have our own room and we just thought we'd died and gone to heaven 'cause we could jump on the beds like trampolines and not get yelled at." Traci paused long enough to display a nostalgic smile. "And there was something about that ice machine down the hall that we thought was the most exotic thing ever created and I have no explanation for why, so don't ask. But we always had a full bucket of ice and those glasses wrapped in that thin, crispy paper. I just loved that. We used to play alligator charge and Marco Polo at night in the pool under that neon light. We thought that was soooo cool."

"Could you get out of the pool or did you have to keep some part of your body in the water at all times?"

"No, you could get out," Traci said. "But if the person who was 'it' said 'fish out of water' while you were out, then you were 'it.'" Traci reached over and took the police scanner from Rick. "Is that how you played?"

"No, for some reason we were pretty strict about having to stay in the pool."

Traci hit a button on the scanner and it squawked, causing them both to jump. She turned the volume down and started dialing the frequency-tuning kob. Having been cut out of the official loop, Rick and Traci were hoping to pick up MBI radio communications that might tell them what was going on inside the motel. Traci wagged the scanner in her hand and said, "Where should I set this?"

"Police and fire are pretty low frequencies," Rick said. "Probably around four, five hundred megahertz."

Traci looked at the frequency display. "This thing tunes way below that."

"That's cabs and delivery trucks down there," Rick said. "Much lower and I think you start getting in the neighborhood of garage-door openers and baby monitors, things like that."

"How do you know that kind of stuff?"

Rick indulged in a nostalgic smile. "Used to be that you had to have an FCC Third Class license to be on the air. You had to go to the nearest city where there was an FCC office and take a test, which, for me, was New Orleans. The test was stuff about amplitude and frequency modulation and radio waves and all that kind of stuff."

As they sat in the truck waiting for Clay to arrive, Traci kept scanning up and down the frequency band. She stopped now and then to listen to the chatter of the McRae Police and Fire Departments. Tuning lower, she picked up a radio call for a taxi. Then, a little farther down the band, they heard a voice say, *"What if he's got a gun?"*

Rick turned and looked at Traci. He knew the voice. "That's DeWayne," he said, grabbing the scanner. "We're picking up his transmitter."

"We're right next door," another voice said. *"He pulls a gun or anything, you just holler and we're in there."* Right about then, Clay's Crown Victoria turned off Bilbo Avenue into the motel. *"Here we go,"* the voice said.

Clay cruised the length of the parking lot then turned around and came back. The car stopped but didn't park. Rick assumed Clay was in front of the room where DeWayne had set the meeting. He said, "How come he's not parking?"

Clay honked his horn a couple of times then waited. "What's he doing?" Traci asked.

Clay leaned on the horn again and DeWayne said something that came through the scanner but Rick couldn't understand it. A moment later one of the motel-room doors opened. DeWayne stepped out and leaned over so he could see into the car. Rick could see Clay gesturing for DeWayne to come out to where he was. The microphone was too far from Clay to pick up his words. But it got DeWayne saying, *"No, you come on in here."* They went back and forth like this a couple of times before DeWayne gave up. He walked over and leaned down to the passenger window. *"We was s'pposed to meet inside,"* DeWayne said, gesturing back at the door to his room.

Clay said, *"Damn, son, stop arguing and just get in. I gotta go take care of something. You can tell me whatever's so damn important on the way. C'mon."*

"He sounds drunk," Traci said. Rick nodded.

"Get in," Clay said. *"C'mon, let's go. Ain't got all night."*

DeWayne glanced back at the room next to his, like he didn't know what to do and was hoping someone might signal him an answer. *"C'mon!"* Clay said. DeWayne just seemed to give up. He slumped a bit then got into the car. *"Air ya go,"* Clay said. Then he gassed the car and shot out onto Bilbo Avenue, heading east, DeWayne staring out the passenger window like a hopeless dog.

Rick started his truck. "I wonder if they were planning on this." He pointed at the room next to the one DeWayne had been in. The door was open. It looked like a Chinese fire drill as MBI personnel spilled out and headed for their cars, which were all parked a block away.

Rick gave Clay a few seconds to get down Bilbo before he pulled out and started following. "I hope they got a good transmitter on that thing," he said. "Otherwise we're gonna have to sit on Clay's bumper to hear what they say." Up ahead, Clay turned south and headed out of town. Rick looked at the scanner in Traci's hand. "Did we lose 'em?"

"I'm working on it." Traci fiddled with the tuner until they heard DeWayne say, *"I thought we was gonna meet in the room."*

"What the hell difference does it make? You can tell me just as good here as there," Clay said. *"And what're you doin' with a room at the Magnolia anyway?"*

DeWayne said, *"Huh? I dunno. Why not?"*

"Shit, it don't matter," Clay said. *"Hey, die ever tell you 'bout that time this gal wanted me to come over to her motel room there and piss on her?"*

Rick and Traci looked at each other and shook their heads. "He just purely loves tellin' that story," Traci said.

"Yeah," DeWayne said. *"I remember you tellin' me about her before."*

"I tell you what, it was—" The sound of a ringing cell phone came over the scanner. *"I swear!"* Clay shouted. *"If that's Lori, I'm 'onna thow the phone out the goddamn winda."* The phone continued to ring. Clay said, *"Shit, it's her all right."*

"You ain't gonna answer?"

"Hell, she can leave me a damn message," Clay said just before it stopped ringing. *"There! Thank you. I tell you what, that bitch is gettin' harder to live with every day. Drivin' me crazy and costin' me good money every time she goes off on those damn shopping sprees uh hers. I swear, I am this close to havin' you take care of her like you did those others."*

They were past the city limits now. Traffic had thinned out and the county road was unlit. "Don't get too close," Traci said.

"I wouldn't worry about it," Rick said. "It's too dark

out here for him to tell if this is my truck or one of the ten thousand other trucks in this county."

"Where're we goin' way out here?" DeWayne asked.

"Oh, I just gotta meet somebody about this deal," Clay said. *"Now tell me what was so goddamn important that I had to meet you at the motel."*

There was a long pause as DeWayne tried to figure out what he was going to say. He hoped that the headlights he could see behind them was the MBI and that he was still in range of their receiver. He decided he better just go for it. *"I need more money for what I done for you."*

There was another pause before Clay said, *"Is 'at right?"*

"Yeah. Uhhh, another ten thousand."

"DeWayne, what're you talkin' about?"

"Y'all didn't pay me enough."

"Whaddya mean, y'all? I'm the only one 'at paid you and—what the hell're you lookin' at back air? Why you keep turning around like 'at?"

Traci and Rick could hear desperation, fear, and paranoia in both of their voices.

"I need help, Clay. Real bad," DeWayne said, snapping under the pressure. *"They on to us and I didn't know what else to do. They was with me all the time so I couldn't call you and they made me do this."*

"Do what? The hell're you talkin' about?"

"This is gonna get ugly," Traci said as she pulled out her cell phone. "I'm calling Sheriff Jackson."

"Hell, I didn't wanna, but I couldn't let my mama see me with that needle in my leg. So they made me wear this microphone and—"

"You what!? You're wearin' a—goddammit! You

dumb son of a bitch!" This was followed by a sound
that Rick assumed was Clay punching DeWayne in the
face or throat or chest, it was hard to tell, but the car
swerved when it happened. Clay started cursing at the
top of his lungs while DeWayne was screaming for
him to stop it and help him out of the mess. That's
when Rick lost sight of Clay's taillights. A second
later, the scanner issued a jarring cacophony of human
and machine noise and then the signal was gone.

Rick was about to accelerate to close the distance, to
get back in range of the transmitter, but then he saw the
yellow traffic warning sign, a cartoon car on two wheels
trying to negotiate a series of S-curves. Rick had to
brake to stay on the road, which curved and dipped and
curved some more. The last bend in the road was a serious hairpin. Rick slowed and made the turn, and as the
truck straightened out and they looked ahead, they could
see where Clay's car had come to rest in the ditch.

Rick pulled to the side of the road and put on his
flashers. He and Traci got out and approached the
wreck. The headlights were still on and the doors and
trunk were open but there was nobody in sight. *Ding-
ding-ding-ding,* a chiming reminder that the keys were
still in the ignition.

Traci was on the phone with the 911 operator. "I
don't know exactly," she said. "Out past French Camp
Road somewhere. Just get the sheriff out here. They've
gone into the woods." Just then they heard the distinct
sound of a shotgun blast. Traci held the phone out toward the trees. "Did you hear that? It was a shot!

Hurry!" She hopped down into the ditch and looked inside Clay's car while Rick went to the toolbox in the back of his truck and grabbed a couple of flashlights and his tire iron. "There's blood in the car," Traci said.

Rick held up his hand. "Shhh!" They could hear Clay shouting for DeWayne to stop, that it wasn't too late to take care of things. Rick said, "He's going to kill him out there."

"Whatta we gonna do?"

"I don't know," Rick said. "I'm new at this. And you're the one who said you wanted to be the supervisor." He turned on the two flashlights and checked their beams. He handed Traci the one with the better batteries and pointed off to his left. "You go that way, try to stay on that side of wherever he is and make a lot of noise, call his name, whatever, so he knows somebody else is out there."

"What good's that gonna do?"

"Maybe it'll make him think. Clay's always slower when he has to think."

"What're you gonna do?"

"Same thing." Rick gestured ahead with his tire iron. "Except I'm going this way."

"Be careful," Traci said.

They disappeared into the woods, heading in different directions. After about a hundred yards, Rick's flashlight started going brown. Fifty yards later it completely crapped out on him. He tossed it and tried to follow the sound of Clay's voice as he kept yelling for DeWayne to stop.

The quarter moon hanging behind thick cloud cover

made it hard to see. In the darkness Rick kept running into things. Low branches on skinny pines scraped his face and neck. Here and there he bumbled into thickets of stickers and brush that he'd have to back out of to find his way around. As he stumbled through the murky woods, he figured that by now, drunk or not, Clay had to know things were pretty much over for him. He had to realize how desperate his situation was, and in a classic case of shifting the blame, he had probably decided to kill the person he felt had put him in this position. Rick wondered if Clay would turn the gun on himself afterward or if he'd run, or, least likely, if he'd stay to face the music.

As Rick picked his way through the trees, he considered the implications of what he figured was about to happen and whether he should put himself in harm's way to try to stop it. A man that the state of Mississippi was keen on convicting of, and probably executing for, solicitation of murder was hunting down the man he had hired to kill two people. The victims, both extortionists, weren't exactly innocents, but neither, in Rick's opinion, were they deserving of the deaths they had suffered. If Clay killed DeWayne and then himself, Rick thought, a fair sum of the taxpayers' money would be saved, and in a great many respects, justice would be served. True, it would be at the expense of issues like due process and innocent-until-proven-guilty, but as had been pointed out many times by many people, life wasn't fair and justice was blind, or at least she sometimes looked the other way. Besides, in addition to the evidence he had gathered in service of establishing guilt, Rick felt that Clay's present behavior spoke for itself and certainly didn't go very far in arguing his innocence. The only reason he could conjure for intervening was the possibility that Clay's and DeWayne's demise might lead to problems in convicting Bernie Dribbling, the man ultimately behind all the deaths.

Rick's meditation on the fitting consequences for capital offenses was interrupted by the sound of voices. He stopped to listen. He could hear Clay and DeWayne but he couldn't tell how far away they were. He started to move ahead carefully, following their voices until he saw a light shining in the distance, moving back and forth across the trees. Rick knew it couldn't be Traci, given the direction she'd set off in, so it had to be Clay.

Rick imagined that after Clay had lost control and put his car in the ditch, DeWayne had jumped out, fueled by terror and adrenaline, and run into the woods. Clay, stoked on alcohol and dread, must have climbed out and gone to the trunk, where he had a flashlight and that Remington 870 Wingmaster shotgun.

Looking ahead, Rick saw that the light had stopped moving. It was trained on the wide trunk of an old pine. He could hear Clay speaking. "Might as well step out and face it, DeWayne," he said. "I'm this close and you know I ain't gonna letcha just walk away. So what's the point?"

Following the voices and the flashlight beam, and trying to move only when they spoke, Rick slipped from one tree to the next until he was only about fifteen feet behind Clay.

"You ain't gotta kill me," DeWayne said. "I can just go away. I won't testify to nothin' and that's the stomped-down truth. I swear! They'll never even find me."

"No good," Clay said.

Rick watched Clay move to his right to get an angle on DeWayne, but DeWayne just circled the other direction, keeping the tree between them.

"How 'bout this?" DeWayne proposed. "How 'bout we make it look like we was all just set up on this thing? You said that Chief Dinkins could help if things got sticky. Well, things is sure sticky now."

"DeWayne, quit suckin' eggs on this and be a man," Clay said. "I'm damn sure sorry it's gotta end this way but . . . that's the way it is. We up against a stump."

For a moment no one spoke. The only sound was the buzzing of cicadas and crickets for miles around. Then, from the darkness of the woods to Rick's left, Traci called out, "Hey!"

It startled Clay so that he just turned and fired a shot in the direction of her voice. As the report echoed through the woods, Rick heard DeWayne turn and run and he figured Clay would take off after him. Rick knew he had to make his move now or start the chase all over, so he charged out from behind his tree with his tire iron poised. He planned to bring it down on Clay's forearm and break it clean, disarming him and leaving him in enough pain that Rick could grab the shotgun and end things without any more death.

And he might have been able to do just that had he not tripped on this big pine branch he didn't see. He landed facedown at Clay's feet.

Clay didn't know what to do or think. He wanted to go after DeWayne but he seemed frozen, startled, wondering who had just yelled from the woods and what the hell Rick was doing out here. As Clay turned and looked down, his posture brought the shotgun to an angle pointing straight at Rick's head.

Rick rolled over and looked up. He could see the last wisps of smoke coming from the end of the barrel. And, even though he wasn't in much of a position to talk this way, he said, "Give it up, Clay."

"The hell're you doin'?" was all Clay could come up with. He was looking down at Rick as if he'd fallen from the sky.

"I found the tape," Rick said. "I know everything that happened and so do the police."

"You did this?" Clay looked off in the direction he had fired the shot. "Who's out there?"

"It's Traci. And I've got a camera," she called out. "Whatever you do is gonna be on video. So you might as well just surrender. Sheriff's on the way."

Clay looked back down at Rick and mumbled, "Goddamn tapes." Rick started to get up but Clay pressed the shotgun to his neck and pushed him back down. "I told you not to nose around in my business." He looked over in the direction of Traci's voice and yelled, "I'll take his head off, you don't come out."

Rick yelled, "Don't do it!"

Clay waited a moment to see if she would come out. When she didn't, he shrugged in defeat and leaned down toward Rick. "All right, Mr. DJ," he said. "Got any last requests? Tch."

Rick closed his eyes momentarily then looked up at Clay. "I really hate to say this but . . . how about 'Stairway to Heaven'?" He flashed an impish grin.

Clay couldn't help himself. As dumb and drunk and

frightened as he was, he still got the joke and his head threw back in one final laugh. That's when Rick swung the tire iron with all his might, catching Clay's tibia in just the right spot to snap it in half. As the bone broke through the skin, the shotgun fired and Traci screamed, "Nooooooo!"

The crickets and cicadas eventually resumed their undulated buzzing. Traci was sitting on the forest floor, leaning against a tree in the dark. She looked vaguely stunned. Rick's head was in her lap, his eyes closed. Her hands were bloody from where she had been applying pressure to his neck.

Clay lay unconscious nearby, the pain and shock of his compound fracture having proved too much for him.

In the distance, Traci could hear sirens approaching. After a moment, Rick's eyes opened and he looked up at Traci. "I hope those are for us," he said.

"Yeah." Traci looked down with a numbed expression. "How you doin'?"

"I'm okay," Rick said. "A little woozy, maybe."

"You'll be all right." Traci rubbed his arm absently as she gazed out into the darkness.

"I've just been lying here thinking about that PD job down in Vicksburg," Rick said.

It took a moment for Traci to understand his words. She said, "I thought you were getting out of radio."

"I said I was thinking about it."

Traci nodded slightly. "You make a decision?"

"I thought I might take the gig while we work on the PI thing."

"We?"

"I'm going to need a partner. You said so yourself."

Traci looked around the woods and said, "Yeah, well, that was before all this happened." She had the sort of doubt in her voice that comes after being shot at for the second time in two days.

But Rick couldn't hear it, his ears were still ringing from their proximity to the shotgun blast. He had rolled to one side as he swung the tire iron and the tight pattern of buckshot at such close range had just caught the side his neck. The experience had an interesting effect on him. Giddy at having cheated death, and with a huge dose of adrenaline coursing through his system, Rick became animated and optimistic. "I was also thinking that as the program director, I'd get to hire my on-air staff."

"Yeah, I suspect you will."

"So, naturally, I thought of you."

"Thought what about me?"

"You said you wanted to work on the air, and I believe you also expressed some interest in moving to a place where you could pick the best parts of your past to tell people or where you could just make up something completely new," Rick said. "You can just leave behind whatever you want. It's *your* past."

But Traci was thinking about the future now. And she was thinking about it in a whole new light as she felt the blood coagulating on her hands. Tempting as it might be to rewrite her past, there was something she couldn't leave behind. But she hadn't told Rick about that and she didn't think now was the time to spring it on him. She could tell him later. He'd understand.

After a few minutes Traci heard the dogs barking.

She glanced in their direction and saw what looked like fairy lights in the distance, dodging and blinking in the trees. "I think they found us," she said.

Now Rick could hear the dazed blankness in her voice. He couldn't tell if she was hearing his words, let alone putting meaning to them. He figured it was a temporary response to the night's events. *She'll be fine,* he thought. "Of course, you don't have to answer now," he said. "Just think about it. Let me know when you decide."

Absently stroking Rick's hair, Traci said, "Yeah, I will."

They caught DeWayne later that night. The dogs treed him like a possum. DeWayne testified against Clay. Clay testified against Bernie. And Bernie said it was all a pack of lies. He was the Booster Club Man of the Year! All three were convicted in the deaths of Jack Carter and Holly Creel and were put in the care of the Mississippi State Department of Corrections.

Once he'd settled in at Parchman Farm, Bernie decided he'd try to make the best of the situation. He formed a 'finance company' that arranged loans for the Aryan Brotherhood and other white supremacist prison gangs. He hired DeWayne as his vice president of collections and protection and they did all right for themselves, all things considered.

Clay was initially welcomed to the institution, where he was held in high regard as a prison yard raconteur. A couple of months later, however, after having told the story about the woman who invited him back to the motel for a golden shower one time too many, he was raped and killed. Guards found his urine-soaked body behind housing unit 25.

Lori divorced Clay and moved to Dallas with the kids. She married the alcoholic chief financial officer of an energy trading company who was later indicted for cooking the books. He fled the country, without Lori, and was convicted *in absentia*. Lori was later arrested for shoplifting a pair of Jimmy Choo pointed-toe slingbacks, in petrol blue.

Autumn received an A for her term paper on the station's format change. It was titled: *Grabbing the Gray: Impact of Format Change on P-1 Listeners in the 35 to 64 Demographic (Average Quarter Hour and Cume)*. Two weeks later her professor discovered that she had plagiarized large portions of the paper. Autumn was "asked to leave" CMU without benefit of a degree. This, however, didn't prevent her from indicating on her résumé that she graduated cum laude. Autumn moved to Jackson and became the assistant communications director for a Democratic state representative.

After graduating from McRae High School, Rob enrolled in CMU's Radio, TV, and Film program. Informed by his experience at WAOR, he opted for an emphasis in film. Two years later he dropped out and moved to Los Angeles to look for work in the film industry. Within a year, he was one of the top-grossing waiters in Hollywood.

Despite Rick's glowing letter of recommendation, J.C. couldn't find another radio gig. He started collecting unemployment while being paid under the table as a local nightclub DJ. He was fired eight months later and subsequently answered a want ad for a position as a nourishment transfer engineer. He delivered pizza and chicken wings to the residents of greater McRae for six months before moving up to management.

The owner of B-Side Vinyl sold *Piper at the Gates of Dawn* on-line for sixty-five dollars. He then took all the albums that Rick gave to J.J. Maguire and sold them for a total of six hundred thirty dollars so J.J. could pay his way into an alcohol rehabilitation program. J.J. then became an instructor at the Paul B. Allen School of Broadcasting in Omaha, Nebraska. He's been sober ever since. He still has The Beatles 45.

A few weeks after Clay was arrested, the ratings book came out. It showed a one point gain in average quarter-hour listeners over the previous ratings period. A month later Clean Signal Radio Corporation announced that it had bought the station. They fired everyone and began simulcasting the syndicated talk format on the AM and the FM sides.

No one knows what happened to Uncle Victor.

The story of Rick's investigation got front-page play throughout the state. Even though his wound was nearly healed, Rick kept the bandage on his neck as long as the reporters and photographers were coming by for interviews. They would come out to the trailer and he'd take them out to the woods and show them where he'd found the body. He talked about his new radio job in Vicksburg and how he was going to open a private investigation service. He said he was toying with names like Rockin' Vestigations, but he hadn't settled on anything. Rick figured all the press would put him in good graces with his new station; nothing like having someone of semi-celebrity status coming on board. And he knew it would get his name out there for potential PI clients.

Still, as busy as Rick was with all the media requests, he wasn't too busy to notice the shift in Traci's mood since their night in the woods. He had the sense there was something she wasn't telling him. It was the same feeling he'd had that night at Kitty's when she seemed on the verge of explaining about her ex-boyfriend, but had held back. When he asked her about it, she changed the subject. She was fine, she said. Don't worry about it. She made vague statements about joining him in Vicksburg, but Rick didn't hear her heart in it. He had started to lower his expectations.

On the day of the move, Rick hitched his pickup to the back of the big U-Haul he had rented. After adding Captain Jack's record collection, his Barcalounger, and the Griswold number-five skillet to his own belongings, there wasn't any other way to do it. Besides, the new station was paying for the move. Rick glanced in the mirror for one last look at the trailer, then he pulled out onto the road.

As he drove across town to Traci's apartment, Rick entertained the fragile hope that she would be waiting on the sidewalk with her suitcases. Upon closer examination, he realized it was more of a fantasy than a realistic hope. He stopped in front of her place around noon but there weren't any suitcases out front when he got there. No Traci either. He climbed out of the truck and went to her door.

Traci met him there with a sheepish grin. "Hi," she said. "All packed?"

"Yeah," Rick said. "What about you?"

Traci smiled but shook her head.

Rick responded with a disappointed nod.

A little girl appeared by Traci's side, looking up at Rick. "Hello," she said.

Rick looked down. "Hi."

Traci said, "Oh, hey, you two've never met, have you?" She put her hand on the girl's head. "Rick, this is my . . . this is Kaitlin."

"Your niece?"

"My daughter."

Rick tried not to look too surprised. He said, "Oh." Like he understood.

Traci seemed a little embarrassed and said, "I was going to—"

Rick shook his head. "Don't worry about it." He squatted down and held out his hand. "Hi, I'm Rick. I've heard a lot about you."

Kaitlin smiled but hid behind her mom's leg. "She's kinda shy," Traci said.

Rick stood up and thought about asking why she hadn't told him, but he let it go. He could imagine a lot of reasons but knowing them wouldn't change anything. "She's got your smile," he said.

Traci sent Kaitlin back to her room to play. After she was gone, Traci looked at Rick and said, "I'm sorry. I should've told you and I was going to, but the timing never seemed right. At first it was . . . well, it doesn't matter. I hope you understand. But that night . . . and the blood? I just kept thinking about her and what would happen if I . . . didn't come home."

"Sure," Rick said. "I understand." He figured this

might be the last time he saw Traci and he didn't want the end too gloomy, so he tried to lighten the mood. "Now, keep in mind that the radio gig I'm offering is a lot less dangerous. So if you think you might want to . . ." He smiled and gave a little gesture to finish his thought.

"Yeah," Traci said with her own sad smile. "I thought I'd let you go ahead and get started anyway, and maybe we could come along later." She turned and looked toward the back of her apartment. "Depending how you feel about it . . ." She looked back at Rick. "Well, you know. We could come visit."

"Sure. That'd be great," Rick said. "We'll take her to the Civil War park and let her play around on the cannons. And the job'll be waitin' for you if you want it."

"Thanks." Traci walked Rick out to the truck and kissed him good-bye.

Rick held her face in his hands and took one last look at the swoop of her eyebrows. Then he kissed her forehead and climbed into the truck.

"Good luck," she said.

Rick looked down, smiling, and said, "Thanks." Then he put the truck in gear and drove away. He saw Traci in his mirror, waving, as he made the turn off her street.

As he drove out of town, Rick tried telling himself it was all for the best, that whatever happens is supposed to happen. That there's a reason things turn out the way they do. He tried all the things people tell themselves when they don't like the outcome of the game and have no way of changing it. Rick figured people believed these things because they found it more comforting to blame fate than to accept the arbitrary nature of life.

Blaming fate while simultaneously embracing a vague implication that something better would spring from it; like Rick's cynicism, it was a philosophy of consolation. In pop Christian terms they would say, "When God closes a door he opens a window." Rick had heard it more than once, and despite there being no apparent basis for the claim, he understood how and why it comforted so many. In fact, he sometimes wished he was among them.

But he wasn't. He would agree that good things sometimes happened after bad things happened but he knew that one didn't necessarily cause the other. When something happened, you chose how to react. Things change and you can change with them or not, the choice is yours. Rick laughed at himself. Radio had changed, but Rick refused to, but at least it had been his choice. He was alone again and heading for another town, another station. But at least he had something to look forward to.

As he drove beyond the city limits Rick picked up his cell phone and hit speed dial for the studio. Rob answered and Rick said, "Just wanted to say one last good-bye and wish you good luck with everything."

"Thanks," Rob said. "You, too. I really appreciate everything you did for me."

"Glad I could help." Rick gave Rob his cell-phone number and told him to call if he ever needed anything or if he came to Vicksburg. Rob said he'd come to visit. "Listen," Rick said, "I have a request."

"Name it."

"How about Buddy Miles, 'Them Changes'?"

1

Durden Tate was a wealthy man. His company had a lock on eighty percent of the specialty-fats-and-oils market for fast-food restaurants in Mississippi, Louisiana, and Arkansas. Durden Tate's company had achieved this extraordinary market share by creating a superior product, a frying fat based on a flavorful blend of deodorized palm oil and refined pork lard. Tru-Fry 2000, as it was known, boasted elevated oxidation resistance, a high smoke point, and true frying longevity. As a result, every time a donut, a catfish, or a basket of fries was lowered into a bubbling vat in this part of the country, the odds were good that it was Durden Tate's fat.

As part of his commitment to quality, Durden spent four days a week visiting restaurants that used his product. After ten years of sampling crispy-fried hash browns at breakfast, corn dogs and fried pies at lunch, and hush puppies with dinner, the once trim and athletic Mr. Tate was pushing three hundred twenty pounds.

His wife, Wanda Lee Henshaw Tate, put up with his obesity and his frequent absence not only because she'd meant it when she'd said 'for better or for worse' but also because Durden had come through on the 'for richer or poorer' part of the deal. But when she began to suspect Durden was cheating, she decided to get out. And she wasn't about to leave empty-handed. She'd put fifteen of the best years of her life into the marriage and felt she was owed something.

But Wanda Lee needed proof. She needed some photos, something that would make the divorce easy and the alimony as fat as Durden's lard ass. So she pulled out the phone book and looked under 'Investigators.'

Rick waited until dusk before sneaking into the weedy field just off Highway 61, on the outskirts of Port Gibson, Mississippi. On the far end of the field was the back of the Pine Grove Motor Inn where Durden Tate had checked in an hour earlier, and not for the first time since Rick had been following him. Rick had a camera bag slung over his shoulder and high hopes that Durden didn't draw the curtains all the way.

It was a typical Mississippi summer night, warm and sticky as a sweet pastry. Rick was sweating before he'd gone fifty feet. Halfway across the field, with burrs scratching through his socks and ticks scaling his leg, Rick stepped into a mud hole, sinking past his ankle. He pulled back, losing his shoe. Sewer gas filled his nose and he struggled not to gag. In the waning light, he looked down and saw the mud oozing into his size ten.

Rick stood there like a flamingo, thinking about the pair of boots in his truck. Sure the loafers were more comfortable, but, well, too late now. It turned out he was standing above an underground waste-water treatment pipe that had been leaking for a week. The rest of the field between Rick and the motel was a rotten-egg-swamp. The mosquitoes arrived just as the sun set. He tried to remember if the West Nile virus had been reported in Claiborne County yet.

Having no good options, he stuck his foot back into the ghastly muck, retrieved his shoe, and continued toward the Pine Grove Motor Inn. By the time he reached the motel, both of Rick's feet were soaked through with sewage, his arms and neck were riddled with insect bites, and he reeked of shit. But he still had a job to do, so he crept along underneath the rear windows of the motel, peeking in each one until he found Durden Tate's room. The good news was that the curtain was halfway open and Rick could see Tate sitting on the end of the bed. The bad news was that he was naked, all three hundred twenty pounds of him. The TV cast a bluish tint onto his blubbery folds. He had a beer in one hand and the remote in the other. Next to him on the bed were two paper sacks and his Dopp kit.

Durden began to talk, though Rick couldn't see who he was talking to. Though Tate's voice was muffled, Rick could tell he was sweet-talking somebody. It appeared the recipient of the honeyed words was lying on the floor. Durden reached behind him and grabbed one of the sacks. It was filled with onion rings from the burger joint across the highway. He continued his sweet talking as he ate the fried onions.

He tossed one to the floor, presumably for his companion. Why was she down there? Was Durden in a domination-submission relationship? Rick hadn't figured him for the type but, as he knew, people will surprise you. Rick popped off the lens cap and waited for the leather hood to come out. Durden ate the onions slowly, eyes closed, lips glistening with grease. By the time he finished there was still no sign of the submissive lover. Maybe she was tied up.

A moment later Durden reached into the other paper sack and pulled out a jar of peanut butter. He unzipped his Dopp kit and removed a tongue depressor. He scooped a wad of peanut butter onto the wooden stick then crossed his legs and began smearing the goo between his toes. It looked to be smooth, not crunchy. Rick exposed a few frames of film.

When Durden finished with the left foot he lowered it to the floor then shouted "No!" at his lover. He crossed his legs the other way and took his time smearing the peanut butter between the toes of his right foot. He licked the tongue depressor and chased it with some beer, then he leaned back onto the bed and said something like, "Okay, c'mon baby."

She was stout. Her hair was black, and she had a tongue the likes of which Rick had never seen on a woman. This was due largely to the fact that she was a Labrador retriever. She gave every indication that she was enjoying herself and, as she licked the peanut butter from between his toes, Durden Tate moaned and flogged himself as though he might win a prize for it. "Good girl," he seemed to be saying over and over. "Good girrrrl."

Figuring with no small amount of dread that this was merely foreplay, Rick snapped off a dozen pics, leaving another twenty exposures before he'd have to change rolls. Fortunately, Durden liked doing this with the lights on so there was no need for a flash. When the poor dog finished with his toes, Durden sat up and reached for the peanut butter again. Rick got a queasy feeling about what was coming and figured right then and there that he'd make two sets of prints, one for Wanda Lee, one for the ASPCA.

Rick decided to switch to a zoom. He was reaching into his camera bag when he heard a man say, "Hold it right there, pervert." All things considered, Rick hardly thought that was a fair characterization. He turned and saw the man from the Port Gibson police department, gun in one hand, flashlight in the other. "Now you just back away from that window and ease on over here, boy."

"This isn't what it looks like," Rick said.

"Yeah? What's it look like?"

"Like I'm a pervert," Rick said.

"That's right, and we call this felonious trespass. That's a fancy term for a peeping Tom, so let's go."

Rick slapped at a mosquito buzzing his ear. "Actually, I'm a private investigator."

"Uh huh." The cop gestured with his gun. "Well, just bring your Rockford Files on over here."

Rick pointed at the window. "There's a man in there about to have sex with a dog."

"And what? You wanna watch?"

Rick couldn't believe this guy. "Did you hear me? I said sex with a dog."

"And who're you to be passin' judgment on that?" the cop asked. "You sayin' you ain't never laid no pipe with uh ugly girl?" He stuck his nose in Rick's direction and sniffed the air. "'At's bullshit. Now, c'mon, you're under arrest."

The guard leaned against the cell bars casting a friendly smile. "You sure you don't want to stay?"

"Much as I love you," Clarence said, "I think I stayed long enough."

"Well, all right then. You 'bout ready?"

"All packed, boss." Clarence stepped out of the shadow of his cell, his tight gray coils like snow on cured tobacco. His face was seventy-five years of troubles, yet it shined with the dignity of a man undefeated.

"Well, all right then." The guard gestured toward the freedom Clarence never should have lost and said, "C'mon."

Clarence walked out of his cell for the last time. Never looked back, not once. No good memories in there. Eyes always forward. He said his goodbyes on the move too. He wasn't going to stop until somebody made him. He'd been waiting too long to get going.

He walked into the administration office wearing the itchy black-and-white striped pants, the ring-arounds as they called them, and coarse prisoner's smock with *M.D.O.C. Convict* on the back. There was paperwork to do and they checked his fingerprints to make sure they were releasing the right man, but they didn't look too close. They all knew who he was. He was an institution within the institution.

A woman behind the counter reached over and pressed something into his hand. Clarence looked in his broad rough palm and saw a small gold cross on a chain. The woman smiled at him and said, "Now is the day of your salvation. You take care of yourself."

"Thank you," he said. "You know I will."

They gave him a hundred dollars gate money and what they called adequate free world shirt and pants. He was glad to wear anything besides the convict uniform he'd worn most of his life. The striped outfit was a cell unto itself, a further humiliation, bars within bars. Clarence had been a fine dresser back in his day, a real dandy. He looked in the mirror after changing and thought 'adequate' was about the best you could say for the clothes they'd given him this time. But that was a small thing, easy to fix once he got to town. He couldn't let that bother him. He had bigger fish to fry.

The warden gestured toward the door. "Somebody meetin' you out there, Clarence?"

"No, suh, ain't nobody out there for me, but I'll be all right. They's a man down in Jackson I'm 'onna see, gonna help me out. I'll send y'all a postcard." They all smiled at that and then it was time to go. They let Clarence out the gate right there on Highway 49 where he'd come in fifty years ago and told him where to go to catch the bus.

He stood there for an hour, watching the traffic, measuring his emotions, not sure if he felt the way he was supposed to feel getting out after all this time. He figured he mostly felt the same, probably take a while for it to sink in. When the bus finally got there, he saw how the people looked at him as he came up the stairs in his thrift store outfit. He didn't guess he could blame them, the bus stopping so close to Parchman and all. But nobody bothered him, probably figured a man his age wasn't going to cause them any trouble. And he wasn't. Clarence was saving the trouble for someone else.

Rick made bail with three other overnight guests of the Port Gibson Police Department. There was Fred, a lanky mechanic, who had been drunk-and-disorderly. (At a bar with his wife, he'd flirted openly with another woman whose husband took exception. Fred lost the fight and the other guy got away.) A roofer named Charlie was busted for breaking-and-entering. (After downing a twelve pack, he broke into an auto parts store, filled his pockets with car air fresheners touting an exotic blend of coconut and forest fruits, then passed out.) And then there was Paul, a small business owner who'd spent the night on a domestic battery charge. (Too much tequila and an argument about whether they were going to watch "The Bachelor" or The Atlanta Braves.)

The four men signed for their stuff and headed for the door. Rick, the only one not suffering from a hangover, was the first outside. He shaded his eyes against a blinding sun then watched in jealous dismay as the other three men shuffled out of the jail and into the arms of significant others. They all hugged and swore they were sorry and vowed it would never happen again. Rick couldn't believe it. A philanderer, a thief, and a wife beater were doing better than he was, and he wondered what it must be like to have a woman like that. One who not only puts up with your stupidity, but who's willing to pay to get you back for more.

It made him think of Traci, the love that circumstance had forced him to leave behind when he left McRae for Vicksburg. Traci would've bailed him out and picked him up if he'd stayed with her. But he hadn't. Rick missed her but he understood why she couldn't come with him. She liked her hometown and didn't want to uproot her young daughter just to chase a disc jockey, let alone one that got shot at, like he had. Rick ran up his phone bill trying to talk her into moving but when she started making noise about reconciling with her ex, Rick figured it was time to move on in his quest for romance. Still, as he watched Fred, Charlie, and Paul drive off, he couldn't help but think how nice it would've been to walk out of jail and into Traci's arms.

As Rick headed for the impound lot to get his truck, he tried not to dwell on the fact that he had no one to blame but himself. He'd spent most of his life dodging commitment and the ties that bind in exchange for the alternative. Of course, early in his rock radio career, there had been some logic to this. But the older he got, the better he could see the advantage of having a solid relationship with someone other than a bail bondsman.

He shrugged off his regrets, got his truck, and headed back to Vicksburg. He'd been there a few months and, so far, it was working out all right. Weeknights he did a shift at WVBR-FM, a classic rock station where he had the freedom to play what he wanted. During the day he ran his private investigation business which he called Rockin' Vestigations.

Rick was a radio veteran but relatively new at the PI game. He'd been in the former all his life and had stumbled into the latter after solving a multiple murder case while working at WAOR-FM, in McRae, Mississippi, where he'd met Traci. In the course of solving that crime, he suffered a serious gunshot wound and had his picture splashed on the front page of every paper in the state. With no small amount of encouragement from Rick, the press portrayed him as a dashing, hard-boiled, rock 'n' roll, flirting-with-danger kinda guy. And without much effort, Rick parlayed his sudden celebrity into the new line of work.

When he opened Rockin' Vestigations, he had a few things to learn. First, most of his work would be done at a computer. But not always. PIs still had to follow people now and then. And most of the people he was hired to follow did their running around at night when Rick was on the air. So he found a couple of younger operatives whose primary qualifications were that they owned camera equipment and a car. They were free-lancers, on call. They did the grunt work, except on occasions when Rick wanted to make sure he got the goods for particularly wealthy clients, like Wanda Lee Henshaw Tate.

After the thing in McRae, during which Rick had found himself without a weapon at exactly the moment he needed one, he decided to get strapped. He bought a .38 and took a concealed-weapons class. He was a good shot, a natural. But given the statistics on firearm deaths, he rarely carried the gun. Still, he kept it, just in case.

His radio job provided a steady, if modest, paycheck. He planned to build his PI résumé and client base to the point that he could get out of radio before Clean Signal Radio Corporation owned every last rock station in the country and played nothing but Zeppelin's *Whole Lotta Love* between fifteen-minute commercial breaks.

So, despite the fact that he was out on bail and smelled like the inside of an outhouse, Rick felt like his train was on the tracks. It's true he wasn't in danger of getting rich as a private investigator but after years of watching the body of FM rock radio rotting in front of his eyes, he felt good that he was at least doing something to improve his future. The way he figured it, rock radio wouldn't live forever, but he could always count on people to lie, cheat, and steal.

So far Rick had caught a bus load of cheating spouses, had tracked down a couple dozen check kiters, and had gathered evidence on a group running a disability insurance scam. It wasn't the cure to cancer, but it beat the hell out of playing *Free Bird*.

Rick glanced at his watch as he eased his pickup onto the Clay Street exit. He had time to get a shower and a nap before starting his shift at eight. He passed the faded green-and-white sign for the Southern Pride Apartments. The building itself was gone but its foundation still sat on the lot as if waiting for that part of the south to rise again. Farther on, the road sloped toward historic downtown. His apartment was ahead on the right, a classic twelve-story, red brick building with "The Vicksburg" painted down the side in big, bold letters just as it was when it was built in 1928, the year before the great Delta flood. Before being converted to apartments, The Vicksburg had been a classic river city hotel like The Peabody in Memphis, though somewhat less grand. And without the ducks.

Rick parked in the lot behind the building but couldn't bring himself to get out. It was ninety-five outside and humid enough to wither a man. So he sat there soaking up the A.C. But then he saw Veronica pull in to her parking spot. She was a cocktail waitress at the Isle of Capri with a one-bedroom on the fifth floor. They'd met the day Rick moved in. He'd flirted, but she was either playing hard to get or dropping hints that she wasn't interested. Rick had a hard time distinguishing between the two. He wasn't sure if he was really attracted to Veronica or if she simply reminded him of Traci. He figured it was the excessive eye makeup they both wore but it didn't hurt that Veronica's waitress outfit was on the skimpy side and she had the legs for it.

Rick got out of the truck. The humidity hit him like a pan of used motor oil. He shook it off and slung his camera bag over his shoulder. He knew he looked pretty rough but figured he'd make up a rollicking story about how he'd just returned from a wild night in New Orleans partying with the Neville Brothers. He headed for the back door, getting there just in time to hold it open for her. "Hey, Veronica," he said. "How you doin'?"

Her face wrinkled as she passed. "Fine," she said. "But you seem to be attracting flies."